# ROADRAGE

M J Johnson (Martin Johnson) was born and brought up in South Wales. He trained at RADA and has worked fairly extensively in all areas of the acting business. He now spends most of his time writing. His first novel *Niedermayer & Hart* was published in 2012. He lives in Kent with his wife Judith. Their son, artist Tom Johnson, is responsible for the cover design. For more information about M J Johnson please visit his website: www.mj-johnson.com

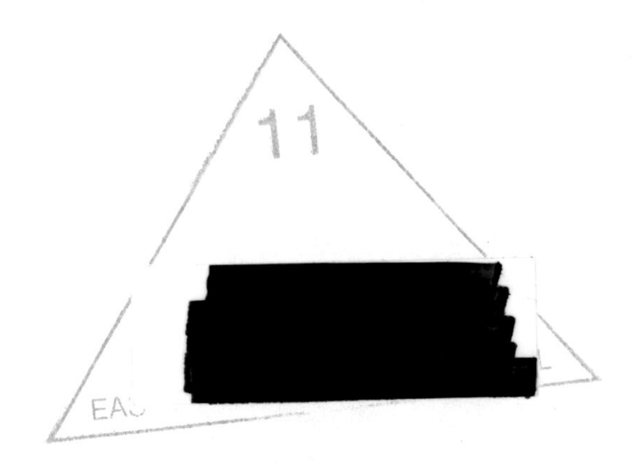

ALSO BY M J JOHNSON

*Niedermayer & Hart*

Jim Latimer reads of fellow photographer John Loxton's suicide in a daily newspaper. An old friend offers Jim an opportunity to take over Loxton's next assignment. He enters the orbit of Niedermayer & Hart, porcelain dealers with elegant headquarters in Hove. Jim's friends Ruth and Erich sense something isn't right and try to warn him. He is brought face to face with a terrifying manifestation of evil that had its inception in mediaeval Acre.

M J Johnson

# Roadrage

First published in 2013 by Odd Dog Press


This is a work of fiction. Names and characters are the product of the author's imagination and any resemblance to actual persons, living or dead, is entirely coincidental.



British Library Cataloguing in Publication Data:
A catalogue record of this book is available from the British Library.

ISBN - 13: 978-0-9562873-4-2

Printed and bound in the UK by Biddles, part of the MPG Printgroup,Bodmin and King's Lynn

www.odddogpress.com

# Roadrage

## Acknowledgements

Books don't get written without an enormous amount of help. Once again I must thank the kind and generous people who have willingly shared with me their time and expertise. I'm certain they know who they are.

However, three people must be mentioned because *Roadrage* is undoubtedly a better book for their contribution: my friend Peter Bolwell for his time, observant eye for any shaky plot detail and invariably good advice, my son Tom Johnson for his continued support of the project and nothing short of superb cover design, and my wife Judith, for her unwavering dedication both to the book and her old man.

You become what you think about all day long.

Ralph Waldo Emerson

Othello:

Will you, I pray, demand that demi-devil,

Why he hath thus ensnared my soul and body?

Iago:

Demand me nothing: What you know, you know:

From this time forth I never will speak word.

William Shakespeare, Othello, Act 5, scene ii.

Hate is a bottomless cup; I will pour and pour.

Euripides, Medea

1 3 5
2 4 R

# FIRST

25 December - 31 January

## 1

The rain was driving hard at the windscreen. In places, pools of flood-water stretched half-way across the carriageway. Gil peered into the murk ahead with a weary stoicism, taking the lane lines as his guide. There were times during the journey when he'd felt he was steering a submersible rather than driving a car. He'd grown tired of the radio some time ago, but now the repetitive hum and swipe of the windscreen wipers was really beginning to irritate.

It was downright unseasonal to be experiencing such a torrent, and on Christmas Day of all days. Not that he cared much; Gil Harper avoided Christmas wherever possible.

"Santa must've caught pneumonia last night," he told Spike, a brown and white wire-haired Jack Russell, whose name pictured him well. An attentive companion under normal conditions, the dog had abandoned his habitual vigil at the passenger window to take a nap; tiny snores were the only feedback Gil received from the seat beside him.

He suddenly felt quite sorry for himself, alone in the wretched dark without even Spike to share the boredom; just an empty road and the interminable rain. Actually, the major part of the journey was behind them. He consulted the dashboard clock, estimated about forty minutes driving time, and reckoned to be home around ten.

Gil was returning from the Somerset coast, having travelled there the previous afternoon in a similar downpour. He had stayed the night and taken Christmas lunch with his in-laws, Marjorie and George, that is if the term in-law still applied to parents of a deceased wife. It was five years since Jules' death and each year Marjorie and George continued to invite him. They still thought of him as family, and never failed to include him at this most poignant of times for anyone who has lost a loved one. They were getting on in years and Jules, christened Julia, had been their only child; Gil could only begin to guess at the pain of their shared loss. It was not an ordeal to visit them, they were kind and sociable, but the whole Christmas thing brought up too many unwanted emotions. He'd considered using the weather as an excuse for not going, but had he done this, he knew he would have felt like a heel.

"It doesn't seem right to be leaving before the day is out, especially with the weather as it is," Marjorie had told Gil as he lent her a hand with the washing up. "You know that you're more than welcome to stay."

"I know that, Marge," he replied, then went on to mumble stock phrases about needing to get back and having things to do. They both knew this was untrue.

Marjorie shook her head, gently reproaching him, "Gil, Gil, what are we to do with you? Both George and I are deeply touched that you loved our daughter, but it hurts us to see you still grieving. Jules has moved on, you know that she would never have wanted you to go on mourning her. Don't you think it's time you allowed her memory to rest in peace?"

Gil scrutinised the dinner plate in his hands with far more attentiveness than he had formerly shown it.

Marjorie misinterpreted the pause, "You must think I'm awful, asking you to forget my own daughter." There was a note of self-chastisement in her voice.

"I'd never think that. You know I wouldn't," he replied, looking into the elderly woman's face with unguarded honesty.

"You'd be quite within your rights to tell me to mind my own business, but we're concerned about you Gil. Nothing any of us can do will ever bring our darling girl back." A large tear appeared at the corner of each eye as she digested her own words.

Gil dropped his gaze towards the floor and quietly said, "Nothing seemed real after the accident. Jules was so full of life, so dynamic. Myself, I've always been a bit retiring … shy-ish … a follower, never the leader. That's why she was so good for me ... she burst into my life like … like … I don't know … like dynamite!"

They both smiled at the awkwardness but accuracy of his analogy.

Gil returned to the sink to deflect attention from his moist eyes and dredged a final plate onto the drainer, poured the dishwater away and began drying his hands on a tea-towel. "I've met someone," he confided.

"And?" asked Marjorie when she felt the pause had lived long enough.

"I like her. I think she likes me too."

"When did you meet?" Marjorie asked tentatively.

"A few weeks ago. Not really much to tell. We met at the library."

"The library?"

"Mm, bit sad, huh?"

They shared a laugh.

"We were both getting some research done."

"What does she do?"

"She designs costumes for stage productions."

"Sounds interesting," said Marjorie, then after a pause, "Well, go on then."

"Nothing more to say, we've chatted over coffee and eaten out twice. That's about it."

"It's a start. Is she a 'looker' like our Jules?" she enquired with a smile.

Gil felt his face reddening, "Well, I think so."

"As long as you think so, that's all that matters. Does this beauty possess a name?"

"Her name is Sally. Sally Curtis."

"I hope it works out Gil, you deserve something good."

He had never thought his late wife had borne much physical resemblance to either of her parents. However, at that moment as Gil hugged Marjorie in what was for him a rare display of affection, he saw something of Jules in her face; it was approving and felt good.

This scene was interrupted by George from the lounge, where up until this point he had been snoring on the sofa, mouth agape like a Venus fly trap with Spike in a similar condition in the crook of one arm. He'd suddenly resurfaced from the arms of Morpheus to announce in a sleepy post-lunch drawl, "I think it's the Queen!"

Gil had remonstrated with himself several times over the journey back for not taking up their invitation to stay, at least until morning.

"All the sane people are home!" he exclaimed. These words were wasted too on his sleeping companion.

Marjorie was right. He had become withdrawn since Jules' death, almost reclusive. Life had lost almost all its sweetness. During the three hours since leaving Somerset, Gil had seen relatively few vehicles on the road, it being Christmas Day on top of weather warnings; he'd been a fool! The concentrated effort required for driving under such conditions was straining his eyes. Driving had never been a favourite pastime of Gil's, even before the accident. For some time afterwards it had been touch and go whether he'd ever go near a car again.

Gil Harper was thirty-nine, married and widowed just the once. He had the kind of features most people seemed to find pleasing: dark hair just beginning to show some grey and a pair of keen blue eyes set in a lean but open face. Despite being quite presentable, and having various dates set up for him by well-meaning friends all of which had come to nothing, five years on from the accident he was still finding it hard to break free of the grief. He had not been ready to form a new relationship.

Gil was quite successful, which always seemed a bit unexpected to those who knew him well, as he possessed very little materialistic drive. He illustrated books, mostly for children, in an anarchic and unique style, often emulated, but rarely executed with anything like the same skill. Success had come early in life and for the past eighteen years Gil had collaborated with one of the world's best loved children's writers. However, this happy partnership was sadly due to end, as Felix Blatt had announced his retirement the previous summer. Gil, with a lot of encouragement from Felix, had begun to write the text of a children's story of his own. When he'd shown him the first draft, Felix had been full of praise, albeit with some positive criticism.

The feeling of isolation from being cooped up in the car for so long, the drone of the engine, constant rain and lack of other vehicles along the route were beginning to produce a sense of mild cabin fever. These vaguely depressive feelings were alleviated a little by Spike, who suddenly opened his eyes, yawned, and went on to perform a languorous dog stretch. His next action was to rise and place his front paws on the window sill to survey the landscape. Clearly unimpressed, Spike sat down again, emitting a sigh much too large for his diminutive stature.

"Only fit for ducks, hey? It's getting me down too, Spikey."

Gil felt cheered slightly when a minute or two later the car's interior was faintly illuminated by the headlights of another vehicle, a good distance behind.

At the same moment Spike gave out an unfamiliar sounding low growl.

"Home before long, boy."

Some people hold to an opinion that animals possess intuitive abilities that we have either lost or never had. Much later, Gil would have occasion to look back at that seminal moment and wonder if Spike had instinctively felt apprehension; whilst he, with his superior brain, had failed to sense a thing.

As the car came closer, Spike seemed to become more unsettled, expelling a series of plaintive whimpers.

Gil assumed it to be toilet trouble. "Not long, Spikey," he said and decided to pull over as soon as they were off the motorway.

It was difficult to estimate the speed of the other vehicle, the rapid approach suggested its driver's foot must have been pressed hard on the accelerator. By now Gil had to avoid his mirrors because the fast gaining car had failed to dip its lights.

Spike, whimpering, pressed his head into Gil's thigh.

"I'll stop soon as I can, boy," he told the dog.

Gil stole a quick glance at the rear mirror but immediately recoiled, his eyes momentarily blinded. "Give me a break!" he yelled. He wondered if the driver was drunk.

Suddenly, without indicating, the car shot past. Gil was relieved. He wanted to flash his lights up and down several times, just to let the other driver know how it felt being blinded. He thought better of this, "If he's pissed that might only make things worse," and decided to let him go his merry way. From the speed the car was moving, Gil would have expected to see nothing more than a set of disappearing tail lights half a minute later, but this didn't happen. As soon as the other driver had overtaken, he decelerated and pulled into the lane just ahead of Gil. Gil was forced to brake and then drop his own modest speed of fifty to below forty.

"What the hell is your problem?" Gil shouted in exasperation. This brought Spike to his feet, and taking a full stretch, he leaned onto the dashboard to let out a growl followed by three warning barks.

"That's right Spikey. He is an arsehole."

No sooner had Gil expressed this opinion than the other car began to pull away at an incredible lick. Considering the treacherous road conditions, such a speed was extremely ill advised. The gap grew between them so fast that it seemed likely the other vehicle had accelerated to a hundred mph at least. Gil was glad to watch as its tail lights reduced to nothing more than red pin pricks in the haze ahead.

"Thank God for that! We can relax again Spike."

Spike however remained on guard duty. And Gil's moment of elation was short-lived when he noticed through the thick sheets of rain that the car ahead must have braked quite hard and that he was rapidly catching up. At first he wondered if there was more flooding, a speed restriction or some obstruction on the road, only to realise unnervingly, once he reached the leading car, that there was nothing. Both were now travelling in convoy at less than thirty mph.

Gil wondered if he'd come upon a bunch of joy-riders out for kicks. If this was the case, then he suspected they would only speed up again if he overtook them. He felt slightly better about things when the car in front started flashing its hazard lights and eased over onto the hard shoulder. As Gil passed the slowing car he attempted to catch a glimpse of its occupant or occupants, but the darkness and rain made this impossible. He briefly entertained the idea of stopping to see what was wrong and whether he could offer some assistance, but swiftly dismissed the notion as a bad idea.

"I'd be no use if they have broken down. Anyway, serves them right for driving like morons."

Gil had managed about thirty yards before he realised to his horror that the other car was tagging alongside. He felt enraged by the inanity of whatever this stupid game was about, and against his better judgement, put his foot down hard on the gas to break away. At first it seemed he might make a clear break and leave his tormentor far behind. Sadly, not for long. The wing mirror showed the other car was getting closer on the hard shoulder. The rain was pummelling the windscreen so fast during this acceleration that Gil needed to strain forward in order to catch a fleeting view of the road as the wipers cleared the streams of water. Spike became more agitated and was growling loudly. As Gil's Volvo touched seventy the maniac was only a car's length behind. Having embarked on this direct action, Gil acknowledged he had little alternative but to see it through. He clenched his teeth, screwed up his eyes and stepped on the gas pedal.

"I'll give you a chase if that's what you want you moron!" he snarled.

Somehow the situation had Spike caught in its grip too. He was rushing to and fro, barking with unaccustomed ferocity, one second at the windscreen, the next at the passenger window. Uncontrollable frenzy had seized the moment and the deafening noise coming from the dog provided an aptly manic soundtrack.

The speedometer needle passed eighty, eighty-five, ninety. At each of these stages Gil looked over his shoulder to see if his pursuer had given up. There was no change. Ninety-five, a hundred, a hundred and five; his adversary was right beside him. Gil was beginning to feel a loss of control in the steering as the wheels found it increasingly difficult to gain purchase on the wet surface. At a hundred and ten Gil had nosed ahead by a few yards, a cold sweat breaking out on his upper lip, the car slithering like a toboggan on a slalom run. Spike was gnashing his teeth, frantically dashing about; the car's interior was bedlam.

"Shut up Spike!" Gil shouted, but Spike, who, as a rule, liked to please, either didn't hear or was too overwrought to check himself.

Gil felt an insanity take hold of him. He put his foot right down until the accelerator was pinned to the floor. The car surged forward; a hundred and fifteen, a hundred and twenty and increasing; it was like trying to manoeuvre a drunk on roller-skates. When the speedometer read a hundred and twenty-seven mph, Gil's control of the steering was so tenuous that to have gone beyond must surely have brought destruction. Even so, the temptation remained when he saw the pursuing car draw level; but sanity won.

Perhaps sensing that Gil had reached his limit, the other car suddenly burst into the lead and cut into the lane with just a few feet to spare. Gil, his heart in his mouth and fearing they might touch, swerved out to the middle. At this point Spike lost his balance and tumbled onto the floor but almost immediately recovered to resume barking at the window. The other car then suddenly veered right, directly into Gil's path. He had no option but to slam his foot on the brake. As they screeched into play, the car began to aquaplane across the wet surface. Fortunately Gil remembered to steer into the skid, although he wasn't certain whether it had been this action or just sheer luck that saved them from hitting the central barrier.

"Oh Christ! Oh hell no! Oh Christ!" he screamed. For a split-second it was like he'd been transported back five years to the accident.

As the car's speed dropped, Gil regained control of the steering. The other car had gotten clear and was now about two or three hundred yards ahead. Gil settled back into the slow lane at forty. It looked as though the machismo game was finally over. This was until Gil noticed the car's brake lights flash up again.

"Fucking idiot! Fucking idiot! Fucking idiot!" he raged.

Spike had hit the deck again when they had gone sliding across the carriageway and this time he stayed there; he'd stopped barking too and lay trembling before the passenger seat giving short heartfelt whines. Gil identified with the dog's anxiety; he too was shaking like a leaf, his breathing shallow and rapid.

Gil was determined not to engage in any more of these lethal games. He would not be goaded into increasing his speed again and would stick to 40 mph whatever. The other driver certainly wanted to play some more and did everything he could to engage him. The first ploy was to plant himself directly before Gil and cause him to brake unexpectedly. The next tactic was to come out of the lane, drop behind, flashing his lights, travelling so close that if Gil's speed had wavered they would have collided. Out of desperation, Gil considered braking hard as a drastic means of disabling the other car. "But I might put myself out of action too, or get off worse. Christ, a maniac like that might be carrying a weapon!" His thoughts betrayed the point close to despair that he had now reached.

A motorway sign brought with it new hope of breaking free. The Clacket Lane Services were three miles ahead. An idea formed: it required the other car to be in front when they reached the exit. There was only one thing to do, speed up as if to get away, and hope his adversary would take the bait.

It worked. Gil shot off as though he planned to make another escape bid and the other car immediately gave chase. Gil had no intention of reaching the dangerous speeds he previously had; this time he would stay in control of the situation. Sensing Gil had reached his top speed, the other car careered out into the middle lane before overtaking and cutting in recklessly close. It was stupidly dangerous but it worked, and although Gil was forced to brake, the speed was far lower than before, only around seventy. And this time Gil was expecting it.

As the services approached, they sailed past the first countdown point with the other car just ahead. At the second marker Gil was praying that whoever was at the wheel of the other car wouldn't anticipate his intention.

"Just keep going you arsehole!"

The final countdown; Gil showed no sign of wavering, shadowing the lead car and playing perfectly the role assigned to him of being the taunted prey. Then, at the very last moment, when it was already too late for his adversary, he took the exit. He couldn't resist flashing his lights in what he knew was an impotent show of defiance as the enemy car sailed off into the dark, wet night.

"I hope you go blind you mad bastard!" he exclaimed with much feeling.

As might have been expected there were only five cars in the parking area. He let Spike out onto a grass verge and scrambled out himself to take deep gulps of air. He was unconcerned by the rain that soon drenched through his sweatshirt, and feeling that his legs might give way, he leaned against the car for support. It actually came as a relief when he began to throw up.

2

Thursday 25 December

I did laugh when I saw you vomit over your car.

You just didn't have the stomach for our brief encounter, did you? Or perhaps a bit too much stomach? (Tee hee!)

I'm content to let you wallow under the delusion that you somehow bettered me by escaping into the services.

It's what I wanted you to think!

I suspect there aren't too many people who'd have the guts to back up along the motorway like I did? Even over Christmas with nothing else around.

After you came out of the toilets you sat in your car for ages, head in hands poor, poor, thing, until you plucked up enough courage to get back on the road. A white van started up and went out directly after you - accommodating I thought. I followed on behind. And you, deluded fool, didn't suspect a thing!

Perhaps you were half expecting me to have parked up on the hard shoulder, waiting to pounce on you like the wicked wolf?

Bet you'd need a change of trousers if you knew I'd followed you - wee wee wee - all the way home.

MERRY CHRISTMAS!

3

Gil arrived home, quite exhausted, just after 11 pm; a journey he generally managed in less than three hours had taken over five.

He had never experienced anything even remotely like the encounter on the motorway and couldn't prevent himself from going over the events in the order they happened.

Had he provoked the other driver in some way?

No. Nothing he'd done could have warranted such aggression.

He brought the car to a standstill on the pea shingle drive before his garage doors.

'Christ, it was like being ten years old again,' he thought. At this age, Gil had suffered some pretty nasty bullying. His family had uprooted from the West Midlands and moved south when he was eight to resettle in a village in Berkshire. For a small boy, with an accent, a different cultural identity and who was appallingly bad at sport, it was alienating to say the least. At primary school, a group of children had conspired to make his every day a living nightmare. The kids who might have gravitated towards the school newcomer were frightened off by the ruling schoolyard junta and Gil became a loner. He learned to fake illnesses to avoid school. His parents despaired; his mother took to worrying about him; his father preferred to believe the boy was congenitally lazy, a trait undoubtedly inherited from his wife's side. Gil never breathed a word to anyone about the bullying.

Subsequently, it had always struck him as odd how nature appears to balance up her weakest points. All those hours alone, looking at comics, drawing grotesque caricatures of his enemies in embarrassing situations, had honed and developed skills that as an adult had provided him with lucrative employment.

Although he knew it was irrational, the motorway experience had awakened some of these bad memories, and had left him feeling impotent and ashamed. This may explain, at least in part, why he hadn't called the police as soon as he stopped at the motorway services. However, he knew he'd been in the wrong too: the law was unlikely to accept that he'd been simply goaded into driving fifty miles beyond the speed limit; it would probably result in an automatic ban.

Not in the mood to get soaked again, instead of putting the car away in the garage, he and Spike made a dash for the front door. Gil opened up, went inside and immediately punched in the code to disarm the security alarm. He made straight for a bottle of scotch in the dining room, and poured himself a large one. The alcohol brought a soothing warmth which seemed to root its way to just the right spot. Gil was not a heavy drinker but on this occasion he didn't mean to stop at one. He took the bottle with him when he went through to sit with a fairly blank expression at the long oak table at the heart of the kitchen.

"What a bastard of a night!" he exclaimed with heartfelt conviction.

Spike appeared with a well-mauled pink toy rabbit in his jaws.

"Glad to get home hey, Spikey? Me too," he said, patting the dog's head. Spike growled playfully, dropped the pink rabbit at Gil's feet and scarpered away expectantly. Gil made a dummy throw, which only fooled Spike for a fraction of a second, then bowled it underarm into the conservatory. Spike recaptured his favourite toy then settled into an armchair in the conservatory for an affectionate chew.

Gil returned his attention to the glass of scotch and took another sip. He let out a deep sigh, there was still sadness attached to coming home. Then, recognising that if he got stuck into the bottle without eating he would end up maudlin and morbid, he found smoked salmon and an assortment of cheeses in the fridge, which together with oatcakes made supper in minutes.

Gil Harper had lived for fourteen years in the same detached Edwardian house on a broad, tree-lined road near the Vine cricket ground in Sevenoaks. The house was sizeable, with five bedrooms and a quarter acre of garden. He and Jules had stretched themselves financially in order to buy it, although its value now made the original sum look paltry. He'd considered selling after Jules' death, so much of her personality was stamped everywhere on it. But so far he had stuck it out.

Gil was in the process of making coffee when Spike dashed past him into the hallway. He assumed the dog's sense of purpose was an entirely canine matter, but paid more attention once he heard him bark. It was the sound he made when someone unrecognised came to the door. Gil felt a twinge in the pit of his stomach as the doorbell rang; it was almost midnight.

"Shush Spike," he said as he strode into the hallway. For the second time that day Spike ignored a command.

A figure was partly delineated through the glass panes of the door, but it was too dark to identify it. Gil remedied this by putting on the porch light before he rushed to open the door.

"Sally!"

"I'm sorry Gil, I hope you don't mind. I saw your light was on. You said you'd be back sometime this evening and ..." Her speech was rapid, almost garbled.

"That's okay. Come in. Be quiet Spike!"

Spike, slightly behind Gil's leg, had adopted a warning-off pose, but on this command he stopped barking and sat down, albeit suspiciously.

"Thanks. I'm really sorry about this." There was an anxious note in her voice. The light jacket she was wearing had been soaked through.

Once she'd entered the well-lit hall, Gil could see the tell-tale signs that she'd been crying.

"Something's upset you?" he asked with genuine concern.

"Oh God Gil, I was really scared," she replied. The tears began to flood from her eyes. "I've been driving around for ages. I thought I was being followed!"

Gil closed the front door, took Sally's jacket and hung it over a radiator. He poured her a glass of scotch and fetched a towel.

As he watched her dry her short dark hair, he realised what a long time it was since any female had performed this simple action in his home. There was something oddly sensual about it.

Sally Curtis was thirty-one, five foot seven inches tall, with a lean and rangy frame. Gil had gleaned, after their two dinner-dates less than a week ago, that her background, like Jules', had been more conventionally middle-class than his own. Sally had been educated at a series of girls' boarding-schools. On their second date, she had talked briefly of her parents' divorce and how her late mother had struggled to make ends meet. She'd studied textiles at St Martin's, but had not found the world of fashion much to her liking. Later on, she had somehow fallen into making costumes for several theatre and opera companies on a freelance basis. She liked the variety of the work and being on the periphery of the theatrical world, enjoyed its bonhomie without needing to be totally immersed in it.

"I must look terrible," she said, attempting to smooth her tousled hair with trembling fingers.

"You look fine," he replied, and meant it.

She smiled and their eyes momentarily engaged; hers he'd noticed at the time of their very first meeting, were brown, doe-like and warm.

She took a sip of scotch, gripping the glass in both hands, shivering slightly. "You're very kind," she said.

"So what happened?" he asked.

She sighed heavily. "Old boyfriend trouble … story of my life. No matter what I do I always seem to end up with dickheads."

Gil felt suddenly crestfallen; although she was not referring to him, the statement still seemed damning.

She looked up apologetically, "I'm sorry, you don't need this."

"If you'd care to tell me, I'd like to understand why you looked so troubled when you rang my doorbell?"

"It's after midnight ... I have to set off for Birmingham in the morning, very early."

"Visiting friends?" he asked.

"Work," she replied, "Costume emergency on a pantomime."

"Then stay the night," he said, and immediately regretted making the suggestion, fearing it might have sounded predatory. He quickly amended, "I mean, there's plenty of room … four empty bedrooms to choose from." He added as a joke, "Spike and I share."

She laughed, "I don't think Spike has taken to me. To be honest, I don't feel very secure with dogs."

"You'll be alright with Spikey then, because he isn't one. He's actually a reincarnated lama from the farthest reaches of the Himalayas taking a bit of time off from too much karmic harmony and enlightenment. Aren't you boy?" Spike wagged his tail and came forward hesitantly.

"I don't suppose there were many girls up at the monastery," Sally said, joining in the fantasy and tentatively offering her hand for Spike to check it out.

"About once a year some nuns from a nearby convent might go past and wave."

"It must be a pretty good thing being your dog," she said. Spike had begun to mellow; Sally had discovered his Achilles heel - a spot just under his chin.

"Mostly it is. But we didn't have a very good time on our way home tonight."

"I bet! That awful rain!"

"That didn't help. There was an idiot on the motorway playing dangerous silly buggers."

"Did you get his number?"

"No," Gil scowled. "To be honest it didn't cross my mind until I pulled into the services. The visibility was dreadful. I probably wouldn't have been able to make it out anyway."

"Oh well, you got back safe and sound, that's the main thing."

"And what about you, you said you thought someone was following you?"

"I think my imagination got the better of me."

"It gave me quite a fright when you landed on my doorstep."

"Poor Gil, I'm really sorry if I frightened you," she laughed.

Gil found the effect laughter had on her features totally absorbing. "So, are you going to tell me about it?"

"The smell of that coffee is intoxicating, may I have some?"

He poured the coffee and filled a jug with cold milk from the fridge. As he put the hot drinks down on the table he noticed that both their whisky glasses were empty, "Would you like some more?"

"You're sure I wouldn't be putting you to too much trouble if I stayed?"

"Course not."

She held out both glasses for him to top them up.

They sipped their drinks for a few moments in silence.

"You probably won't be interested in seeing me again if I tell you about myself … when you find out just how stupid and neurotic I really am."

She had said these words half jokingly, but Gil could see that underlying this she was quite troubled.

"You don't have to tell me anything unless you want to," he reassured her. "I'd like us to get to know each other better no matter what."

Sally was clearly touched by this declaration, and she replied, "I'd like to at least try and explain, if that's okay?"

"Fine by me," he answered.

"About four years ago I met someone. To begin with it was fun, he was successful, urbane. I felt I deserved a break on the relationship front. To begin with it had all seemed very different, so romantic. He'd send me bouquets every day for a week, take me to lavish hotels for romantic weekends, one time he even booked a weekend in Vienna just to surprise me. I suppose I found all the attention flattering, but as the months went by he became more and more possessive; he didn't want me to work away from home, didn't like me doing anything much unless he was there to hold my hand." As she spoke she made two fists with her hands and brought them up to her temples in a gesture of frustration. "I felt like I was being suffocated. His personality was so dominating," a look of despair came over her face, "and I'm so bloody weak and vacillating."

"Don't talk about yourself like that, we've all found ourselves vulnerable at times," remonstrated Gil.

She grew calmer again. "I allowed him to take over my life. He insisted I move in with him. He took over my finances. He put my house up for sale, bought me a new car, though I loved my old one. He even started buying clothes for me, like I was his property or something. He went so far as arranging the time and place for our wedding without consulting me. Can you imagine that?"

"But you didn't marry him?" Gil asked uncertainly.

"No. In fact it was the wedding that brought me to my senses. When I had the temerity to protest that I should have been asked, he went berserk. He became so aggressive, I was ready to cave in just to appease him, which usually worked; but this time he just got madder." Sally paused; Gil could see the tension on her face. "He started using me as a punch-bag." She was shaking now. "Then ... he raped me."

"Christ, what a bastard!" Beyond this Gil found himself speechless.

"I took off next morning after he'd left for work. I left the car, clothes, jewellery he'd bought. A friend collected me and took me to her home for a few weeks. He'd found a buyer for my cottage, but fortunately the contracts hadn't been exchanged and I managed to hang on to it."

"Was he charged?"

"I took out a non-molestation order against him. He wasn't allowed to come within three miles of my house for a year. All my friends wanted me to take him to court. I wasn't sure. Michael has a habit of getting out of scrapes."

"That's his name then, Michael?"

"Yes. He's quite a big-shot in the city. He could easily have afforded a good lawyer. I took legal advice from a friend who reckoned Michael would get a suspended sentence at most."

"That's appalling."

"Apparently it's still true that judges aren't keen to sully the reputation of a formerly upstanding citizen, especially someone with all the right credentials."

"That's awful!" exclaimed Gil.

"I can't say I was too eager to go through the legal process, suffering all the humiliation it might entail, only to come off the loser. I've already told you what a coward I am."

"I don't think it was cowardly, you sought advice and after consideration chose the best course available."

She smiled, leaned forward and kissed Gil's cheek.

"What was that for?" he asked.

"For listening, and being considerate."

"Not all of us men are arseholes, you know."

She nodded, "I admit that for a time I wondered."

Gil changed tack, "So he's been troubling you again? I mean, since all that happened?"

"Yes, for about a month now. I left him just under two years ago. He kept well clear of me after the order was put in place. I thought it was all over. Then one evening in late November, I saw him across the road; he was watching me getting off the train from London. I thought it might have been coincidence. Then a week later the same thing happened again, only this time he followed me home. I was scared stiff."

"I bet you were."

"Since then it's happened twice more."

"Did he attempt to talk to you or anything?"

"No. I think he just wanted to unnerve me. He can be a vindictive sod! He's been ringing me too from time to time, at least I'm certain it was him, he never spoke."

"What, heavy breathing or something?"

"Just nothing. I'd pick up, and silence, as though he wanted to make sure I was at home. He's an incredibly jealous man."

"Did you try to trace the calls?"

"Public telephones."

"And tonight?"

"Tonight he spoke. He rang me on his mobile. He was very drunk. He said he wanted to come over and put things right between us. I told him that if he came anywhere near me I'd call the police. Then he got abusive, called me an effing whore, said I was still engaged to him and that he knew I was seeing someone." Sally paused before adding, "Presumably that meant you, because I haven't been seeing anyone else. More than likely it's all in his head; he used to suspect me of seeing other men if I spoke to the paper boy."

"But you were afraid he might come over so you got in the car?"

"Yes, and for a while I thought he was following me, but I think it was just that I was so worked up by then. He was very drunk on the phone. I drove around for well over an hour, through villages I'd never been to before. Eventually I found myself in Sevenoaks."

"You did the right thing. I'm glad you decided to come here."

## 4

The next morning, Gil woke just after nine. Sally had left a note on the kitchen table which read:

*Thanks for being there last night. If you're still interested*

*in seeing me again, I should be back on Tuesday.*

*Say hi to Spike.*

*Sally x*

Gil smiled. Even though the note was concise, he knew from its tone and what it left unstated that she was declaring an interest in him; he was very attracted to her.

"It's mighty strange this romantic business," he told Spike, who was watching his master attend to a pot of simmering porridge. "It's nowhere near as simple for me as it is for you, dog, sniffing around any accommodating backside. We humans have romance, courtship and there's such a thing as subtext to contend with."

Spike responded with a quizzical look, cocking his head to one side.

Gil replied as though a genuine question had been posed, "Subtext ... what isn't said. A bit like when you take to your basket and sulk if I'm late with your walk."

Spike's tail began to wag at mention of the 'w' word; there was nothing more to learn about subtext.

"You are utterly transparent, dog."

The rain had finally stopped during the middle part of the night and had not resumed. After breakfast, he let Spike out into the garden while he sat in the conservatory with coffee and settled down with the novel he was reading. But however much he tried to involve himself in the book Gil found that his thoughts kept returning to Sally's unannounced appearance. They had chatted until just after 2 am. He was glad they had not ended up sleeping together; he suspected it might have happened given different circumstances, but after she'd confided in him about the rape it would have been utterly the wrong moment.

Unable to settle, Gil went upstairs to dress, followed by Spike, who'd grown tired of the garden. After dressing, he went into his office, a large comfortable room purpose-built above the garage. Along the wall beside the door was a nineteenth century draughtsman's desk built out of solid oak. He had bought it at a junk shop in Kilburn out of the first advance he had received as an illustrator. Beneath the window on the opposite wall was another desk with a monitor and keyboard. To one side of this modern desk was a comfy chair draped with an old blanket showing grubby paw marks and liberally covered with white hairs. At the study's farthest end were French windows opening onto a small verandah with cast iron steps leading down to the rear garden.

He sat at the desk and logged on to his computer. The first thing he did was to check his emails, mostly spam and nothing of any importance. Then he typed in the password and opened up his diary. It was good to catch up; the last entry he'd made was on 23 December before leaving for Somerset. For Gil, getting stuff off his chest in this way had always had a cathartic effect; it was probably the reason why he had kept a diary for so long. On this occasion he wrote:

> Had the misfortune to meet a complete arsehole on the motorway tonight. Luck of the draw I expect. I was certainly at the wrong place at the wrong time ...

After this, he replied to the half dozen or so letters from children waiting in the in-tray to be answered. Although he employed Megan to assist with general paper work, he tried to respond personally to letters from children.

By midday Gil had completed all the correspondence. Spike was getting restless; the dog's body clock never failed. Gil put on his wellies and a coat and allowed Spike to eagerly lead the way from the front door to the car.

The sight that met his eyes caused his jaw to drop.

The car windscreen, side, rear windows and bodywork were streaked white: trails of paint, long dry, had run in all directions; the rain had interfered with the paint's solvents, causing it to dry in ugly pustules like chicken pox. The quality gloss was guaranteed to remain durable for up to five years; at least this is what it proclaimed on the can now sitting on the car roof with several holes punched in its base.

A gasp was all Gil could manage.

## 5

Within the hour a policeman arrived.

'Blimey, it's true,' Gil thought, observing the bright-eyed constable on his doorstep, 'They do get younger.'

This youthful officer introduced himself as PC Dave Rowe.

"Your Volvo certainly looks *unique*, Mr Harper," Rowe said with a wry smile.

Gil wasn't ready for humour about his trashed car yet, especially coming from the mouth of a Botticelli cherub. "I'll get my coat," he replied in a rather surly tone.

"Did you make the discovery, sir?" the constable asked as they crunched across the pea shingle.

"Yes, just before I rang the station, about ten past twelve."

Constable Rowe went to his own car first. He put on a pair of latex gloves and took a plastic bag from a roll. After this Gil followed the younger man as he returned to the Volvo. Rowe removed the paint can, placing it carefully into the plastic bag which he secured along its sealing-strip.

"Pretty much dry," said Rowe testing a finger to the atoll of white paint that had surrounded the can. "You heard nothing?"

"Nothing at all, but my bedroom is at the back." Gil thought a moment, "A friend stayed over and slept in that room." He pointed up to a window left of the garage, "She couldn't have heard anything either."

"Surprising," Rowe replied, "Pea shingle makes quite a racket when it's walked on."

"Perhaps she's a heavy sleeper, or maybe it happened before we went upstairs?"

"Is your friend still asleep?" asked Rowe.

The question seemed stupid at first, before Gil realised that the bedroom curtains were still drawn. "No, she set off early, before dawn," he explained.

"Were you in the house all evening together?"

"No, my friend turned up late … around midnight."

If Rowe was surprised by the late visiting hours of Gil's female friends he didn't show it, "Did she come by car?"

"Yes."

"Where did she park?"

"Here on the drive I'd imagine."

"Then she'd surely have seen the damage to your car. Once she'd started the engine, put on her lights, it would stick out like a sore thumb, don't you think?"

"Maybe she parked on the road. I didn't see her arrive or leave." Gil suddenly felt defensive; the way innocent people often can when questioned by the police.

"Being Christmas, I expect you'd been at home until your friend arrived?"

"No. I only arrived back last night too. I'd been staying with my in-laws, in Somerset."

"You and your wife," Constable Rowe corrected.

"Alone. My wife is dead."

Rowe looked uncomfortable, "I'm very sorry to hear that sir," he said.

The young man's awkwardness made Gil feel instantly sympathetic towards him, "There's nothing more to see here. Shall we go in?"

"Good idea," said Rowe.

Gil went in and put the kettle on. The constable packed the tin of paint away in his car boot before joining Gil in the kitchen. The atmosphere became quite relaxed as they sat and drank mugs of tea. PC Rowe checked and noted down Gil's car registration documents and took some notes.

"I expect the journey home from Somerset was pretty grim."

"Visibility was awful. There was a lot of water on the road. I didn't get above fifty for most of the journey." Gil hesitated before adding, "Then, as if things weren't bad enough, I had a run-in with a nutcase on the M25 who kept cutting in and out. He tried to goad me into racing him."

"Did you get the registration?"

"Sorry."

"Make, model?"

"Dunno. My late wife used to claim I was 'vehicularly challenged'. I'm afraid I know nothing whatsoever about cars."

Rowe smiled.

A terrible idea then occurred to Gil which he couldn't help voicing, "You don't think he could have followed me home and done the paint job?"

Rowe perked up, "Did the car follow you off the motorway?"

"No. I lost him at Clacket Lane services. He stayed on the road."

"Not likely then, is it," said Rowe a little disappointedly.

Gil agreed; the hairs on the back of his neck were able to stand at ease again.

The conversation moved on to the time after Gil arrived home.

"Miss Curtis was anxious you say?"

"She thought she was being stalked by an old boyfriend."

"Did she see him last night?"

"No, but he rang her. She said he sounded extremely drunk. He wanted to visit her. He's been violent in the past. She was scared."

"Understandably," said Rowe.

"She drove around for an hour, thinking he was following her, before landing up here."

Rowe seemed unconvinced, "Bit unlikely wouldn't you say? That he managed to pursue her for an hour if he was extremely drunk?"

It did sound implausible.

"Sally said she panicked after he rang. She acknowledged it was probably just in her imagination that he'd come after her."

Despite this, Rowe still seemed to consider it a worthwhile line of investigation, "Even if he wasn't following, he may already have known where you lived." Biro poised, he asked, "What's the boyfriend's name?"

"Ex-boyfriend," corrected Gil. "I only know his first name - Michael."

"Where can I reach Miss Curtis?"

"She's away for a few days, but I can give you her mobile number."

"Fine," said Rowe.

Once everything had been covered Gil led Rowe to the front door.

"I'll contact Miss Curtis and have a word with this other gentleman."

Rowe bent down and patted Spike's head, "You can get your walk now, boy."

Spike's tail got busy at mention of the 'w' word.

# 6

Gil was not expecting to hear from Sally until Tuesday; he planned to ring on the evening of her anticipated return. Having been devoid of any romantic feelings for so long, he thought it surprising how much he longed to see her.

It was about four hours after Rowe's departure. By this time, Gil had walked the dog, read a few pages of his novel, taken a catnap and was in the process of peeling the plastic film off a microwave dinner when the telephone rang.

"Hallo," he cheerily responded.

"Gil?"

He recognised her voice immediately.

"Hi Sally. How's Birmingham?

His question was met at first by silence. After a moment, she said, "I was contacted by the police."

"I gave your number to them. I've had some trouble. I'm sorry, I should've let you know they'd be ringing you ..."

"That might have been considerate." Her reply was frosty.

"I'm sorry Sally, but I had to call them ... you'd understand if you saw my car."

"Why did you accuse Michael of vandalising it?" Her voice was rising, "You've absolutely no idea what he's like!"

"He's been pestering you again. You thought he'd followed you. Perhaps it's time to get this sorted out."

Sally started to cry. "That is so arrogant of you!" she said, "You discussed with the police what I told you in confidence last night. I am so angry about it! I thought you were different, but you're just the same as all the bloody rest!"

"Sally, you're upset ... if you'll let me explain ..."

"Explain what? That you don't want to take over my life like he did ... like every other man I've ever come across!"

"Sally, I don't want to take control of your life, I would genuinely like to get to know you better, on equal terms. I don't want to own you ..."

"Yeah, like I haven't heard that one before?" She fired the words at him scornfully through her tears, "Sorry Gil, but you're not going to get the chance!"

"Let's meet up when you get home. You're angry at the moment ..."

"Well done, you've managed to comprehend that much at least."

Immediately after this the line went dead.

Gil took the corner of his microwave lasagne and flung it at the bin. He missed.

## 7

Saturday 27 December

I wonder how you reacted to my little Picasso touch. Strange, isn't it, what some people leave in their car boot when they go away on holiday?

I haven't slept very much for days. All the excitement of the chase I expect. I feel alert, in command. I have such an incredible energy inside. I know I could achieve anything I wanted to.

I daresay there are those who would call me deranged. I can easily imagine their disapproval as they sit watching soaps on TV, living under the delusion of being alive, whilst gorging their bloated bodies and feeble minds on rubbish.

"GIMME MORE!"

It's Christmas! A time for pouring sugar and fat into their putrid carcasses, another piece of cake, a mince pie, another multi-pack of 'cheesy thingys' - and the real world passes right on by beyond their cosy lace curtains.

"I'm feeling a little dissatisfied with my life.

"If only I could lever my lardy fat backside out of this triple-seat sofa, I know what would satisfy me. One of those king-size bars with nuts and marshmallow on a crunchy biscuit base covered in creamy chocolate. I've seen it advertised. Sexy. I got such an erection when I watched the TV commercial for it that I thought I was going to soil my pants.

"OOH! YUCK!

"What's this on my telly screen, pictures of children with bloated stomachs like mine, only the rest of their bodies are skeletons. I can't bear to look! It's ugly!

"Must change channel and cram something into my mouth to take the bad thoughts away!

"That's better!

"Shocking stuff like that shouldn't be allowed! Might put people off their food! Anyway, they aren't the same as us! It would be terrible for a civilised person to be underfed like that! They don't feel things same as us.

"I know what I'm talking about. I read about the world in 'The Daily Scumbag'. It's a challenging blend of sport, leisure, with information about all my favourite soaps and just the right amount of news. It keeps me well informed, with the added bonus of nubile young lovelies exposing their breasts on every other page - slags! I wouldn't let a daughter of mine take her kit off, to be lusted over by perverts!"

## 8

The sun came out for a few hours on Saturday, but it failed to lift Gil's spirits.

He knew Sally had been unreasonable on the phone, but conceded that he might have checked with her before implicating a man, who, judging from what she had confided in him, she had good reason to be wary of.

"I finally meet someone I like and I wreck it straight off. What an ass! And for what? Rowe implied that the episode was unlikely to conclude with much of a result anyway!"

Sally had told Gil that Michael had been very drunk when he rang. Was it possible that, drunk and incapable, he had managed to follow her for over an hour, then magically produced a tin of white gloss from the boot of his car? The more Gil thought it through, the more unlikely it seemed.

Gil could think of a few people he didn't like much, and where quite possibly his low opinion of them was reciprocated. However he was unable to think of anyone likely to undertake such a rash act, especially as the miscreant must always run the risk of humiliation if caught.

'Perhaps it was just a bunch of kids who'd been out ransacking garden sheds and came by a cache of paint,' he thought.

After some time listening to his head running on like this, he finally reached a point where he stopped trying to figure out what had happened. He rang his insurers; after all, the repair costs wouldn't even cause them to raise a corporate eyelid. As anticipated, they viewed the incident with a dispassionate professionalism. They would arrange for an assessor to visit, and provide a courtesy car.

On Sunday, Gil tried to work at his children's book in the vain hope that it would help take his mind off Sally. For two hours he laboured, only to produce one slim paragraph with the flow and consistency of suet pudding.

"Shit ! Shit! Bugger and bloody shit!" He raged at his computer screen as though he meant to do it grievous bodily harm.

Spike, as usual when there was writing to be done, took it easy on his chair. On this occasion though, he seemed to sense Gil's inner tension and from time to time let out a sigh. Gil believed the dog was voicing his disapproval, and found it extremely distracting.

"Will you stop that!" he lashed back at the dog after hearing what he perceived to be a particularly accusing exhalation of breath. Spike raised his head, his face bore the look of noble suffering.

Gil scowled, highlighted all the text on screen, decided it was irredeemable crap and pressed delete.

"Okay, toe-rag, you win!"

The indomitable Spike perked up at once.

## 9

Felix and Kate Blatt lived in a beautifully renovated oast-house, just on the edge of the village of East Peckham, about twelve miles south-east of Sevenoaks.

The Blatts' door was rarely, if ever, locked during the daytime, so Gil and Spike went straight in as they always did. "It's only us!" he called out.

Spike charged through the entrance hall and disappeared up the flight of stairs ahead. A moment later Gil heard Kate's voice raised in adulation.

When Gil reached the kitchen on the first floor, Spike was already stretched out on Kate's lap. She was sitting alongside a pine table at the centre of a light and airy kitchen.

"That dog is a slut," said Gil.

"He's a lovely boy," Kate defended, "And how's my other lovely boy?"

"Not happy," he replied as he reached down to plant kisses on both her cheeks.

Kate Blatt was in her mid-sixties. Her almost translucent skin and sparkling deep blue eyes ensured that she would always remain an enchanting woman. Gil had never known her make any effort to disguise her age, her shoulder length hair was grey, drawn back into a pony tail, and she never wore make-up. Her clothes were casual, jeans and a white shirt with a red and gold scarf about her neck for colour and that indefinably feminine touch.

"A generalised post-Christmas ennui, or does this melancholy have deeper significance?" Kate asked.

"Take a look at my car," he said, fishing out from his pocket a print of the digital photograph he'd taken that morning.

Kate gasped at the sight of his vandalised car.

Gil explained about finding it in this state on Boxing Day. He told her too about Sally arriving scared on his doorstep.

"Sally? Who's Sally?"

"She's a girl I met at the beginning of December."

"You dark horse! Sounds like romance may be in the air, Harp."

"I thought so maybe too, at least until she rang up and blew me out of the water."

"Angry? At you? Why?"

Gil explained. "Seems I should've consulted her before suggesting her 'ex' was the budding Leonardo."

"More Jackson Pollock, I'd say," said Kate referring to the print of the car in front of her.

At this point, they heard the front door open and close downstairs. Spike sped off excitedly in response. This was followed by the sound of greetings, footsteps ascending, and Spike's re-entrance in Felix's arms. Felix was dressed for outdoors in waterproof coat, hat and scarf, having been for a Sunday morning stroll.

"Harp!" the elderly man cheerfully cried out as he entered, "I suspected we had guests. But didn't recognise the car. Feared the worst. Thought of my detestable nephew and his appalling wife. Almost didn't come in, briefly considered running away to sea." Felix gently transferred the supine Spike into Kate's arms and gave Gil a welcoming hug.

"Harp's had car trouble," understated Kate.

"Mechanical?" inquired Felix.

"Hardly," said Kate passing the print to him, "See if you can diagnose."

Felix peered down at the photo and without registering even a flicker of surprise said, "There have been reports of low-flying pterodactyls over Sevenoaks."

"I can believe it. If extinct flying reptiles came to life you can bet my drive would be their number one site for target practice."

"Harp needs cheering up," said Kate, slipping an arm under Gil's and depositing a kiss on his cheek.

"Right. Come with me, Harp. We're going to the cave for some male bonding," he told Kate as they started to descend.

"Lunch will be ready in about an hour. Leek and potato soup," she announced.

"Soup? Men like us need meat!" exclaimed Felix; Felix Blatt was a lifelong vegetarian.

"There are a couple of bison steaks in the freezer," Kate volleyed back.

"Rare!" asserted Felix.

Spike made no effort to leave the kitchen with its culinary possibilities and Kate, so easily corruptible by such a charming fellow as himself. The two men went via the back door into a courtyard surrounded by one storey brick outbuildings. They took a door to the right. The space they entered, originally stabling for horses, had been converted a quarter century earlier into a workspace for Felix.

The room itself was about fifteen foot wide by thirty foot long. It was divided into two distinct areas: a carpentry workshop at the rear, where Felix often whiled away the early hours restoring furniture or carving bowls on his lathe, and his writing study where they now stood. A slim glass partition separated the two spaces. Unlike Gil's workspace and its nod at least in the direction of technology, here, there was only a telephone to suggest the room belonged to modern times. There was a couch strewn with cushions and a dishevelled array of blankets in case Felix required a nap during a writing session. There were two comfortable armchairs, a wall of shelves bearing reference books, an antique writing desk on which was resting a pad of lined A4, a fountain pen and a pot of ink.

Despite having visited this space many times during the years of their collaboration, Gil never failed to experience a sense of awe and wonder when entering the great man's domain; to Gil, Felix Blatt was not only a fine writer of children's books but also a staunch friend, and as Gil would readily acknowledge, something akin to a father figure too.

Felix Blatt would reach eighty years of age in the summer, and although the years had bowed him slightly, at six foot three he was still an imposing presence. His marriage to Kate had lasted forty contented years. It was one of those happy unions that had only been slightly marred by an unresolved wish to have had children.

The two men sat across from each other in the armchairs. Felix asked, "How were Marjorie and George?"

"They were fine. I tried to look like I was having a good time. I really don't understand why they put up with me."

Felix smiled, "Well, Harp, you're not altogether a disagreeable type, even if you do find it a bit hard to look cheery about Christmas."

"Marge thinks it's time I let go of Jules and found myself a new partner."

Felix nodded but said nothing.

"I told her I'd been seeing someone."

"You're a bit of a dark horse, aren't you, Harp?"

Gil smiled, "That's exactly what Kate said."

"Where did you meet?"

"Tonbridge Library. She was doing historical research on costume design and I was brushing up on my physics for *Pete's Pirates*."

The answer struck Felix as marvellously absurd. His fertile imagination immediately conjured up images of discotheques and singles bars losing out to public libraries, along with muscle-bound librarians in velvet tuxedos and frilly shirts imposing a strict dress code at the door.

"The green shoots of romance perished under an early frost, I'm afraid," said Gil. He went on to explain in less florid detail exactly what had happened.

"I can see you were really smitten with her."

"I suppose I was. She's the first person I've met since the accident that I actually wanted to be with."

"Then it's down to you, old thing."

"What can I do? She doesn't want anything to do with me."

"All's fair in love and war. Take a crack at wooing her back!"

"How?"

"For heaven's sake Harp, how should I know? Ring her. Get talking again. Tell her how keen you are. You think of something, you're the one with the problem!"

"Thanks for the benefit of such profound wisdom."

"Not such bad advice," laughed Felix, amused by the look of despondency on his friend's face. "I do have some experience in these tender matters, you know. Nobody wanted me to marry Kate; I think her father would almost have preferred giving her away to white-slavers. My own family seemed to regard me as barmy at best.

"Kate's father had connections in the Foreign Office and organised a job in Canada for her lasting a whole year. Kate, to her credit, wasn't about to be pushed around like that. I proved the softer touch, so they went to work on me. They made what seemed at the time quite reasonable appeals, pointing out the difference in our ages, which I was of course already well aware of.

"Her father invited me to his club one evening, it was the first time he'd been anything other than openly hostile towards me. In fact, on this occasion, he was extremely civil. I should have guessed what was coming, 'Kate's still very young, if you truly care about her you'll allow her this year to think things over, for the duration of which you must agree to have no contact with her. If at the end of one whole year, you both feel the same about this match, which both her mother and I know will prove disastrous, then I will not stand in your way'."

Gil had never heard any of this before, "Did Kate go to Canada?"

"Not on your frickin' life, Harp! I wasn't prepared to lose the first woman I'd ever wanted to marry to some damned Mountie in his cabin out in the back of beyond."

## 10

At lunchtime, over soup, salad and garlic bread, they had talked about what Felix claimed would be his final written work, his autobiography, which was to contain illustrations drawn by Gil. After lunch, they adjourned to the downstairs sitting room, appropriately decked out with a Christmas tree etcetera, and exchanged presents. The Blatts insisted that he stayed to dinner, and he and Spike finally returned home around nine.

## 11

Gil was thinking about turning in for the night when the doorbell rang. It was shortly after 11 pm. He had left the light on outside in the porch when he got back, so this time it came as no surprise who his late caller was.

"Hallo Sally, you got back earlier than expected then?"

She looked uncomfortable, "Yes, I'm sorry to call on you so late again, Gil. I wanted to see you. I thought perhaps we could talk things over ..."

"Of course we can. Come in."

She remained on the doorstep, head drooped on her chest, staring at her feet. "Gil, I feel really awful about the way I spoke to you, I wanted to apologise. You must think I'm a complete bitch."

"I don't think that at all, I think I can understand why you got so upset ..."

She looked up at Gil; she seemed so vulnerable standing there, "If you meant it, what you said on the phone … about getting to know me better ... I just want to say, I'd like that too. In fact, I can't think of anything I'd like more."

Gil took Sally gently by the arm and pulled her into the hallway, flicking the front door shut behind her. A moment later they discovered themselves in each other's arms, embracing with a passion Gil had not known for a very long time.

## 12

Sunday 28 December

Just think, all I had was your house number and street name.

It took about two minutes to get your postcode, with this I got your name off the electoral register and then your telephone number. The satellite pictures of your house and garden are charming and informative – just so nice to see how it's all arranged.

You are Gil Harper. You appear to live alone. You are an artistic type – a book illustrator. You are mostly associated with the work of a children's author called Felix Blatt. Judging by the number of hits on your website you must be popular. Your house suggests you must be successful too.

Never heard of you myself!

But isn't information technology a marvellous thing?

## 13

Gil awoke shortly before eight. In the first moments of consciousness he recalled the passionate scenes of the previous night, the intensity and heat of love-making. He felt wholly content; he just wanted to lie there, to watch her sleeping, bathe in the shared warmth of their bodies as they embraced. It was so long since he had lain with someone in his arms, an Ice-Age.

Gil would probably have remained exactly as he was if it hadn't been for Spike. The dog nudged open the bedroom door, with what Gil interpreted to be a disdainful look on his canine features. He let out a low growl which usually meant he wanted something; possibly the toilet.

Gil extricated his arm from beneath Sally without disturbing her, took his dressing-gown down from a peg on the bedroom door, and followed Spike who led the way.

The dog showed no interest whatsoever in stepping out into the garden when Gil opened the back door. Spike had been letting Gil know it was their breakfast time.

Throughout the making of their porridge Gil felt the need to voice feelings of resentment, "You just couldn't let me enjoy the moment. You're like some kind of mini dictator, a canine Napoleon," and wondered how to draw a dog with one paw across its stomach.

An hour later, Sally surfaced. By this time, Gil was reading the paper in the conservatory.

"Hi," she greeted him tentatively.

"I thought I'd let you sleep. You seemed tired."

"I wonder why?" she replied with a knowing smile.

At this, Gil was unable to suppress a boyish grin.

Sally was wearing a bathrobe of his; somehow the masculine design and the coarseness of the towelling increased her femininity. She planted a kiss onto his lips.

"Mmm ... coffee flavour," she said, smacking her lips together.

"Want some?"

"Can't a girl get any rest around here?" she asked.

"Coffee too, if you like," Gil replied, getting in on the double entendre act, but a touch late on timing.

She laughed, "Yes, please. Hallo there you gorgeous boy!" she told Spike.

Spike, sprawled on the chair beside Gil, offered up his tummy.

'Low life!' thought Gil.

After pouring coffee, Gil made Sally some scrambled eggs. They chatted and joked while he got them prepared.

"So why exactly did you have to rush off to Birmingham?"

"I'd designed and made these rather complex ballgowns for the Ugly Sisters. They had lights sewn all over them."

"Sounds technical."

"I didn't have anything to do with all that stuff, 'the sparks' got the lights to work. It was very effective. They flashed on and off whenever Prince Charming walked past. Unfortunately, and unbeknown to anyone else, the actor playing Buttercup, that's the sister in question, had put on about a stone and a half since his costume fitting in October. Somehow, he'd managed to shoe-horn himself into the dress, but on Christmas Eve, during a very physical dance routine, he burst forth, so to speak. Unfortunately, the actor was wearing hardly anything underneath."

"Bloody hell!" exclaimed Gil, "They weren't dancing to *Great Balls of Fire* by any chance?"

"No. But you're getting the picture."

"What did the audience make of it?" he asked.

"A few complaints but mostly they loved it apparently. They appeared to think it was part of the action."

"So you needed to do a rapid dress repair?"

"No. The girl who runs the wardrobe could have done that. The director thought the moment worked so well he wanted the dress rigged so it could fall apart at every performance.

"Presumably with the addition of some appropriately over the top underwear?"

"Of course. In the true spirit of British pantomime, girls being boys and men grotesquely prancing about as women."

"All in the best possible taste."

"The best," Sally echoed, "Incidentally, the number they'd been hurling themselves about to, which probably clinched the moment, was *June is bustin' out all over*."

"You're having me on?"

"No, I'm not," she chuckled.

Gil put the plate of eggs on the table before her.

"Any ketchup, please?" she asked.

"Yes, I think so."

He found an unopened bottle, and watched with fascination as she dribbled it across the eggs.

"Do my eating habits gross you out?" she asked anxiously, "I've eaten them like this since prep-school."

"Not at all, it reminded me of someone ... that's all." He felt embarrassed; it seemed a dead-cert romance-killer to mention his late wife at this early stage in the relationship.

"Julia?"

"Yes, sorry."

"Nothing to be sorry for. We've both had relationships before. From what I've been able to gather, your marriage was really good, a genuine marriage of minds," Sally shrugged, then smiled philosophically as she nibbled the corner off a slice of toast, "whereas all my relationships have ended in tears."

"Surely not all?"

"No, not quite all … but the truth is I've done a pretty neat sabotage job on every man who didn't want to hurt or abuse me."

"You must have a fairly low opinion of men?"

"I hope not ... least, not anymore. Although, I took a pretty good shot at wrecking our chances of ever getting together when I bawled you out on the phone." She smiled wryly, before going on, "By my late teens I was well on the way to becoming whatever the female equivalent of a misogynist is. I'd inherited such a lousy pattern from my parents. My mother was prepared to suffer any humiliation to save her marriage to a man who set out to bed, without exhibiting an ounce of remorse, any tart that ever wiggled her rear-end at him. Her submissiveness didn't work though ... he still dumped her, just as soon as he found a replacement doormat - a younger version of my mother. I never saw him again after he left. I was thirteen."

"He really did desert you."

Sally shook her head, "Actually it was me. I wouldn't let him come anywhere near me. I wanted to punish him for what he'd done to her … and me."

"Do you regret taking that action?"

"Probably," she replied. "Both my parents died within a month of each other. Mum died of a rare form of stomach cancer, it consumed her in a matter of twelve weeks from the time it was diagnosed. He telephoned me right out of the blue. He wanted to come to her funeral. But I still couldn't forgive him for what he'd done to us. He actually pleaded with me, said I could never understand how much he'd loved her. After he said that I really let him have it, proceeded to list all his crimes and misdemeanours ... at least the ones I knew about. By the time I'd finished, he was sobbing." She scanned Gil's kindly face with the dark pools of her eyes, tears had collected in them. "But you know about my temper, don't you?"

"It was insensitive of me to give that policeman Michael's name."

Sally made a gesture to suggest the whole thing should be confined to history. She collected her thoughts again, "Twenty-eight days after my mother passed away ... Dad was dead too."

"How did he die?"

"He had a boat at Plymouth. He'd been a naval officer, sailing was second nature to him. He'd been drinking, according to the coroner. It was reckoned he'd most likely fallen overboard, and passed out when he hit the water."

"Tragedies happen. Believe me they do," Gil said.

"Is it possible to ever forget the past, do you think?" she asked.

"No, not forget, but perhaps it's possible to come to terms with it, resume living."

"You don't sound one hundred percent certain?"

"I'm not, but 'being here', getting on with the little things that give our lives meaning, is all we've got."

Instinctively, they both knew that to go on any further would be demanding too much from a relationship in its fledgling stages. As for Gil, he was not ready to discuss the details of his personal tragedy with Sally yet.

She returned her attention to breakfast and nothing more was said for a time. Then she asked, "Do you have work planned for today?"

"I probably would have worked, but being here with you is much better."

"I've got to do some chores and stuff later but I don't have to leave 'til two-ish." Her eyes twinkled seductively at him.

"Let me see, did I manage to show you every one of my etchings last night?" he asked, feigning a lascivious look.

"You certainly did, but I'm sure another viewing would do no harm."

## 14

### Monday 29 December

I had to go to a supermarket today. It was sickening. Like watching a swarm of locusts descending, or flies landing on some extremely choice piece of excrement. Here, in the midst of people I feel the most alone, an individual amongst automatons.

Today as they turned out in droves from their stinking boxes, panic about the eyes, aggressive, territorial, fearful there may be nothing left to buy, filing like rats from a thousand sewers, stockpiling provisions. What ugliness, men and women drowning under oceans of flab, unashamed by their grossness, glorifying in the crassness of their vacant minds. Like it was "PROUD TO BE FAT UGLY AND STUPID WEEK".

I am alone. Forced to inhale the reeking stench of stinking bodies, stomach churning body odours, rancid sweat disguised beneath deodorant.

Am I the only one?

If our leaders and politicians were anything but useless themselves, they'd speak out. But they know better than to upset the apple-cart, flattery is more expedient. Tell people how fine, how intelligent they are, how valuable and worthwhile their tawdry little lives are. Encourage their stupidity, promise anything, anything they are able to conceive in their minuscule brains. Let them cram their bodies to bursting with all the junk they drink and eat, watching pornography and masturbating themselves stupid. Let them fill themselves up with the banalities of early twenty-first century life.

Let them feast on their burgers and cola until their foul offal bursts at the seams of their stretch marks. A society filled to the brim, unable to delay gratification, wanting for nothing; yet starving.

Is this my species? God's Creation? If so, then the child turned out a bastard! What a delusion, to believe a Divine Being, capable of creating the heavens and the earth, decided after only six days to make Man? Lo and behold, His crowning glory! Moulding Adam out of clay, and in His own likeness no less!

Am I expected to believe these buffoons, staggering behind loaded trolleys, were designed by God?

A man with eyesight so dim he had to bring each item up to his germ-infested nostrils before he could see what it was; or the middle aged woman wearing make-up as thick as the icing on a birthday cake. A truly gorgeous sight! Who would ever want to have sexual relations with that you ask yourself? A mother who looked about twelve, with two brats in tow, one gratefully restrained in the shopping trolley while the other went rampaging about with chocolate like smeared excrement around its mouth and teeth, which blended nicely I thought with the two strings of mucus dangling from its nose. Or the elderly married couple, plodding zombified through the aisles, bored into a living death long ago by each other's company. Their week's most major dilemma, which brand of fish fingers to get?

BEHOLD THE LIKENESS OF GOD!

## 15

It was Tuesday morning when Sally raised the subject of the proposed party. Sally had left Gil for a few hours the previous afternoon but had returned later on to spend the evening and subsequent night with him.

"I'd love it if you'd come with me to a New Year's party I've been invited to. Klaus Williams is a very good friend and I know you'll get on together."

Gil, unable to think of any decent reason why not, thought what the hell, and said, "Great, yes."

"Brilliant."

"Where is the party?"

"Wandsworth."

"London?" Gil asked, instantly exhibiting less enthusiasm.

"Klaus has a house there."

"Er … I'll arrange somewhere for Spike. I'm pretty sure the Blatts won't mind." He made it sound problematic, without trowelling it on too heavily. He could be almost certain that Felix and Kate would be happy to play host.

In social matters Gil was invariably reluctant to get involved, though generally he entered into the spirit of things once the initial inertia was overcome.

He couldn't help adding, "As long as Felix and Kate aren't doing something!" knowing full well that every New Year's Eve the Blatts entertained at home.

Sally, uncannily, just as Jules had invariably done before her, paid no attention to the problems he'd duplicitously raised, and just said, "Great!"

Gil rang and explained to Kate about being invited to a party. She told him they were only having a few local friends round and that Spike would be guest of honour, "I take it you scored with the library girl then, Harp?" she said.

He wondered how women always knew so damned much. He said, "How did you deduce that?"

"When did you last celebrate a New Year, Harp? This has to be her."

"Mmm, I'll drop Spike round late afternoon, five-ish okay?" he said grumpily.

"Come a bit before that for coffee, and bring *her*."

"Mmm. Maybe, if we're not too pressed for time."

Kate laughed, far too knowingly in Gil's book.

Changing the subject he said, "You can't think of a hotel in London we could stay at, can you? So far everywhere I've rung was booked up months ago."

Sally had said they could stay in Streatham at a tiny flat belonging to her friend Roz if all else failed. Gil couldn't say he felt very enthusiastic about this idea.

Kate said, "Hang on a minute, Harp."

Gil could hear her discussing the problem with Felix.

After a minute or so she came back to ask, "Felix wants to know how many rooms?"

"One," he replied.

"Oooh!" said Kate with a giggle before disappearing off the line again to report back.

After this Felix came on, "Leave it with me, Harp. I'll see what I can do."

Twenty minutes later Felix rang back with a booking arranged, "It's all sorted out. It's where I lay my head whenever I need to stay over since I gave up the flat. They'll make you comfortable there I'm sure."

"Thanks Felix. You're a pal."

"I'm trusting you, now, Harp," began Felix, sounding intensely serious, "This is my favourite hotel. And I believe I'm held in fairly high esteem there. Please don't go wild and end up trashing the room! No rock-star antics, please!"

"I'll do my best to contain my rock star alter ego," laughed Gil.

16

The insurance assessor rang Gil shortly after he'd finished speaking with Felix and arranged to see the car on Wednesday morning. Unless he deemed it to be an uneconomical repair, which judging by the age and value of the car seemed extremely unlikely, the re-spray would probably go ahead the following week. Gil had kept the car locked away in the garage since the paint attack.

When he'd shown it to her, Sally had exclaimed, "My God, it's a total mess!"

"No doubt the work of some budding artist," he said sardonically.

"In that case it couldn't have been Michael, because he doesn't possess an artistic bone in his entire body."

Gil hesitated before asking, "Could it have been him?"

"I don't know. He's rather indolent, especially when pissed. He certainly wouldn't have driven home to Hadlow to fetch a tin of paint. By some strange quirk of fate he may have had a tin stashed away in the boot, of course."

"Seems a bit unlikely, doesn't it?"

She thought about it, "He's certainly vindictive enough."

"The chap the police sent round, Constable Rowe. He said he was going to have a word with him ... perhaps they didn't bother. The insurance company are footing the bill, so perhaps it's best forgotten."

Sally smiled, but the underlying tension remained, "Not bothered about getting your pound of flesh?"

"I think pinning it on him, even if he was guilty, is unlikely. And as for getting my pound of flesh, I probably feel more animosity towards him on your behalf than on my own. I mean, beyond the Michael part, I don't even know what he's called."

"Chilvers ... Michael Chilvers."

"You're still quite scared of him, aren't you?"

"Not when I'm with you."

17

Tuesday 30 December

You're quite a sad character.

I've just been reading some archive accounts relating to the accident that killed your wife. When you consider what happened to her, I think it's quite remarkable how much spirit you showed on the motorway when we met.

I wonder how you felt about your wife's killer getting off so lightly. I think I would have needed to intervene if the murderer (let's call a spade a spade) of someone I cared about got away with only two and a half years in prison. So, high marks for how you behaved on the motorway but poor marks for accepting an unacceptable verdict.

I suppose some might say, 'Poor chap, he's suffered enough, walk away, let him get on with his wrecked life.' Many people might think like that – but you know what Gil, you aren't dealing with them. I always see everything I do right through to the end.

By the way, your house is worth a fortune. I found out what the asking-price was when you bought it and what it's likely to be worth now. Almost five times what you paid for it!

I've said it before and I'll say it again, isn't information technology a marvellous thing?

## 18

New Year's Eve began on an uneasy note when Gil and Sally were woken at 7.50 am by a phone call from Constable Rowe. He had been to see Michael Chilvers the previous afternoon. Apparently, Chilvers had been so drunk when Rowe called, that the constable had found it necessary to caution him about his abusive language.

"As you might expect, he denied damaging your car. However, he did admit ringing Miss Curtis on Christmas Day but claims he fell asleep immediately afterwards." The constable went on to say, "If he was as drunk on Christmas Day as he was yesterday, I doubt he was capable of much. Anyway, if he was involved, now I've talked to him, he'll think twice before doing anything like that again. I suggest, for the time being at least, we let sleeping dogs lie. He'd be crazy to bother you again."

The assessor for the insurance company came to see the car at 9.30 am, and he arranged for a recovery vehicle to pick it up less than an hour later. Because of the holidays, the re-spray would take a few days, but in the meantime Gil was perfectly happy with the courtesy car.

For the rest of the morning Gil and Sally passed the time pleasantly in each other's company. That afternoon, Gil followed Kate's explicit instruction and took Sally along with him when he dropped Spike off at the oast.

Now, several hours later, they were on their way to the party in London.

"I'm glad you liked the Blatts," Gil told Sally, as he brought the car to a stop at a red traffic light.

"They're delightful. It's so romantic, meeting two people who've been together for years and years that are still devoted to each other."

The lights changed and they moved off.

"Do they have children?" Sally asked after a lull in the conversation.

"I think that's possibly the only sadness in their lives together. They both wanted children. Poor Kate had a series of dreadful miscarriages."

"How awful," Sally hesitated then asked, "Did you and Jules plan on having kids?"

For a moment Gil affected more attentiveness in his driving "I think we both would have liked a family," he replied then quickly came back with, "How about you?"

Sally laughed, "Not me. I like kids, but other people's are better. You get the nice bits without the angst. Most of my girlfriends are either already mums or about to be. Do you still want to be a father?" She asked the question almost too earnestly, as if she feared his answer might be affirmative.

"Not anymore. I can't imagine it would be much fun being constantly mistaken for your kid's granddad."

"You're not old, lots of people start families late these days."

"Not me. I'm too settled, too selfish." Gil pointed to a signpost, "Wandsworth."

"You need the next right," directed Sally.

As he prepared to make the turn the clock on the dash said 8.40.

The conversation was making him uncomfortable, so he changed the subject, "So our host, Klaus Williams? How do you know him?"

"When I was a student at St Martin's, he gave a series of guest lectures and workshops. He told me to get in touch once I'd graduated. We've worked together quite a bit since. He designs sets for most of the leading opera companies. He's quite prestigious - Covent Garden, La Scala. He recently designed a new production of Bizet's *Carmen* at the Met."

"He gets about then."

"He's a sweetie. He's been really helpful in my career ... very supportive back in the days when Michael didn't want me to work. 'You must work, darling,' he kept saying, 'it would be a crime to let your talent go to waste.' Michael and Klaus loathe each other. Almost came to blows once or twice."

Sally had just used the two most clichéd words associated with the theatrical lexicon: 'sweetie' and 'darling'. Gil wondered if he was about to spend the evening adrift on a vast ocean of slush and lovie-ness and felt a rush of apprehension.

## 19

Klaus's home was an impressive double-fronted Victorian property over four floors. They were let in by a girl in her mid-twenties who greeted Sally as an old friend. Gil missed her name when introduced due to the vocalisations of David Bowie's *Changes* blaring out from the room to the right. A sudden stampede of teenagers clambering down the staircase before him was no aid to hearing either. Later, he deduced the friend's name was Roz. Sally had already mentioned her; she often assisted Sally with costume-making and sometimes provided her with a place to stay over in London.

Roz shouted above the competition, "Our Sal has been very secretive about you Gil. For instance, she didn't think to mention how tasty you were."

Gil half-gathered what the girl said through party osmosis; which is, gleaning the barest gist of a remark and nodding appropriately.

Sally brushed her friend aside with mock aggression and linked an arm under Gil's, "Hands off, slattern!"

"Thought he might appreciate a bit of variety, that's all."

"I can provide all the variety he requires, thank you."

A dancing man about Roz's age came out of the room playing the Bowie, grabbed around her waist and started to propel her towards the music. "Hi Sal," he greeted with a wave.

"Hi, John. This is Gil," called Sally.

"Hello there Gil," said the younger man, releasing a hand from Roz's waist to shake Gil's before continuing on his way. At the door he spun the happily-consenting Roz about and slapped a hand down on one of her pert buttocks, protruding like a sun-ripened peach beneath a short, black, spray-on dress.

"He's a sweetie," commented Sally.

At first, Gil found himself noting every 'sweetie', 'darling' or 'love' he heard. However, his uncertainty about being thrust into this alien environment quickly passed, and he was soon discovered laughing, joking and generally enjoying himself. The evening was not exclusive to people from the world of opera, and the number of children present suggested a family event. These children were generally seen marauding up or downstairs like a troop of demented Von Trapps.

Food and drink was in plentiful supply in the large basement kitchen area. Sally, leading the way downstairs, was greeted by a cheer from the crowd already gathered there. A Neanderthal-browed, short, stocky, curly-haired man, about fifty, in jeans and a t-shirt that bore the slogan 'Opera kicks ass', threw his arms affectionately around Sally. On the back of the t-shirt was a photograph of the late Luciano Pavarotti in defiant pose, with a superimposed hand and a raised middle finger.

"Sally, I'm so glad you made it."

"We thought we should see the year in in style."

"You've definitely come to the right place then, plenty of that here, darling," replied the man, affecting a more camp delivery.

"I'd like you to meet Gil Harper, Gil this is Klaus Williams."

Klaus took Gil's hand in his bear-like paw, "Welcome Gil," he boomed in a deep baritone voice, which would have made it easy to believe if he'd been introduced as a singer. Then he whispered in a playful aside to Sally, "So, this is the one you've been missing heartbeats over?"

Sally flushed pink.

"She's been obsessing about you for a couple of weeks, Gil."

Gil felt a little abashed too, even if it was flattering. Chuckling he asked, "Do you always go in for the ritual humiliation of your guests?"

Klaus gave a wicked laugh. "I always say, if you can't embarrass the guests at your own 'do' then what's the point?"

A man in his mid-thirties, a foot taller than Klaus but with a contrastingly slight build approached the group.

"Hallo David," greeted Sally, placing kisses on both the man's cheeks.

"How are you Sal, did you have a nice Christmas?" The young man's voice was gentle and Gil observed that his mannerisms were quite naturally feminine.

"Christmas was alright ... the holiday since has been immeasurably better," she replied clutching Gil's arm.

"Uh-oh, she means filthy sex, David. Best cover our ears," interjected Klaus.

Sally playfully punched Klaus on the chest, "Gil, I'd like you to meet Klaus's partner, David Simpson."

"Very pleased to meet you, Gil," said David, offering his hand more formally than Klaus had done.

"Hello David, nice to meet you."

Sally asked, "How was New York?"

"Hectic!" answered David.

"Absolutely bloody marvellous," answered Klaus simultaneously.

"Which one?" asked Gil.

"Both," laughed David.

Having introduced themselves their hosts went off. Sally led Gil through the throng of people who had congregated around the room's central table, the main source of food. Over the next hour or so Gil found himself introduced to untold numbers of people whose names he didn't stand a chance of remembering. Sally was clearly well-liked and popular.

In his feverish illustrator's imagination Gil had pictured rooms packed like sardines with operatic heavyweights, like singing sumo wrestlers. He was surprised to discover that the majority of the guests were not performers; like Sally and Klaus a good many had ancillary roles. Some were connected to David through legal work and nothing whatsoever to do with opera; a lot of those present were the friends or neighbours of their hosts.

"Klaus and David know cartloads of people!" Sally told Gil as she fanned an overheated cheek with a floppy hand.

"I know what Klaus does, how about David, do they work together?"

Sally found the suggestion amusing, "I don't think they'd survive long if that was the case."

"It's just that you asked how New York went and they both replied, so I thought that perhaps ..."

"David took a sabbatical to be with Klaus. He's a solicitor, legal aid mostly. He's very socially committed. He's a real love … gentle, calm. Not a bit like Klaus who's totally extrovert. Remember I told you a friend had given me legal advice after my trouble with Michael? That was David."

"You look absolutely gorgeous tonight," said Gil, not meaning to change the subject, just suddenly struck by her attractiveness.

"Play your cards right, and well, you never know …" she said as she raised her eyebrows.

Their chat soon came to an end when Roz came down the stairs. Her eyes alighted on Sally and she forged a path to them through the animated crowd.

"Sorry. I've got to borrow your girlfriend," she said to Gil taking Sally by the arm.

Sally resisted, looking bemusedly at Gil.

"Come on Sal, I need your help. He'll be safe for five minutes." Roz assumed a mock seriousness, "There's this prat, who says he works for the ENO. He clearly doesn't know his arse from his gonads. He's been dissing the work of Matthew Bourne." Roz laughed, then gave them both a quizzical look, "See. It's really serious."

"I think you'd better go," advised Gil, who had not long before been introduced to Matthew Bourne's name in a Sunday paper. He decided to trade on this knowledge and add Brownie points to his street cred, "The honour of dance is at stake," he said.

Roz appeared to give him a perplexed look. Gil felt a moment of self-doubt about whether he'd made the right connection. Then she exclaimed, "See, Gil agrees!"

"Sure you'll be alright?" chuckled Sally, the two glasses of red wine she'd consumed beginning to show.

"Yes, of course."

Sally handed Gil the empty plate of canapés they'd been sharing and planted a gentle kiss on his lips.

"True Love," expressed Roz, eyes rolling heavenwards as she led Sally away.

Gil, alone with an empty glass, cut a course through the crowded room to the young man and woman serving drinks at the bar at the garden end of the room. Mission accomplished, he moved on to browse the buffet table.

"These are rather good," said a blonde in a vibrant dark red evening dress he suddenly became aware of beside him. This was entirely typical of Gil, who although observant by trade, had the peculiar knack of sometimes missing the blindingly obvious. She was the kind of woman it was very hard to miss.

Her dress gleamed with sequins that twinkled hypnotically as she moved, particularly in her generously over-prescribed chest area.

"Yes? Then I'd better sample them," said Gil, thinking 'massive breasts' and flushing at the thought of making even the slightest unintended double-entendre. He bent and peered at some Japanese-style canapés with almost forensic interest, then took a plate and made his choice. When he straightened up to speak to the woman again he tried to avoid the breasts, but couldn't be certain whether his eyes had fluttered onto them during their nervous flight past.

"Are you a friend of Klaus and David's?" he managed, looking at the woman's face with an unnatural keenness; he really wanted to drop his eyes and gawp, not in any way lasciviously, only to digest the phenomenon they truly were.

"Klaus has designed some of the opera productions I've sung vith," she replied.

Gil noted her accent, Eastern European, he thought. "You're an opera singer!" he exclaimed, restating what the woman had just told him.

"And vot are you?" she asked, her chest appearing to inflate after the question mark, which Gil couldn't fail but notice with his peripheral vision.

"I draw," he replied timidly.

"Vot, are you gunfighter?" she smiled playfully, as a pussycat might with a mouse in its sights.

"Sorry?" he asked lamely.

"You draw, like gunfighter in cowboy films?" she quipped, performing a little mime of pistol drawing, shooting, then with puckered lips cooling the imaginary gun barrel with a laconic out-breath.

"Ah! I see," he managed with an unconvincing laugh, his legs starting to feel unsteady, "No, the *art* kind of drawing."

"You are painter?" she asked, and before Gil had time to put her right, added, "Perhaps you paint me?" She turned and indicated her body in profile, "How vould you have me pose?" she asked.

Gil's mouth suddenly felt as parched as a desert landing strip. "I ... illustrate … books."

"How fascinating," she said, moving closer.

Gil felt himself deflate, her chest appeared to monopolise most of the available air space.

"Gil!" came the happy sound of reprieve. It was Klaus. He wore a bemused expression. "I see you've met Marika and her pet seals."

"You're incorrigible, darling," giggled the diva, placing a hand, many sizes too small, onto her capacious bosom for the sake of modesty. "Ve discuss art."

"Sorry to be a party-pooper at my own party but I'm afraid I need to take him away," said Klaus, taking Gil's arm.

"Shame. Perhaps ve meet later."

Klaus led the relieved Gil upstairs. "You looked like you needed rescuing," he smiled.

"Who was that?" asked Gil.

"Marika Novotny. She's playing Lady M in the new production of The Scottish Opera that Sal and I are about to start work on."

"Scottish Opera?"

"It's considered bad luck to say the name, you know ... *Macbeth*," said Klaus, suddenly not seeming to mind being accursed.

"Should I have known her?"

"Not unless you're an opera buff. She's up and coming, from Budapest, a fine soprano. Unfortunately, a lot of singers with clout won't work with her."

"Why?"

"Rottweilers."

"What?"

"Her unspeakably large puppies - they tend to upstage everything. Audiences are mesmerised by them. 'Never mind the singing, did you see those tits!' Dressing them down is going to be Sally's biggest headache."

"They are seriously unavoidable," gulped Gil.

"I suspect she crushes her victims between them like a Bond villainess."

Gil found the idea amusing.

"Was she coming on to you?"

"I'm not sure."

"Marika Novotny is a woman with large appetites." Klaus underlined 'large appetites'.

Gil sighed with relief. He began to wonder where Klaus was leading him as they ascended the stairs from the hallway to the first floor.

"Sal mentioned that you illustrated books. But it was only tonight, after being introduced, that the penny dropped and I realised who you were. Sorry."

"Don't worry. Most people haven't heard of me even if they're fans of Felix's."

"I remember reading about your car accident. Several years ago now, I think?"

"Five," said Gil.

"Really? As many as that?"

They were now approaching the second floor landing and had to step around a boy and girl in their mid-teens snogging on the top step. Klaus and Gil might have been invisible.

"Evening!" exclaimed Klaus as they passed.

The teenagers broke off momentarily and replied with a cheery, "Hi, Klaus," then resumed kissing.

To the right of the landing was a games room where a group of youngsters was gathered around a billiard table.

Klaus took a key from his pocket and opened a door directly opposite the room where the kids were playing into what immediately revealed itself to be his study, "It's not normally locked, but thought it better to tonight. Come in. I'd love to hear your views on some designs I've been working on with Sal."

"I know very little about theatre design," replied Gil.

The space was more eclectic than Gil's own work area. Shelves packed with reference books lined one whole wall; posters, mainly for opera productions, adorned most of the free wall space, and the ubiquitous computer was stationed at a desk in one corner. The focal point was a large table, and placed around the room's periphery were a couple of Chesterfield sofas. This room suggested collaboration.

"Have a seat," Klaus pointed to a sofa, "It's good to escape for a bit." He opened the door of a free-standing cabinet and produced a bottle, "Brandy okay?"

Gil peered down at the empty glass in his hand; he'd unwittingly drained it after his rescue from the Hungarian prima donna. "Thanks," he said.

Klaus poured the brandies, then sat on the Chesterfield beside Gil. "What's the time?" he asked earnestly, raising his wrist to show that he didn't have a watch.

"Eleven-O-five," replied Gil.

"Good. I've got to do the fireworks at half past."

"Fireworks?" enquired Gil.

"We generally start the New Year with a few bangs. The kids like it."

"Great."

"Do you have children, Gil?"

"No. My late wife and I didn't quite get there."

Klaus seemed to consider for a moment before saying, "My own kids are grown-up."

"You have children?"

"Don't look so surprised," laughed Klaus.

"I didn't mean to ..." fumbled Gil.

Klaus gestured that it was okay, "My ex-wife and the two youngest are here tonight."

"No bitterness then?"

"Not now. But I caused a lot of pain. There had been attractions, a few minor infatuations, but nothing too serious. I'd realised the truth, but lacked the courage to do anything about it. I was happily married, believe it or not. I constantly fought with myself. I didn't want to lose the good things I had. Then, David came along and everything changed, for everybody."

"Not the first time that's happened," said Gil.

"I was lecturing when we met. David was one of my students."

"Sally said David's a solicitor."

"I lectured in law. Becoming a stage designer was one of many changes I made."

"Sounds like you underwent a major re-think."

"I'd been groomed for legal stardom. My father was a barrister before moving into politics. He grew up in the South Wales coalfield, a grammar school boy from a mining family who dragged himself up by his bootlaces. Christ he could be a hard bastard! I did what I was told. After Cambridge I suppose my first rebellion was to become a lecturer rather than choosing to practise law. I thought the veins in his forehead would explode when I told him."

"So you're Welsh ...that explains the Williams part. But where did the Klaus come from?"

"My father met my mother in Germany during the post-war years."

Gil said, "My mother was Welsh, but you couldn't tell. She'd grown up in Birmingham. My grandparents went back to Wales after they retired."

"Where?

"Llandysul, Ceredigion. Do you know it?"

"No, but I've heard the name."

"I used to spend my school holidays there. They had a smallholding, not much, a few chickens and a pet pig. Actually, I still keep a little place in Wales."

"At Llandysul?"

"No, on the coast, a bit further north. It's a tiny cottage on cliffs overlooking the sea, between Llangrannog and Newquay."

"A bolt-hole?"

"I suppose it was."

The tone of Gil's reply prompted Klaus to ask, "Don't you get there much?"

"Not anymore. I should sell it."

Gil hadn't visited the cottage in Wales since Jules' death.

"Take Sally sometime."

Gil nodded, "Perhaps."

"Sal's very taken with you."

"I'm very taken with her."

"I don't know if she's mentioned it to you, but she had a very hard time with an ex-boyfriend a little while back. Poor thing, it nearly destroyed her. Sally's a wonderful girl, Gil," Klaus looked directly at him before adding, "I don't think she could handle an emotional ordeal like that again."

It suddenly occurred to Gil that the whole reason behind this little tête-à-tête might possibly have been to check him out.

If so, Klaus skilfully covered his tracks in the next breath by saying, "I'd better show you these designs." He fetched a leather-bound portfolio and unzipped it to reveal his drawings for the Verdi opera, which he spread out over the table. He let Gil peruse these while he fetched a 3-D model of the main structure. "Mostly bits fly in and out to change the scene. It has to be relatively light and easy to handle for touring."

Gil recalled the play from school and assumed the overall story remained much the same. "It certainly has a claustrophobic feel, a definite sense of foreboding."

"Good," said Klaus.

"I love these shapes, like tree roots," Gil added, referring to the organic shapes that made up the castle walls, like the ribs of some gigantic beast. Gil was reminded of the HR Giger designs for *Alien*. Of course, he didn't mention this, nobody appreciates it being pointed out that their work is derivative.

Klaus peered down at Gil's wristwatch, "Shit, I'm sorry to rush you after inviting you to see my work, but I really must get on and organise these fireworks. David's not very practical, couldn't light a candle. He'll be frantic."

"That's okay. I look forward to seeing the production."

The sketches and model were left on the table as they exited the room.

A couple of boys appeared from the room opposite, one asked, "What time are the fireworks, Klaus?"

"One-forty-seven precisely," replied Klaus.

"Huh?" said the other boy.

"Midnight, you donkey!" corrected Klaus as the two men started to descend.

"I thought so," said the boy.

"Then why'd you ask?" Klaus called back, turning to exchange a smile with Gil.

"I dunno. I just didn't know the time."

"Donkey!" exclaimed Klaus.

There was a slight pause, then came a less distinct, "Ass," and an extended, "Ho-o-o-ole," followed by giggling.

"Cheeky little sods," said an amused Klaus, "these spawn of the chattering classes."

"Where did you get that t-shirt?" asked Gil coming a step behind him.

"Like it?"

"It's terrific."

"It's a one-off. The hand is mine incidentally."

There is something about voices raised in anger that brings instantaneous alertness. Both men were aware there was something amiss a few steps before the turn of the staircase brought visual confirmation.

Before he saw her, Gil heard Sally; unable to make out any words but aware of the plaintive note in her voice.

There was another female voice, more distinct, angrier, screaming, "Leave her alone you bastard! Are you too stupid to get the message? She doesn't want anything to do with you! Just fuck off!"

There were two male voices amidst the cacophony, one low and sneering, the other light and calm.

Klaus rushed ahead out of sight. Almost at once, Gil could hear him shout, "Get out of my house!"

Gil turned the bend in the staircase. Klaus had already reached the hallway floor, where, prompted by all the commotion, a sizeable crowd was gathering. His face was flushed with rage, body weight centred down like a Welsh forward waiting to enter the fray.

"Fuck off!" Roz shouted directly into the face of a tall man with his back set against the front door who wore an expression of contempt. There was a dullness about his eyes that suggested he was drunk. The man's attention appeared to be concentrated on Sally, who was standing beside the balustrade at the base of the stairs. Roz and David had formed a protective first line of defence; Gil didn't doubt for a second this was Michael Chilvers.

"Are you getting out of my house, or do I have to kick you out, you stupid shit?"

Michael Chilvers gave a condescending laugh, "And what are you planning to do, attack me with your annual subscription to Chanel No. 5?" sneered the interloper.

"Right!" exclaimed Klaus as he rushed at the man ready to do as promised.

"Please Klaus, let me handle this!" interceded David who got between the two warring parties. Two other men, one of them Roz's boyfriend, stepped alongside to lend support.

Gil was now beside Sally and had taken hold of her arm. He wasn't sure she was even aware of his presence. Her face was ashen, the look in her eyes like that of a panic-stricken animal. Gil, unsure of what to do, merely held on to her.

"He's got thirty seconds to get out that door, David," warned Klaus, boiling with rage. There could be no doubt he meant to carry out his ultimatum.

Michael Chilvers appeared not to heed this warning at all. Gil had become the new focus of his swaggering glare, a fact Gil was conscious of but tried to ignore. Sally, suddenly aware she was no longer the target of Michael's attention, said in a tearful voice, "I'm sorry this had to happen, Gil."

"*Gill*?" mouthed Chilvers, "Like the fish have?"

David came in, "Michael, you've forced your way into a social gathering that you most definitely aren't welcome at. You have been asked to leave and I should advise you that if you don't go immediately ..."

"Save your breath 'legal eagle,'" said Chilvers, opening the front door, "I'm going, see." He turned unsteadily then pulled himself up to his full height, assuming the dignity every drunk believes with an unshakeable conviction they naturally possess. "I came here to wish some old ac ... acquain ... acquaintances," he smiled at his difficulty, "... a Happy New Year and I'm treated with contempt. So I'll be gone." He took another faltering step, only to turn again once he reached the threshold. His attention was still on Gil, who was looking directly back at him.

"Go then you bastard," said Roz, calmer now than before.

"Good luck, *Gill*! You'll need it. I suggest you have a word with her therapist..."

"I'll kill the bastard!" exclaimed Klaus, who made a spirited attempt to get by the little group that had him marked.

David pleaded, "Please Klaus, that'll do no good."

But Chilvers, drunk though he was, did finally seem to know what was good for him and he began to stagger down the steps, calling, "Happy New Year!"

Roz strode forward and closed the door after him.

Sally began to cry, broke away from Gil and fled upstairs. He was in two minds whether to follow.

Roz, seeing his dilemma, said, "Let me go first. She'll be alright, I promise."

Gil nodded.

The assembled guests didn't seem to know what to do with themselves.

Klaus gazing up at the hallway clock, announced, "Now for the fireworks!"

1 3 5
2 4 R

# SECOND

1 January – 19 January

## 1

It was past midnight before Sally felt calm enough to return downstairs. By this time the firework display was underway and the partygoers had decamped into the garden. Gil remained at the bottom of the staircase, his lone vigil punctuated by whoops and cheers coming from the garden.

He heard the approach of feet on the stairs, rose from the step where he sat, and turned round just as Sally reached the landing above.

"Hi," he said.

"Glad to see you're having a really good time too," she said with an ironic smile.

"Never was much for fireworks."

"Too many fireworks tonight," agreed Sally, descending.

"What an arsehole that man is!" exclaimed Gil, deciding it was time to voice an opinion.

"Let's not talk about him," she said, "He did the damage he set out to do. I'd just like to finish this evening the way I always intended."

Now she was close, Gil could see swelling around her eyelids and redness in the eyes themselves.

"What do you want to do?" he asked.

"I just want to be with you."

Gil stroked her hair then brought his mouth to her lips and kissed her softly.

## 2

Apsleys was everything Gil would have expected of an establishment recommended by Felix, who had always enjoyed comfort, luxury and good living in equal measure.

"Ah yes, Mr Harper. Reservation for two, Mr Blatt's favourite suite. Two nights."

"Two nights?"

"Yes sir, two. Mr Blatt telephoned to extend your stay. His treat. He said to tell you, that you needed the break," smiled the receptionist. "Mr Blatt is a long-established guest of ours. We're a family business. We tend to see the same faces, like old friends."

Gil shook his head and laughed, "Is that okay?" he asked Sally, "It seems the old rogue has arranged a short break for us."

"Fine by me."

The receptionist rang for the porter, who duly arrived within moments. "Palmerston Suite, Robert. May I wish you both an enjoyable stay with us."

"Thank you," they both responded.

The young porter took their bags and led the way to the lift. Their suite was on the fourth floor. "This is the sitting room," the porter informed as he held the door for them to enter. He deposited their bags on a low table next to the door then crossed the room to draw the curtains across a pair of French windows. The room was spacious, and decorated in keeping with the hotel's Regency period. It was impossible not to be enchanted by its elegance.

The porter took them through a set of double doors that opened out into the bedroom.

"The bathroom is just through there, sir, madam," the porter said, indicating a door at the top of a short flight of stairs. If you should need anything, don't hesitate to call."

Sally went off to explore the bathroom. Gil slipped a note into the young man's hand.

"Thank you very much, sir."

Once the porter had left Gil cast himself down onto the bed which proved extremely comfortable. The sound of running water was coming from the bathroom. He closed his eyes for a moment and began to reflect on the evening; how it had started uncertainly, then gone well, before going very badly awry; now, thanks to Felix, it was ending on an upbeat.

'Beginning,' he thought, 'Not ending. The first day of a New Year.' And he was starting it in a romantic setting with a woman he believed he was falling in love with.

The rap on the door, although gentle, caused him to sit up with a start. He strode back into the sitting room and opened the door to find the man from reception, bearing a silver tray with a bottle of champagne on ice and a pair of glasses.

"Compliments of Mr Blatt."

"Was that someone at the door?" called Sally from the bathroom.

"Yes," he answered, "Felix sent us champagne. Care for some?"

"Mmm, yes please. I never say no to champagne."

"Are you half decent?" he asked at the bathroom door.

"Come in," came the reply.

He followed instructions.

"Is this half decent?" she asked, reclining in the largest sunken bath Gil had ever seen.

"Very," he replied. He set down the tray, popped the cork and poured.

"It's got a whirlpool and jacuzzi. There's plenty of room. Why don't you join me?"

He passed her a glass of champagne and began unbuttoning his shirt.

"You wouldn't be planning on taking advantage of an innocent book-illustrator would you?"

"Most definitely," replied Sally, flicking a small turret of bath foam at him.

## 3

Gil lay awake in the dark with his arm about Sally savouring the moment. He listened to her breathing as she slept. He called to mind how great and long his hunger had been for tenderness. It was not the sex - not that he was objecting - but all the tiny things unavailable to him since Jules' death, taken for granted moments, shared intimacies.

There had been a few women, physically attractive, personable women. Yet these brief liaisons had only served to exacerbate his ever increasing sense of isolation. The women themselves hadn't been to blame. Perhaps it was a case of time being a healer, like the old adage, or simply a matter of finding the right person. Whatever it was, he was certainly beginning to grow strong feelings for this girl. Gil closed his eyes and was soon asleep.

They woke around ten; early considering how late it had been when they went to sleep.

Gil's eyes flickered open then shut again. He saw that Sally was already awake, lying on her stomach, chin resting on her hands. She was watching him.

He didn't open his eyes but smiling sublimely, asked, "How long have you been there?"

"Long enough."

"Not right. Spying on people."

"Did you know you were snoring?"

"Was I?" Gil asked sleepily.

"You were gurgling like a very bad drain!"

"Oh my God! Was I? Do I snore?" Gil was suddenly wide-eyed and thoroughly awake.

"No, I'm lying," laughed Sally, "You were sleeping like a pussycat. I just wanted to wake you up."

"That's very bad of you, very bad indeed," said Gil, screwing up his eyes to affect disapproval.

"What do you intend to do then?"

"Make you apologise," he said, at the same moment whipping her hands out from beneath her chin and throwing her down onto her back.

"Never," she laughed.

There followed various threats and counter threats, laughter and general horse-play. It would inevitably have led to love-making if there hadn't been a sharp rap on the door that stopped them in their tracks.

"What's that?" whispered Gil, suddenly concerned that their messing around had disturbed some fellow guest.

"Better find out," giggled Sally, pulling the sheet over her head. "Best conceal your ardour though!"

"Oh, Christ!" exclaimed Gil, once he realised his condition was not presentable. "Just a moment!" he called.

"Just coming!" mimicked Sally from beneath the bedclothes before squealing in paroxysms of laughter.

"Bad thing," said an amused Gil as he got out of bed and belted down his embarrassment in a white towelling robe with the Apsleys logo embroidered on its breast pocket.

Sally could hear only the vibration of exchanged words, the sounds of the door closing and the pad of feet returning.

"Who was it?" she asked, emerging from her cocoon.

"Breakfast," said Gil, wheeling a trolley before him, "Felix again ... house speciality, scrambled eggs and smoked salmon, served of course with more champagne and orange juice."

"How brilliant!" said Sally, sitting up enthusiastically.

## 4

The two nights at Apsleys were just what the doctor might have ordered. At times, they felt like teenagers in the first flush of a new passion. There were no declarations or promises yet. Neither of them wanted to crush this fledgling relationship; both carried a lot of emotional baggage from the past.

They took a walk through Hyde Park in the late morning. They watched the Horse Guards exercise on Rotten Row and drank coffee while ducks dabbled and bobbed on the Serpentine.

Not wishing to be diverted from each other, they had left their phones at the hotel. This made no difference in Gil's case, whereas Sally had a dozen messages waiting for her when they returned. These were mainly from concerned friends who had been at the party, including one from Klaus: '*Sally, darling. How are you? David and I are concerned about you. Roz made your apologies for rushing off. We totally understood. Michael is a complete bastard ... unforgivable! As if he hasn't done you enough harm already. He's an evil little fucker, or rather big fucker! I could murder him. Please, if you have a moment, let us know how you are*?'

Sally looked across apologetically at Gil after listening to the recorded messages. "If you don't mind, I'd better answer these."

"I need some coffee stimulus after all that walking. I'll find a paper to read in the bar," he smiled, planted a kiss on her cheek and left.

Gil ordered coffee and took up residence on a comfortable sofa tucked away in a corner of the lounge. He took the opportunity to ring the Blatts. Kate answered.

"Hallo Kate."

"Harp! How are you getting on at Apsleys?"

"Marvellously. I just wanted to say thanks. Sally and I were genuinely touched by your generosity."

"Our pleasure, Harp. Was the party good?"

Gil sighed, "Mmm, until the ex-boyfriend turned up!"

Gil explained.

"Blimey! I bet that went down like the Titanic! Poor Sally. Is she okay now?"

"Yes, fine. We had the loveliest day today I can remember having in ages."

"You and Sally look just right together, Harp."

"Oh shucks!" said Gil, feigning coyness.

"I know you're thinking, what can Kate know, she's only met her once? But there's something about you two. Even Felix commented that you looked happier yesterday than he'd seen you look in years. And let's face it, as a writer, he's hardly the most on the ball person when it comes to observations concerning real life!" she quipped.

Gil laughed, "How did your New Year get-together go?"

"Changing the subject, huh? It was lovely. Felix was on top form but got a little too well-oiled for his own good. He's paying the price today, padding about like a ghost he is. It feels a bit like being haunted. He announced that he was going off to do an hour's carpentry, but believe me there's no carpentry - he's probably napping. Shall I put you through?" she asked rather mischievously.

"No. Don't. Let him sleep," pleaded Gil.

"Big soppy date!" she said.

## 5

Gil spent almost an hour in the bar before Sally joined him.

"Sorry I took so long," she apologised, "Everyone wanted to chat. Klaus hadn't realised we were staying over. He and David have invited us to dinner tomorrow evening. I said I'd check with you first."

The suggestion immediately prompted Gil to exclaim, "The car! I meant to pick the damn thing up this morning!"

So while Sally got herself ready, Gil took a cab over to Wandsworth to sort out the courtesy car. It had been fine to leave it in a permit-holder zone over a public holiday, but the traffic wardens would definitely be back on the streets looking out for transgressors early in the morning. Once he'd driven the car back to South Kensington, the hotel reception took the keys and parked it up for him.

Gil and Sally were in ebullient moods. Although Apsleys had comfort, sophistication and boasted an excellent menu, they wanted to roam about the city streets hand in hand, sit side by side on buses, recapture that freedom they had known as students. This city which they had both left behind seemed charged with an energy, a joie de vivre, which had for some time been missing from their lives.

"Got it!" exclaimed Sally. They were travelling east on a bus along Oxford Street, fast approaching Tottenham Court Road, "How about Chinese?"

Gil liked the idea. They got off at the next stop, walked down Charing Cross Road, turned right at Cambridge Circus into Shaftesbury Avenue, then took a left that led them into Gerrard Street at the heart of Chinatown. The street, as ever, was bustling with people and noise. They did a little window shopping, browsed in a Chinese supermarket and bought half a kilo of lychees and a box of uncooked prawn crackers. The restaurant where they chose to eat was on Wardour Street. The service was brusque which they found amusing, especially after Apsleys, but the food was indisputably good. Afterwards they went on to a bar in Camden that did jazz, one of many things they discovered to be a shared passion.

## 6

<u>Friday 2 January</u>

Today I bought a car with tax and MOT for the best part of a year (I won't need it for anything like that long). It's a Ford Galaxy in good condition and with low mileage for its age. I wanted something inexpensive (no return to be made on this!) that wouldn't look out of place parked-up on the nice street where you live. It also had to be comfortable enough to sit in for hours at a time. Needless to say I bought it under a false name from a private seller – no possibility of ever tracing it back to me!

I spent a lot of time this afternoon customising it to requirements. The windows need to be virtually opaque. I began by attaching a roll of tinting to the side and rear windows. This mostly solved the problem, but it was still possible to see a shape silhouetted against the light. Tricky one ... solved with track and some black landscaping material from a garden centre.

Guess what?

I have become invisible.

# 7

"So, while David and I have been concerned for your well-being, you've been languishing at some posh establishment in South Ken!" Klaus joked as the four of them took an eating break. They had just finished a first course of melon balls and Parma ham. The combination had prompted Klaus to pronounce that he hadn't known melons possessed balls and that in future he would approach the fruit more delicately.

David shook his head at Gil in amused dismay.

Sally, entering into the spirit, said, "I'm not sure melon is a fruit."

"What is it then?" enquired Klaus.

"I think it's a gourd," she replied.

"Can't a gourd be a fruit?"

"I dunno."

"Listen, if it has balls, anything is possible!"

They all laughed with the exception of David, who clearly had other matters on his mind. Seeing that Klaus had done a good job relaxing their guests, he chose the moment to get straight to the point, "Have you considered what you might do about Michael?"

"We've been trying hard not to think about him," replied Sally.

David paused for a moment before saying, "I think you should consider taking a fresh non-molestation order out against him."

Sally looked uncertain. "I'm not sure ... do you think that would work?"

"It worked last time; for the duration of its tenure, he left you alone."

"True, but there's all the rigmarole, going before a judge. I'd rather not go through all of that again."

"I can certainly appreciate that," replied David.

"Can you afford to let this rest though, darling?" joined in Klaus. "I mean, judging from what he did to Gil's car it sounds like the man is losing his marbles."

"I'm not convinced it was Michael who did that," replied Sally.

"But in all honesty, who else could it be?" Klaus asked rather incredulously.

Gil said nothing, but on this matter he was with Klaus. It had to be Chilvers.

Sally tried to explain, "I'd certainly agree with you that it sounds like he's lost the run of himself. The other day he had to be cautioned for swearing at the policeman who went round to talk to him about Gil's car. It's uncharacteristic of Michael to lose control like that, especially before an authority figure."

"Rowe's very young, just a constable," said Gil.

David shook his head, "I have to say I agree with Sally. It is odd behaviour ... Michael's a master of presentation ... laid back, sophisticated. I was surprised to see him quite so out of control on New Year's Eve."

"He has a history of being violent and disagreeable though," put in Klaus.

"Yes, but not in public like that," said David, "The man, as we know, is a control freak."

Gil looked confused. Sally made an attempt to clarify, "Michael grew up in a tower block in Canning Town. His teenage mother brought him up on state benefits. Is that the background you imagined he came from when you saw him?"

Gil had pictured the sneering Chilvers always in a world with money, an independent education, Oxbridge perhaps. His look of surprise ruled out the need to voice this.

"See. Nobody who meets him ever sees the council estate! Simply because Michael doesn't want anyone to. He's a con artist and a street angel."

"Has he always drunk a lot?" asked Gil.

"Except when working," nodded Sally, "Always knew what was good for him did Michael."

"He'll need to sober up soon, once the wheels of commerce start to roll again after the holidays," said Gil.

David and Klaus exchanged a glance with each other, then David began, "We don't know how much truth is in this ... an acquaintance of mine who was at the party recognised Michael. She passed something on she'd heard from another merchant banker who works at the same firm as Michael. Apparently there's a rumour going round that Michael has been suspended."

Sally gasped, "Why?"

Klaus answered this time, "Not sure ... misplacing funds ... creative accounting. Whatever bad boy City types get up to … she honestly didn't know, but she reckoned it had to be something very serious."

David added, "I suppose being suspended might explain the insane drinking, why he started ringing you again ... perhaps even his behaviour with the young constable."

Sally looked relieved. "Suddenly losing his status, his routine, all the structure of his life … he'd fall apart!" She laughed ironically, "All this nonsense isn't about me at all. It's a diversion. It's helping to take his mind off the really important thing … him … and losing face!"

"So. Am I right in thinking you'd like to wait a while before considering a fresh non-molestation order?"

Sally nodded, "I think so, David."

"We'll leave it like that then, and see what happens." He didn't look entirely convinced.

"Thank you, both of you, for your concern," she said, placing a kiss on David's cheek and reaching across the table to squeeze Klaus's wrist.

"Judging by the state he was in on New Year's Eve," said Klaus, "There's always a chance the bastard might be mown down by some unsuspecting motorist as he sprawls into the path of their car ... with a bit of luck, anyway! I don't think I'd be able to resist the temptation myself if I ever caught sight of him in my headlights."

## 8

Saturday 3 January

I was genuinely pleased to watch you arrive home last night. You had overnight bags. Been away?

I saw that a woman was with you. I don't know why, but I have this gut feeling that the relationship is fairly new. Of course, I'll find out everything in due course.

I can absolutely guarantee one thing, whether this relationship is new or established, it certainly won't last.

## 9

After the nights shared in the serenely pleasant atmosphere of Apsleys, they still had a whole weekend together before returning to work. To begin with, Sally would do the initial preparation from home, as she generally did at the start of a new job. When it got busier and the production demanded even more of her time, she would stay at Roz's flat in London.

As midnight approached on Sunday evening, all was peaceful. They were snuggled together on a sofa in Gil's sitting room before the dying embers of a log fire. Only two sounds prevailed: the solemn tick-tocking of the grandfather clock in the hallway and the tiny snores coming from Spike, fast asleep on the hearth rug.

Sally sighed, a contented sound mostly, but with a note of resignation too, "I don't feel the slightest tingle of enthusiasm about starting work."

"Don't go then. Let's just stay here," smiled Gil, planting a kiss on her forehead.

"If I don't there won't be any bread and butter on my table," she yawned.

"Then resistance is useless," agreed Gil with drowsy resignation.

## 10

### Monday 5 January

12.34 am - I arrive to begin my vigil. I park in a good position just ten metres or so from your property. I'm just in time to see the lights go out downstairs.

7.51 am - Boy delivers newspaper.

8.03 am - First signs of life. You open the curtains downstairs. The bedroom you sleep in must be at the back of the house as the upstairs curtains weren't drawn.

8.55 am - The woman you came home with on Friday night leaves. Romantic scene on drive (thoroughly nauseating).

9.04 am - Postman makes his delivery.

9.27 am - Another woman arrives, middle-aged, late fifties/early sixties, too well dressed to be the cleaner. She parks her nicely preserved MG Midget directly in front of the garage, so she can't be expecting you to leave. She has her own key to let herself into the house. The pooch is expecting her. This looks like a routine. Does she come every day?

12.31 pm - Middle-aged woman comes out and drives away.

12.50 pm - You come out in wellington boots – not a good look! Open the garage doors. You allow the dog to scramble across the car upholstery into the passenger seat. I don't suppose you're bothered about the arse-sniffer making a mess because it's not your car. I see you keep this (hire/courtesy?) car locked up in the garage. Very wise. You wouldn't want it to be the victim of another Art Attack! Ha! Ha! Ha!

I think about following. Decide not. More important to stay on task. I'm not in any rush.

Anyway, you're probably only tramping along some muddy track, avoiding the steaming heaps of dog filth, waving cheery hellos to familiar dog walkers, perhaps pausing for a friendly chat. No doubt you exchange fascinating anecdotes, like visits to the vet to get anal glands squeezed, or share a jolly moment as your charges sniff each other's backsides? What fun!

1.57 pm - Midget woman returns. Lets herself back in.

2.11 pm - You and dog get back.

4.32 pm - Midget woman leaves.

5.58 pm - Girlfriend arrives home. She has to ring doorbell. Forgotten key perhaps, or doesn't have one because the relationship is new? Romantic Noel Coward moment on the doorstep. Excuse me for wanting to THROW UP!

7.47 pm - You leave with the woman in her car. Both have changed clothes, smartish/casual.

Note: Gil employed a different routine with the front door than he did at lunchtime. He left it open, then went back inside and punched some numbers into a panel set on the wall over to the right (my right that is). After locking the door he waited for a beep or signal before getting into the car.

## 11

"Am I the first?" Sally asked.

"You mean, the first since Jules?"

"Yes."

"Would it matter?"

"Of course not."

"Why do you want to know then?" he asked with a smile.

"A woman likes to know these things."

Gil took a sip of black coffee and smacked his lips together in appreciation of its bitterness. "Not many," he replied sheepishly.

Sally giggled. They were in a jokey mood, in fact the whole restaurant seemed to be in high spirits. The restaurant, La Boissonière, a local establishment offering French cuisine, was unexpectedly busy for a Monday, especially so soon after Christmas.

"I wasn't having much luck, until ... I can't quite believe we actually met in a library!"

"What's wrong with libraries?"

"Nothing. But, I mean it doesn't happen, does it? I mean, of course it does, it must do, like us. Everyone always says they met at a dance, in a bar, at a club, on holiday or something. Nobody ever says, 'we met in the reading room at Tonbridge Library,' do they?"

She started to laugh, it did seem preposterous. Then she asked, "How'd you meet Jules?" She kept her eyes averted from looking directly at him as she put this question, nonchalantly stirring a little sugar into her coffee.

"Ah!" he exclaimed triumphantly, "Proves my theory. We met at a pub. See."

"Why? Was the library closed?"

Gil suspected that Sally was taking this opportunity to learn more about Jules. He didn't blame her, she'd been incredibly patient with his reticence on the subject. He only wished he found it easier to open up.

"It was at a pub called the Marlborough Arms. I was at the Slade and Jules was doing English at UCL. It was a great place for meeting people. It was at the Marlborough where I first met Felix too."

"That's extraordinary, don't you think? Meeting two people who went on to play significant parts in your life at the same place?" She thought for a second, "Not at the same time?"

"Not quite. When I met Jules I was in the second year of my Fine Art degree. She'd only just started her course. We kept meeting, or rather I engineered meetings. You know how it is, 'Oh, what a surprise! I wasn't expecting to see you again!' Of course, she knew."

"She was probably doing a bit of engineering herself."

"Probably, but I was far too shy to take the next step. If it was down to me we'd have been there years later … you know, meeting by total coincidence, twice daily. Finally, exasperated, she said, 'Look Gil, I happen to like you a lot. So are you going to ask me out, or are we going to fuck about like this for ever?'"

Sally burst out laughing, "She sounds great. Like my kind of gal."

"You'd have got on well."

He reached across the table and took her hand. He wanted to say more, open up. He wanted to tell her everything there was to tell, tell her how much his wife had meant to him, tell her about the accident, how desperate his life had been in the intervening years, until she, Sally, had entered his life. But he didn't, couldn't, and on reflection, considering how new their relationship was, thought it prudent.

Sally seemed to understand at least something of his difficulty and let him off the hook by asking, "Felix? How did that come about?"

"Jules fixed it. You see I was a big fan of Felix's. I'd read every single one of his books many times and done about two dozen illustrations based on them. His first nine books were published without any drawings at all. They'd often thought about it. His publisher had commissioned a few illustrators for a try out, but the writing and artwork never quite gelled."

"So, how did she introduce you?"

"Well, I immediately recognised him. In fact, I'd seen him in there quite often. He kept a flat in London at that time. It was just around the corner from the British Museum. I suppose the Marlborough was his local. He'd pop in for a pint and sandwich at lunchtime. By that time I was actually going out with Jules but we weren't living together yet. She was still in halls of residence. I'd shown her the illustrations."

"What did she think of them?"

"Yes. Good. She kept urging me to introduce myself. I could never quite pluck up the courage. Eventually, exasperated, she muscled her way into the seat beside Felix and did the job for me."

"He didn't try to make a run for it then?"

"Surprisingly, no."

"A pretty face never harms."

"Felix was polite and charming and, whether it was genuine or not, he certainly looked interested. Actually, knowing Felix, he probably was. We arranged to meet the following day. I brought in my portfolio to show him. To my surprise he actually showed up. He loved the stuff I'd done."

"So, the meeting of the two great men was all thanks to the wiles of one little woman," joked Sally.

"'Fraid so. Don't think I'd get any medals for bravery though."

"Are you a man or a mouse, Gil Harper?"

Gil considered the question, then with a nod and grin at the cheeseboard said, "Pass the Camembert."

## 12

10.23 pm - Return of Romeo and Juliet. They were laughing a lot.

Note: he unlocks door, goes straightaway to press some buttons again. The alarm probably has a code that must be fed in within a certain time limit.

This will make for interesting research.

12.14 am - All lights extinguished. Presumably enjoying sexual relations with his tart in the dark.

## Tuesday 6 January

7.56 am - Boy delivers newspaper.

8.06 am - First signs of life.

8.12 am - Curtains opened.

8.57 am - Postman.

9.01 am - Kisses girlfriend. She goes off in her car.

9.27 am - Glam Gran arrives in the Midget. I get ugly picture in my head of you doing the business with both of them. No sooner have you waved loving goodbyes to your girlfriend than you're fornicating with the older woman. Grim thought! Think I'll carry on believing the old one is your secretary rather than your sex slave! Ha! Ha! Ha!

12.32 pm - Woman goes off in Midget.

12.46 pm - You in wellies, pooch in tow, car taken out from garage. Wonder what has happened to your trashed car?

Note: Gil does not set the security alarm just like yesterday.

1.59 pm - Midget woman gets back.

Note: one hour and thirteen minutes - One-seven yesterday.

2.12 pm - Return. Man. Dog. Barely indistinguishable (Joke!).

4.39 pm - Older woman goes.

7.47 pm - Girlfriend arrives. You either hear the car or have telepathic powers (another joke!) and come to meet her. Romantic interlude. I am dismayed - you are wearing an apron! As you go into the house you playfully slap her backside.

13

Gil was by no means a culinary master but with application and a good recipe he could generally put together something edible. He hadn't cooked a meal for another person since Jules' death.

"You look like you've had a busy day," he greeted Sally. He'd gone outside when he heard her car arrive.

"There's so much to do. I've been cutting out patterns all day for the chorus and barely done half. We're seeing the principals next week for their fittings and I still haven't finalised all the designs with Klaus."

"I expect it's always that way isn't it?" he asked, stroking her hair.

"Always," she smiled, "Probably why we do it. All the adrenaline."

"There's ages to go yet, so just come inside and relax. I'll pour you a glass of wine and if you survive my cooking, you can forget all about it until the morning."

"Great!" she said, planting a kiss on his lips. "You know something?

"What?"

"That apron really suits you," she giggled as they went through into the hallway.

"Bitch," he laughed slapping a hand to her bottom.

14

11.02 pm - All lights extinguished.

Wednesday 07 January

7.48 am - Paper boy.

8.34 am - Later getting up today.

8.59 am - Postman.

9.25 am - Midget arrives. Gil introduces girlfriend to older woman. More certain than ever that this relationship must be new.

15

Megan Hollingsworth and her late husband Terence, a Foreign Office man, had enjoyed a marvellous life together in enviable Far Eastern locations. However, not long after they returned from their years abroad and bought a splendid Georgian house in nearby Seal, Terence suffered a massive and fatal coronary.

A widow at fifty-two, Megan was determined to retain her independence. She was capable, resourceful, intelligent, and could still turn a head or two, not that sex was of much interest to her, after thirty years of marriage, four children and a miscarriage.

This change in circumstance had led her to Gil's door, when he had placed an ad in the local paper seeking an assistant with typing and computer skills. Her typing was rusty but basically sound, and she had bribed a granddaughter to secretly instruct her in the arcane science of computing. Gil, never certain about exactly what his needs were, had enlisted Jules' help. She had picked Megan; Gil, unsure, had offered her a week's trial. Although the typing was slow to start with, she was eminently literate, numerate and articulate and Gil made the position permanent after three days. For this act of generosity and faith she had reciprocated with unswerving loyalty. She had become much more than just a typist or telephone responder; she drafted almost all Gil's business letters, liaised and organised book signings, the occasional lecture tour and did his book-keeping.

Megan immediately guessed who the Vauxhall Astra parked in Gil's driveway on that crisp January morning must belong to. The fact it was parked untidily in the spot where Megan had for the past nine years habitually left her Midget, was most irritating.

"Hello. I'm not in your way, am I?" asked Megan, seeing Gil coming towards her as she got out of the car.

He looked confused by the question, "No, you're fine. I'll be off to pick up my car later, but I'd leave it where it is for the moment. Sally will need to leave shortly, but you're not in her way, either."

"That's good then," replied Megan, hackles rising a little.

"We came out to say hello," he said, looking round for Sally, who'd been beside him a moment ago. She emerged from the house with Spike, who immediately launched himself excitedly at Megan. "Megan Hollingsworth, Sally, Sally Curtis. I very much wanted you both to meet."

Megan, patting Spike, looked up and smiled graciously.

"I'm very pleased to meet you, Megan," said Sally. "Gil's told me all about you. He describes you as indispensable."

Megan laughed off the compliment and took Sally's outstretched hand. She knew she was being foolishly possessive. However she understood herself well; it always took her a little time to get used to change.

Sally read the older woman's coolness.

Gil saw nothing. "Sally doesn't have to leave immediately. I made a pot of coffee."

"That's very good of you Sally. But we mustn't keep you too long. You make clothes don't you?"

"I design costumes," replied Sally, smiling through slightly gritted teeth.

"How clever of you," said Megan taking Sally by the arm, "You must tell me all about it. I see we share a taste in cars."

Sally didn't understand.

"Both red!"

## 16

10.35 am - Young woman leaves. Is waved off by you holding pooch.

10.47 am - You get car out of garage and go off alone.

11.01 am - New pawn arrives. This must be the cleaning woman! She's more commonly dressed than the other woman, jeans, t-shirt, etc. but about same age, late fifties. I'd be surprised if she turned out to be the accountant as she brought a vacuum cleaner!

(After a cold bright start, it has just started to rain.)

12.04 pm - You return in your Volvo. Hurrah!!! They've done a lovely job - can't see the join (joke). You bring cleaner and Midget woman and pooch (held by the cleaner - how unhygienic!) to take a look at the re-spray. I entertain wicked thought about doing it again. But this would be repeating myself, and I'd hate to be unoriginal.

12.40 pm - Midget woman goes (for lunch?).

12.42 pm - Dog takes man out for walkies (joke). The cleaner is left in house, therefore once again you don't set alarm. Now raining v. heavily.

Question: will he cut the dog's walking time down because of the rain?

Note: where do they walk? Is it the same place every day? Where does Midget woman live? Not far I suspect if she goes home at lunchtime.

2.00 pm - It's a photo-finish as Midget woman and you arrive back simultaneously!

Note: despite rain Gil and the dog ventured out for a heroic hour and eighteen minutes.

3.40 pm - Cleaner woman leaves.

I'm beginning to feel the strain. The amphetamines have helped me get through but must get a proper sleep soon. I've been extremely careful, never getting too close, and I've changed my location daily. The infra-red night glasses have proved invaluable.

I expect my feelings of paranoia are largely caused by the speed.

Note: so far, unless the cleaner comes on different days each week, it'll need to be done on Monday or Tuesday.

4.52 pm - Midget woman leaves.

7.27 pm - Girlfriend home.

11.46 pm - Lights out.

## Thursday 08 January

7.55 am - Paper boy.

8.02 am - Up and about.

8.56 am - Girlfriend leaves in her Vauxhall Astra.

9.14 am - Postman.

9.24 am - Older woman arrives.

Note: The morning routine has only varied slightly from day to day.

12.41 pm - Woman leaves in Midget.

12.55 pm - You take pooch. You set the alarm before leaving.

Note: why this variation?

2.06 pm - You return from walk. The older woman does not return.

Note: could this be a regular Thursday routine or is it a one-off?

7.32 pm - Girlfriend arrives back.

## 17

It was just after ten in the evening. Gil was at the computer in his office making an entry in his diary. Sally, whom he'd last observed lazing in the bathtub, appeared in the doorway in an old dressing gown of his that she had taken a shine to.

"How're you doing, Mr Pepys?"

Gil looked up and smiled, "Pepys? Pepys is no threat. He only managed nine years. I've kept this up since I was fifteen. I suppose Pepys might arguably have the edge, ever so slightly, as far as content goes ..."

"But not by much, you reckon?"

"Secretary to the Admiralty, knowing the great and the good, dropping by on royalty when the mood took him ... as opposed to walking Spike or popping up to Waitrose for a pot of hummus."

"Sounds fascinating. And how's your kids' book coming on?" she asked.

"So, so," he replied half-heartedly as he clicked with the mouse on the save icon. He swivelled the chair around so he was completely facing her. "Sometimes I think I should stick to illustration."

"So the writing went badly, did it?"

"Not really. It's just that I've worked so long with Felix, I can't help emulating his style at times."

"What's wrong with that?"

"It's just that it has to have some stamp of originality about it. I can't have people say I just copied Felix."

"I'm no expert but I honestly don't think you're doing that, and I've read all his books too. You have a discernibly different voice from his. The passages you've let me read were really funny. You should trust yourself. You write well."

"You sound just like Felix."

"There you go then."

"By the way," said Gil, "Megan asked if we'd like go over for drinks one evening next week."

"Okay. Great."

"See. I told you she was a good egg."

"I'm sure she is. I just thought I'd stepped on her toes a bit."

"I don't understand. Why?"

"Why?" she laughed, "'Cos you're a bloke … men never understand. It's a variation of the eternal triangle."

"She's old enough to be my mother!" he protested.

"No, silly. Not that."

"Thank God. I thought for a moment you meant she was after my body!"

"Women are creatures of habit. Also, we've enjoyed an inferior status in society, so we're possessive about the things important to us. Megan has been with you for years, feels protective towards you … doesn't entirely appreciate me muscling in. Look at mothers-in-law and all the jokes they've spawned!"

"I always got on very well with Marjorie."

"Yes, but you're a bloke. Every daughter-in-law has a mother-in-law and will one day possibly become a mother-in-law, so how come their relationships are often so tense?"

"I don't know. Why?"

"Because they're both vying for the attention of the boss man!"

"So is this an introduction to Freud or Feminism or something? Are blokes to blame then for the abrasive state of affairs between mothers and daughters-in-law?"

Sally rolled her eyes, "You can't ever hope to understand us … we're a different species. Megan will come round. Just leave her to me."

## 18

11.57 pm - Lights out.

Friday 9 January

7.47 am - Newspaper.

8.00 am - Awake.

8.52 am - Girlfriend leaves.

9.17 am - Postman.

Note: no Midget today.

12.51 pm - Walkies. You set alarm.

2. 03 pm - Arrive back.

Note: Gil is in the habit of setting the alarm each time he goes out except on days when the woman in the MG Midget returns before he gets back with the dog.

Thursday or Friday I'd be up against the alarm and Wednesday would probably mean giving Mrs Mop a little tap on the head.

Realistically, if I'm going to break in, it will have to be Monday or Tuesday.

5.50 pm - Girlfriend gets back.

6.43 pm - Drives away in her Astra. You set alarm.

## 19

Gil and Sally decided that completing the first working week of the new year warranted a celebration. After a brief discussion about the options, they chose La Boissonière again. It was quite early, before seven when they arrived; even so the restaurant was quite full and once again they hadn't booked.

They were greeted by Robert the patron, who hadn't been present during their previous visit. "I'm afraid, Monsieur Harper, I shall not have a table free for a little while," he explained in a French accent just short of being a cliché, "That is, unless you wouldn't mind dining in the other room?"

Eating in the rear room was not a problem.

"That'll do us fine, Robert. Thank you for squeezing us in."

"Not at all. It is a pleasure to see you again Mr Harper. It was my evening off, but my son recognised you when you dined here the other night." Robert composed himself before adding discreetly, "We were all very sad to hear of your tragedy."

"Thank you Robert." Gil made an involuntary gesture, touching Sally's shoulder as if for reassurance.

"Are you okay?" Sally asked Gil after Robert had shown them to their table, "You look a little disorientated."

"I must be feeling tired," he replied, then thought better of it and added, "Actually, I was a little shaken by Robert ... what he said."

"About Jules?"

"Yes. I'd forgotten that we used to eat here quite regularly. Isn't that incredible? After her death it's like I stopped thinking or something."

They were interrupted by the wine waiter. Gil didn't feel like drinking much and Sally was driving, so they ordered half a bottle of red wine and some sparkling water. After he left them, Sally asked, "So why did you and Jules move out of London?"

"George and Marjorie lived here then … that's her parents."

Sally nodded that she already knew this.

"Jules grew up in Sevenoaks, went to school here. Also Felix was close by."

"See, it was different for you. You and Jules had a purpose here. You weren't just doing a runner. I had a nice little flat in Battersea. When my mother died, swiftly followed by dad, I suddenly felt terribly unsafe. All I could think about was getting away. I mean there was nothing wrong with where I was. I just felt this awful insecurity. I desperately wanted some knight in shining armour to ride by and offer me his protection ... arguably, how I got myself mixed up with Michael. Although, I'd long established a pattern for being attracted to shits."

"Not still, I hope?" Gil enquired tentatively.

"I hope not. The therapy was pricey," she laughed as she said this. "I suppose that's what he was alluding to on New Year's Eve, about my shrink."

Sally glanced over at Gil and smiled.

"What?" he asked.

"I was just thinking that on a shittiness scale of one to ten, you'd barely register."

"That's good isn't it?"

"Very."

"As long as it doesn't in any way correlate to physical attractiveness and sexual prowess?" he told her, puffing out his chest.

"Don't fish!" she said.

They had both experienced a busy week, and the food and modest amount of wine consumed began to have a soporific effect somewhere between dessert and coffee.

Gil tapped his PIN into the card terminal the waiter brought to the table.

"Thank you, Monsieur Harper," he responded to Gil's generosity.

"Thank you," replied Gil.

Gil slipped the credit card and payment slip into his wallet and followed Sally who was already on her feet. They went through an arch which led into an area that served as a coffee-making station. At the end of this corridor was another arch which brought them back into the main restaurant. It was very full, with three waiters busily navigating their way with nimble expertise around the diners. Robert was standing behind a counter near the door checking bills. Sally's body-language alerted Gil that something was wrong when she stopped abruptly.

"You evil bastard!" she called out.

Gil was now alongside her, and able to identify the problem himself. There, grinning broadly, holding out a glass of red wine towards them as though proposing a toast, was Michael Chilvers.

"Why? Why are you doing this? Haven't you done enough?" Sally cried.

"I've no idea what you're talking about!" he said, his seeming incredulity only just enough to mask an underlying sneer. "I came here to enjoy a quiet meal." He took in and played to the acquired audience at the tables round about. "My ex-fiancée thinks I have nothing better to do than follow her and her new boyfriend about," he confided to the couple at the next table.

"You're sick!" Sally screamed, before turning to flee from the restaurant.

Gil was left facing Michael Chilvers. There seemed little chance this could be a coincidence coming so swiftly on the heels of their previous encounter when Chilvers had gate-crashed Klaus and David's party.

"You really have a problem on your hands there Gil," confided Chilvers, "Wouldn't you agree that her behaviour is neurotic?" He asked this question of an elderly couple who were sitting a few tables away and who immediately looked away in embarrassment.

"Shut up!" said Gil, now seething with anger.

"Come on Gil. This is embarrassing ... sit down, let's talk things over."

Gil leaned down at Chilvers and growled, "Keep out of my way. Do you hear?"

"I think I'm being threatened," said Chilvers, innocently looking round at the other diners.

Gil's eyes remained on him.

"Monsieur Harper, please."

Gil felt Robert's hand on his arm.

"Monsieur Harper, please. My restaurant. Please."

Gil came to his senses. He broke eye contact with Chilvers, who looked, if anything, disappointed.

Robert held Gil's coat for him. "I am sorry about this Monsieur Harper," he whispered as he helped him into it, "I assure you, that gentleman will not get a table here again."

"Thank you," Gil replied, "I'm very sorry about the scene."

"Pfoo!" The patron said dismissively, "Sometimes a little scandal ..." he joked with a Gallic arm gesture.

Gil managed a brief smile.

"The lady ran out without her jacket," said Robert.

Gil placed Sally's coat underneath his arm and left. He didn't glance back.

## 20

9.47 pm - Hello! Gil arrived home alone - on foot! And he didn't look very happy! He glanced uncertainly up and down the road several times before he went into his house. Lovers' tiff?

## 21

Gil was surprised to find no Sally and no car when he reached the parking place. He walked home; it wasn't far, just fifteen minutes away. He'd kept meaning to give her a spare set of keys but so far had forgotten to do so. When he didn't find Sally waiting outside the house, as he'd expected to, he became quite concerned for her.

Spike made to greet Gil, who for once ignored him and went straight to the telephone.

There was a message from Sally.

'*Gil. Forgive me running out like that. I just had to get away. I'm at home. I hope you understand ... I'd like to be on my own tonight. Please, I'd rather if you didn't ring me after you play this. I'll speak to you tomorrow.*'

The message ended and an unavailable tone replaced her voice. Spike who had been gazing up at him turned tail and left the room.

Gil felt very alone.

## 22

10.30 pm - All lights extinguished.

That's me finished too. I'm exhausted. I've been getting by on about two hours' sleep. Feeling very paranoid. See you again on Monday, Gil Harper.

## 23

Gil slept badly. The scene at the restaurant had shaken him up. It somehow triggered the revisit of an unwelcome night terror he hadn't experienced for some years now, but which had plagued him for many months following the crash. It portrayed, in clinically accurate detail, what he remembered in the moments immediately after the collision. This ordeal sometimes recurred over several nights. It had driven him to the brink of despair, and in his darkest moments he'd considered taking his own life in order to break free of it.

The nightmare happened exactly as the events were recorded in his memory. Upon impact, he'd blacked out, perhaps for a minute or two:

His eyes are shut, he is aware of physical constriction but no pain. He is disorientated, thoughts all jumbled-up, unable to recall where he is or what has just occurred. A warm stickiness bathes one side of his face, the side nearest to Jules.

Yes, Jules; where is Jules?

Concern for her encourages him to open his eyes. What has just taken place? Why is the car bent and distorted out of shape around his body?

He blinks several times as if to cast away the obfuscation in his mind. He looks out through the shattered windscreen; it makes no sense; the tangled mass of wrecked machines, the brilliant afternoon light bathing his face.

That looks like blood, he thinks. So much; is it his own blood? Then he realises he can turn his head. He looks across to Jules and suddenly he remembers. He sees and remembers everything.

At this point he always woke up screaming.

It was a minute after 5 am. Gil turned on the bedside lamp. His heart was pounding and he was drenched in sweat. He knew it would be impossible to return to sleep again and headed for the bathroom. Spike, at the bottom of the bed, raised an indignant eye and snorted before promptly going back to sleep.

The heat of the water in the shower brought soothing and comfort. Gil dressed, made coffee and began writing up his diary, which he'd felt too despondent to attend to after getting home. There was certainly plenty to say. He recorded 'the horror' too, which was the way he'd always referenced the nightmare in his diary.

Of the encounter with Chilvers at La Boissonière, he wrote:

> ... everything had been good up until then. Poor Sally must be feeling rotten about herself. The whole thing had to be engineered by the thoroughly vindictive, shameless Michael Chilvers .... but for Robert's intervention I came close to punching him. Actually, I think this is just what Chilvers would've liked. I can't deny that smashing his teeth might have brought some satisfaction. However, had it come to this, I daresay Chilvers would have slaughtered me. I was never much good at any of that macho stuff, my most recent pugilistic experience being as a pre-pubescent at school; I lost. At least my embarrassment is not compounded by recalling myself as one of two bloody-nosed men rolling about on the restaurant floor.

Spike rose around 8 am and looked in on Gil. "Ah, yes, I suppose the little lord will be wanting breakfast," he commented on the dog's look of expectancy.

He'd finished his diary entry, so he made porridge for himself and Spike. He desperately wanted to contact Sally. However, she had been clear about needing time alone and he knew he must respect this. He passed the morning listening to the radio and reading the newspaper.

When the telephone eventually rang he pounced on it.

"Hello," he said, trying to project casualness into his voice. He was certain it must be Sally.

"Gil?"

He was thrown by the initially unrecognised male voice and mumbled something in response.

"It's Klaus Williams."

"Yes, of course," he replied with some relief. For a moment he'd thought it was Chilvers, "Klaus."

"I'm ringing for Sally."

"What's happened?" asked Gil anxiously, his mind's eye picturing Sally sprawled on her cottage floor amidst spilled wine, pills and vomit.

Klaus, already on his wavelength, reassured, "She's fine ... well, as fine as you'd expect under the circumstances. She told us what happened. That man is a complete shit!"

"I'd have to agree with you there," replied Gil. "I expect he followed us."

"Of course he did."

"Is Sally at her cottage?"

"Actually, she's with us. She rang last night. She was very upset, and terrified that bastard might've followed her. We suggested she came to stay."

"Can I speak to her?"

Klaus paused, "She's sleeping at the moment. Poor love didn't get much rest last night. I'm sure she'll want to speak to you soon. I think she needs time to think everything through. Believe me, it's got nothing to do with anything you've done or said. She asked me to stress that. Can you bear with her, Gil?"

"Yes, of course," he replied; he felt he was being dumped by proxy.

Once more Klaus appeared to read his mind, "She asked me to tell you this is not an indirect way of giving you the brush-off."

"That's good to know," said Gil, unable to mask a hint of sarcasm.

"Try to understand it from her point of view, Gil. Michael is not the sort to give up. It's been over eighteen months, for Christ's sake!"

"Maybe we should call in a hit man?" Gil joked sardonically.

"Believe me, I thought of it first. The trouble with murder is being caught, and although Michael is eminently worthy, I don't really relish serving life for him. But seriously, let her come through this in her own time. David will help with all the legal stuff."

"Okay, Klaus. Thanks. I'll wait to hear from Sally."

For the remainder of the conversation they spoke generally; after it ended, Gil brooded a while.

He came to the conclusion it would do him no good to sit around waiting. He drove Spike the mile to Knole Park to pace out one of the walks in their repertoire. This passed an hour. The morning was dull and the familiar parkland was smothered beneath dense, grey cloud, but not actually as gloomy as it seemed to Gil.

Once back at his house again, he immediately checked the answerphone. He was disappointed, and decided the best thing would be to absent himself from home for as long as possible. And anyway, Sally could reach him at any time on his mobile. He walked up Dartford Road to the High Street, bought a sandwich, then browsed for an hour in the Sevenoaks Bookshop. He finally emerged with two novels and a children's book stunningly illustrated by someone he'd never heard of. From the local Waitrose he bought two ready meals, a DVD, some ground coffee and perhaps most tellingly, a box of cream cakes.

Just after he'd embarked on the homeward trek, he heard someone call out his name.

"Hey, Gil!"

He turned and recognised at once the gangling figure of Nigel Paddick. Nigel was married to Sue, who had been Jules' best friend since prep school.

"Christ!" muttered Gil. He was in a rather misanthropic mood by now. Nigel was a likeable chap, who displayed an enthusiasm for just about everything. However, to be in his company for too long could prove exhausting. Without even trying, Nigel Paddick generated enough energy, albeit of the nervous kind, to keep a small town powered through a Russian winter.

Nigel was waving and smiling inanely at Gil as he carelessly cut his way through the bottle-necked traffic along the High Street. Despite the lack of speed, Nigel's inattentiveness caused a driver to step on his brake and yell, "Idiot!" and for several other cars in a line behind to buck. Nigel was padded out in a postbox-red ski jacket. Gil thought, uncharitably, that perhaps it was a safety measure to make him visible to the naked eye. On Nigel's frame, a skin-tight suit in lycra might look oversized.

"I thought it was you," said Nigel as he reached the safety of the pavement.

"Nigel!"

"Fancy a coffee, old mate?"

Constantly being referred to as old mate was another irritating thing about Nigel.

Gil accepted and they went to a nearby café. Nigel ordered a latte for himself and a double espresso for Gil. Gil asked after Sue and the girls. Sue was pretty and petite, but somehow between them they had produced three wild-eyed ungainly daughters. Gil, who had demolished his espresso before Nigel had time to explore the froth on his latte, asked, "Another one?"

"Not for me, old mate. If I had another, I'd go into planetary orbit."

Gil returned with his coffee and asked, "How was Brittany?"

The Paddicks owned a cottage near St Malo. Nigel loved all things Gallic with a passion, be it bread, wine, film, poetry, chansons or smelly cheese. Despite this love of all things French, he actually taught English at a local prep school with a true sense of vocation, appreciation and deep knowledge of his subject. However, as soon as the holidays came, Nigel, Sue and the Valkyrie (Gil's secret name for their girls) headed at break-neck speed for the Channel.

Nigel shook his head despondently, "Didn't make it. Sue's mum. Unwell."

"Sorry to hear that. Nothing serious?"

"On the mend," said Nigel, lowering his voice, "Delicate matter. Women's stuff … you know, er, plumbing trouble!"

"Oh, yes," replied Gil, nodding sagely, fully appreciating that anything medical below the female waistline was utterly *Verboten*. "I'm glad she's better."

Nigel took a sip of latte to relieve a sudden dryness of throat. Then he changed the subject, "Sue rang you at the New Year to see what you were up to."

"I wasn't there."

"She gathered that, old mate. I suggested you'd stayed down west with 'the outlaws'. Sue reckoned not."

"Sue was right."

Nigel nodded, "She generally is … even when completely wrong as a general rule."

"I stayed at a hotel for a few days."

"On your tod?"

Gil hesitated, "Er ... no."

Nigel's eyebrows suddenly perched themselves like spectacularly arched felines above the rims of his spectacles.

"I met someone. We've been seeing quite a bit of each other."

Nigel discharged the captive eyebrows and began to grin, ear to ear, "She said you had … found a woman that is."

"Sue? How did she know?

"Dunno. Been reading the entrails again I expect."

"I met her at Tonbridge, in the library."

Nigel didn't bat an eyelid at the concept of seeding a romance this way.

"'Bout time you found a new woman." Nigel immediately displayed great embarrassment following this spontaneous remark, "Sorry," he mumbled into the remnants of his latte, "Didn't mean ..."

"Don't worry, Nige. I know exactly what you meant. It's been a long time. Even George and Marjorie have been telling me I should move on."

"So what does she do?" Nigel asked, perking up again.

"She designs costumes, for opera mostly."

"I love opera."

"I know absolutely nothing. You'll have to give me a bullshitter's guide sometime. In my teens I saw an avant-garde piece by Stockhausen at the Royal Opera House … *Donnerstag aus Licht*, I think."

Nigel blinked, "Perhaps a little hardcore. Bit off-putting perhaps?"

"You're right there. I thought never again."

Nigel took Gil's casual remark about a bullshitter's guide seriously, "I'll put together some light books as an introduction and lend you some recordings. You can learn opera the Paddick way!"

"Sounds good," smiled Gil, who liked Nigel a lot, despite finding him annoying at the same time.

"All fixed for the thirty-first?"

"Huh?"

"My birthday?"

Gil had completely forgotten that the last Saturday in January was a standing fixture to celebrate Nigel's birthday.

"You can bring your new lady-friend. What's her name?"

"Sally. I'm not sure," Gil replied, uncertain whether he'd have a lady-friend, new or otherwise, in three weeks' time. "She's very busy … just started on a job … but I'll ask."

"Sue will be over the moon. Drives me mad … compiles lists of available females each time you come over. The list has got smaller, mind, because you rejected most of them."

"Not rejected!" protested Gil.

"You'd be a terrible subject for organ transplant, old mate."

Gil smiled.

"Let Tarzan find his own Jane, I say," pronounced Nigel. "Women! Can't help themselves! Social engineers all of 'em." He thought, before adding stoically, "Got four to contend with … wouldn't change them for the world, mind … women, hey? Drive you nuts!"

Were it not for the females in his life, Nigel might easily be imagined in some shabby bachelor's flat, surrounded by piles of books, mouldering coffee cups and dust.

"I'll mark it in my diary," promised Gil.

"Great," said Nigel, who catching sight of his wristwatch speedily explained that he was overdue for an appointment with his daughters and a swimming pool. And within thirty seconds he was gone.

Gil, feeling decidedly less cranky after seeing Nigel, bought another coffee, non-espresso this time, then found a paper to help him pass the next half-hour.

It was almost dark by the time he reached home. Sally's car, parked in the driveway, was almost invisible in the murky twilight. She had been waiting forty minutes for him and was beginning to lose hope. She knew she could have reached him on his mobile but felt it was appropriate to speak face to face.

Gil's feet came to an abrupt stop on the crunching shingle when he saw her car.

"Sal!" He exclaimed as she emerged from the driver's door. He moved forward to embrace her but her body language spoke of tension. Gil let his arms drop.

"I'm so sorry, Gil ... for what I did."

"Michael's the one who should be sorry."

"I overreacted, embarrassed you, at a place where you're known. I feel ashamed."

Gil took her hand. He was close now, their breath visible in the chill air. He could smell the familiar perfume she wore. He was close enough to read her face, see the tears welling up in her eyes, feel the shivers as they ran through to her fingertips in response to the cold.

"I don't care," he said, "Michael Chilvers is a pain in the arse, but he'll give up eventually."

"You don't know what he's like ..."

"When he realises that whatever it is he's trying to achieve isn't working, he'll let us be."

Sally didn't seem convinced by these assurances, "I'd understand if you didn't want to see me again after last night. It was unforgivable, to run off and leave you there."

"Sal. Read my lips. I don't care about last night. I was worried … angry too … but at Chilvers, not with you! I admit I was a little hurt because you went to Klaus to be consoled and didn't seem to need me ..."

"It wasn't that ... I just needed some time to work things out. Since Christmas, you're about the only person I've really seen. I'd virtually moved into your house ... your life. Please, try to understand, Gil, I can't afford to lose my personality in a relationship again."

Gil nodded, indicating that he understood the sentiments behind her statement.

"Take all the time you need, Sally. But I hope you believe me when I tell you I like you just the way you are. You don't need to change in any way to accommodate me. I think of relationships as being two way, and I've greatly valued our time together." He paused. He was aware that he had reached a defining moment with no choice but to go further. He smiled at her softly, "I believe I've fallen in love with you."

Sally's lip trembled as she tried to choke back her tears.

"Oh, Gil!" she cried as he embraced her.

## 24

Monday 12 January

6.02 am - Up early this morning. Something must be happening

6.43 am - They emerge. Gil is wheeling a suitcase. I'm a bit concerned they're going away somewhere. My breaking and entering plan might be scuppered! Panic over - he puts the case into the Astra, then we get, 'sad you're leaving' body language. As usual the scene is painfully slushy. Where is she going? She's about to drive off, stops, lowers her window. Something important? Could national security depend on it? No, just a last kiss! Oh, please!

7.39 am - Newspaper boy.

9.02 am - Postman Prat delivers large bundle of mail.

9.23 am - Older woman arrives by Midget power.

I'm tense. I can almost feel the adrenaline bubbling in my veins. Must stay focused. It's understandable being excited, after all the preparation and watching I've done.

## 25

Gil was invariably busy at work by the time Megan arrived each morning and today was no exception. He heard the key turn in the lock, the front door opening and the sound of four small paws scampering on the wood flooring of the hall. He raised his head from his monitor and called out, "Hi!"

"Morning!" Megan shouted back. Not even the greetings altered much from day to day.

Spike at her heels, Megan picked up the mail from the doormat and headed for the kitchen to make coffee. While the kettle boiled she opened the mail, sorting it into four piles, personal, business, fan-mail and junk.

"Good weekend?" she asked on entering Gil's studio, tray in hand, only to realise her words were entirely wasted.

Spike immediately located his missing pack leader and scratched at the base of the French windows. Gil let the dog through. At the same time he popped his head into the room and asked, "Good weekend?"

"William and Jessica brought the children over on Sunday and took me out to lunch."

"Sounds nice."

"Lovely not to cook. How was yours?"

"Bit like the weather. Started badly but got sunnier," he replied. There was a resigned tone about his answer which Megan duly noted.

"Well, I'm pleased things improved. It's a fantastic morning. Shall I bring the coffee out there?"

It was indeed a fine morning. They often had their morning talk on the verandah, whenever the British weather showed its smiley face; however, it was January and Gil was beginning to shiver.

"Too cold," he said. He looked for Spike who had purposefully bounded off down the steps into the garden. He thought of calling, but dismissed the idea with a backhanded wave then drew the door to behind him.

Their informal business chats generally lasted about twenty minutes. They often meandered between professional and personal matters. Gil had already told Megan about Sally's ex-boyfriend problem. He updated her on what had transpired at the restaurant. Megan was appalled by the man's tenacity.

"Sally's decided to stay with a friend. Anyway, she's getting so busy, there'd only be time enough to get home, eat and sleep before travelling back to work."

Megan realised Gil was putting on a brave face, "Very sensible," she agreed.

"The space might be good for both of us. We've seen a lot of each other since Christmas."

"Sounds wise."

"I'll see her at weekends. And, hopefully, in the meantime, he'll lose interest and give up troubling her."

"Poor thing," she said sympathetically, "That man sounds like an utter scoundrel."

Gil could think of several other words to describe Michael Chilvers.

Their briefing completed, Gil asked, "Shall I make us another cafetière?"

"Not for me," replied Megan, who rarely stretched beyond one cup.

Gil went downstairs. He let Spike, who was waiting outside the conservatory door, in.

"What have you been up to?" Gil asked suspiciously.

Spike breezed past. It was clear from his blackened legs and tummy that he'd been digging; his favourite pastime.

"Look at the state of your trousers!" remonstrated Gil.

Spike appeared not to hear.

## 26

12.28 pm - Midget leaves.

12.52 pm - You go with dog in car. <u>As anticipated</u>, you don't set the alarm.

I experience a rush of excitement. I reckon I have an hour. I don't wish to be seen by any prying eyes. I climb over into the driver's seat, drive off and park in the next street.

1.01 pm - I enter the drive. I put on latex gloves. There is a side gate, not locked, ornamental, apart from function of keeping dog in check. Attractive garden, v good shape and size.

I check all the windows along the sides and rear of the house. All secure. I'd hoped to find at least one open, which by applying a little force, might be made to look like an opportunistic burglary. I try the conservatory door. Firmly locked. By now I have examined every window. I consider the situation.

Approx 1.03 pm - I'll need to break a window. I look around for the likeliest candidate. There's a window to the left of the conservatory that appears to open into a small hallway. I decide to force my way in here. I open my rucksack that holds my toolkit. I'm about to do it, then I stop, consider what I'm about to do and decide I should try the fire escape before I irrevocably damage anything.

It seems unlikely, a waste of precious time perhaps, but I abhor recklessness!

The cast iron staircase rises to patio style doors located on a sort of balcony. There are places to sit. I feel exposed as I climb the steps. Even though the garden is secluded I might be visible to the neighbouring houses.

I try the door.

<u>I can't believe my luck!</u>

"You fool!" I say (not too loud!).

I am standing inside your office. I feel light-headed, unable to contain an outburst of laughter.

I regain control of myself.

"What an idiot!"

You really aren't proving much of a challenge.

## 27

Because it was such a bright day, Gil took Spike for a walk at Oldbury Hill. It was one of their favourite walks and often, though not today, they met up with Megan and her two dogs who lived nearby. The sunshine had brought dog-walkers out in force. Spike greeted humans and their charges with equanimity; unfamiliar dogs he approached more carefully.

Apart from the benefit to his physical health, Gil found this time creatively therapeutic too. During walks he'd dreamt up many of his best ideas. Besides his work with Felix, Gil had written and illustrated two award-winning picture books for younger children. The text for these was very simple, so he didn't feel it lent him any advantage at all with his current undertaking, *Pete's Pirates*, also conceived whilst walking the dog, about which he was beginning to feel more optimistic. Felix's nurture throughout the project's crucial earliest days and more recently reading passages to Sally and receiving her approving laughter had been encouraging. The basic premise was one often adopted by writers of children's literature, where a child hero encounters something from another place or time which breaks through into their world. In Gil's story, a band of cut-throat seventeenth-century pirates had fallen through time.

As he strode along the muddy well-trodden path, exchanging the time of day and a few words with those walkers he recognised, and a nod and smile with those he didn't, his thoughts were mostly of Sally. Over the weekend they had expressed their mutual feelings and exchanged that peculiarly all-important little phrase of affection. Today, there was a certain inner contentment about him as he strode along.

'Everything would be great,' he thought, 'But for that bastard Chilvers.'

# 28

Approx 1.05 pm - Thanks for leaving me your computer already booted-up. A nudge of the mouse and I had your morning's work on screen.

The world of illustration can't be very challenging, judging by all the awards that adorn your office. There are several photographs of you with the ridiculously named Blatt.

I have done my research meticulously. Whilst watching your house, I read every one of the titles you illustrated for Blatt. I wish I could claim the experience was enjoyable!

I loathe the unrealistic pap dished up as children's literature. I particularly hate the way things turn out well or for the best. Let's face it, how often is goodness rewarded in real life? If that were so, then all those bankers, commodities dealers and all the others who earn fat cat salaries, paid for by the toil and misery of the world's poorest, must be the finest people alive? Veritable saints!

Hardly surprising there are so many fantasists about if they get raised on the diet of utter tripe you and Blatt churn out, is it? Grown-ups seem to think that telling lies to children is somehow part of childhood, eg "Santa lives at the North Pole and if you're good, he'll come down the chimney on Christmas Eve and bring you toys."

Let's face it, any old man who broke into a child's bedroom at night wouldn't be there to give them toys!

By the time I was no more than five or six, I'd already worked out that Christmas must be nonsense. How could a senile old fool get around the world on a sleigh pulled by flying reindeer in one night and deliver presents to everybody?

It's all a bit like believing in Jesus, whose Father, God, let him die so that everyone else could be saved. Some Father, don't you think? And saved from what? Talk about dysfunctional families – an unmarried mother and an absent father who allows his own child to be betrayed to the cops of the day! But in the end it was alright because Jesus rose again and made a few guest appearances to his friends. After this he went off to be happy forevermore in heaven with his Dad.

Eventually of course every child learns that Father Christmas is a fairy story, (sob, sob)

"And the Easter Bunny, too?"

"Yes son, that too."

"And Jesus, Daddy? Did you and Mummy make up Jesus?"

"What the hell are you talking about? I'm surprised you could even think such a thing! In fact if you don't believe Jesus was born of a Virgin, and died on the cross because all Jews are evil, you'll die and fry in hell."

Even as a child I wanted to know the facts, not the racist twaddle adults tried to instil in me.

However, I digress:

Approx 1.05 - 1.30 pm - I anticipated you'd have a computer. Bit surprised to find a PC. I thought an illustrator would probably work on a Mac. I don't care. I brought in my rucksack of many tricks a 500 gigabyte external hard drive. I had considered bringing something bigger but I knew that even 50 gigabytes of data would take far too long to download within my time limitations. You have about thirty gb of files and images. It should be possible. Isn't external data storage a wonderful thing!

I connect to a USB port and set it up to copy everything: the writing on screen, your online accounts, address book (very helpful).

Once the download gets underway, I search your desk. In the top drawer you keep several sets of keys. Thoughtfully labelled in clear block capitals FRONT DOOR, CONSERVATORY, GARAGE, SPARE CAR KEYS. I borrow the front door keys (a dead-lock and rim-lock) for copying.

In the drawer below is another cache of gold – a little black book that contains just about every other key to your life. I can't quite believe it. I want to let out a yell but don't of course! You have listed in this skinny A5 book every computer password you use. I am holding the means of accessing: your email, ISP server, the social networking sites you belong to, your website admin, even (I am almost speechless!) the passwords for your online banking. I take a raw jpeg of each of the four relevant pages with my digital camera. See, everything I think of.

I look through the other areas of your office. There is a stack of portfolios containing your art work, some I recognise from the books. No interest to me!

Your unlocked filing cabinets prove more worthwhile. In a file marked IMPORTANT PERSONAL DOCUMENTS, I come across your paper driver's licence along with your birth, marriage certificates etc. I may be required to produce some proof of identity when I get the keys copied, so I take your Driving Licence and Birth Certificate.

Approx 1.32 pm - Your assistant, the woman with the MG, has an office next door. She has established the space as her own, woolly cardigan on hanger on back of door, pictures of grandchildren (I presume) on the wall by her desk, mug with the words 'To Gran'. I scan her computer files, but everything I really want is on yours.

Approx 1.40 pm - I do quick tour. Your bedroom is at the back, nice room, nice view, bed unmade, dog hairs on the duvet - disgusting. The other bedrooms have no regular occupants. You've chosen simple but elegant furniture, Arts and Crafts period, nothing self-assembly. Children's books must pay!

There is a flight of stairs up to the attic but this door is locked. The key is most probably in the desk drawer. I'll return if time but I want to see downstairs more. As I might've expected the furnishings downstairs display a similar simple taste, block-wood floors, more Arts and Crafts furniture. There is a grandfather clock ticking in the hall.

I perform whistle-stop tour of remaining rooms; a room with bookshelves, library of sorts; dining room, oak table, six chairs, elegant sideboard; sitting room, television, magazines and newspapers in a rack, two sofas, nice lighting, logs sitting ready to light in the fireplace, on the mantelpiece are two dark wood candlesticks and between them a signed photograph of a woman (mid-twenties) in a silver frame. Dead wife? There is a small corridor leading off the hallway, straight ahead is the kitchen and to the left is a small cloakroom and toilet (where I'd considered making my break-in).

I glance around the kitchen and conservatory; much evidence of the pooch - bowls, cushions for its hairy backside.

Approx 1.44 pm - I return to your office. The copying has finished. One thing has eluded me. A folder that requires a password before I can open it. I wonder why someone who lives as openly as you do keeps a protected file? Have you got secrets to hide, details so personal you'd curl up and die if they leaked out? I hope so!

I try everything – nothing in the A5 book – I try every stupid title of every inane book you ever worked on with Felix Blatt - Bladderghast, Brian Franglestein, Hollowpimples, Penelope's Perfect Pizzas, The Annoying Bumblewart, Harlow's Flying Hamsters. I go through the whole dreary list and not one of them works! Access denied.

I want to hurl your computer through a window!

1.49 pm - I must leave. I experience a powerful urge to violate your home. I know this isn't rational. I compromise. I defecate in your en-suite bathroom. My bowels appreciate the gesture after all the excitement. After flushing I check the bowl for marks.

Nothing remains but my stench.

## 29

Tuesday 13 January

Your mail is so boring and inane.

'dear gil harper, i am riting this letter to yew from hosbitle as i am ill and haven't been very wel either. i like your drawins, theyr funni. and i still like you even though it hurts me when i laff. i miss being at home with mumy and dady and my dog 'poo-sniffer'. do you have a dog?'

And you always reply personally.

"Yes, little Johnny. I too have a leg-shagger. His name is Spike."

You're too good to be true!

Adults get Megan Hollingsworth, Mr Harper's Personal Assistant (Midget-rider sounds better).

7.44 am - Newspaper boy.

9.16 am - Postman Prat.

9.26 am - Megan arrives.

12.48 pm - Megan leaves.

12.59 pm - Gil and Spike go walkies. I move car, park in next road.

1.07 pm - Enter via front door. If you'd set the alarm I still could have got in! You must have a rotten head for figures. The four digit security code for your burglar alarm is kept in a computer file cryptically labelled (sarcasm) "Home Security". You should have heard me whooping last night when I discovered it!

First jobs: return the keys I borrowed from your desk (I have my own set now); I put back your birth certificate too but I've held on to your driving licence (I have a plan formulating). If you go looking for it, I daresay you'll only think you've misplaced it.

I hardly slept last night, going through your files, planning my next moves.

I gave a lot of thought to the password for that secure file. I became even more excited about getting into it after discovering just how cavalier you'd been with your security codes. It must be awfully personal.

I compiled a list of seventeen words that crop up regularly in 'Pete's Pirates' (rubbish story by the way!). You like inventing names, so I'm convinced it's a name – numbers you tend to write down.

Within minutes of entering your office I'm testing my list.

(Incidentally, I checked the patio doors. Locked! I am such a lucky opportunist!)

Approx 1.20 pm - V angry. None of my words work. I experience almost uncontrollable urge to destroy everything you own.

Look around downstairs to ease my tension.

I wonder if the library might hold the key?

Your books are organised in sections: autobiography, smallest; biography, slightly larger; history, yes, interested in history; art books and fiction vie for most space.

Approx 1.27 pm - Fiction is in two sections, Children and Adult. Do you have a favourite illustrator, a role model? I look along the alphabetical names, Ahlberg, Bestall, Blake, Briggs. There must be two hundred names. This is impossible, it could be anything, an artist, a writer, or nothing whatever to do with art or literature, a place name perhaps, even his dog!

Dog! SPIKE. Of course, the dog! You talk about the pooch incessantly in your letters to children.

I rush up to the office.

PASSWORD REQUIRED

Here goes, I say.

I type the name in lower case letters.

s p i k e
ACCESS DENIED

I'm sweating. It has to be. I try again.

S p i k e
ACCESS DENIED

Don't lose it now, I tell myself, stay focused. Try block capitals.

S P I K E
ACCESS DENIED

<u>It was a good thing nobody arrived back early from lunch at that moment or I would have torn them limb from limb</u>.

Approx 1.35 pm - I go downstairs again. I'm running out of time.

I go into the sitting room - to calm down more than anything. I sit on the sofa directly opposite the fireplace. I feel despondent. So utterly crestfallen I find it hard to raise my head from looking down at the floor. I feel it's personal. Gil has deliberately affronted me! Then I notice the mantelpiece, the wooden candlesticks, the photograph of the young woman in its elegant frame. It reminds me of a shrine. Then I see it. Yes!

An affectionate message with signature at the edge of the portrait: "To Gil, All my love forever, Jules."

I take the stairs a dozen at a time (exaggeration). I type the name.

J u l e s

And I'm in!

And what a find! Your diary! A record of everything you've done from age fifteen. It's pure, unadulterated, twenty-four carat gold. I'm ecstatic!

Approx 1.43 pm - All this excitement has left me with certain biological needs. I relieve myself in various ways in your private bathroom.

Approx 1.49 pm - I exit same way I arrived.

## 30

The week passed quietly. Sally and Gil communicated by telephone each evening and sent short, affectionate text messages to each other throughout the day. As for his book, Gil began to feel he was finally taking ownership of it. The words were beginning to flow easily, and at times even seemed to materialise of their own volition. He found he could actually return to a passage written previously and make any necessary corrections, without giving in to the impulse to pick the whole thing to bits.

Felix was pleased Gil was finding his feet. They spoke on the phone most days, "You're learning the business of writing, Harp. Sometimes a passage appears as if by magic, but mostly it requires sheer graft. This can, of course, be rewarding too. One seemingly inconsequential word can miraculously balance a hitherto wayward sentence and what was formerly base is gold. Alchemy has taken place!"

Gil had heard him say much the same on book tours when asked about the processes of writing. It struck him that Felix's words had sunk in at last.

## 31

Wednesday 14 January

I'm working through your diary. What an egocentric bore you are. Your diary makes worse reading than your indulgent flight of fantasy for children, 'Pete's Pirates', which at best might amuse a child with Special Educational Needs!

The diary is however, detailed, frank and unguardedly honest. The first fifteen years were written in longhand. It was most considerate, scanning it into your computer so I could conveniently download it. Thanks.

In the early years you were scared your mother, who you had little respect for (tut, tut) and considered a snoop, might discover it. There are childishly inane codes for the un-appetising practices you constantly indulged in at fifteen, eg: March 3, '85:

*'I think Mum has been snooping again. When I got in from school I noticed my stuff had been moved. You'd think the sign on the door, PRIVATE KEEP OUT, might've got the message across!*

*'Don't think she found this though, or my horde of X rated nubiles. You remain perfect my lovelies, my angels of deliciousness, in my secret harem beneath the floorboards! ... flayed the beast four times tonight while I should have been revising history.'*

There are passages and passages of teenage angst. You record for almost a year, the number of times a day the beast got flayed, monkey got spanked, salami got slapped, gherkin was jerked, bishop got beaten or you took a J Arthur – I had to look that one up!

There are coy accounts of attempted seductions, fumblings with panty-hose and bra straps in the back rooms of youth clubs or rear seats of cars, agonised meditations on the delicate matter of premature ejaculation.

Although a torture to read, I will have a clear picture of you, your deepest most anxious thoughts, innermost concerns and more importantly, your weaknesses.

Remarkable, one little word opened the door to your life - J u l e s - I suppose you weren't to know how dangerous a name could be.

## 32

During the second half of the week the prospect of being re-united with Sally brought a distinct spring to Gil's step.

"You're looking all bright-eyed and bushy-tailed," commented Megan as she delivered the coffee and mail on Thursday morning. Gil was whistling to himself whilst perched on top of some kitchen steps. He was hanging a canvas, about five-foot square, on the wall alongside the French windows. It explained the banging she had heard downstairs. "Ooh, I like that, reminiscent of Klee." Megan possessed a broad knowledge of twentieth-century artists.

"Yes, I was going through a Klee-love-fest when I did it."

"You painted it?" she asked, not meaning to sound so surprised.

Gil chuckled at her response. "When I was at the Slade. Before I met Felix and gave up being a penniless painter to become a well-paid illustrator."

"It's really good."

"Thanks."

"Where was it hiding?"

"Up in the attic."

"Any more?"

"Dozens."

"May I see?"

Gil led her out of the office and up the flight of stairs leading to the attic. The key was kept on a cup-hook screwed to the side of the door frame, not immediately visible.

"I'm impressed," she said, after touring the fifty or so abstract canvases stacked against the gable-end walls. Her eyes were inevitably drawn to an easel set up in the middle of the space which held a painting covered by a dust-sheet. "Is that something you're working on?"

"I haven't painted for some time," he replied with some diffidence, "it's the last piece I completed."

Megan hesitated; somehow she knew it was this final work that she had been brought here for. "May I?" she asked, tentatively extending a hand towards the dust-sheet.

He gave a little nod to affirm it was okay.

Megan was aware that Gil was reading her face as she removed the cover. He was watching keenly as her eyes roved across the painting, absorbing every nuance, examining the brush-strokes, appreciating how skilfully colour had been employed to bring life and depth to the face of his late wife.

After what seemed to Gil an interminably long time, she looked across at him; tears had formed in her eyes, she nodded and smiled in speechless approval.

She spoke softly, almost in a whisper, "It's beautiful, Gil. You captured the dear girl in every detail. Was it painted after ..."

"Before," he interjected. "I completed it about two weeks before."

"She was so lovely."

"Never lovelier, to me at least ... so full of life."

## 33

Thursday 15 January

You won a scholarship to the Slade. Should I be impressed?

During this time you met Julia. Shortly afterwards you start referring to her as Jules. I detect a hint of social inadequacy. She grew up in a middle-class home in Sevenoaks and went to a posh school. You struggled through the state system, and grew up in a home that only aspired to be middle-class.

Your parents were, as described in your tiresome adolescent words:

*'Snobbish bores ... they worship at the altar of consumerism and pray only to Gods with a recognisable brand name. Their idea of heaven has a fitted kitchen and a Georgian style conservatory in brilliant white UPVC.'*

What agony you suffered taking Jules home to meet your appalling parents.

You possess a sizeable chip on your shoulder.

## 34

Sally telephoned late Friday afternoon to say she was running late. Gil was disappointed.

"I'm really sorry, darling. We're up to our eyeballs. I have to tie-dye forty shirts, surcoats etcetera for the English chorus. If it isn't finished tonight I'll have to come in tomorrow. The fittings are Monday."

"Can't be helped, price of art," he mused philosophically, "What time shall I expect you, then?"

"Ten ... eleven possibly."

She got in shortly after eleven. Spike alerted him to the arrival of her car and Gil popped the Indian meal for two he had standing by into the oven. He managed to reach the door just before she pressed the doorbell.

Spike got first attention. Sally picked him up which seemed like the only way to placate him.

"Hallo," she said to Gil, who was wearing a broad smile from one ear to the other. Sally had completed all tasks and raced for her car without consulting a mirror. Her hair was waif-like and dishevelled, she was wearing a baggy old sweater with jeans torn on both knees, not nice designer tears, and brown lace-up boots that hadn't seen polish in years. To Gil however, she looked delightful.

"Ah, yes, front door," he said, handing her a set of keys he'd deliberately left on the hall table to remind himself, "I finally remembered and got a new set made, yesterday."

While their food heated they shared a bottle of wine and rapidly told the small everyday events of their days apart.

"I haven't finished before ten once, there's so much to do. Roz has been great. We've had lots of girlie chats. If you don't mind slumming it, you could stay over for a night or two. Roz and John wouldn't mind. The flat's small, but cosy. My room's tiny but I've got a double bed," she winked to emphasise its potential and laughed. "Spike could come too."

"Okay, great. I'll do that."

"How's the writing?"

Gil nodded, "I feel I'm finally getting somewhere. I completed five thousand words this week."

"Brilliant. Will I be allowed to see it?"

"Of course."

Neither of them had eaten since lunchtime, so they sat down to their supper with enthusiasm.

"I didn't realise how hungry I was," said Sally as she mopped up the last drop of sauce off her plate with a piece of naan, "That went down without touching the sides."

"Shall I open another bottle?"

"Not for me."

"Coffee?"

"No, utterly replete I am. No longer hungry or thirsty," she replied with an emphatic crossing of arms. Her eyes began to smoulder as they engaged with Gil's, "However, a girl can experience other appetites."

Gil raised an eyebrow, "I'd better see what I can do," he said.

## 35

### Friday 16 January

It was while at the Slade that you met Felix Blatt.

Can that really be his name?

I'm fascinated. This older man takes you under his wing and gives you the approval you've been crying out for all your life. He not only values your work but nurtures your talent and educates you, knocks off some of those rough edges.

In March 1992 your father's duodenal ulcer perforates. You attempt to be a good son and lend support to your mother, dutifully hold her hand while you both watch him flat-line.

A month later, in your hackneyed style, you wrote:

*'... strange to think, how the man who brought me up, who should be a major figure in my life, passes on and leaves me feeling so little ... We were like travellers in an old tale who meet by chance and are forced through circumstance to stay a while in each other's company. However, it's clear they have little in common, and when the time comes, both parties move on; indifferent as to whether they shall meet again, un-touched by their association.'*

Yawn-yawn-yawn!

Of Blatt you say:

*'... Felix is the warmest, most kind-hearted man I have ever known ... in a recent interview for the Sunday Times, he said his books had been enhanced by his association with me and quoted increased sales to back this up. Felix is far more than a colleague. He epitomises everything I always pictured a proper father son relationship should be ...'*

Isn't that touching?

On the subject of your long collaboration you say:

*'... Although I'd always been interested in illustration, sometimes I regret meeting Felix at the moment I did. I can't help but wonder how I might have developed as a painter if I hadn't been side-tracked into illustration. It sounds like I'm whingeing ...'*

Yes, Gil, it jolly well does!

## 36

They spent Saturday lazing in bed until late morning, laughing and chatting between bouts of dozing and love-making. In the afternoon they took Spike for a walk and talked about the things that fascinate lovers but evoke yawns in the rest of the world.

On Sunday they'd been invited to Felix and Kate's for lunch. They left earlier than necessary because Sally wanted to call at her place to pick up mail and collect some things she needed.

Sally's home in Hildenborough was part of a short terrace of Victorian cottages, the outer dimensions of which appeared to be far smaller than the area within.

"The Victorians were brilliant with space," commented Gil.

"I know. I'm like Doctor Who in his Tardis. Mind you, it would fit about five times into your gaff."

"My place is too big. I only hang onto it because I'm too lazy to move."

At the end of a long but narrow galley-type kitchen was a ground floor extension, built by the previous owner who had described himself as a DVD fanatic. What had been his surround-sound TV lounge now served as Sally's work-room.

Gil had been there for coffee once but had never seen this room before. It was fascinating to see where other people worked. The large number of pins all over the laminated wood floor was the thing he noticed first. He picked Spike up to protect his paws.

"Not the best place for yoga practice," he quipped.

There was a purpose-made work table in the middle of the room and on its counter were three sewing machines with half a dozen tall stools tucked beneath. Sally often said the work appealed because of its companionability. Built under the table was storage space, packed with numerous rolls of cloth, black bin bags, their multi-coloured innards spilling, a mix of neatly-labelled plastic storage boxes and dog-eared cardboard ones branded Heinz Beans, Jacobs Crackers, Mr Muscle etcetera, scrawled over in marker pen with descriptions like 'tapes', 'braiding', 'buckles' and 'straps'.

Sally had begun to seek out the items she required by digging through an assortment of more boxes and tins that were distributed along two walls of stout shelving.

"Can I help?" Gil asked.

"I'm fine. Make a coffee if you like."

Redundant, Gil took himself and Spike off to the kitchen. From time to time they could hear Sally, whenever her hopes of finding a required object were thwarted, exclaim, "shit" or "bugger" or "fuck" even; and when a really promising box proved a giant failure, all three expletives together.

## 37

Sunday 18 January

Poor, poor Julia; and poor, poor Gil.

To think the love of your life was killed so tragically. I genuinely felt moved as I read your account of the crash - such a waste.

And the trauma remains with you. You take comfort from the leg-shagger and the supportive Felix and Kate. George and Marjorie, Julia's parents, have been very understanding too. Remarkable, considering you killed their daughter!

I've learnt you were on your way home from visiting them when our paths crossed.

Nothing has been the same for you since the accident, has it? How you wish you could re-connect with life. You avoid old joint friends because they bring back too many memories.

Pages and pages of your diary are constantly on about, what Jules meant to me, or my dreadful loss, or the guilt I feel.

Talk about wallowing in it! Get a life, please!

## 38

An hour and two cups of coffee later, Gil loaded two hefty boxes into the back of his Volvo.

"Sure you haven't forgotten anything?" he asked with amused sarcasm.

"Enough cheek, Harper. Just drive."

From Hildenborough, Gil took the road to Tonbridge, then turned onto the Maidstone road. Gil glanced across at Sally as they passed the Hadlow village sign. All ease had suddenly vanished from her face and only apprehension remained.

"Bad memories?" he asked.

"It fills me with dread just travelling through. These were the bounds of my prison when I was his hostage. Each day when he was expected home, I'd panic. He'd ask for details about everything I'd done. Where I'd been; who I'd talked to."

"Christ, that's so paranoid."

"Paranoid! You can ..." Sally suddenly broke off and shrank down in her seat, "Shit! His car!"

Gil misunderstood at first and glanced up at his rear mirror before realising she meant ahead. He followed her eye-line to a pub called The Harrow, which was now alongside them on the right.

"Which one?"

"Silver Merc."

"He's starting early," said Gil watching the car in his side mirror as they left The Harrow behind.

"Probably isn't in there. Trevor, the landlord, takes his keys and won't let him drive home if he's over the limit. It's only about a quarter of a mile up there," she said pointing to a lane that curved off to the left.

Sally shook her head and sat back up, "The car's outside the pub more often than it's parked in his garage."

## 39

While Sally helped Kate with lunch, Gil went off to find Felix. He discovered him busy at the wood-turning lathe in his workshop. Spike, ruled by his stomach, had stayed with the ladies.

Felix, catching sight of Gil as he entered, lay down the chisel in his hand, switched off the lathe's motor and raised his goggles.

"Harp, m'dear," he said stretching out a hand.

"Hallo Felix. What are you up to?"

"I was just assisting this piece of walnut in its ambition to become a bowl."

"Sure it wasn't happier as a tree?"

"Had its life cut short by the hurricane."

Felix and Kate had lost two dozen trees during the hurricane of '87. Gil had seen photographs of their beloved ten-acre garden utterly devastated.

"This is the last of our old walnut."

Felix, after the pain subsided, had set about saving the timber. He enlisted a small army of helpers and every useable scrap was salvaged. The table in Gil's dining room had been a wedding gift to him and Jules from the Blatts, crafted from their most beloved oak by Felix himself.

"I remember thinking Kent would never look the same again. You must have thought so too?"

"I thought it likely I might not live long enough to see things restored," replied Felix before going on to ask, "The dear girl and little feller with you?"

"Helping Kate."

Felix placed one of his shovel-sized hands on Gil's shoulder and smiled, "Kate and I think Sally is delightful," he said, then added, "Shall we join our womenfolk and partake of a pre-lunch snifter?"

The weather was too good to miss, so once lunch was over they donned coats and hats to go walking in the crisp but glorious afternoon. They went through the Blatts' garden initially, clambered over a stile into an adjoining field then on into woodland. Felix, a keen daily walker despite carrying a stick these days, led the party with Sally, arms hooked together. Kate, preferring a more moderate pace, walked behind with Gil; Spike rushed back and forth patrolling the gap.

It was evident to anybody who had known Gil as long as the Blatts, that he was happier now than in an awfully long time. It is always difficult for a new partner to sit comfortably with old friends but Sally had slotted right in.

Kate, who'd taken a little more wine with lunch than she usually did, was in jocular spirits. As Gil helped her down from the stile she asked with a Bacchanalian gleam to her eye, "Thought about popping the question yet?"

"What question?" he disingenuously asked.

"Don't play the innocent, Harp. You know what question it is gets popped."

Gil, cheeks reddening, shook his head and laughed so loudly, that Felix and Sally, now forty yards ahead, turned to see what was happening.

"You two carry on!" Kate shouted at them, "We're talking about you, not to you!"

Felix made some off-the-cuff remark to his companion, clearly an amusing one, and they continued their walk.

"Well?"

"Isn't it a bit early days for that kind of thing?"

"I didn't ask when the happy day is going to be, I merely asked if you'd thought about it?"

"Why, do you think I should?"

"Doesn't matter what I think, Harp."

"I've thought about it," he confessed. Then, suddenly a new seriousness took hold of him, "But, before anything, I need to tell her ... about what happened ... about Jules, the accident. I've tried, I'm just not able to ..."

Gil was a subject Kate Blatt was well-versed in; she knew how much the crash still haunted him. Along with Felix she had stood helplessly by as grief had overtaken his life. Kate had concluded that his wounds were beyond the skills of any human agency, and being a woman of quiet personal faith, she had often prayed for him.

She now took Gil's hands in hers and re-assured him gently, "You'll get there, Harp. I know you will."

## 40

Two names crop up in your diaries that alert me to some possibilities. The first is the man Owens. The other is your whore's ex-lover, Michael Chilvers.

How much would it take to get you angry?

Who knows, a few nudges and you may tip right over the edge. I doubt it though. You don't have the guts. You're too weak.

## 41

Sally awoke with the feeling that there was something important she'd forgotten to do. The sensation was not uncommon, especially when starting on a new show. She sighed, turned over and stretched her arm towards Gil. It came as a surprise to find his side of the bed was empty. The clock told her it was 3.07 am. The bathroom was dark, but she noticed a sliver of light beneath the door to the landing.

A clear-skied day had been succeeded by an icy cold night, and as she left the warmth of bed the temperature-drop caused her to shiver. She put on Gil's old dressing gown and opened the bedroom door. It was immediately apparent that the only light was coming from the door to the loft, left slightly ajar. The seeming oddness of this discovery in the middle of the night caused Sally's heart to miss a beat.

She recalled asking Gil when he'd given her a tour of his house, "What's up there?"

And his casual reply, "Just storage stuff and junk."

"Gil?" she called tentatively.

There was no reply. She started to ascend. As she approached the landing her eyes were drawn and momentarily blinded by the powerful halogen work-light. She nudged the door open with her hand. Then as her vision returned to normal she saw Gil. He was sat quite still on a paint spattered chair before the easel which supported the portrait of his wife, its dust-cover in a heap by his feet.

Sally suddenly felt like an eavesdropper.

She assumed he hadn't heard her either calling or climbing the stairs.

However, this uncertainty was dispelled, when Gil, not averting his attention from the portrait, said, "I was driving."

Sally took two steps; she knew this was not a moment when any words were required from her.

"It was September, a beautiful autumn day," Gil recalled with a grim laugh. "Bright and sunny with just enough chill in the air to let you know it wasn't still summer. We thought we'd drive about, not plan a route … find a pub for lunch." He sighed. Averting his gaze from the portrait for the first time, he dropped his head, "I'm sorry. Did you wake-up and find me missing?"

"It doesn't matter," said Sally. She took another step and put her hand on his shoulder, "I'd like to know."

Gil sighed and lowered his head again.

"I'll go downstairs and make a hot drink," she said, "Why don't you come and talk."

In the kitchen, Sally warmed some milk. Gil arrived just as the cocoa was ready and took a seat at the table. Sally set a mug down before him and another for herself opposite.

Gil lifted his drink and blew softly across its surface before testing with his lips. "I like cocoa," he said, "Didn't know I had any."

"Warm and soothing, isn't it?" she replied, but immediately felt irritated by her own words, she hadn't meant them to sound like a lead in.

"Did Felix or Kate mention the accident to you?"

"No." Sally paused then added, "And I would never have asked."

Gil smiled, he liked her integrity. He took a deep breath, "Jules was expecting a baby."

Sally wasn't able to suppress her gasp, "Oh Gil, I am so sorry."

"The pregnancy had run almost full-term. The baby was due in three weeks."

"That's appalling," she felt his pain so palpably it required great effort to hold back her tears.

"The bump was very big. We were convinced it was a boy … I don't know why, we were both certain. We used to joke about what a bruiser he'd be. Jules had reached the stage where carrying the baby was uncomfortable, even some of her maternity dresses were too tight. Every time we went out in the car, she kept fidgeting with the seat belt, trying to position it so it didn't cause her discomfort … I thought it would do her good to get out in the sunshine," Gil paused as if to punctuate the irony.

"I think she'd have been happier sitting in the garden. After driving around, we found ourselves about a mile from Tunbridge Wells. We had lunch in a place near the High Street, and afterwards we looked round some shops. I bought her a new maternity dress." Gil smiled as he remembered his wife's little foibles, "Jules had a vain streak; she loved to be well turned-out. There was no way she would've set foot outdoors without make-up, even heavily pregnant. Anyway, after shopping, we headed for home. The day was still nice, so we detoured. We thought we'd explore … cut across country."

Gil broke off, bit down on his lip and turned his face to avoid the look of compassion in Sally's eyes.

He continued, "She kept the new dress on. Blue, with a green trim at the neck and hem it was. She was pleased with it. I caught her admiring herself in the mirror on the back of the sun-shade. I told her she was vain. She laughed and said it was a woman's prerogative. We took a narrow road that wasn't sign-posted that we reckoned would bring us up into Langton Green. We planned to head towards Penshurst. Neither of us had taken that route before.

"There was a sign to say the road narrowed up ahead. I wasn't going fast, about thirty, maybe thirty-five. There was a Water Board trench dug out along Jules' side for about a quarter of a mile. We drove down into a dip and came to a sharp bend around an old bridge. Then we started to climb up a gradient. There was another bend a little way ahead. I saw Jules fidget with her seat-belt. 'You okay?' I asked. 'This bloody belt is cutting me in two,' she said. Then as we approached the bend, out of the corner of my eye, I saw her release the catch."

Gil stared at the mug before him on the table, "I've seen Jules repeat that action a thousand times in a thousand different nightmares."

Sally nodded, understanding the reason behind Gil's often troubled sleep.

"I shouted 'A car! A car!' But it wasn't a car, it was a pick-up truck. It hurtled around the bend … strange, you can tell in a split second the other driver hasn't seen you. His wife was beside him in the passenger seat. They were arguing with each other. I slammed my foot on the brake. I caught sight of Jules fumbling to re-connect her seat-belt. The wife saw us first. She screamed. I saw the blind panic in his eyes, the sheer terror in hers … it must've been a mirror image of the expressions on our faces.

"The crash was inevitable. No escaping it … a deep trench on our side and a wall on the other. I recall the screech of brakes ... the impact and the irresistible force … being propelled forward. I must've reached out my arm to try and protect her. I remember the sound of breaking glass, of metal grinding into metal … the smell of burning rubber ... but I don't remember her flying into the windscreen ... or the screams of the Owens children as their father's truck bulldozed into us before it overturned in the ditch."

Sally possessed no words to console after hearing such an atrocity. There were tears in her eyes. There were none in Gil's; he had wept so long and hard there was nothing left.

"Jules' baby?" she asked quietly through her sobs.

"Jules died instantly. They did an emergency Caesarean … the baby ..." Gil faltered, "... our son ... dead too … too late."

"You were conscious?"

"I was knocked out for a few minutes, concussed, my left arm was broken, a few cracked ribs. I was trapped in the wreckage and had to be cut free. I was black and blue with bruises but none of my injuries were serious. The rescue took an age."

"What about the pick-up truck? You mentioned children?"

"A boy six and girl eight, sitting in the back of the truck, no belts, nothing. They were crushed when the truck turned over."

"Oh, God! But you weren't to blame."

"The inquest exonerated me of all blame. Geoff Owens had been drinking and was over the limit. He was convicted of causing death by dangerous driving."

"He deserved it."

"He received a life ban from driving and a five year prison sentence. He was released after two and a half years on parole."

"That can't be right. He caused the tragedy and got off so lightly!"

"I never thought he got off lightly. He and his wife witnessed the death of both their children. Mrs Owens became more and more distraught. Six months into Owens' sentence she took an overdose. Paracetamol. She was discovered and revived but there was a delayed reaction. The poor woman died of liver failure a few days later."

1 3 5
2 4 R

# THIRD

19 January – 13 February

1

Gil was grateful to Sally for not overwhelming him with questions about the crash, or for attempting to fix him emotionally. Rationally, he had always known that he was not to blame for the accident; unfortunately, the mental processes of those who survive traumatic events don't always conform to cool, clear logic.

After they returned to bed for what remained of the night, Sally held Gil tightly in her arms. Once certain he was asleep, only then did she allow herself to drop off and catch the final hour.

2

Monday 19 January

I know so much about you.

You are shockingly honest. You donate ten percent of everything you earn to children's charities, which you do anonymously. Even your tax returns are legit, probably more than could be said of your average politician.

I know your likes and dislikes: favourite foods, places to eat, taste for Arts and Crafts furniture, music, art, even the types of book you read. I know more about you than anyone living. Through your diary I've had access to the darkest reaches of your mind, the desperate times, and how close you've come to ending it all.

If I wanted to, I could embezzle an enormous amount of money from your bank accounts. However, I'm not a common thief, and this is not about anything as vulgar as robbery.

There is a superb plan forming in my mind. You'll appreciate the necessity of preparation. Over the days ahead I'll be turning more and more of my attention away from you directly, Gil. I'm going to be busy. I'll be wearing my most appealing smile and will have to exploit everything I've ever learnt about how to win friends and influence people. Tee hee hee!

You'll find out later, when it's time.

For now, all you need to know is that the package I'm putting together for you is quite a masterpiece.

## 3

The week passed quickly. Gil and Sally stayed in touch by texting and speaking on the phone for at least an hour each evening.

On Tuesday, during their nightly chat, Sally suggested, "Roz and the girls keep telling me I must take a night off."

"Sensible idea."

"I could come down tomorrow evening, or you could come up?"

"I'll drive up, that way we'll get extra time together. Megan will take Spike."

He met her at six at the company rehearsal rooms near Highbury and Islington tube and they ate before going on to see a film. They spent Wednesday night together in Sally's tiny room at Roz's place in Streatham. Work permitting, they hoped to do the same the following week.

On Saturday night, Sally managed to escape the clutches of *Macbeth* relatively early, which enabled them to get out for a drink. On Sunday Megan invited them to lunch. Gil was delighted to observe that whatever reservations Sally and Megan had initially had about each other appeared to be resolved and they now got on like a house on fire.

'Women!' thought Gil.

## 4

Sunday 25 January

I've been very busy on your behalf. I wish I could fill you in on the details. But I love a surprise!

I don't suppose you've missed me, though? Tut, tut, how ungrateful!

But then, you don't know I exist, do you?

You soon will though.

Time perhaps to start with a little mischief.

## 5

Another Monday morning came round. It was becoming routine for Gil to start the week by lugging a suitcase out to Sally's car.

"Seems like you've got a busy week ahead," he said. At breakfast he'd watched her prepare a formidable list of things to do.

"Don't remind me. The Tech looms ever closer, followed by the Dress and previews. Don't know how we're going to cope."

"You'll cope. Doctor Stage and all that!"

"Oh Gil," she said, nestling into his shoulder, "I don't want to go. I'd much rather stay with you." She was play-acting, looking helplessly up at him with her big brown eyes.

"And then I'd have Klaus breathing fire down my neck. He'd insist I'd taken you hostage."

She deposited a kiss on his lips, then got into her car and started the engine. Spike, who had been sniffing around the borders, suddenly realised he was required and rushed across to rest his front paws against the base of the driver's seat. "I hadn't forgotten you Spikey," she said patting his head, "I'll see you in a few days."

Gil picked Spike up and tucked him under his left arm. "See. You have two male admirers at this address."

She laughed.

Sally closed the car door and blew a kiss before accelerating out of the driveway, slowing briefly for a final wave.

Once out of sight, Gil looked down at Spike. He took his companion's forlorn expression to be brotherly solidarity; rather than a statement on the humiliation of being a dog sandwiched between an elbow and an armpit. Spike, barely twelve inches from ground-level in his socks, always reckoned himself to be six-foot-four.

## 6

### Monday 26 January

7.06 am - Sally leaves. Off to sew a few wimples I expect. I assume she is staying with Roz. You inform that she does this when productions get busier.

7.48 am - Newspaper boy.

9.19 am - Postman.

9.26 am - Megan.

12.50 pm - Megan leaves.

12.56 pm - Gil and Spike take off.

Approx 1.05 pm - I enter your house. Three things to do:

1 – Download new entries to your diary. And copy any new files for 'Pete's Pirates' (yawn!).

2 – I want to see your attic. See your portrait of Julia. I wasn't sure where to find the key before I read:

*'March 4, 2001 ... because I kept mislaying the key, I've screwed a cup hook into the doorframe to keep it safe. Not being renowned for my DIY skills, I felt quite proud of myself. Jules, of course, took the piss!'*

3 – A little job to do in the garden.

I suppose what I'm about to do could be described as an unnecessary act of pure, pre-meditated malice. Quite wicked!

# 7

It was before dawn on Wednesday when Spike's symptoms emerged. He'd been a bit listless the evening before but Gil hadn't taken much notice. However, now there could be little doubt something was seriously wrong. Shortly after 4.30 am Gil was woken up by his dog vomiting on the bathroom floor. He put on the bedside lamp, and went into the bathroom to see what the matter was. The sight was pitiful. Spike, eyes half-closed was swaying on his legs with barely enough strength to stand. He had just expelled the contents of his stomach, but what frightened Gil most was the sight of the blood in it.

He kneeled and stroked him gently, "Poor Spike."

He observed there was bright fresh blood around the dog's tail and hind legs.

"Back in a minute, Spikey," he said, recognising that he needed to get help. As he walked through the bedroom he noticed a patch of watery blood on the duvet where Spike had been sleeping.

Gil kept important numbers on the notice board in his office. His fingers were trembling as he dialled the vet's number. It rang half a dozen times before it was picked up.

"Hello ..." began a male voice, clearly just surfaced from sleep.

"Jim? It's Gil Harper."

"Mmm."

"Spike's been sick, there's blood in it … and bleeding from the backside ..."

"I'll meet you at the surgery in ten minutes."

Gil put down the phone and went back to the bathroom. Spike, lying down, eyes still half-open, expressed no recognition at his master's return.

He stroked the dog and explained, "I'm going to take you to the vet to make you better, Spikey."

Gil got dressed in under a minute. He rushed downstairs, retrieved his car-keys from the kitchen table, grabbed a jacket from the hall and sped outside into the dark. It was freezing and he shivered as he fumbled with the key to open the garage door. Once he'd started the car he backed out. He left the engine running with its passenger door open. He rushed upstairs again, took a blanket from the linen cupboard on the landing and placed it alongside Spike, avoiding the vomit.

"I'm going to lift you up and put you on this blanket. Okay, Spikey?"

The dog made no response as Gil transferred him, folding the blanket's corners around him securely before raising the bundle. He carried Spike carefully downstairs and set him down gently on the passenger seat.

He reached the veterinary practice nine minutes after making the phone call.

Jim Cooper was backing into a space in the practice's car park as Gil was arriving. He parked directly opposite the vet's car. Jim came across, Gil lowered his window. "Give me a minute to do the alarms and switch on the lights," Jim said.

Gil's attention was divided between watching Jim open the surgery and listening to Spike's panting which was rapid and shallow.

The vet indicated with a wave through the surgery window to come in. Gil carried the sick animal through the waiting room, past the reception and dispensary, into an examination room beyond. Jim, an acquaintance rather than a friend of Gil's, was in his mid-thirties. He possessed boyish good looks and a genuine empathy for animals and their people. He was something of a local pin-up for middle-aged females with pets. "Hi," he said.

Gil placed the blanket on the table-top and lifted Spike out from it. The dog attempted but failed to rise to his feet.

Jim looked keenly at the dog's eyes and into its mouth. Spike put up no resistance. His eyes were bloodshot and his gums were bleeding.

"How long's he been like this?"

"I heard him being sick, just before I called. He was a bit quiet last night, a bit under the weather I thought," said Gil, starting to feel he'd been irresponsible.

Jim Cooper went on to re-assure him, "Dogs get off days like the rest of us. Anyway, it's impossible to tell until the symptoms appear."

"You know what it is?"

"Yes," said Jim. The vet's swift response caused something to clench in the pit of Gil's stomach. "Ninety-nine percent at least. Looks like rat-poison."

"Rat poison!"

"It thins the blood, literally leaks through the capillary walls." Jim gently pulled back the dog's lips to reveal Spike's bleeding gums. His finger traced the line of a capillary to illustrate the point. Spike's gums were anaemically white and the capillary was bright red. "Any idea how he came into contact?"

Gil shook his head.

"Been walking somewhere different?"

"We vary our walks, but they're all places we've been a hundred times." Gil needed to know the prognosis, "Can you do anything?" he asked, dreading the reply.

"I can't make any promises. The treatment is vitamin K. I'll give him a shot."

Gil had been so distracted by Spike's condition during the conversation that he hadn't noticed that Jim had already prepared an injection.

"There's a chance it won't work?"

"Afraid so. Sorry. It depends when he ate it, how much, and how long it's been in his system."

"I see ... thanks for seeing us so fast."

"It's my job," said Jim with the look that had won him the devotion of the local ladies. "Can you hold him?"

Gil put his hands across the dog's back to steady him. Spike had been known to become uncharacteristically fierce in veterinary situations with needles about. On this occasion, however, he didn't so much as flinch or signal he was even aware that anything was being done to him.

## 8

<u>Wednesday 28 January</u>

4.40 am - Dear me, you are up early!

I knew the greedy little tyke wouldn't be able to resist my 'treats'. While you're taking 'baby' to the vet, I'm going to take the opportunity to spell things out for you.

IF YOU DON'T SPOT MY TRAIL NOW I'D RECOMMEND GETTING <u>YOUR EYES TESTED</u>!

## 9

Gil didn't know what to do with himself once he got back from the vet's. He was reminded of Spike everywhere in the house. It was going to be a long day until 5 pm, when Jim Cooper suggested he ring the surgery.

Gil needed to talk to someone. He rang Sally just after seven. He woke her up.

"I'm really sorry, I thought you'd be awake," he said.

She could tell by the sound of his voice that something was wrong, "I set my alarm for ten past because I foolishly got hooked into a game of

Monopoly with Roz and John last night and didn't get to bed until midnight."

Sally was upset to hear the news. From a position of indifference to dogs she'd become quite attached to Spike.

"He's so special to you, Gil. I'll drive back. I should be there around nine."

"Please, don't, you're too busy and ..."

"I don't want you to be on your own."

"Megan will be here shortly."

"Promise to ring, soon as you hear?"

Gil promised. Their conversation led on to the question of where Spike might have picked up poison.

He had almost the identical conversation with Megan three hours later.

"So it could only have been Oldbury Hill or Knole Park?" pondered Megan.

"It would have to be one of them."

"Poor boy," said Megan, who, not given to displays of emotion, blew her nose discreetly on a tissue. "C'mon Gil. It's not doing us or Spike any good sitting around, getting maudlin. We've got plenty to do."

As he generally did, Gil heeded her advice. Megan set to work immediately. He didn't notice at the time that she came to him with an inordinately large number of queries that morning.

Gil attempted to get creative with *Pete's Pirates*, but it required too much effort. At eleven he went downstairs and made a pot of tea, poured cold milk into a jug, found a packet of chocolate biscuits and together with crockery returned with it all on a small tray stacked high. Megan was on the telephone so he deposited the tray on an empty area of her desk and went to the window to stare out at the bright crisp morning. He wasn't looking at anything in particular. It was impossible not to picture Spike out on patrol in the garden.

At first he thought it was a brown pebble lying on a border, before noticing another, then another. The pebbles were spread around the borders at spacings too equally distanced to occur naturally. He felt a strange tingling in his scalp and along his spine and allowed his legs to follow where instinct led. He returned to his own room, unlocked the French windows and walked down the fire-escape to the patio.

What had looked like pebbles at thirty feet he now recognised were dog biscuits, the kind that has a hard-baked outer casing and a soft meaty centre. He picked one up and held it in his palm for a moment before turning it around for examination. He saw the soft centre had been partially removed then replaced. He examined half a dozen of the biscuits; they were all the same.

10

In the office, Megan had finished her phone call. She could feel a draught coming from Gil's room and assumed he was taking a breath of air. She poured the tea and lifted the tray. As she reached the French windows she just caught sight of Gil rushing down the side of the house. Half a minute later she heard his car start and drive off with an uncharacteristic roar.

'Where's he going in such a hurry?' she thought.

11

11.17 am - You race off. <u>Nothing wrong with your eyesight then</u>!

I just can't resist seeing where this might lead, and decide to follow - <u>at a safe distance, of course</u>!

12

Gil had scant recollection of his journey to Hadlow. Later, when he considered how mechanical his driving must have been it brought him out in a cold sweat. Sally had pointed out the general direction of Chilvers' house and described a Georgian farmhouse. However, it's possible that Gil's mission may have run out of steam had he needed to make judgements like identifying the correct property.

As it happened he didn't need to go any further than The Harrow pub to find his man. Chilvers was enjoying the sunlight, leaning with one hand against a wall, clutching a pint and cigarette in the other. He was talking to a man who was polishing the chrome bumper of a vintage Jaguar. Gil presumed this man to be the landlord; an irresistible urge to shine things and ownership of a Jag were clues.

Gil swerved into the pub car park with a screech of brakes that grabbed the immediate attention of both men. Surprise was superseded by a smirk once Chilvers saw who was behind the wheel. Gil came to a halt a few yards from them. He left the engine running, drew on the handbrake and shoved the gear stick into neutral.

"Gil, my dear fellow, this is an unexpected pleasure ..." began Chilvers sardonically as Gil emerged. It was necessary to speak above the sound of the engine which started the scene off at quite a high pitch.

"Shut up!" Gil snapped.

The landlord, recognising a situation, dropped the rag from his hand and straightened up to accentuate his height, "What is this, Mike?"

Chilvers didn't reply. He had his eyes fixed on Gil, "You really are an aggressive chap. I'm sure Sally could recommend a good psychologist to help you deal with it."

"You're beneath contempt," Gil shouted. He reached a hand into the pocket of his cardigan and drew out a handful of biscuits. "Yours!" exclaimed Gil, throwing them at Chilvers' feet.

Both men burst out laughing at the seeming ridiculousness of Gil's action.

"They look like dog biscuits," remarked a bemused Chilvers, "It's kind of you but when I'm not working, I prefer a liquid lunch."

"What kind of sick bastard are you?" Gil asked, his voice full of rage.

The publican decided it was time to intervene, "Look pal, this is private property. It's time you left."

Gil looked at the man's unsmiling face, then pointed at Chilvers and shouted, "He poisoned my dog!"

"What?" asked the landlord with a look of incredulity.

Michael Chilvers, grinning with nasty delight, shrugged his shoulders, "I did what? Poor chap's crazy, Trevor. Poisoned his dog? He's absolutely barking!"

Trevor smiled.

"You and Sally must be well-suited," continued Chilvers. "She imagines stuff too."

"You leave her out of this. I'm warning you, don't come anywhere near her or my house ever again ..."

At that moment the door to the pub opened and three regulars who must have heard the commotion came out. Chilvers looked pleased to have a larger audience.

The publican moved closer, squaring up to Gil, "I don't know what this is about and I don't care. I won't warn you again. Get off my premises. Go on. Get the fuck out of here!"

A ripple of excitement passed amongst the onlookers.

For Gil there was little option but to back off. He already knew that acting on his anger had been a mistake. He'd only succeeded in making himself look foolish before Chilvers and his rent-a-crowd of cronies.

He opened the car door, put a foot inside and said, "Keep away from us. If you ever trouble Sally or me again I'll ..."

"Are you threatening me?" interjected Chilvers, backed by jeers from his gallery of allies.

Gil replied through gritted teeth, "I'm warning you ... If you persist ... I'll put a stop to you!"

Gil got into the car amidst much guffawing. As he backed up to turn around, he saw sheer delight written across Chilvers' face, who stood arms folded at the front of the group. Behind him two of the acolytes, laughing inanely, were making jerking actions with hands and wrists at Gil.

## 13

The encounter made Gil feel quite wretched. On his return, he described it to Megan.

"What the hell was I thinking?"

"You did what anyone might have done. I saw the biscuits and came to the same conclusion. I tried to reach you on your mobile."

"I didn't have it with me."

"I know, I heard it ring." Megan patted Gil's shoulder and smiled, "You mustn't be too hard on yourself. I might have done the same in your shoes."

Gil considered it unlikely but appreciated her solidarity.

"I was concerned for your safety, Gil. Heaven knows what that reptile's capable of," she said with feeling. "I had visions of you being duffed-over!"

Gil thought being duffed-over a likely possibility had he remained in the company of Chilvers and pals.

"You must report it to the police."

"I didn't get very much for my trouble the last time," he replied despondently, recalling the paint incident.

"This is different. The man has poisoned your dog ..."

"He denied it."

"You believe him?"

"'Course not. The man has systematically harassed Sally, followed us to the restaurant ... tried to ruin New Year's Eve at Klaus and David's."

"So you have to report it!"

The idea worried him; not the fear of reprisals from Chilvers, but of upsetting Sally, "You're right, but this affects Sally too. She's suffered so much at that bastard's hands. If you'd seen her Megan, on those occasions when he's turned up. Poor thing's terrified of him ..."

Megan looked sympathetic but unconvinced.

Gil knew what Megan was advocating was right. But he had already acted rashly once today, and he was not prepared to jeopardise a relationship with the only woman he'd loved since Jules over dog biscuits. After all, seeing justice done meant nothing to Spike.

Megan looked concerned, "You can't let a thing like this pass ..."

"I will report it ... but, I must talk it through with Sally first."

Megan nodded.

"First, I'm going to collect up those damned biscuits. I'll ask Jim to recommend a lab to analyse the stuff inside. When we know for certain, we can take it to the police."

## 14

I followed discreetly. When you took the road to Hadlow, I knew you'd swallowed the bait just as certainly as the pooch did. Sadly I couldn't eavesdrop on what was said. I was forced to watch the row from forty metres away. Despite this, it was still gratifying to know I'd orchestrated the whole thing. I was hoping you might actually assault him! Sadly, not. Lacked the cojones for it!

Even so, it was très amusant.

## 15

Sally was horrified when she heard about the dog biscuits.

"Deliberately poisoning a little dog … I didn't think even Michael would sink that low," she said.

Gil hadn't suggested anyone was responsible. "So you think he did it?"

"Who else could it be?"

Gil admitted he'd come to the same conclusion. He went on to confess about the confrontation outside the pub.

Sally was concerned for Gil, "He didn't threaten you?"

"No ... but he denied doing it ..."

"Of course he denied it! You're sure he didn't attack you? He's very strong and prone to violence after drinking. I'd bloody well murder him if he touched you!"

Gil appreciated her sense of loyalty.

## 16

With great apprehension, he rang the veterinary practice at 5 pm on the dot.

"Hello, this is Gil Harper. I brought my dog Spike in this morning ..."

"Spike Harper, poisoned Russell?" asked the receptionist.

"Yes. Jim told me to ring at five."

"One moment please," the receptionist replied sympathetically.

Gil could hear some whispering at the other end. He anticipated this might be a bad sign.

"Gil? It's Jim. He's definitely more stable. No promises, but I will say, it looks more hopeful. If his progress continues, you should be able to pick him up in the morning," there was a note of restrained fulfilment in Jim's voice; everyone likes to be the bearer of good news.

Gil punched the air with his fist and let out a cheer.

Megan, who had stayed later than usual to learn Spike's fate, greeted what she assumed must be good news with a quivering bottom lip.

## 17

As a means of thanking her for her support and helping him get through a stressful day, Gil took Megan out to dinner. He picked her up at eight, and they settled on a local pizzeria. They had needed a planning meeting anyway, to discuss arrangements for his forthcoming tour with Felix of the US and Canada. It was scheduled for August to coincide with the American publication of Felix's autobiography, illustrated by Gil.

"End of an era," commented Megan, "You'll miss working together."

"We've had a good run for our money," he replied, "I suppose, truth be told, I'd love for it to go on, but at nearly eighty I can't begrudge him his retirement can I?"

"This is a time of major change for you."

"You sound like a horoscope," Gil said, "Been reading the tea leaves again?"

Megan laughed, she enjoyed these occasional evenings with Gil. He was more like a son than an employer. She couldn't recall him giving her one boss-like instruction ever. And, as she sometimes reflected, if it weren't for Gil she might've been confined to the world of ash-blonde widows of comfortable means, weekly appointments at the hairdressers, coffee mornings and cake-baking for the WI.

A teenage waitress brought the desserts. Gil's eyes opened wide, as expectantly as a nine year old boy's, when he saw the large slice of cassata being set down before him. Megan exchanged an amused look with the girl before allowing a dash of cream to be poured over her fruit salad.

"Stephen and Lizzie have asked me to consider moving closer," said Megan. Stephen was her youngest son who ran a GP practice in North Devon.

Gil looked up from his ice-cream, "You aren't planning to leave me?" he asked plaintively.

"Not for the time being. But a year or two from now, who knows?"

Gil rested his spoon, "You are thinking about it then?"

Megan was somewhat amused, "I'm not getting any younger Gil. I think they find it a strain having an ageing mother quite a journey away from them. I think they'd like me nearer so they can keep an eye on me."

"Why?"

"In case I start talking to my toothbrush or something!"

"I talk to the radio."

"We all do that," she giggled, "I have ferocious rows with John Humphrys in the mornings."

"What about your friends?"

"They can visit, but remember I have four grandchildren who are growing up fast."

"I can understand that," he replied, then added, "First Felix, now you!"

"You have new things too. Sally for instance."

Gil looked at Megan and said with heartfelt sincerity, "I really like her. There hasn't been anyone else ... not since Jules ... I really care about her."

"I know," she replied, "it's wonderful to see you happy again. I mean, you've never been anything other than pleasant company, but you were so sad, deeply sad. It's like watching a bud open again after a terribly harsh winter."

Gil nodded, he could see that picture. He returned to his cassata and bit the corner off a fan shaped wafer, then with a twinkle in his eye he asked, "So, exactly how old are you, Megan?"

Megan smiled, her reticence on the subject of her age had always been a matter of amusement, "That information is only available on a need-to-know basis."

"And I don't need to know?"

"Exactly!"

## 18

Spike was clearly pleased to see Gil when he picked him up from the surgery, although he was still quite frail.

The vet advised, "If he exhibits any symptoms, contact us immediately."

Gil showed him the dog biscuits. Jim was horrified. He took them off Gil and promised to get them analysed.

Once away from the dreaded vets', Spike attempted his favourite car position, back legs on the passenger seat, front paws on the dash. However, he'd fallen over twice before they were out of the parking space. After some encouragement from Gil he settled for sitting semi-reclined, and proceeded to lick his testicles, or at least the area where they had once been.

Gil had no idea a welcome home party awaited them. Megan had attached a dozen multi-coloured balloons around the front door and invited Felix and Kate. Felix popped a bottle of champagne to greet the diminutive hero's arrival accompanied by cheers from the other two. Spike appeared hesitant, probably because he only got this much attention after doing something naughty. And uncharacteristically in the presence of all his most ardent admirers, he took his pink rabbit off for a mauling in a quiet corner. It was unanimously agreed that after such an ordeal, Spike was entitled to a bit of peace and quiet.

## 19

Thursday 29 January

I'm disappointed to see the dog back. I feel cheated, like I was sold something under false pretences. The product claimed it killed vermin!

I shouldn't be downhearted. I achieved my goal. I convinced you Michael Chilvers was responsible.

Yes, I was disappointed to see balloons and a welcome home committee.

<u>For a dog! Has the world gone mad</u>?

A dog eats rat poison disguised in a biscuit because it has an IQ of two, then because it doesn't turn its paws skywards everyone's over the moon. Is it me? What's wrong with these people?

Somewhere in the world, about once a minute, a child starves to death.

It's a <u>dog</u>, you morons!

Okay, I admit I feel cross about this. I'm coming to accept that the dog is still alive and for the present this will have to do.

Talking of the present, you have behaved entirely predictably.

Let's see what you do when I raise the pace?

For now the little rat can live. I've bigger vermin to eradicate.

But don't fret. I'll be returning to pest control. And I won't forget little Spike - Spikey, as you say.

## 20

Sally had been on target for accompanying Gil to Nigel's party, when a large consignment of leather accessories arrived, which, instead of being finished a muddy dark grey, was discovered to have been dyed an insipid shade of pea-green.

"It might do for *A Midsummer Night's Dream* if the director wanted butch fairies with a militaristic slant," said Sally.

"If it's your supplier's fault, can't they fix it?" asked Gil.

"They were doing us a favour. They let us have the leather at cost, for a mention in the programme."

They were having this conversation over the phone around breakfast time on Saturday.

"There's no way I can make it tonight. I'm really sorry, Gil."

"Can't be helped," he said, trying to conceal his disappointment.

"Tell you what … I'll do the re-dyeing and drive back late."

"Really?"

"It's the only way I'm going to see you this weekend."

Gil felt flattered, "What time shall I expect you?"

"Very late … but at least we'll get to spend half the night together."

"Sure you won't be too tired?" he asked with some concern.

"I won't be able to sleep anyway till I've had time to unwind. I'll have a head full of belts, boots and hauberks."

"Nigel and Sue's 'dos' go on quite late. I generally exit about one or two-ish … but I could get away earlier?" he suggested hopefully.

"Two sounds realistic. There's such a lot to do, and Roz isn't able to work tonight. I can't really ask any of the other girls to work Saturday night. So I'll be all on my lonesome."

"Okay," said Gil, "Long as you're certain you won't be too tired to drive?"

"Positive. There'll be nothing about on the road."

"So I'll have to fly solo through another of Nigel's birthday parties!"

"You'll have a good time," she assured him.

"Actually it's generally okay. It's me, not them. They're nice people."

## 21

Although he was pretty much himself again, Megan had given Spike board and lodging for the night.

At eight, Gil set off for Nigel and Sue's place. He always went on foot to their parties. It was under twenty minutes' walking time, and meant he could take a drink without any worries about alcohol limits. It was a cold, clear night, perfect for a stroll.

The Paddicks inhabited a large Victorian semi-detached house, roughly west of Gil's place.

Nigel opened the front door to Gil with a pair of large pink bunny ears attached to his head. He was accompanied by the two youngest Valkyrie, Françoise and Eloise, aged eight and ten respectively.

"Hello, old mate," greeted Nigel, ears bobbing.

Gil observed that even kitted out with pink fluffy rabbit ears, Nigel somehow missed being funny. As an observer of life, Gil found this quite amusing in itself.

"Where's the lady friend?" enquired Nigel, looking right and left along the road, which caused his ears to bounce.

"Couldn't get away. Sends her apologies."

"Blimey, must be worse than teaching! Never mind, you're here, old mate."

"Hi girls," said Gil.

"Hello," replied an impassive Françoise and Eloise, who spoke unnervingly in unison and without any detectable trace of enthusiasm.

Gil found himself unable to suppress an unkind thought that the Valkyrie looked pretty unconvincing disguised as little girls in their party dresses. He generally enjoyed popularity with youngsters but these were the exception to the rule. However, he'd observed that their older sister Garance, at fourteen, had become considerably more earthling-like; there might be hope yet.

Françoise and Eloise stood to one side to let Gil enter.

"Best get dancing," said Nigel, leading the way.

'Not bloody likely,' thought Gil, 'Specially not to Culture Club.'

Nigel and Sue, refined and educated in ways beyond Gil's comprehension, had always shared, in his view, execrable taste in popular music.

The party was much the same as it had been throughout the preceding years. Gil could recall being present at more than ten, although he'd been excused attendance in the year immediately following Jules' death. And despite having felt like a wallflower for much of the time, he was grateful to the Paddicks for persevering with him.

The Paddicks' friends, some fifty or sixty already there, were invariably convivial. They were mostly either teachers like Nigel and Sue, or friends made when their girls had been younger.

The party sprawled over the two lowest floors of the house. The strains of George Michael, Chris de Burgh and Elton John blared out of the sitting-room on the ground floor. It was a room Gil didn't feel called upon to enter, not even once, all night.

At a Paddick party there was guaranteed to be someone interesting to talk to. Gil recognised the majority of guests, although he knew relatively few by name.

Nigel led Gil downstairs, the girls forming a cohort behind.

Sue greeted Gil with great affection. She was small, blonde, attractive and possessed a razor-sharp mind. She taught Politics and Economics.

"Hallo, Harper," she said, depositing a welcoming kiss directly onto his lips, "Why haven't we seen you lately?"

Nigel, ears akimbo, anticipating Gil's reply to Sue's promptings three or four questions ahead blurted out, "She can't come, too much work on!"

"Thank you, Nigel, as always displaying princely tact," said Sue sarcastically, eyes rolling for Gil's benefit.

Nigel smiled inanely.

"Now, why not be a good bunny and hop the fuck off!" she exclaimed.

Gil couldn't help but smile.

Sue - mother, teacher, highly-educated and erudite - possessed a mouth that could, when the mood took her, be as profane as a bricklayer's mate's.

The good-natured Nigel turned on his heels and said, "Hopping off now!" He headed upstairs again, the girls following.

"Sometimes my dear husband is an insensitive arsehole!" said Sue, smiling.

"He's okay," defended Gil.

"Oh, he's okay, but he's still an arsehole," she laughed.

"So, you weren't going to ask me about Sally, then?" enquired Gil, an eyebrow arched.

"Sally? Sally who?" said Sue, feigning innocence, adding, "Ooh, is that the name of your new girlfriend, Harper?"

She reminded him so much of Jules. They had been best friends since their first year at prep school.

"What do I need to tell you?" Gil asked.

"Everything, of course," Sue replied. "But first off, what will you have to drink?" She gestured towards the area of kitchen dedicated to alcohol.

"That red looks like it might hit the mark."

She poured him a glass of wine, then led the way through a little hallway into a small study she and Nigel shared. During the hours of daylight the room looked out onto their well-tended garden.

Sue pushed Gil into a leather office chair, took a stool for herself and said, "Now, spill the beans, tell me everything. I want you to describe her in enough detail so I could pick her out from the crowd at a Selfridges Winter Sale."

"She's a costume designer in the theatre."

"I already know that," laughed Sue, "I got that much from effing Nigel! I want to know important stuff!"

Gil responded with an uncomprehending look.

She flicked her eyes heavenwards, "Men are hopeless! Start at the beginning! Where did you meet?"

Gil went through his history with Sally. Sue was someone he trusted completely and he told her the whole story; about her past with Chilvers, her surprise visit late on Christmas Day after his dreadful drive home, and all that had transpired since, right up to Spike's poisoning.

"You don't think it might've been him? This Chilvers chap - on the M25 - do you?" she asked, displaying some concern.

"Unlikely, don't you think? He'd have had to follow me all the way from Watchet. Anyway, he was pestering Sally at the time, apparently pissed out of his brains!"

"He sounds foul. Poor Spike. Be careful, won't you, Harper."

"I keep my car locked away safely in the garage these days, and I bought a sturdy padlock for my side gate yesterday. I'm not taking chances."

They chatted on, losing track of time, until Sue, glancing at the clock on the wall, exclaimed, "Shit! It's nine-thirty. Everyone must be wondering where the fuck I am!"

They both rose and she hugged Gil to her. "I'm really glad for you, Harper. Sally sounds just the ticket. You know, don't you, this is exactly what Jules would have wanted … for you to be happy?"

He nodded.

"I can see you're in love with her."

"Can you? That transparent, am I?"

"It's obvious, Harper."

"Blimey!" he said.

Gil followed Sue back through the hallway into the kitchen, now heaving with guests.

"Hello! Hello!" a male voice called out with mock indignation, "Where've you been?" His questioning was backed-up by good natured jeers from some of the other guests.

"I've been in the Study enjoying unnatural sex with Gil," replied Sue casually.

"Never mind any of that," replied the indignant male, "Nigel wouldn't let us start the bleedin' buffet until you gave the nod!"

"Is he still wearing those stupid frickin' ears?" asked Sue.

"Yes!" came the weary reply from at least a dozen of those gathered.

"What a plonker!" she said, plodding off upstairs to find him.

Although Gil was pleased he'd come, he still wished Sally could have made it. He was beginning to feel, despite the bad stuff with Chilvers and Spike, that something deep down inside of him was finally being healed; once again it felt good to be alive.

Gil poured himself a glass of wine and joined a small group he recognised.

## 22

It was round 1.15 am when Gil started for home. The party had barely begun to thin out. He planned to be back in plenty of time for Sally and reached home just after 1.30 am. He'd drunk more wine than he usually did, although the food he'd consumed at the Paddicks' generous buffet had helped soak up the extra alcohol; he was swaying ever so slightly. Gil made himself a coffee, sat at the kitchen table and began to wonder if Sally had left the workshop yet. He tried her mobile but only got her voice-mail and deduced from this that she was probably driving.

After arriving at this happy supposition, he promptly fell asleep.

## 23

Gil woke to the sound of the doorbell. Although groggy with sleep, he made his way enthusiastically to the front door. He forgot in those confused first moments of waking that Sally now possessed a key.

He was taken aback to find two men standing in his porch. They were soberly dressed, and both were wearing dark grey overcoats. The older and taller of the two was a man in his mid to late forties, the younger one was probably somewhere in his late twenties.

Gil opened up.

"Mr Harper?" enquired the older man, stretching out a hand that proffered an ID card, "I'm Detective Chief Inspector Mullings and this is Detective Inspector Jackson. Kent CID."

"Oh yes?" was all Gil could manage, his mind jumbled-up by alcohol and broken sleep.

"We understand you recently had a disagreement with a gentleman by the name of Michael Chilvers?" enquired the Detective Chief Inspector.

Although he couldn't have explained the reason why, Gil felt the tiny atavistic hairs on the back of his neck suddenly rise.

"I … er, yes … yes, I did," he muttered.

DCI Mullings drew himself up to his full height before stating, "Mr Chilvers died last night in a traffic accident."

Gil found the moment so shocking it caused him to let out a sudden, involuntary, exhalation of breath.

"Are you alright, sir?" asked Mullings.

"Yes … yes … Michael Chilvers is dead?" The idea seemed incomprehensible.

"Could I ask you where you were last night, Mr Harper?" asked Mullings.

Gil recovered enough composure to voice, "At a party."

"Did you drive, sir?" asked Jackson, speaking for the first time.

"No, it was local … I walked."

"Finished late, did it, sir?" enquired Jackson.

"I left around one."

"Don't plan on going to bed tonight, Mr Harper?" asked DCI Mullings.

Gil didn't quite understand the question, until he glanced across at the grandfather clock and saw the time was 6.15 am. "Christ!" he exclaimed, "I fell asleep."

At the same time he thought, 'Where's Sally? What could have happened to her?'

"I sincerely apologise for disturbing you so early, Mr Harper," said Mullings, "But would you mind if we took a look at your car?"

Of course Gil didn't mind. All he could think about was Sally, his mind anxiously racing through a series of imagined scenarios that might possibly have prevented her arrival.

He fetched his keys and led the detectives across the gravel drive to the garage. The air was freezing; dawn was still well over an hour away. Gil opened the garage door and fished with a hand for the light switch. The car was as he always left it, driven in front end first, its rear facing them.

Mullings and Jackson quietly moved to the far end of the garage.

Gil, still thinking about the reasons for Sally's absence, didn't observe the meaningful looks being exchanged between the two police officers.

"You say you didn't use the car at all last night, Mr Harper?" Mullings asked.

"Like I said, I went to a party, walked there and back."

He was very concerned about Sally. Where was she? What would her reaction be to this news about Chilvers?

"How did you damage the front of your vehicle?" asked Jackson.

"Damage?" asked Gil, displaying a little irritation now. He wondered what the hell the Detective Inspector was talking about. "No damage! It's just been re-sprayed!"

Gil strode down the side of his garage along the car's length to join Mullings and Jackson at the car's front end.

His jaw dropped when he saw the caved-in radiator grill and smashed left headlight.

"I don't understand ..."

"Mr Chilvers was the victim of what appears to have been a hit and run incident at approximately 11.30 pm last night," advised DCI Mullings, before adding, "I think you'd better come with us, sir."

Gil found he could only gawp at the police officers in glassy-eyed amazement.

Mullings turned to his colleague, "Get Forensic to cover this area ASAP."

DI Jackson immediately responded by taking out a notebook, pen and phone to start making the arrangements.

All Gil could think about was Sally. Why hadn't she arrived?

## 24

### Sunday 1 February

I don't understand why you're wearing such a long face. You should be delighted. The man your bitch claims abused her is now worm food.

My first idea was to despatch Sally into the arms of God instead. To join Julia and be one more in Jesus' harem of little sunbeam brides forever!

But it would have meant too much pain too soon.

I've invested a lot of time and energy in this. So you can appreciate I'd like you to go the distance. I mean, if you were cooking someone alive, it wouldn't be making the most of it to just dunk them in boiling water, would it? Far more rewarding to start over a gentle heat and build slowly!

It's a matter of patience.

Believe me, it required a great deal of planning to conjure up this little nightmare. To have you hauled in by the police because your girlfriend's 'ex' got pancaked by your car! Exquisite, don't you agree?

I did, of course, leave you a cast-iron alibi. Not even someone with an IQ as low as the average policeman's would try to build a case against you. However, the next few hours should prove satisfyingly uncomfortable for you.

I expect you're already fretting.

"First my effin' car, then my effin' dog, now this? Why? Who can have done this? What have they got against me?"

Your brain must be overheating.

But I'd be awfully upset if you gave yourself an embolism.

## 25

A police car arrived swiftly and Gil was taken to CID headquarters in Maidstone. For this journey he was accompanied by a male and female police constable. The woman drove, whilst her male counterpart sat beside Gil in the rear. The journey was undertaken mostly in silence.

From that first shocking moment when Gil had seen his recently restored Volvo wrecked, to the arrival of his police chaperones, was largely a blur. He recalled Mullings spelling it out, that his vehicle may have been involved in what was likely to be a criminal investigation. But Gil had guessed this much for himself.

DCI Mullings appeared to view the evidence with total impartiality and displayed no change in either his approach or manner. However, this offered no insight into what the Detective Chief Inspector was actually thinking. By contrast, the younger man, DI Jackson, looked increasingly bemused at Gil's professed innocence.

Mullings instructed Jackson to take down the Paddicks' details, "We'll try to verify your whereabouts as quickly as possible, Mr Harper."

Gil took heart from this.

# 26

Roz woke with a start. The bedside clock said 7.03 am. She'd heard the intruder tip-toe across the laminated floor of the hallway and go into Sally's room.

Roz nudged John in the ribs.

"Ugh?" he groaned, directing an eye at his tormentor.

"Someone's in the flat," whispered Roz, "They just went into Sally's room."

"It's Sally," said John, closing his eyes and rolling onto his front.

Roz reached across his back and shook him with both arms, "She's with Gil. Go and see who it is!" she insisted.

"Why me?"

"Because you're a bloke and supposed to protect me!"

"Mmm." He wanted to remind his girlfriend that he was a humble postman in real life, but said nothing. He swivelled his body up to a sitting position, retrieved his boxer shorts from the floor and stepped into them. Before he'd reached the door, the interloper was heard crossing the hall again and switching on the bathroom light.

John, wondered what he would do if Sally really was with Gil. He hesitated, hand hovering above the door knob.

"Go on!" said Roz in a muffled whisper. She'd drawn up the duvet to just below her nose as though it offered protection.

John tentatively opened the door and called in a thinnish voice, "Sal?"

There was no reply.

John tried a little louder, "Sal?"

This time he heard a sob, then Sally's tearful voice, "Hi, John!"

"You okay, Sal?"

"Yeah," came the reply, "I need a shower."

"Okay," said John.

By the time Sally had taken her shower, Roz, concerned for her friend, had got up and was making coffee.

"What are you doing here?" Roz asked her as she entered the kitchen.

Sally immediately burst into tears.

"What's wrong, Sal?" she comforted, "You haven't quarrelled with Gil?"

"Nothing like that," wept Sally, "It was Michael. He rang me last night!"

"Why?"

"To gloat about Gil … after he'd accused him of poisoning Spike."

"Nasty little shit!" said Roz.

"He was out of his brains. I refused to talk to him, but he kept ringing back. The calls got more abusive ... he kept calling me an effing whore."

Roz hugged her friend.

"In the end I switched off my mobile. I was so upset and so bloody tired ... I must have fallen asleep." Sally thought a moment before she broke into a fresh bout of sobbing, "Now I've let Gil down ... and he was expecting me ..."

"Gil will understand," Roz consoled.

Sally had left her bag in the kitchen when she'd entered the flat. The mention of the mobile phone prompted her to fish it out and turn it back on again. There were two messages and one missed call from Gil.

The first was a garbled rant from Chilvers, the phrase, '*fucking whore*', was easily identifiable amongst the few comprehensible words.

"Bastard!" commented Roz.

The second message had been left at 4.30 am.

It was a Detective Inspector Jackson from Maidstone CID. He left no specific details but he was emphatic that Sally should return his call as soon as possible.

She immediately felt worried for Gil and rang Jackson.

Roz observed her friend's verbal exchange.

"Hello, this is Sally Curtis. You left a message ... yes ... I am ... I was ... Oh my God!"

Sally listened for a short time, then began to reel off the address of Roz's flat. She listened to another instruction for a few more moments, before concluding with, "Three quarters of an hour, that's fine."

"What's happened?" asked Roz, who knew something serious had occurred because Sally's face was ashen.

Sally looked quite stunned as she slowly stated, "Michael's been killed."

"Christ! How? What happened?"

Sally shook her head as if to wake herself up, "He said ... road accident. Michael was hit by a car at around 11.30 last night ... the driver didn't stop."

"That's dreadful!" Although Michael Chilvers was a complete shit in Roz's view, she was not a malicious soul.

Sally suddenly recalled the previous evening, Michael's repeated calls to her mobile, four before she had turned off. She stared imploringly at her friend, "They're coming to interview me. Christ, they're going to think I did it!"

"Don't be silly," reassured Roz. Then she thought about what Sally had just said; how she had been alone at the workshop, for the entire evening and night. To Roz, after all Sally had suffered at Michael's hands, it seemed diabolically unjust to think she might now be under suspicion as his killer. She said, "You couldn't have done it, could you?"

Sally looked enquiringly back at her friend.

"Because you were here with me and John. You got back from the workshop around eleven, completely exhausted, had a brandy and hot chocolate and went to bed. You were probably asleep before eleven-thirty!"

## 27

Gil was in a state of partial shock. It didn't help that he'd had so little sleep. He looked fragile, eyes bloodshot, blackish-grey stubble unflatteringly contrasting with pallid skin. These days, even moderate drinking needed recovery time.

Feverish images assaulted his mind. Could he have been drunker than he'd realised? Had he returned from the party earlier than he could recall in some kind of alcoholic blackout? Then taken his car and used it as a weapon to kill Michael Chilvers? These recurrent questions boiled down to the same thing: had he suffered some kind of temporary memory lapse coupled with insanity? In other words, completely lost the run of himself and gone barking mad? Deep down, Gil knew the gymnastics going on in his head could only be rubbish; even so, just entertaining such ideas not only proved to be unsettling but quite exhausting too.

However, it wasn't exclusively thoughts of his own culpability that troubled him. Since he'd first glimpsed the car, with its caved-in grill, bumper and smashed light, he'd been filled with concern for Sally. No matter how hard he tried he couldn't account for her absence. He knew there had to be a plausible explanation, and refused to acknowledge a picture of her, mad-eyed behind the wheel of his Volvo. In his heart and gut he knew the idea was ludicrous and couldn't believe her capable of cold-blooded murder. Despite this, he still wasn't able to prevent the seeds of doubt from being scattered in his mind.

# 28

Whatever will the neighbours say?

"Tut! Tut! Tut!"

"As secretary of the local residents association, I am disgusted! There are police vehicles, all shapes and sizes, sitting on your drive and parked along the road!"

"One doesn't like to be uncharitable; but one had always suspected you weren't exactly the 'right sort'. In fact, I told my husband when you moved here that I didn't think you were really of 'the Best People'. However, I must say, your late wife was charming. Heaven knows why she chose to marry beneath her? I'm not one for malicious gossip but I've heard little whispers that her death may not have been an accident?"

"One doesn't wish to be unkind but type invariably reverts to type. One understands you went to a comprehensive school? Please, don't think one has anything against state education. It's only humane to teach the poor how to write their own names and manage rudimentary addition and subtraction. However, I can assure you we don't want your council estate tribal wars here!"

"I read in the 'Daily Scum' (not my copy) that you killed your girlfriend's ex-lover. Typical of your sort! No doubt fuelled by your addiction to alcohol and drugs. The same newspaper implied that together with your girlfriend (no stranger to men apparently!) you'd attended a number of sordid parties recently, and that you'd been at a sex rave, high on drugs, on the night of the killing?"

"Really! This isn't the sort of attention we like to attract for our nice residential area! It's the kind of focus that could easily depress house prices! Frankly, one is appalled!"

Tee hee hee!

My Ford Galaxy is tucked up neatly about forty metres away, parked between a Citroen Picasso and a VW Touareg. I couldn't look more innocent if I tried.

There are men in overalls erecting a tent-like structure across the front of your garage. They are about to explore an enigma! I was very careful when I took your car. My hair was covered. I wore a mask over my mouth and nose. In fact my hands feel a little itchy today from the latex gloves. I've always had sensitive skin.

Such a lot of manpower and effort for nothing!

## 29

Gil had a long and frustrating morning ahead of him. At Maidstone CID headquarters he was booked into a cell, read his rights and entitlements, and told the interviewing officer would be along shortly. After about an hour, a constable brought him some tea and biscuits.

Another hour passed before anything else happened. He was asked from time to time if he needed anything, and apart from a glass of water the answer was always no. Beyond these brief exchanges little else was said. With a head pounding like a kango hammer, Gil went over and over events in his mind; the time at the Paddicks' party when his car must have been taken, Sally's failure to show up, as well as the scant details he knew about Chilvers' death.

Shortly before ten, DCI Mullings appeared. He popped his head round the door to say in an unexpectedly cheery fashion, "Sorry to keep you, Mr Harper. You'll appreciate, there's a lot to coordinate at the start of a murder investigation". He then disappeared for another twenty-five minutes.

The Detective Chief Inspector's seemingly casual use of the phrase 'murder investigation' set Gil's brain off in a frenzy of activity. Mullings, as anyone who knew him would attest, never said anything casually or without due consideration.

When Mullings returned, he got the interview formally underway immediately. He appeared sublimely relaxed, as if he'd spent the morning gardening.

He began by putting Gil's mind at ease, "Mr and Mrs Paddick have verified your whereabouts. As I recall, you reached home around 1.30 am?"

"Yes, I left about 1.15 ... it takes about fifteen to twenty minutes to walk."

"You left their house alone?"

"Yes."

"Miss Curtis wasn't with you last night?"

Gil paused, "No, Sally's swamped under with work. She designs costumes for the theatre. She's on a new production … working round the clock. She's been staying in London with a friend." Gil felt heat rise through his face.

"We've spoken with Miss Curtis," replied Mullings.

Gil was relieved to learn Sally could be reached and hoped he was about to find out what had happened to her. Unfortunately, this was not to be the case.

Mullings continued, "Mr and Mrs Paddick said they'd been hoping to meet her."

"It was never certain she'd come … deadlines, pressure of work."

"Of course," replied Mullings softly as he scanned the page of handwritten notes before him. The DCI then suddenly changed the mood, "Was Miss Curtis aware you'd confronted Michael Chilvers and that you'd accused him of poisoning your dog?"

"Yes, she was."

"Why did you think he was responsible?"

Gil explained about the paint, Chilvers' gate-crash on New Year's Eve and the incident at the restaurant.

"Beyond personal conviction, do you have any evidence that Michael Chilvers poisoned your dog?" asked Mullings.

"The garden was littered with biscuits containing rat poison!"

"Did anyone see Mr Chilvers in your garden?"

Gil shook his head.

"Why didn't you report it to us?"

Gil sighed, "I planned to, once the biscuits were analysed."

"Haven't you had the results back?"

"Yes … as expected, rat poison."

"But you still didn't report it?"

Gil shook his head. "I meant to … Megan kept prompting me to." Then, rather uncharacteristically, Gil played the blame card, "I reported the paint damage immediately … for that Chilvers got a ticking off for using bad language!"

Mullings nodded, not unsympathetically.

Gil considered what he'd just said and looked directly across at Mullings, "I felt embarrassed … rushing off after Chilvers like that. It was pretty stupid! I could see that afterwards … I was angry, I'm very attached to Spike."

"It was a dreadful thing to do," agreed Mullings, who thought before adding, "Personally I'm surprised there were any biscuits left to find!"

"Sorry?"

"I have two dogs myself, Mr Harper. If they found treats dotted about the garden, I doubt they'd stop till they'd snaffled the lot!"

Gil nodded and indicated with a shrug that he had no explanation for this. Frankly, it seemed irrelevant. He said, "Michael Chilvers had already shown himself to be cruel and vindictive. Who else would have poisoned Spike?"

Mullings raised his head and said flatly, "Michael Chilvers didn't take your car last night, Mr Harper."

It was the indisputability of Mullings' statement that sent Gil metaphorically reeling. "I just don't get it," he said.

They sat in silence for a few moments. Then Mullings asked, "What happened to the tin of paint that was used on your car?"

"The constable who called on me took it away with him."

"Good. It will have been recorded. I'll get forensics to go over it again," the Detective Chief Inspector noted this down. "What about the biscuits?"

"Like I said, I took them to my vets' to get them analysed."

"Do they still have them?"

"You'd have to contact them."

DCI Mullings made another note.

"Mr Harper, did you notice anything unusual when you got home last night?"

"What do you mean?"

"Anything different?"

Gil shook his head.

"Is the garage connected to your security system?"

"Yes."

"Did you set the alarm before going out?"

"Yes, definitely. I needed to disarm it when I got back."

"Who knows the codes besides yourself?"

"My assistant, Megan ... Deirdre, my cleaner. They've worked for me for years, I trust them completely."

"And Miss Curtis?"

"Huh?" Gil's ears began to warm.

"Does Miss Curtis possess a set of keys?"

"Er, yes ... she has a front door key." Gil suddenly realised something important, "Not one of them has a key to the garage."

"Do you keep a spare?"

"Yes."

"Where's it kept?"

"In my desk."

"Always locked?"

Gil felt uncomfortable again, "Not generally."
"Do you have the house security codes written down anywhere?"
"No."
"You're certain? Nowhere at all?"
Gil considered the question again, "There is a file with the four digit code on my computer."

The interview concluded about 12.30 pm. Gil was glad he hadn't needed to lie directly about Sally's whereabouts. He believed there had to be a reason for her absence and it was academic whether or not he'd lied by omission.

There was no offer of a police chaperone to take him home. Gil took this to be a good sign. He'd left home without any money or his mobile but he did have a wallet with plastic in it. He located a cash machine and withdrew some cash. After this he found a greasy spoon, ordered a bacon sandwich and washed it down with a couple of large mugs of tea. Finally, he sought out a cab.

## 30

I don't think your bitch went to Nigel's party. Too busy?

Now here's an amusing thought: she might at this very moment be top of your list of suspicious candidates!

If so, that would be priceless!

Who, after all, hated Chilvers most?

Oh deary, deary, me!

### SUSPICION!!!

It might so easily drive a wedge between you!

I wonder: can you imagine Sally behind the wheel of your Volvo, targeting Chilvers as he staggers home drunk?

Are you getting all this?

Picture how thrilled she becomes as the car bumps and rises over his injured body? See her callously eye him in the rear-view mirror lit by reversing lights? Then backing-up over his prone body? Vicious, cold-blooded, calculated ... perhaps even sexually aroused by it all?

Just think of the wry smile she may have been wearing when Michael Chilvers suddenly sits up reeling like something out of a zombie film, coughing, spluttering out frothy, bright blood from his burst lungs.

I certainly hope you can visualise the hard line of her mouth as she puts her foot on the accelerator and drives straight at him?

Perhaps not. It takes a special kind of person to do something like that.

His crushed, bleeding arm and hand were raised to protect his eyes from the headlights. The force of the impact was really quite unexpected.

I cursed my own recklessness for the smashed headlight!

The noise as Chilvers' face met the grille was incredibly loud.

Ouch!

It was followed by a muffled thud as the back of his head spread out like a mashed peach on the tarmac.

Yuck!

But then, you see, someone had to do it. I felt ashamed of you when you walked away from Chilvers and his drinking gang.

I simply carried out what you would have liked to have done yourself.

Honour has been served.

## 31

The taxi brought Gil along the wide avenue that led to his house. Directly ahead, an assortment of vehicles, each marked Kent Police, had congregated about his property. Whatever thoughts he'd entertained about getting home to some peace and quiet were instantly dashed to pieces.

"Must be something serious going on up there!" commented the taxi driver.

"Drop me here," said Gil.

They drew up behind a Citroen Picasso.

"Someone dug up a body?" the driver, until then a taciturn character, chirpily inquired.

Gil distractedly drew some notes from his wallet to cover the fare, stepped out of the taxi and began to walk in the direction of all the activity with a heavy heart.

"Very kind!" commented the man, seeing he wasn't required to give change.

After Gil had made about a dozen hesitant steps the taxi cruised past him, slowing up just ahead as it drew level with his home. A constable materialised out of the driveway and waved the cabbie on with unequivocal firmness, which made Gil feel irrationally pleased.

An area around the property had been cordoned off with a low barrier. Several members of a forensic team in hooded overalls could be seen milling about in the background. A Mobile Incident Room had been parked on the drive itself. The garage doors, no longer visible, had something resembling a gazebo erected across them.

Gil, about to be challenged by the fierce-looking constable who had sent the inquisitive taxi-man packing, was rescued by DI Jackson as he emerged from the MIR, "Okay, Sams," he called, "That's the householder!"

The constable smiled considerately and opened the barrier to let him through; Gil looked like a man who had stumbled into an alternative universe.

"Mr Harper, I'm sorry about the intrusion," said Jackson.

"I appreciate it's necessary," replied Gil.

The way Jackson spoke suggested the Detective Inspector no longer considered him the prime suspect.

Gil continued walking towards his house.

Jackson kept alongside him. "DCI Mullings instructed me we'll need to look in your office too. Is that okay, Mr Harper?"

"Yes, of course."

"The team should find time to get in there by the end of today."

"Fine," said Gil who had now reached his front door.

"We'll require fingerprints and DNA samples from you too, Mr Harper."

Gil looked surprised.

"To exclude you from whatever else we find."

Gil mumbled his assent.

Jackson organised a forensic officer to take the samples. Gil gave a full set of prints and allowed a swab to be taken from inside his cheek.

Once he was alone, he checked the phone for messages. There was nothing on the landline; however, his mobile had been busy.

At 9.53 am there had been a concerned message from Sally, '*Gil, I just rang your house ... the police were there! They said you were helping them with their enquiries. Why? They can't honestly think you're involved? When you get a chance, ring me.*'

She'd rung again at 10.32 am with, '*Me again ... I don't understand, what's going on*?'

And again at 12.38 pm, '*I've just spoken to Megan. She hadn't heard about Michael ... she said she'd been expecting you to pick up Spike. I just don't understand why the police need to talk to you. Why are they keeping you so long*?'

It was obvious from her messages that the police had given Sally no indication that Gil's car had probably been used to kill Michael.

The next message was more unexpected. It was left at 1.47 pm by Klaus' partner, David, '*... Klaus has spoken with Roz who told him that Sally is worried about you. If there's anything I can do, any assistance I can give, legal advice, or help in any way, please don't hesitate ...*'

'They must think I did it!' he thought.

It was after 4 pm by the time Gil tried to reach Sally on her mobile; the number was unavailable.

Next, Gil tried the phone number for Roz's flat. John picked up, and immediately recognized Gil's voice, "Hi. You okay, mate?"

Gil, who certainly didn't feel okay, replied, "Yes, thanks."

"We were told you were helping the police with their enquiries?"

Gil had no intention of reminiscing about his day, "Is Sally there?"

"Sorry. Not here."

"Could you let me have the number of the workshop? I can't get her mobile."

"She's not at the workshop. Roz and some other friends are helping out with her work stuff. She's on her way down to you. Klaus and David went with her. As you'd expect she was quite upset. We couldn't let her drive herself!"

At that moment the doorbell rang. Gil strode into the hall. Although it was almost dark outside, his front drive was lit-up like Las Vegas; Sally was delineated against the light.

"She's here, John," he said, and pressed the call-ended button with uncharacteristic abruptness.

Their meeting was inhibited by the sudden appearance of DI Jackson at Sally's side. There was no sign of Klaus and David.

"Hi Sally," said Gil, with an uncertain smile.

"Hello Gil," she replied.

Then Jackson interjected, "Sorry to butt in … forensic would like to start on your office in about half an hour?"

"Fine," answered Gil.

Jackson nodded to them both and went off to the bright lights beyond.

Sally rushed inside, pushed the door shut and hugged Gil with great feeling, "Oh Gil, this is dreadful!"

"It's appalling! I'm sorry I couldn't contact you before. But I left my phone here when they took me off to Maidstone."

She looked up at him in disbelief, "Why did they do that?"

"I think I was public enemy number one."

"That's ridiculous!" She shook her head, "I don't understand. What's going on? Why are the police all over your house?"

"It looks like whoever killed Michael did it with my car."

Gil was glad he'd been the one to break this news. Her reaction convinced him that she could not have been involved; he did, however, feel a little ashamed of himself for ever considering it possible.

It was difficult to credit that when Sally had been interviewed by Jackson about seven hours earlier, it wasn't mentioned that her current boyfriend's car was probably instrumental in the death of her troublesome 'ex'.

Gil explained what had happened to him since the police had arrived.

Once her initial surprise had subsided and she'd had time to consider the facts of Michael's death in this new light, Sally said anxiously, "I expect they'll think it was me now!"

"Why on earth would they do that?"

"Because I detested him."

"But you didn't kill him."

"They aren't going to believe me, are they?" She considered a moment before continuing, "Klaus and David came down with me …"

"I know. John said."

"… Klaus probably thinks I killed him … possibly, David too."

"I'm sure you're wrong! You're just upset," he consoled.

"Gil, I don't have an alibi for last night … and I've already lied to the police."

# 32

Faggot - n. Brit. a ball or patty of seasoned offal, baked or fried. N. American. informal, derogatory, a male homosexual.

I'd planned to leave shortly. Then Cinderella arrived with her ugly sisters! I guessed Klaus and David.

They must've believed themselves invisible in the dark. When the younger of the two caressed the older one's hair and they exchanged a kiss, I felt like smashing my infra-red night goggles!

Pervy writers would probably have referred to it as: 'gentle, understated and affectionate'.

I wanted to vomit!

The integration and acceptance of such deviants into our society simply points to the erosion of our moral values over decades. Why don't people wake up to the liberal coup that has crept like cancer throughout the western world?

It hurts my ears when I hear phrases like 'loving relationship between consenting adults', and 'everyone should have the right to express themselves according to their sexual orientation'.

HOMOPHOBIC???

Like it's suddenly a bad thing to detest queers???

You know, Gil, I'd like to have got out of my vehicle, walked across the road to where they were parked, and put them out of their misery by bludgeoning them to death. If it hadn't been for my dedication to 'our little thing' (and the fact the street was crawling with policemen! Ha Ha!), I might have done.

After about an hour you and your bitch came out of the house. You shook hands with the deviants. I'd have worn gloves! You got into their car and drove off.

I followed.

## 33

Klaus went with Gil to the bar to order some meals and drinks. A log fire spat and crackled in an inglenook, its flames dancing on walls and ceiling, wood-smoke pervading the air.

At the bar, Gil could see multiple images of Sally and David, through a profusion of mirrors that proclaimed the finest ales and spirits. They were engaged in an earnest dialogue at a table in the farthest corner of the room.

As Klaus recited their food order, the Eastern European barmaid's manner suddenly changed from affable receptiveness to a look of deep concern.

"I don't know if ve have two beef ale pies left," she announced.

"I can order something else," offered Klaus.

"No, you vait! I check!" commanded the girl.

Klaus exchanged a sheepish grin with Gil as she went off.

The two men appeared lost for words for a few moments, then Klaus stole a glance in the direction of their companions and said, "Sal told you she fell asleep at the workshop last night?"

Gil nodded, "Yes."

"Roz claims the alibi was her idea … sounds about right!"

"I don't understand why they felt it necessary to make up a story," said Gil.

"They had no idea you'd been implicated! I suppose 'hit and run' suggests a driver unknown."

Gil nodded.

Klaus went on, "It's easy to imagine: the girls, hearing about the accident, picturing Michael pissed - not hard, he was most nights - swaying across the road as he wended his way home … getting ploughed into by a car! I expect Roz, who's pretty sharp, saw it as a potential headache for Sally … alone, without any witnesses."

"Yes, I can see that."

"This kind of thing generally gets resolved when the driver goes to the police claiming the accident was so traumatic, they'd panicked, rushed home, hurled back a bottle or two, then come to their senses."

"What happens in cases where the culprit doesn't appear?" asked Gil.

"The police keep a close eye on body-shops. They have a good idea from the crime scene what damage to expect. It's not too easy to hide a smashed-up car!"

Gil took a moment to consider how far from Klaus's hit and run scenario Michael's death had already strayed. "I don't get the deliberateness of it all!" he announced.

"Michael was not a popular man."

Gil looked across at the others, "Sally believes you think it was her?"

Klaus shook his head. "I don't think anything of the sort. Poor thing was terrified to go near the bastard, let alone pull off something like this." Klaus thought a moment, "More importantly, *you* don't think she did it, do you?"

Gil replied without hesitation "I admit at first I wasn't sure, but now I am."

"Good," said Klaus, who went on to say, "I knew very little about Michael's City life ... who knows, if he was as unpopular there as he was in my world, might be more candidates for the killer role than in an Agatha Christie country house thriller."

This may have been so, but Michael's disagreeable personality didn't explain why Gil's car had been chosen as the murder weapon or why the killer had deliberately implicated him.

Before Gil could voice this, Klaus had started again, "As you know, I hated him ... heat of the moment, I might easily have lost it and laid into him ... accidentally killed him perhaps. But this is altogether different ... pre-meditated!" Klaus broke off, he looked uneasy. He leaned on the bar, drew himself closer to Gil and asked softly, "Is it possible someone is pursuing a vendetta against you?"

"What?" asked Gil, momentarily stunned by the suggestion, gazing at Klaus in disbelief, "Are you suggesting someone killed Michael to get at me?"

Klaus shrugged, "Unlikely, but worth considering. Does anyone hold a grudge against you?"

Gil didn't reply because their conversation was interrupted by the return of the barmaid.

"Yes, beef okay, two left," she earnestly explained, adding, "Sorry for delay, Chef not in kitchen!"

"No problem," smiled Klaus, as he gave her the remainder of their order.

While the barmaid went over to the other end of the bar to pull a pint, Klaus whispered conspiratorially to Gil, "Best if you don't mention anything to David about Sally sleeping at the workshop. As you know, he's represented her in the past. It would compromise his position, make it impossible for him to offer help if the police ever learnt her alibi isn't sound."

"Yes, of course," nodded Gil.

# 34

"Does anyone hold a grudge against you, Mr Harper?" asked Mullings.

This was the second time the question had been put to Gil in one evening and it made him feel distinctly uncomfortable.

"However slight the incident? Someone you unintentionally hurt, perhaps?" put in DI Jackson.

Anyone observing the scene around the table in Gil's kitchen might have assumed they were three friends chewing the fat over a mug of tea. It was 10.05 pm and each man bore signs of weariness. The day had been a long one.

Gil shook his head.

"Let us know if you do think of anything," said Mullings, who went on to say more reassuringly, "It's unlikely, but we have to explore each and every possibility."

Mullings had rung Gil on his mobile to propose the meeting while he'd been walking home from the pub, '*... just a call to keep you up to date...*'

The three men each took a sip of tea and silence reigned for thirty seconds or so.

Mullings broke the spell, "So far all the prints in your car appear to be your own."

Gil looked concerned by this.

"It's what we'd expect," assured Mullings. "Whoever took your car wore gloves – latex, apparently a type worn by the medical profession."

"Especially vets, apparently!" added Jackson in quite a jocular way.

"We don't suspect your vet by the way," Mullings added swiftly with a smile. "They're widely available, can be purchased online, like everything else these days," he sighed wearily, as if he yearned for life before broadband.

"So there can't be any doubt it was deliberate?" said Gil.

"None whatsoever," interjected Jackson. "Whoever took your car undoubtedly meant to kill Mr Chilvers with it."

"Plus an intention to implicate you in some way," added Mullings.

"In some way?" retorted Gil, as if he'd just heard the understatement of the century, "I'd say they definitely wanted to point the finger at me!"

Mullings hesitated, "Mmm, possibly," he replied.

"Possibly?" asked Gil, exasperation in his voice, "Surely it was meant to look like I'd done it?"

"I suspect whoever did this knew you'd be at a party all evening and be seen by lots of people."

Gil thought about this, then asked, "You're saying, whoever killed Michael didn't want the blame to stick to me?"

"But they certainly wanted to involve you," said Mullings. "It would have been much easier to steal an anonymous vehicle and abandon it after the killing."

"The killer took a big risk driving back from Hadlow. The car had sustained considerable damage, the offside headlight wasn't functioning at all," put in Jackson.

Mullings went on, "Whoever did it knew your plans well enough to be able to enter your home, disable your security and take your car for the necessary time. Two hours minimum I'd guess, then drive back, return your car to its garage and reset the alarm."

Jackson took up the baton again, "Their planning was thorough. They appear to have known a great deal about you."

The colour drained from Gil's face; he was momentarily speechless.

"How could they learn so much about you?" asked Mullings.

Gil could only mutter a few incomprehensible sounds. Sally floated up into his mind again; he shook his head to dispel the thought.

Then Jackson spoke, "We suspect the codes to your security system were stolen off your computer. What about the party details? Do you keep an online diary like Outlook?"

Gil had always set a high value on personal privacy; the implications of such an intrusion were truly monstrous. He said, "I've kept a diary since I was fifteen. The earliest stuff I scanned in some years back … everything about me, past and present, is on my computer."

Mullings and Jackson exchanged a meaningful glance.

"But I just can't see how this could be possible. I mean, my diary is set up with a password … I've never told a soul!"

"Something obscure and difficult?" asked Mullings.

Gil thought a moment, then shook his head, "Jules … it's what I called my late wife."

Jackson looked at Mullings, "It might be worth examining the computer. Check whether any files have been remotely accessed."

Mullings nodded, "Okay with you Mr Harper?"

"Yes, of course," said Gil.

DCI Mullings rose to his feet, followed by DI Jackson.

"Try and get a good night's sleep, Mr Harper," advised Mullings, "I'm afraid your offices must remain out of bounds until forensic can finish off."

Gil suddenly remembered something that had been troubling him since he'd left the pub, "Look, this is probably nothing, but tonight after the pub … my friends were driving back to London, I intended to walk home and get some air. I waved goodbye to them in the car park entrance … then seconds later, another car started up along the road. I thought nothing of it until it stopped alongside me …as if they were going to lower their window and ask directions. Then they suddenly just roared off."

"I appreciate it was dark, but did you get a glimpse of the driver … an impression, male, female?" asked Jackson.

"No. I think the windows were tinted. I couldn't see a thing inside."

"Notice the make or model?" asked Mullings.

Gil smiled, "I'm afraid I know absolutely nothing about cars. All I can say is it was a people carrier of some kind … I couldn't be certain, but I think I may have seen it before … parked on the road outside my house occasionally. I'd observed in passing how opaque the tinting on its windows was. It's probably nothing, possibly belongs to a neighbour who thought about offering me a lift."

"Let us know if you see it again. And if you do, try and get its number," said Mullings.

Jackson recorded Gil's recollection in his notebook. He also noted down the name of the pub and the time the incident happened.

Mullings had one final request, "Could you spare an hour … not right now, in the morning … to look round and see if anything is missing or out of place?"

"Yes, of course," replied Gil.

## 35

You remained in the pub for almost two hours. When you re-emerged, you kissed Cinders and shook hands with the Ugly Sisters.

You stood in the car-park entrance to wave them off.

When I started my engine, you looked across at me. I wanted you to take me in properly. So I stopped right beside you.

We were staring eyeball to eyeball. <u>Exhilarating!</u>

I think you were trying to figure out where you'd seen my car before.

RIGHT OUTSIDE YOUR HOUSE YOU DOLT!!!

Hopefully you got the car fixed into your fat brain so you'll notice it next time. Needless to say, I shan't be driving it much. I daresay I'd soon be helping the police with their enquiries if I parked it outside your house again. Nevertheless, it has an important part to play in my beautiful plan.

Your queer friends dropped your girlfriend off in Streatham, and then drove on to a very nice house in Wandsworth. I checked your diary - the place you visited on New Year's Eve. Just as I thought - Klaus and David!

As I watched them stroll along the street, I considered putting them out of their misery!

I remembered my priorities.

I may slot them into my busy schedule later on. Ha! Ha! Ha!

The fact you are friends with deviants only makes you more deserving of what's coming your way.

## 36

After Mullings and Jackson had left, the house seemed to ring with an unusual hollowness. Before going to the pub Gil had rung Megan, who had volunteered to keep Spike until the police vacated his home.

All activities had been suspended until the morning; however, two officers had been left on site to guard the integrity of the evidence. After all the earlier talk about an intruder disabling his alarm system, their presence made Gil feel safer. Despite this, he knew he wouldn't be able to sleep easy until he'd followed Mullings' instruction and carefully looked over his house for signs of intrusion.

After forty minutes of searching, except the offices of course, he found nothing to suggest that anything had been touched, let alone stolen. It was 11.30 pm and by now very tired, he considered leaving the attic until the morning.

"In for a penny ..." he muttered wearily as he climbed the stairs and took the key off the door frame.

At a glance everything was fine.

The portrait of Jules was centrally positioned on its easel, protected by a dustsheet.

As he drew back the covering his heart missed a beat and he gasped.

In a bold if unsteady hand with a thick black marker pen the word 'Jules' had been scrawled across the portrait.

## 37

He hurtled backwards from the painting, horrified, gasping for breath, a pain erupted in his chest, his ears screamed and the room began to spin. If he'd been struck by lightning the shock could not have been much greater.

It is difficult to conceive of many situations where a proper noun, Jules - three consonants, two vowels - might produce such a powerful reaction. Until then, the view that Gil was being personally targeted had seemed fantastical. When it was suggested by Klaus and Mullings, Gil had considered the idea plausible but unlikely. He had clung to the belief that Chilvers was responsible for the original damage to his car and for poisoning Spike.

Suddenly everything altered; the scales dropped from his eyes as dramatically as the sheet had revealed the portrait.

After a minute or so the palpitations diminished and he began to calm down. He was glad to realise that he would probably not require the services of an A & E department for tonight at least. The fact there were still policemen on site was comforting and he rushed downstairs to unburden himself.

It was one of life's quirky moments of synchronicity that one of these men turned out to be Rowe, the constable sent to him on Boxing Day.

The hum of the car window as it lowered was accompanied by the young man's cheery greeting, "Hello, Mr Harper."

The night temperature was two below freezing. Gil had rushed out of the house in a t-shirt and jeans, a pair of espadrilles on his feet that he slopped around the house in. He started to shiver and his teeth were chattering. There was a look of bewilderment about his face.

Rowe exchanged a look of concern with his companion, "You okay, Mr Harper?" he asked.

"S-s-s-someone b-broke in," stammered Gil, "D-d-don't u-u-understand … they …"

Rowe opened his door and stepped out.

Gil took in a deep draught of the freezing night air; its icy sharpness drove a note of clarity back to his mind. "I need you to see something," he gasped.

## 38

Mullings and Jackson came out of Gil's house and crossed the driveway. They didn't speak until they were seated in an unmarked car that was parked along the street. It was 9.50 am on Monday.

Mullings took the passenger seat. He had a reputation amongst colleagues for being a dogged and thorough investigator. Many believed he might have gone far higher in the force but for a refusal to get involved with internal politics and the fact that he lacked the honeyed tongue of a self-promoter. In a crowd he was more likely to be mistaken for a bank manager than a policeman with long experience in the world of violent crime. Beyond work, he was father to three children, painted watercolour landscapes as a hobby, shared an interest in gardening with his wife Joy, and attended church on Sundays.

DI Jackson had little in common with his senior officer. The younger man was very keen to get on, was unmarried and had so far ruthlessly extricated himself from any relationship that competed with career. He worked out regularly, was at the peak of physical fitness, and enjoyed a spectacularly hectic sex life with girls who always looked like models. Despite a tendency to personal vanity, he was no fool; he recognised Mullings as an excellent policeman and was glad of the opportunity to learn from him. Jackson had a degree in criminal psychology. Despite having been partnered together for almost three years, Jackson didn't have a clue what Mullings really thought of him.

The two detectives sat with their thoughts for a few moments before Jackson broke the silence, "The first thing that struck me was how awkward it was, uncoordinated … like it was written with the hand they don't normally use."

"I wondered that too," replied Mullings.

"It's feasible of course that it was Harper himself."

"To make us think someone else is behind it?"

"It's possible."

"Harper didn't kill Chilvers," said Mullings.

"Yes, but he and his girlfriend may have arranged for someone else to do the killing. It's been done before."

Mullings nodded, "Find a handwriting expert, get samples from Harper and Miss Curtis."

Jackson made a note.

"I want Harper watched round the clock," said Mullings.

Jackson exhaled audibly, "We'll be popular. We're short-staffed as it is!"

"I don't care. It's essential Harper is watched at all times."

"You think he may not be as innocent as he claims?"

"Oh," replied Mullings with a note of surprise in his voice, "I don't know what to make of him yet, David." Mullings was the only person who ever referred to Jackson as David, the rest of the world called him Dave. "Harper is either an ice-cold manipulator, capable of organising a murder, or else a man badly in need of our protection."

"What about his late wife? Could there be any link to her?" suggested Jackson.

"We know she died in an accident … certainly worth looking into. Whoever defaced her portrait certainly wanted us to believe it was personal."

"The choice of word was significant … Jules … they were letting us know they'd accessed Harper's diary."

"Which Harper would undoubtedly want us to believe if he was behind it!"

"What about CCTV footage?"

Mullings nodded at his young colleague, "You mean the people-carrier last night? Good idea. Get any footage from Sevenoaks town centre round the times Harper mentioned."

Jackson quickly made a note; he didn't look up as he said, "I was thinking about Christmas Day, the stuff Harper told us about ... being baited by another car … might be worth looking into?"

"Definitely."

## 39

While DI Jackson went off to set these lines of inquiry in motion, Mullings remained on site. His first job was to discuss their findings with forensics.

"Anything more about the paint-pot?" he asked.

The head of the forensic team was sitting opposite him in the MIR.

"Dozens of prints all over it, unfortunately nothing we've been able to match up. The majority probably belong to stock handlers in the delivery chain."

"No help there then," said Mullings, "What about the car?"

The forensic man shook his head, "Still nothing," he replied.

"Nothing?" echoed Mullings, giving the word nothing extra emphasis.

"Whoever was behind the wheel took no chances. I reckon whoever did it must have been kitted out like one of my team when they enter a crime scene. They left no trace of themselves ... had to be wearing some kind of suit and a mask."

"Has Harper's office revealed anything?" Mullings' tone contained a note of despondency. He was getting used to there being no leads in this case.

"So far, same as the car."

"Predictable," said Mullings. "Have the IT people looked at the computer yet?"

The forensic man flipped over a page on the clip-board before him, "Everything on the hard disk was copied over two consecutive days, Monday the twelfth of January at 1.12 pm and Tuesday the thirteenth at 1.37 pm."

"They broke in twice?" asked Mullings in disbelief.

"On the first occasion everything was copied except for one personal file that required a password."

"The diary," nodded Mullings.

## 40

The forensic people were still at work in Gil's office and had started on the attic.

Sally rang around ten.

Inevitably, their conversation led on to the hit and run. "When I think how Michael died it makes me go cold," she admitted.

"It's bound to be a shock," replied Gil.

"But at least I can immerse myself in work," she admitted, "I feel guilty that I'm not there with you ... you're the one suffering most, getting interviewed by the police ... your car stolen, and then used ..." she broke off.

Gil had decided not to tell her about Jules' portrait; it seemed unfair, she was already concerned about him and stressed out because of her enormous workload. It was also the final week of preparations in London before the whole company moved to Manchester for the production week.

"I told Megan not to come in today," said Gil, "but we're going to take the dogs for a walk together. Afterwards I'll drop by to see the Paddicks. They've left several messages on my answerphone.'"

"If you can't work, why don't you come up here for a few days?" she suggested.

"I'd only be in the way. You've got plenty on without having me moping about! I mean, what would I do?"

"You could go sight-seeing?" she retorted.

Gil imagined her making this remark with the kind of throw-away, deadpan delivery he'd grown to love about her. He laughed.

"P'rhaps not then," she said.

## 41

After they had walked the dogs, Megan suggested a pub lunch. Gil jumped at the opportunity to avoid going home. Again he decided not to mention the portrait; he felt Megan, living alone, might be unsettled by it. After lunch he visited Sue Paddick; it was her half day, Nigel and the Valkyrie were still at school. He filled her in on what had happened after he'd left the party; again, omitting Jules' picture; no good excuse this time, just a reluctance to talk about it.

He got back to his house around six and was pleased to discover the MIR already gone. By the time Mullings and Jackson called by around 6.45 pm the last of the forensic vehicles was leaving and the house and its environs were silently familiar again.

Mullings and Jackson accepted coffee.

"Still no thoughts regarding anyone who might hold a grudge against you?" asked Mullings.

"No … not really."

Mullings and Jackson both pounced on the note of hesitancy, "Not really?" they asked in unison.

Gil looked apologetically down at his coffee, "I wondered, when I saw the word 'Jules' … whether it had something to do with the accident?"

"Your wife's accident?" interjected Jackson.

Gil looked up, something in the way Jackson said it suggested he was already aware of the circumstances.

"The only person I can think of is Geoff Owens."

"Why do you think Mr Owens might be involved?" asked Mullings.

"I don't. You asked if anyone bore me a grudge … when I saw the portrait defaced, I thought of the accident, that's all."

"You think Mr Owens might blame you for what happened?" inquired Jackson.

"I heard he suffered a breakdown after the accident. His wife killed herself. The driving ban cost him his livelihood. I didn't cause his problems, but I know about feelings of guilt and remorse. I've relived that accident many times ... I've no doubt Geoff Owens has too."

"I'm sure he has," agreed Mullings sympathetically, "We'll certainly make enquiries about Mr Owens' whereabouts on Saturday evening, and last night."

"Last night?" asked Gil.

"We found CCTV footage from Sevenoaks High Street ... a Ford Galaxy at the time you described. We got its number plate."

Gil looked optimistically at the two policemen.

Mullings went on, "Unfortunately, the vehicle registration was under a false name. Let's hope he drives it again!"

"You think he might not?" asked Gil.

"Whoever it is has been very careful. You thought you'd seen the vehicle before, but it was only last night you really noted it. Perhaps because they wanted you to."

Gil looked horrified by the suggestion.

"We've uncovered motorway footage from Christmas Day too," put in Jackson. "We have a recording of a car backing up on the M25, then following you into the Clacket Lane Services."

"What?" asked an incredulous Gil.

"The car was reported stolen after the Christmas holidays. Its owner had been on a family holiday to Goa. It was taken from outside their home in Winchester, and discovered in early January burnt-out and abandoned in woodland near Watford."

"North of London?"

Mullings nodded, "We're dealing with someone who is being very careful."

## 42

Gil's views about his personal safety had undergone something of a sea-change. He started to sleep badly, to wake up feeling sick with anxiety and drenched in sweat. He found this depressing, as if he'd regressed to the bad days immediately following the crash. And he began to feel nervous and uncomfortable in the company of strangers.

It seemed incongruous, almost absurd, to feel frightened here; after all, this was Sevenoaks, where conservatories were multitudinous and garages generally double. He had always gone about his daily business secure in the world that surrounded him; he hadn't experienced a situation that felt edgy or dangerous in years.

Gil contacted the firm that had installed the burglar alarm and asked them to review his security system. In light of what had happened, this amounted to changing the locks on the external doors and windows and upgrading the alarm itself.

Although he possessed an inbuilt aversion to them, he even considered having security gates installed, thereby converting his discreet home into something akin to a fortress. It was only when he found himself trying to calculate exactly how high a gate would need to be to provide absolute safety that he finally dropped the idea. He did however agree to cameras.

Gil also had new computers installed for himself and Megan. These were in fact long overdue. For the very first time, passwords were introduced for logging on. The old easily-remembered, easily-breached password which had accessed his diary was changed to an unrelated set of numbers and letters in higher and lower case. The only things unchanged were his email addresses and the domain name to his website.

The effort of making these changes was beneficial inasmuch as it took his mind off events and at least gave him a sense of being in control. The only thing he procrastinated over was buying a new car. His old one was being held indefinitely as physical evidence by Kent Police, and even if repairable, there was no way Gil could ever drive a car that had extinguished someone's life.

Over the course of the next eight days he overhauled everything: changed bank accounts, credit cards and altered his pin numbers. No sooner had the police left than a small army of tradesmen began to stomp through his home. There was no point attempting any creative work, and he told Megan not to come in until everything had been completed. He was glad she was keeping Spike, although it was quiet without him, but the little chap would have loathed the disruption. Gil went for a daily walk with Megan and the three dogs. Spike seemed content and didn't go in too much for guilt-tripping him. Each day he took Megan for a pub lunch after the walk, when any necessary business was discussed.

He put on a brave face, but anyone who knew Gil could tell he was troubled. After the police left there had been some hassle from newspaper reporters. A brief statement was read out by his agent, Patrick Small. This had been suggested and crafted by Patrick to help dampen speculation. Basically, it stated that Gil's car had been taken on the night in question, without his consent or knowledge.

## 43

"Any more trouble from the news people?" Megan asked as she perused the pub menu.

"Not since Patrick read the statement Friday morning," replied Gil. Over a week had elapsed since Michael's death. "What about you?" he asked.

"Oh, you know," she said with a dry laugh, "They try. I expect they imagine an elderly woman living alone might be a soft target for their journalistic probing."

Gil gave a broad laugh, "Bad mistake!"

"Indubitably," she agreed wryly. Megan continued to watch Gil as he took a sip of beer. He looked pale and unusually haggard. "How are you sleeping?" she asked with concern in her voice.

Gil shrugged, "Oh, okay."

"I take that as meaning badly," she retorted, "Not surprising, is it? I'm not sleeping well either. I can only imagine the strain you must be under, Sally too. How did her move to Manchester go?"

"Fine I think. She was disappointed I didn't get to see her before she went … but I've had so much going on … alarms, computers. We speak every day. She says working flat out helps keep her mind from dwelling on stuff. She says her friends have been brilliant. I've been lucky in that department myself," said Gil, briefly patting a hand on Megan's arm.

"When this is over, you and Sally must take a holiday."

"We'd planned to go to the cottage once the opera opened in London."

Megan had to think for a moment, "Do you mean your cottage in Wales?"

"Near Llangrannog, yes."

"I didn't realise you still had it."

"I haven't been there since before Jules died."

Megan nodded in approval, "What a good idea. Get away from it all!"

"I guess it won't happen now, not unless the police can wrap things up … get Chilvers' killer."

"Oh well," commiserated Megan, "I'm sure you'll get there later on."

## 44

By the end of Wednesday the security improvements had been fully implemented and Gil had the house to himself again. On Thursday he took a cab to Megan's earlier than on previous days. They walked the dogs as usual, then Megan drove him to a restaurant a few miles from Felix and Kate's oast where they had arranged to meet up with Patrick Small, Felix and Gil's agent. This was a long-postponed meeting to discuss arrangements for their forthcoming tour of North America.

Felix was his usual affable self, despite retaining the remnants of a cold. His eyes had a rheuminess about them and he occasionally suffered a mild coughing fit; in spite of this, he entertained the group for half an hour after lunch by recounting jokes sent to him by child fans.

"I received this one from a little girl," began Felix, surfing along on a wave of laughter, "A girl goes to see the doctor. She has a carrot sticking out of one ear, a stick of celery in the other, and a radish poking out of her nose. She says, 'I haven't been feeling very well.' The doctor says, 'I can see straightaway what's wrong with you … you're not eating properly!'"

This joke, undoubtedly aided by red wine, evoked a massive laugh. Poor Felix went a purplish-red when his laughter turned to coughing. This brought Kate in to remonstrate with him, "You'll end up in bed again if you're not careful."

Felix, appearing chastened, looked over at Gil and winked impishly. However, Kate's intervention prompted them to get down to business, and the requirements for the tour.

Felix and Kate had been in touch every day since Michael Chilvers' death to check how Gil was bearing up. They had invited him to come and stay, but he assured them he was fine; every one knew this wasn't the case.

As Kate said to Megan in a whispered aside, "Who wouldn't be overwhelmed by what's happened? Poor Harp, Felix and I are terribly worried about him."

"Have you noticed how he drifts off mentally?" asked Megan.

"Yes, when he thinks none of us is watching."

"Sometimes when we've been walking the dogs, I've seen a real sense of apprehension come over him whenever someone he doesn't recognise comes near."

"It must be terrible … not knowing who's done this," replied Kate.

"I wish he'd go off to visit Sally in Manchester," said Megan.

"Why can't he?" asked Kate.

"To be honest, I think he's frightened to leave home, probably in case something else happens."

"Let's work on him," whispered Kate conspiratorially.

## 45

That evening, shortly after Gil had been deposited home by Megan, DCI Mullings rang and arranged to drop by in an hour's time. He was punctual, arriving just after 8.30 pm. He was alone.

"I see you've had a camera installed in the porch," observed Mullings.

"Two at the front of the house and one at the back," said Gil. "I can see whoever calls on this," indicating the monitor on the table left of the door. "I've also had the locks changed and alarm upgraded."

"You've been busy," said Mullings.

"You don't think I've gone too far?"

"Not under the circumstances."

"So you think I have good reason to be concerned about my safety?" asked Gil, voicing his fear.

Mullings thought before he spoke. "In light of what has happened, it would be wise to remain vigilant."

"Would you like a cup of coffee?" asked Gil.

"Thanks."

Gil led Mullings through to the kitchen. While he made coffee they talked generally. Gil told Mullings he'd been to lunch with his colleague Felix Blatt, and explained they'd been making arrangements for a forthcoming tour of the US.

"Our kids were big fans of your books. The wife and I had to read them over and over."

"In that case I'll understand if you're not too enamoured yourself."

"Not at all," said Mullings warmly, "I think Mr Blatt manages to get right to the heart of what matters to children, but at the same time is able to entertain and amuse their parents too. Your drawings complement his writing brilliantly!"

"Thanks," said Gil, placing two mugs down on the table.

Mullings, after tasting his drink, returned to business, "I just wanted to keep you up to date with our investigation." He paused and took another sip, "You mentioned Geoff Owens as someone who might hold a grudge ..."

"He was the only person I could think of," corrected Gil.

Mullings nodded, "We investigated, but he's ruled out. He spends most nights round his local pub, and it seems that Saturday the thirty-first was no exception. He is of course banned from driving. Frankly, Mr Harper, the man is a mental and physical wreck. I don't think he'd be able to motivate himself into organising something like this even if he had the desire to."

Gil nodded, "I'm sorry I …"

"No need to apologise," interjected Mullings, "It was a worthwhile course to pursue. I'm sorry it took so long to get back to you."

"So there's nothing new, then?" asked Gil. It was hard to disguise the disappointment in his voice.

"Our enquiries into Mr Chilvers' professional life have uncovered certain discrepancies. He'd been suspended from his job …"

"Yes, a friend of Sally's mentioned that some time back."

"It appears he may have had dealings with certain unsavoury types."

Gil listened attentively as Mullings spoke.

"It's alleged he may have been laundering money for a Russian crime cartel … very nasty people … drugs, human trafficking, prostitution."

The possibility excited Gil, "Do you think it's likely? I mean, stealing my car, damaging my wife's portrait? It all seemed so personal!"

"It does seem uncharacteristic … but stranger things have happened. These people aren't generally known for their subtlety … but then, Mr Chilvers wasn't killed in a terribly subtle way."

"I suppose making it appear personal may have deflected attention away from them?" said Gil, feeling a surge of hopefulness that he may not have been personally targeted after all.

"It's certainly possible," replied Mullings.

The sense of relief was profound; it prompted Gil to reconsider Manchester. He explained the situation to Mullings; how it was a very important job for Sally.

"If your lady friend would like you to join her in Manchester, then it's probably a good idea to be there," smiled Mullings.

## 46

The suggestion that he'd been used as a pawn to breed confusion and disguise the real motives behind Chilvers' murder brought Gil considerable relief. Next day, he booked himself a seat on the midday train to Manchester. It was Friday 13 February, an appropriate day, its producers felt, to open an opera that told such an eerie tale.

Gil had left home early that morning to purchase a new car. Being completely ignorant on the subject, he'd asked Megan to go with him. She read magazines about cars and liked nothing better than watching all the blokish TV programmes about them.

"I reckon a Skoda Octavia estate would tick all your boxes," she'd advised.

He accepted her assessment without question. Megan drove them to the nearest dealership, he took a test drive, found the car agreeable, and signed the dotted line in just over an hour. The silver model he ordered would be ready to collect Monday afternoon.

After this, they went back to Megan's for coffee and a slice of cake, after which he gave Spike a pat goodbye and was driven to the station.

He reached Manchester with just enough time to check into his hotel, eat a sandwich and get to the theatre by 7.30. He rang Sally to let her know he'd arrived. There was no possibility of seeing her before curtain-up. She had arranged a seat for him in the third row of the stalls, and he discovered himself sitting next to David Simpson.

"I'm really glad you made it," said David. "Last time I spoke to Sal, she seemed to think you weren't coming. I could tell she was disappointed."

"I thought it would do me good to get away. And I wanted to support Sally, and Klaus too. Is he joining us?" asked Gil, pointing to the empty seat beside David.

"Oh no, he'll spend the night treading the Dress Circle carpet like the ghost of Hamlet's father, terrified everyone will loathe his set!"

As a novice to opera, Gil was unable to make any informed criticism. He detected no bum singing notes, and the audience, who he assumed were all more knowledgeable about opera than he was, appeared to greet each scene with approval. The subject matter, in light of Michael Chilvers' recent violent demise, was not entirely to Gil's taste. However, it was an operatic melodrama played out in a pseudo-medieval setting that really only existed in Klaus Williams' imagination. The set, once populated with its principal singers and chorus, grew into a spectacular organic whole. Sally's costume designs were understated to great effect within the powerful setting. Occasionally a costume, particularly those worn by Lady M, played by the extremely well-endowed Marika Novotny, lent an epic quality to the scene. At the final curtain call she received a standing ovation.

There was great excitement backstage where Gil found himself being reluctantly led by David. Guests were already streaming into the principals' dressing-rooms and there was the unmistakable sound of champagne corks popping. They saw Klaus in the middle of a great throng of people in Dressing-Room One pouring drinks. He caught sight of them and gestured for them to come through, but David took Gil up a flight of stairs to a room marked Wardrobe. Inside, Sally, Roz and another girl were hanging up costumes. Sally, facing away from the door, didn't hear them enter. Roz signalled her comrade to say nothing, and led the girl and David out of the room.

Sally must have sensed some change to her surroundings. When she looked round and saw Gil she let go the costume she was holding and rushed over to him.

She was wearing a pair of old faded jeans and a baggy jumper. She watched him observing her and announced, "I look a fright, don't I? Haven't had time to put on my party frock yet. Don't worry, I clean up okay!" she laughed.

"You look lovely," Gil said.

1 3 5
2 4 R

# FOURTH

13 February - 19 March

## 1

Forty minutes after the curtain came down everyone, with the exception of the stagehands who were busy dismantling the set, had de-camped to a restaurant a few streets from the theatre. Here they were greeted by waitresses dressed in witches' garb serving Bloody Marys in plastic goblets; a Gothic nod to the bloodthirstiness of Verdi's opera. Most members of the company had walked the short distance in large enthusiastic groups and it seemed to take no time at all before the first-night party was in full swing. There was a prevailing view that the production could not be faulted by very much, if anything, and that all involved had contributed to its success. The company's self-belief, an accomplished band fronted by an excellent vocalist performing classic soul numbers, a plentiful buffet and freely-flowing alcohol made it a brilliant night.

Despite his inbuilt diffidence, Gil found the evening great fun too. He was glad he'd overcome his reluctance about leaving home. Once he'd taken up his seat on the train at Euston, his anxiety and foreboding immediately began to dissipate. He'd grabbed the opportunity to become better acquainted with his newly acquired lap-top. Gil hadn't actually made a single entry in his diary since Chilvers' death, and had even considered abandoning it altogether. However, the man possessed a quietly understated tenacity of spirit that only his oldest and closest friends might really attest to; the files on his computer may have been breached and his privacy invaded, but he would only give up recording his life, when he, and he alone, chose.

During the journey to Manchester he had written:

> ... As the countryside flies past it feels like I am casting off the tensions and pent-up emotions that have been crowding in on me recently. I know where these thoughts would drive me if I let them ...

The place was Gil's private hell, sometimes obliquely referred to in his diary as 'the crater'. He dreaded revisiting this barren moon of deepest hurts and darkest thoughts. He had always understood that too long spent brooding there might take him beyond despair to self-annihilation.

Sally's claim that she cleaned up well was accurate. She looked great in a sparkling black dress bought for the occasion. Gil was barely able to take his eyes off her. At a moment when they found themselves alone, he whispered lasciviously in her ear, "You look terrific in that dress, but all I really want to do is get you back to my hotel, tear it off and ravish you."

Sally's eyes shined with anticipation, "All that dark passion has brought out the brute in you! Can't wait!"

Although the party was enjoyable, their dilemma was judging how much time would be deemed respectable before they made their exit. Despite an aching desire to be alone together, they managed to look relaxed, which under the circumstances wasn't hard.

As 1 am approached they considered they'd stayed an acceptable amount of time.

Sally announced their departure to the group of cast and production people they were seated with at a large circular table, "Gil and I are going to leave you!"

There followed shouts of protest from the others.

Gil, like a new-born babe in the face of theatrical worldliness, mistakenly thought it might help to say, "Yes, we're both quite tired and an early-ish night is called for."

This only produced ribald jeers and much guffawing from Sally's friends who seemed fully aware the pair didn't have sleep down as top item on their to-do lists. Sally merely laughed along with them, as in fact did Gil, although his face flushed beetroot red.

Klaus was sitting beside a standing Marika Novotny, who had floated over to visit the group. He had an arm about her waist while his head rested against Novotny's monumental bosom, proudly displayed in a low-cut gown. At Gil's innocent comment he looked up at the opera diva, "They want to go for an 'early one'," he said with a rude wink.

The leading lady, who on stage just hours before had convincingly incited murder and been driven to madness by her evil deeds, laughed as uproariously as a fish-wife, then said in a very loud voice, "Yes, darleengs ... have an 'early one' for me too!"

As the group shrieked with laughter Gil's mouth ran as dry as Arizona at the thought of having any kind of euphemistic 'one' with Marika Novotny, who according to Klaus was a woman with huge appetites. There are some jobs a man knows he's just not up to.

## 2

Despite getting to sleep late, they woke early and lay in bed laughing, talking and caressing, in complete contrast to the frenetic love-making of the night before.

They ordered breakfast in bed, and chatted while they ate.

During the previous week, although they had spoken daily, their conversations had largely amounted to lists of things done during their day. Although he'd already mentioned it, Gil talked in more detail about the improvements to his home security, although he played down its real significance. On the subject of Jules' portrait he remained silent.

"Was your alarm faulty?" asked Sally.

"I don't think so," he answered, "I just wanted to be certain."

"You read about this kind of stuff, identity theft etcetera," said Sally.

"It certainly felt like a violation," he added.

"Poor love," she said with feeling, "I've been surrounded by friends the whole time and had the show to keep me occupied. For what it's worth, I think you've coped really well."

"I've muddled through," he said.

Inevitably, the seeming lack of progress made by the police in their investigation into Michael's killing cropped up, and this dampened their mood for a while.

"I'm surprised you still want anything to do with me," Sally confessed.

"Why would I feel that?" Gil asked, astounded that she could even think such a thing.

"Because you'd never have even heard the name Michael Chilvers if it wasn't for me!"

"That doesn't make any of this your fault ... you might as well blame Public Libraries or something!"

Sally nodded and managed a weak smile, indicating that she knew he was right. Nevertheless, Gil could tell she still considered herself in some sense to blame for what had happened.

He thought for a moment before he spoke. He'd been uncertain about exactly how or when to mention the matter discussed with Mullings on Thursday evening. Gil had no idea how Sally might react to this unexpected information and he didn't want to upset her. He considered the moment appropriate and said calmly, "The police told me they are investigating a possible link to the Russian mafia."

"The who?" she asked, with more than an air of disbelief.

"They think Michael may have been doing a spot of creative accountancy for some Eastern European criminals."

"I find it hard to believe that even Michael would have done anything quite that stupid!" she said, nonplussed by the revelation.

"Apparently, this was what was behind his suspension at work."

Sally paused for a moment's consideration before asking, "But why would the Russian mafia go to such a lot of trouble to lay the blame at your door?"

"I asked the same question. The police seem to think it's worth investigating though."

Sally, clearly not too convinced, went on to say, "I suppose if the Bulgarians could assassinate someone with a poisoned umbrella on Waterloo Bridge, or Alexander Litvinenko could be given a fatal dose of radiation in a London Sushi restaurant … anything's possible!"

"Who knows, it may be of value to these people to deliberately mislead the authorities ... lay some kind of false trail!"

Sally nodded, there was some credibility in this argument but she remained sceptical.

"I've been over every detail a hundred times," replied Gil, "Seems to me everyone who ever met Michael Chilvers ended up despising him. But to murder him? And to go about it in such a cold, calculated way? I mean, even if it crossed your mind to do away with someone, and over-riding any personal moral code that says it's wrong to murder, it would be very risky … far too many things might go wrong …"

"And you might get banged-up in prison for a hell of a lot of years!" agreed Sally.

Gil nodded.

"Did you ever consider that it might be me … that I could have killed him?" she asked.

Gil glanced sideways at Sally and gave a shamefaced nod, "Not for long. I think it would be the same for you as for Klaus or David or Roz, or the dozen others who despised Michael … me too! I mean, if you happened to be there in a car on a deserted road at night, and he just happened to stagger into your sights … nobody to witness it … all it needed was a bit of pressure on the gas … for a split second it might be hard to resist!"

"When I was Michael's … domestic prisoner, I used to fantasise about killing him ... mad things like hitting him over the head with a cast iron pan while he dozed in a drunken stupor at the kitchen table. Once, he passed out in his car in the garage with the engine running … I actually considered closing the doors to gas him."

"That's what I mean," interjected Gil, "We all have such thoughts."

"Do you know why I didn't?" she asked.

"Because you're not a murderer?"

Sally shrugged, "I wanted to, believe me, I really wanted to! But the truth is, I was terrified of him!" As she spoke a solitary tear ran down her cheek, "Even if he'd been alone, as you described, drunk and powerless … and I was behind the wheel of a car … I'd still be scared of him. Scared that in spite of his feebleness and my relative position of strength, he'd still somehow be able to exert his power over me, control my actions, cause me to swerve and fail at the last moment."

3

Sally was not required to be at the theatre until midday. This was for the production team meeting or post mortem as Sally referred to it. Apart from Saturday afternoon, the remainder of the weekend was theirs to do as they pleased.

They went out for dinner in the evening with Klaus, David, Roz and ten other mates from the company. They were a warm and chatty group of people who it would have been extremely difficult not to get along with. A good time was had by all, especially by Gil, eager to enjoy himself after his recent troubles. He did wonder if Klaus and Sally had asked their friends to avoid mentioning the investigation, as no reference was made to it during the entire evening. He meant to ask Sally later whether this was actually the case and offer his thanks, but forgot and never got round to it.

## 4

On Sunday they rose at the moderately early time of 8.30, had breakfast in the hotel dining-room, and drove to Blackpool. Neither had been to this most famous of British seaside towns before, and afterwards concluded it was unlikely they'd experience any pangs of longing to return.

They enjoyed a bracing walk along the promenade, pummelled by a powerful headwind beside a turbulent gunmetal-grey sea. Everything about the seafront seemed unremittingly drab, but the salt air was fresh and the exercise felt good. They ate seafood for lunch and took afternoon tea in Lytham St Annes. Despite finding Blackpool rather stark they still had a nice time.

That night they dined alone at an Indian restaurant, recommended by the permanent staff at the theatre. Their only complaint was with themselves for ordering too much. They finished the evening in the hotel lounge on a large leather sofa with double brandies to help ease the pains of excess.

Sally had two more performances at Manchester in the forthcoming week. Although everything looked fine to Gil, there were still changes being made and it looked as though Sally would have a busy time ahead of her before the company moved on to Bristol.

Monday morning, she drove Gil to the train station to see him off.

"Thanks for coming, it really meant a lot to me. I've had a lovely time."

"Me too. See you in a few weeks."

"Take care," she called, blowing a kiss at him and stepping quickly along the platform to keep up with the train that had begun to move off.

"You too," he shouted back.

## 5

It was nearly 4 pm when he reached Sevenoaks. His first port of call was the dealership to pick up his new car. It was already dark by the time he drove away from the showroom. The original plan to go for a spin in the new Skoda was postponed until the morning. It felt strangely disorientating to be home again, especially with Spike still away.

He remedied this by calling Megan after supper.

"You're back! Enjoy yourself?" she asked.

"Very much."

"How was the opera?"

"Fabulous!" replied Gil.

"And how was Sally?"

"Tired, overworked, but in good spirits."

"When did you get back?"

"A few hours ago. I picked up my new car on the way home."

"And?" she asked excitedly. Megan truly adored cars.

"Great," he replied, trying not to sound too phlegmatic. For Gil Harper, a car was only ever going to be a car, "Your recommendation of course … I knew it would suit me," he tried to enthuse.

Megan chuckled to herself, he was a hopeless case. "Shall I come tomorrow? Any danger of us starting work again?"

"It is rumoured there's a chance."

"What shall I do about my house-guest?"

"I think it's time for the King to return!" announced Gil.

## 6

The next morning, Spike was back from exile. He breezed in, head held high, self-confident, assured of his place in the world. However, the recent intrusive activities of the Kent Police provided the diminutive canine with a stack of information to decipher. As self-appointed guardian of the house it was Spike's duty to sniff out wherever these interlopers had been. This demanded a thorough investigation of the premises, requiring an in-depth olfactory review of every surface below knee level. By late morning the poor chap was staggering under the burden of responsibility. He had to be woken up when the time came for his walk.

As for Gil, a return to routine brought a focus back to his life. The sense of foreboding had not entirely dissipated, and there were still moments whilst out and about that caused him to think he was being followed. However, each time this occurred, his assumed pursuer had blithely veered off on some innocuous course. Megan, conscious of this, suggested they continue to exercise their dogs together, which lent a feeling of some solidarity at least.

On Wednesday morning Gil rang the Blatts. The phone was picked up by Kate, who was her usual chirpy self.

"We were glad to hear from Megan that you'd gone to Manchester."

"I was going a bit stir crazy," replied Gil.

"How is Sally?" Kate asked in her gently-spoken way.

"She's great. The opening night was a big success. The reviews have been good. Her costume designs looked fantastic."

"Did you manage to get some time together?"

"We went to Blackpool on Sunday," he said.

"Felix and I love Blackpool."

"Really? I thought it was bloody awful."

"Well come on Harp, the seaside, in February?"

"I have a feeling I'd probably dislike the place even more in August."

"Perhaps it's a generational thing," she said. "When Felix and I first went there it was the very early sixties ... before flower-power or psychedelia ... the country was still recovering from World War Two. Everything was grey and dull, but Blackpool was alive ... garish, brash, vulgar, but unlike the rest of Britain, in Technicolor."

"Technicolor?" questioned Gil, adopting a sarcastic tone, "Wasn't that around at the same time as steam locomotives?"

"You're being a digital snob," laughed Kate.

"No matter what names you call me, you'll never get me to say I liked the place. The seafront at Hastings will in future seem like St Tropez after visiting Blackpool."

"The lord and master will be shocked when I tell him how badly we've underestimated your taste and judgement all these years, Harp," she joked.

"Is he around?" enquired Gil.

"'Fraid not, gone for his constitutional."

"Bit late for him, isn't it?" said Gil, consulting his watch.

"He's been a bit troubled with a bad chest since getting shot of that cold. The doctor gave him some antibiotics, but he's not right yet. And the antibiotics only seem to make him tetchy. You know how he is, he hates to take anything."

"I suppose he refuses to take it easy?" proffered Gil.

"I get accused of nagging!"

"Sounds like I'm going to have to come round and take you both out for lunch," said Gil.

They arranged to do this on Friday.

"I'll get Megan to book us in somewhere nice," he said.

"Will you be bringing Megan along too?"

Gil replied hesitantly, "I thought I would. Is that okay?"

"More than okay," answered Kate, "I'll be desperate for some female company by Friday!"

## 7

Sally rang Gil each evening at 10.30 pm. On performance nights this was twenty minutes after the curtain came down. When the phone rang on Thursday evening just five minutes before this appointed time, Gil picked up in happy anticipation.

"Hi, darling," he said.

There was a momentary pause.

"Am I talking to Gil Harper?" asked the man at the other end of the line.

"Oh … yes … I'm sorry … "

"Mr Harper, my name is Martin Harrison. I'm the emergency doctor for the East Peckham area."

"Felix!" exclaimed Gil automatically.

"Yes. I'm sorry to say Mr Blatt has been taken ill. He's been taken to Maidstone Hospital. He's suffered a suspected heart attack."

"Is he going to be alright?"

The doctor paused, "I'm afraid the only reassurance I can give you at present is that he's in the best place and his condition is stable."

"Would it be alright to go there, to be with him?"

"Mr Harper, I was ringing to ask a favour of you. I'm afraid Mrs Blatt became a little overwrought when Mr Blatt was taken ill …"

"The sight of Felix having a heart attack must have really disturbed her," said Gil who had never known Kate remain anything other than calm under pressure. "Poor Kate!" he added.

"I've given her a mild sedative to help her settle down. She suggested I ring and ask you if you'd mind driving over here to be with her?"

"I'll come at once," said Gil.

"And perhaps later on you'd be good enough to take her to the hospital?"

"Yes, yes of course."

"I'll let Mrs Blatt know you're on your way."

## 8

Later on, apart from his sense of urgency about getting there and frustration at not yet being fully acquainted with his new car, Gil remembered only the scantest details about the journey that night.

He remembered being filled with an almost overwhelming sense of powerlessness. He, of course, knew and accepted that at nearly eighty,

Felix must be drawing ever closer to the inevitable; yet the unexpected suddenness with which his friend had been taken ill still shocked him.

A bitter snap of icy weather had been superseded by mild damp days and nights. The incessant drizzle left a residue on the windscreen, it lay on the glass like thin, unappetising, broth. Although he drove right up to the speed limit, he felt he was travelling at an excruciatingly slow pace. Gil actually made it to East Peckham in eighteen minutes, a time well below his average.

The lights appeared to be turned on in every room of the Blatts' house. He pulled up sharply across the drive and rushed from the car. As usual he didn't knock and predictably the door wasn't locked.

"Hello?" he called out. He waited for a response but none came. Before trying again he reconsidered and thought better of it. If the doctor had given Kate a sedative she might have dropped off to sleep. The bedroom doors on the ground floor were open, but there was no sign of her. He quickly ascended and searched the two floors above but found no trace here either.

He returned to the ground floor and took the door that led to the garden and Felix's workshop. It made a curious kind of sense to him that Kate might be waiting in the room where Felix had done most of his creative work over the last forty years.

When he reached the workshop, its door was slightly ajar. That was the first thing that struck him as odd; despite the mildness of the night it was still winter. Perhaps it was a kind of prescience that caused him to hesitate before pushing forward the door.

His uncertainty was justified. The door opened onto an unimaginably appalling scene.

His great, beloved friend, Felix Blatt, was dead.

At just one glance, there was no disputing it. Felix was sitting on his sofa in a pose far too unlikely for someone still alive. The head had lolled back with eyes staring, clouded and unfocused. Felix's mouth hung wide open in an ugly, unfamiliar expression, his features drawn and blank, as inanimate as the objects in the room.

There was a disturbingly large amount of blood; it would be a forgivable exaggeration to describe Felix's workroom as awash in it.

Gil somehow found whatever strength was needed to propel himself forward until he was now standing before Felix. He saw there was a deep wound on the left side of his late friend's head. The blood from here had flowed over his clothes, drenched the sofa and created a small pool about his feet, all beginning to coagulate.

Gil was by now far too shocked to think with any clarity. He didn't immediately notice the trail of blood leading off diagonally across the room. It was only when his confused eyes followed its course, just a few feet or so from Felix's corpse to the farthest corner of the workroom that he became aware of Kate. The reason why she had been dragging herself away from the man she was so thoroughly devoted to was not immediately clear.

Gil rushed over to her, crying out, "Kate. Oh God! Oh, no!"

She was laying face down and completely still. Gil assumed there was no life here either.

Then, in response to the sound of his familiar voice, there came an enormous heave from Kate's ribcage and a rattling gasp for breath. It was totally unexpected, and it seemed impossible that she could be alive after the loss of so much blood. Gil recoiled in horror at first; before he remembered that this was still Kate. He gained control of himself and kneeled beside her.

"I'm here … it's Gil … don't try to move …" he said gently, trying his best to sound calm.

Kate appeared not to hear his words, or if she did, didn't heed them. She drew herself up onto her elbows and propelled herself over onto her back. Gil winced at the sound as the back of her head struck the polished floorboards upon landing. Then reaching forward with a hand he began to stroke her face. He wasn't at all conscious of the tears that now filled his eyes.

Kate reached out her blood-drenched hand towards him. This hand, tightly clenched into a fist, had been stemming the blood that seeped from the wound in her chest. The hand clutched something. It took a moment before Gil realised that she was holding the disconnected end of a telephone cable. Her journey across the room had been an attempt to reconnect it with its socket in the corner. This had been Kate Blatt's final effort to save the man she had adored for half a century.

He took her hand in his, sticky and slippery with blood.

Kate's anguished eyes focused on his face, "Gil … Gil …" she feebly whispered, attempting at the same time to lever herself up again but to no avail.

"Don't move, try and keep still," he said, drawing himself in closer to her.

"Gil … help … help Felix…" she groaned.

She hadn't realised that Felix was already dead.

Gil could never be certain, but he wondered afterwards if his eyes might have communicated this fact to her. It would not have surprised him; Kate Blatt had always shown unerring accuracy when it came to interpreting his face and body language. Why should this ability be lost in the final moments of her life?

He thought he saw her expression of anxiety waver before fading into resignation.

A second later and Kate's eyes, like her life partner's, had glazed over in the opaque vacancy of death.

Gil began to shake uncontrollably.

## 9

### Friday 20 February

00.35 am - It was thrilling to speak with you tonight.

Our first contact! After everything that's happened, isn't that incredible?

I suppose it was a bit naughty, misleading you like that. Making you think you were talking to the nice woodcutter, not nasty Mr Wolf!

I recorded our conversation. I've played it over again and again.

Alright, a bit sad I suppose!

You know, Gil Harper, sometimes I wish we could have been friends. You are loyal, faithful and rarely have a bad word for anyone. It's refreshing to find someone like you who is largely uncontaminated by jealousy. There is so much about you that is admirable. I even find your self-doubts quite attractive.

(No, please, not in a gay way!)

Personally, I've always found people fickle and untrustworthy. Once, when young and naïve, I deluded myself into believing that someone I'd met was different. Unusually for me, I felt driven to open up. My unguarded honesty, the depth of my character and the strength of my convictions were met by an awkward silence, uncertainty and vacuousness.

I've learned better since then. I don't do relationships. What is to be gained by consorting with inferior types?

'Don't cast pearls before swine,' a rare piece of worthwhile advice from that collection of lies and fairy tales, The Bible.

So, joking aside, I can say in all sincerity: I wish we could have been friends.

Please, don't imagine I'm unable to empathise with how much pain you must be suffering right now. I can picture your grief very well. Coming upon your friends, butchered like that. It must have caused you terrible distress.

Sometimes, it feels like you and I are mythological heroes, opposing each other, driven by the wiles and whims of the Gods. I've been set upon a course to wreck your life and nothing will stop me.

When I arrived at the Blatts' oast-house, as anticipated, your friend Felix was in his workshop. I must congratulate you, your diaries were very accurate when it came to planning my timings. They not only detail your own sad existence but comprehensively timetabled your friend's life too:

*'Felix always likes to unwind by spending the last few hours at the end of each day in his workshop/study, either working in wood or quietly editing the work he's produced in the morning. He's generally at one or other of these activities from 9 pm till at least midnight. Felix doesn't get the concept of 'taking an early night'.'*

So generous and thoughtful of you to help me out like this.

I opened the door cautiously. Blatt was fast asleep on the sofa. I crept in until I was standing directly in front of him. He remained sleeping. His head had fallen back against the headrest, his mouth was hanging loose and he was snoring. The old are even less attractive when asleep than when they're awake. Nasty!

I was carrying a knife in a leather holster attached to a utility belt around my waist. But it suddenly struck me as far too simple to draw the knife and slit his throat, him resting there, presenting his neck like a sacrificial lamb (except this lamb was mutton!).

<u>I'll take any opportunity to be more creative</u>!

I crept past the comatose old fool and went into the carpentry area of his study. I quickly chose and removed a club hammer from the place where it was neatly organised amongst a range of other kinds of hammers. Then I returned.

I expected I'd need to wake him up with a good prod or something. But this wasn't necessary. He was already stirring. I don't know why, perhaps the draught from the door as I entered, or possibly my movement into the other room and back had disturbed his sleep. Anyway, he was showing signs of waking.

Tee hee! I wish you could have seen that look in his eyes when he saw me!

It was priceless! Blatt just sitting there in stunned bewilderment, a dumbfounded look of utter stupidity on his face. I can't help but smile to think of it.

I'm certain he thought he'd died and gone to heaven!

He was probably trying to work out why St Peter was wearing a surgical mask and gloves, wellington boots and a white bio-suit.

I raised the club hammer. I'm not ashamed to admit that I felt a thrill run through me. Blatt's eyes widened and for the first time I saw terror grip them. He suddenly realised his mistake: instead of reaching the gates of heaven, God's mobile abattoir had come a'callin'! Hallelujah!

I swung. Strange, he made no attempt to avoid it.

It didn't land with conclusive force, but it was powerful enough to cause a dull crunch as it connected with the bones of his temple. He swayed where he sat but didn't really move much. A trickle of blood started to flow from his ear. I was surprised, almost impressed, that the blow didn't send him flying. An odd, disconnected groaning sound began to come out of his mouth, quite weird and a bit macabre. It didn't sound quite human. The look in his eyes was like a stunned animal.

At the risk of sounding sadistic, I must admit, I found his facial expression mildly comic. Had it not been for his wife's intrusion, I daresay I'd have savoured the moment a little longer. Fortunately she'd telegraphed her arrival by calling "Felix" as she crossed between the oast and workshop.

At the moment she entered I was delivering the fatal blow. This time I didn't hold back. With a loud crack like the sound of a nutshell breaking, Blatt's head hurtled back onto a pile of cushions. His body started to twitch, accompanied by a rattling noise from his lungs. Fascinating!

Unfortunately, Kate Blatt was not dispatched anything like as easily as her husband. She'd entered holding a tray with what looked and smelt like two mugs of hot chocolate. She looked up, saw me and screamed.

Then, and I say this in her praise, she demonstrated incredible presence of mind and hurled the drinks tray straight at me. Fortunately, her aim wasn't as clear as her intention and it mostly missed apart from a little of the chocolate spraying my left arm.

But showing no hesitation, she turned and made a dash for the door. Needless to say, I was on top of her before she could get out of the room. I dragged her back and swung her about, shoving her hard into the door, which slammed shut behind her. I let the hammer drop to the ground. I hate to repeat myself. I drew the knife, and drove it into her chest with every ounce of force I could muster.

The knife has an eight inch blade and it plunged in up to its hilt. She sank to her knees, gulping for air like someone drowning. She was gazing straight up at me in disbelief. I withdrew the knife and she collapsed face down.

I assumed she was either dead, or very nearly there, when I let her fall and I suddenly realised I'd have to drag her away from the door before I could leave the room. I felt more than a little annoyed with my management skills.

Nevertheless, I'm proud to say I still managed to call you.

You'd have to agree I displayed remarkable composure.

Apart from the knife, my utility belt also held a pouch that contained a recording device and some bleach wipes which I now used to clean the telephone mouthpiece. I didn't remove my mask to speak, because you can never be too careful about leaving evidence. I'd had a number of practice runs, recording and playing it back many times until I felt the sound of my voice was as clear and unimpeded by the mask as possible.

Once our exciting little chat was over I packed my recording device away again, wiped the phone carefully, then replaced the used wipes back in the pouch on my belt.

I'm sure you can appreciate my amazement when I saw that Kate Blatt was not only alive but actually crawling towards her husband.

What luck! No need to drag her body out of the way after all! I tugged the cable out of its wall socket and hurled the phone away into a corner. Then I left.

Frankly, it would only have seemed malicious if I'd finished off Kate Blatt. After all, she wasn't part of my original plan. She was just unfortunate enough to make an entrance at the wrong moment. Unlike her husband and his dreadful stories, I harboured no animosity towards her.

Anyway, she'd lost a lot of blood, and it seemed unlikely she'd still be alive by the time you arrived to summon help. Even if she did happen to survive by some absolute fluke, what then? Approximate height or colour of my eyes perhaps? Nothing more I reckon.

What a shame.

## 10

Within a minute of witnessing Kate Blatt's final breath, Gil had rung 999 on his mobile. It suggested a reserve of inner fortitude, that despite being deeply traumatised, he possessed enough presence of mind to act swiftly. Even so, his mental faculties were by no means functioning with anything like their normal agility. Had this been the case, his suspicions would have been aroused when an armed police officer arrived only three minutes after making the call.

It took nearly four hours for the penny to drop.

"I was followed, wasn't I?" asked Gil flatly; his voice expressing nothing more than the straight observation of this fact.

"Yes," confirmed Mullings, "For your safety mainly."

Gil immediately looked across at the Detective Chief Inspector and adopting an uncharacteristically bitter tone, replied, "But I wasn't the one in danger."

Mullings nodded with grim deliberation. At 3.40 am he looked older, greyer, the jowls on his broad face baggier and its age lines deeper. Jackson, who was sitting alongside him on a sofa in Gil's sitting-room, remained impassive; the time of day appearing to have no ill effect on him. Also present in the room was a uniformed policewoman, who had remained with Gil ever since he'd been escorted home. She was sitting directly behind Mullings on a high-backed chair taking down notes.

Gil had already made a statement to the police some hours earlier. Since he'd been followed, it was very straightforward to corroborate timings. It was quickly established that Felix had been killed and Kate stabbed, at least twenty minutes before Gil arrived.

A doctor had come by shortly before Mullings and Jackson's visit. He'd examined and then talked to Gil about traumatic experience, its effect on the emotions and the impact of stress, nothing of which Gil actually took in. He'd left a couple of pills, "To help you get to sleep when the time comes," the doctor had said.

Gil heaved a great sigh. At that moment he saw no likelihood he'd possess the desire to sleep, with its possibilities to dream and relive experiences, anytime soon.

"I was planning to take them out to lunch today." After speaking Gil paused for a moment to reflect, "Felix would have been eighty in a few weeks time." The words were not directed at anyone, he was merely thinking aloud. "We'd been planning a book-signing tour of the US," he said.

"I know how hard this must be, Mr Harper, but it would help if you could answer a few more questions," said Mullings gently.

Gil nodded, at the same time his frame went into one of the brief spasms of shaking that for the last few hours had taken control of him from time to time.

"I'd like to know more about the voice on the phone."

"Like I said, it was definitely a man's voice."

"Any characteristics?" asked Jackson.

Gil looked confused.

"A particular accent, something memorable about the voice?" clarified Mullings.

"Not really. There was no accent." replied Gil.

"Was it like RP then, received pronunciation ... like a BBC newsreader?" asked Jackson.

Gil nodded. His mental confusion and general disorientation made thought seem like wading through mud. He considered the question for another moment then said, "Just as you'd expect a doctor to sound."

Jackson helped fill in the picture, "What, calm, authoritative and clear?"

Gil nodded.

"Age lends weight to a voice," said Mullings, "Did the voice suggest any particular age to you?"

"Not particularly young ... over thirty, possibly older ... but not an old voice," said Gil.

Mullings pondered these facts for a moment before speaking again, "Suppose he was disguising his voice somehow, does anyone spring to mind?"

Gil's brow furrowed deeply as he thought about the question.

Half a minute must have passed before Mullings prompted him again, "Maybe it belonged to someone you haven't met in a while ... someone whose voice sounded younger the last time you heard it?"

Gil looked across at the Detective Chief Inspector. For a split second Mullings might have been optimistic, before Gil replied, "I can't be certain of anything ... I really don't think so."

## 11

05.40 am - I'm so excited I haven't been able to sleep.

Everything has come together beautifully. Even if I say so myself and at the risk of sounding vain, the success of this venture is all down to great planning.

Even so, things have still gone wrong. Inevitable I suppose.

Truth be told, I'm a little disappointed about the Blatt woman. Just can't help feeling it makes me look bad, a double killing with lashings of blood, like I was a deranged maniac!

Simply the wrong place, wrong time. Shame.

Anyway, I certainly feel no remorse.

(Please read next sentence in a Californian accent! Tee hee hee!) Nevertheless, I think I can say that out of this experience, I've grown as a person and that I've attained a greater degree of humility in my life!

As you know, I don't believe in any kind of God nonsense, salvation or universal cause for goodness. There isn't any divine retribution to fear. I won't be serving a sentence for the naughty things I've done dressed in prison pyjamas marked For All Eternity. Even so, despite my contempt for God-botherers, and those who endlessly search for spiritual meaning and rubbish like that, I'd be the first to admit that life holds a few interesting lessons.

Which begs the question: what have you learned from this little escapade Gil Harper?

You've certainly discovered one thing at least that I knew already, that pain and life are synonymous. When I first observed you, you'd just met the bitch and the wounds from your past were starting to heal. But now you will be able to fully appreciate that for as long as you live, the pain can never stop.

Life, pain; pain, life. Same thing, see.

Our adventure, although not over yet, is drawing to a close. It has been, without a doubt, exhilarating.

Ten years, or perhaps even a hundred from now, criminal psychologists will still be discussing what happened in this case. Why was one man so vindictively targeted they'll ask? Why was the perpetrator never brought to justice?

I noticed a few newspapers yesterday were beginning to explore a link between my old victim Michael Chilvers and Russian criminals. What fertile imaginations! Isn't that precious? The conspiracy theorists away with the fairies again!

Nothing new there!

Of course, they'll go round and round the houses, use up forests to write reams of award-winning drivel. I can imagine academics agonising over the reasons why you were chosen.

But nobody will ever quite grasp it.

My little project has been successful almost entirely because I had no axe to grind.

I specifically chose you because you're nice. Because you care. You even acquired bonus points because you donate a tenth of everything you earn to children's charities, without seeking publicity or recognition. Had you been a tireless worker for some loony campaign, like Gay Rights for Vegan Hamsters, I'd probably have moved on and let you be.

It is because of people like you, the liberals, placaters, peacemakers, moderates, appeasers, the truly permissive in society, which enables the loud-mouthed, gross, crass promoters of mediocrity to thrive. You aren't innocent or blameless. It is because of people like you, the (not so) innocent bystanders, that these peoples' contagion is allowed to breed in our midst. You may well be a decent person, even so, you are still a compliant fraction of a poisonous whole.

I expect the moment you found your friend Felix with his head caved in and his wife stabbed, was the point of no return. I don't believe you can ever recover from it.

It's fairly easy to imagine the nightmares you'll be having in the future ... taking that telephone call again, turning up at the oast, finding them ... again and again. Just like all those sleepless nights and tortured dreams after your wife's death that you describe so vividly in your diary. Each time you'll attempt to get to their oast faster in order to try and prevent the inevitable. Faster, faster, faster ... over and over ... night after night ... trying to staunch the blood.

Let's face it. You just aren't going to make it.

I predict you'll revert to being reclusive. After the crash, you had your friends to draw you back from the brink. But oh dear, they've suddenly become extinct!

So what exactly does the future hold for you?

The bitch will probably dump you. She won't be able to bear the gibbering wreck you've become. Unfortunately, my timetable won't allow the situation to develop entirely naturally. So I'm going to be called upon to do a little string-pulling in order to assist and compound your sense of loss. Let me put it another way, your bitch's DNA isn't going to be merging with yours for too much longer.

Not unless you're a necrophiliac that is!

More tears ahead. Sorry.

Poor old Gil!

I reckon you'll be lucky (or unlucky) to be alive in five years time. Self-neglect could all too easily be the cause of your demise. There will most definitely be no more relationships for you, unless they're abusive ones. Just like that time after Julia's death when you toyed with the idea of seeking out a prostitute:

*'... to find physical comfort and warmth again.'*

How pathetic and sad!

Frankly, I think it will all prove too much for you and you'll end by taking your own life.

I don't really need to do any more. But then, I've always been ready and willing to go the extra mile.

I wish you were able to appreciate the superb construction of the closing scenes I've got planned for you.

All subject to certain conditions being in place of course!

Before the end, I hope to give you a chance to reflect on what has happened to you.

But long before that, just as everyone is willing to believe Michael Chilvers was bumped off by the Russian mafia, it's all got to make perfect sense. At least you and everyone else will think it does! Tee hee hee!

## 12

The dawn finally arrived. But for Gil it didn't bring those feelings of relief, hope and renewal so often associated with a new day. As the morning drew on, a stream of people attempted to contact him: friends and colleagues who wanted to commiserate, the police with still more questions, and journalists, who, not content with besieging his home from the outside, were electronically bombarding it via telephone and email.

The young female constable who had remained with him throughout the night had batted off any unwanted phone calls, just as the police officer stationed outside had done with physical callers. During the night, Gil had undergone mental torment, constantly returning to and reliving that hideous scene. He'd been so utterly preoccupied that he hadn't even thought to ask this helpful young woman her name. In fact, it only occurred to him to ask when she was about to be relieved.

"I'm sorry, you've been very kind … I should have asked your name …"

The girl smiled sympathetically, "That's okay, Mr Harper. You've had quite a lot on your plate, so I'll forgive you. I'm PC Amy Shaw."

"Thank you for your help, Amy," he said with genuine gratitude.

Patrick Small heard about the double murder in the middle of the night from journalists. He in turn had rung Megan and had broken the news to her with a great deal more sensitivity than he'd been afforded by the press. She had driven round to Gil's at once.

It was Megan who contacted Sally, who in turn called Klaus Williams to explain why she must suddenly desert the production. Sally then drove from Manchester, without making any stops en route, and got to Sevenoaks by midday.

Gil sprang to his feet when she arrived and they clung to each other in a long embrace. Sally sobbed. Gil shook. He felt completely numb.

"Oh Gil, Gil … Felix … Kate … you poor thing!" she wept.

He lowered his head onto her shoulder.

Gil felt like an observer rather than an active participant. He wanted more than anything to comfort her, but didn't seem to have any of the right words. He patted her gently on the back but the gesture felt empty, impotent and futile.

## 13

Throughout the days ahead, true to her nature, Megan made herself useful. She contacted everyone Gil needed to communicate with and skilfully kept at bay pack-hunting predators, like the tabloid press. To assist in this, she helped formulate a statement on Gil's behalf, which was released via Patrick Small's office. Like Sally, Megan was terribly worried about Gil. Both women feared he might easily crack from the intolerable strain he was under.

Gil was of course both grateful and glad that Sally had abandoned her busy schedule to be with him. However, any ability to express how he felt either by word or deed now seemed to abandon him. At times, he was rather tetchy with Sally, even though he had never meant to be. Occasionally, he gave the distinct impression that she was superfluous, even crowding his space.

Four days on from Kate and Felix's deaths, gloom, despondency and an indescribable tension seemed to pervade the house. Even Spike spent these days curled up at Gil's feet, silent but for an occasional sigh.

On Monday morning, Sally burst into Megan's office sobbing, "I just w-wanted to be with h-him … but he doesn't seem to w-want me around …"

"Of course he does," placated Megan, "He's undergone a dreadful experience and his mind's been thrown into confusion. Believe me he cares about you a very great deal."

Amongst her many other roles over these unhappy days, Megan had become Sally's confidante and counsellor, "He just needs time to assimilate all that's happened. Let's face it, we all do … but he was there, he found them …" Megan was unable to suppress an involuntary shiver as she thought about the sight that must have met him.

"I know, I know. I'm just being selfish," Sally began upbraiding herself, "Thinking about myself and my own feelings, not how much Gil must be hurting."

Megan shook her head, "Now you're just putting yourself down … there's no need, it's not easy for you either."

"It's just that it's hard to watch that lovely man looking so desperate," said Sally, beginning to cry again.

Sally had cried so much. As indeed had Megan privately, often disappearing into the loo when her tears could no longer be held back. The house had seemed awash in tears. The majority of Gil's friends who had come to offer sympathy had shed a few before leaving. The sheer brutality of the crimes seemed to exert a powerful effect upon everyone. Throughout these visits, Gil had been present physically, but certainly not mentally or emotionally. Nevertheless, he somehow managed to maintain a polite impassivity; but inside, he remained altogether numb. And despite the grief and sadness being openly expressed around him, Gil discovered himself unable to shed a single tear.

"I know he'll get through this," consoled Megan, "He's far stronger than people give him credit for. A lot thought he'd never recover after Julia, but he did. He bravely plodded on through some very dark years. He got quite depressed at times, but he clung on, continued to work. His world lightened a little, then he met you and his spirits really began to lift. You made him truly happy once more."

"And look at what I came with … nothing but bad luck!" wept Sally.

"Don't say that," scolded Megan, "Whoever was behind this, had nothing whatsoever to do with you." She paused momentarily before going on, "He may give the impression of ambivalence towards you … but that's only because he's feeling so dreadful. You must surely know how much in love with you he is?"

Sally burst into deep sobs again. Megan hugged her and whispered soothing words of comfort. There were tears in the corners of the older woman's eyes too as she considered the positive spin she'd attached to Gil's ability to recover. She recalled how worried his friends had been about him after the crash; how fundamental Kate and Felix had been to his recovery; like towers of light when he had been adrift in an ocean of darkness, pillars of strength at moments of deepest despair.

Yet, for all these brave words of encouragement, Megan wondered if Gil could truly get over what had happened. And deep down, though she kept her own counsel on this, she wasn't certain at all.

## 14

Sally stayed until the following weekend. Then she rejoined the company to prepare for the London previews and first night. She had found it a hard decision to make. It felt like she was abandoning Gil in his hour of need. But then, it wasn't fair to let Roz and the other colleagues who had so resolutely stood in for her at Bristol, make final preparations and shoulder responsibility for the London opening.

The steadfast Megan had encouraged her to go. From the older woman's perspective, the present situation was putting Gil and Sally's relationship under a colossal strain. Megan believed a time apart might help Gil focus, see the good thing his unintentional neglect might be in danger of losing.

Although Gil said nothing to Sally directly he understood her reasons for going. He was aware too of how dreadful it must be for everyone to be around him; he felt cut off from life, emotionally shut-down and unable to communicate. However, being in this frozen state didn't mean he couldn't actually experience emotions or feel the pain associated with them. The idea of Sally being stalked by the killer, unidentified and still out there, gripped him at moments with a paralysing terror.

Strangely, the only person Gil felt able to confide in was Mullings, "I'm worried for her safety, Chief Inspector."

"Of course. I can assure you that Miss Curtis will be the subject of round the clock surveillance," replied the policeman.

"I know a lot of people," said Gil. He stated this as a grim fact before going on to say, "There are over three hundred names on my Christmas card database, at least half that number I'd call friends." He felt like a plague-carrier, bringing destruction to those unfortunate enough to enter his orbit, a harbinger of death.

Mullings nodded sympathetically.

"Do you intend to watch over all of them? Can you offer everyone I know protection, or is it going to be the luck of the draw?"

The tone of Mullings' voice hinted at the pressure and burden of responsibility he was experiencing as officer in charge, "This is not an enviable position to be in … not for you, the victim of crime, or for us its investigators. It would be dishonest of me to suggest that we are even close to solving this case. Having said that, a piece of evidence might appear and change everything, forensic might suddenly discover something … you can never tell when a case is going to break."

Mullings paused to clear his throat, "But I can assure you that every avenue of investigation, however remote or seemingly implausible, is being vigorously pursued. So far, I admit every lead has got us nowhere. Whoever is behind this prepared meticulously, they haven't left us much of a trail to follow. We can only advise everyone close to you, to be vigilant. We're concentrating our resources on people you mention in your diary regularly. The Paddick family is being shadowed to and from school and work … the same goes for Mrs Hollingsworth and your agent, Mr Small. The Somerset force is keeping an eye for us on your late wife's parents."

"I feel responsible … to think just knowing me could get you killed!"

"We don't know that's the reasoning behind these killings, but I can understand how you feel."

"Do you think you can?" asked Gil. He put the question straightforwardly without a trace of self-pity.

Mullings pursed his lips, "Let's say I empathise, then."

Gil sighed. Although desperately frustrated with the investigation, he wasn't angry with Mullings. He had never doubted the man was leading a thorough inquiry, doing everything in his power to apprehend the killer.

"Any luck with the names you asked for?" enquired Gil, without holding out much hope of a positive reply.

Mullings shook his head, "Nothing so far."

Five days earlier, Gil had been asked to compile a list. It included anyone who may, at any time, have harboured a grudge, real or imagined, against him. It was to include kids he hadn't got on with at school, students at the Slade, contemporaries or rivals who might be jealous of his success, past difficulties and disputes with neighbours, minor prangs he'd had in cars, even altercations in shops and any obsessive fan mail he or Felix had ever received. The list had taken hours to complete.

Inevitably, the name Geoff Owens had cropped up again in the course of this. Kent Police had checked out Owens' whereabouts, as a matter of course, within hours of Felix and Kate's deaths. Several eyewitnesses had seen Owens walking home from the local pub along a footpath around 9.30 pm. It had been early for him to leave the pub as he generally stuck around until closing. He had told the barmaid he was expecting a phone call. Geoff Owens didn't own a mobile phone apparently. It was just about feasible for Owens to travel the twenty odd miles from Speldhurst, to reach East Peckham in time to have committed the murders. However, Geoff Owens not only didn't possess a driving licence, but far more significantly didn't own a vehicle. If Owens had been driving about illegally, and to the extent suggested by the case, Mullings felt certain someone would have seen him and come forward; he was not a popular character locally. There was also a question of motive. It was difficult enough to see a reason for murdering the elderly children's author and his wife, let alone connect Owens with Michael Chilvers. Lastly, the murderer had left imprints of his wellington boots in the soft grass verge outside Felix and Kate's oast. It was one of the few bits of tangible evidence the police possessed; Owens wore size nine shoes but the killer had been wearing size eleven.

"I read a newspaper article this morning which implied I may have had more of a hand in Felix and Kate's deaths than appeared to be the case at first glance," said Gil. He was referring to a foul little piece in one of the daily rags renowned for its invective. "Did you read it?"

"I read it," replied Mullings, "I suppose these people have to write something contentious every day to guarantee readership and keep their big fat pay cheques rolling in."

The paper had revealed that Gil was the main beneficiary in Felix and Kate's will, a fact which had stunned Gil when he'd been contacted by Felix's solicitor only twenty-four hours before the article was printed. The source of poison was obvious: the paper had interviewed the Blatts' nephew, a man Felix had found detestably creepy and insincere. The nephew's wife, also quoted in the article, and who in Felix's view had been as equally loathsome as her husband, was reported as saying, '*Poor Uncle Felix was taken in for years by the fairly talentless Harper.*'

"You don't think I orchestrated this, to get my hands on the money?" asked Gil.

"Mr Harper, I'm a copper, I check everything," replied Mullings. "You own a big house that's all paid for and you earn a lot more money than you spend. I'd find it hard to see a money motive. I expect your bank manager is always pleased to invite you to lunch, which is more than can be said for my relationship with my own bank … I doubt the manager even knows I exist."

Gil smiled. It was probably the first time since Felix and Kate's deaths. "I think the reference to 'the fairly talentless Harper' is what rattled my cage!"

An uncommonly vindictive thought then suddenly occurred itself to Gil. He looked up about to speak.

But the Chief Inspector was already there, "Like I said … I'm a copper. Mr Blatt's nephew was having dinner at his old Oxford College."

Gil managed to share a wry smile with Mullings.

## 15

Two hours later, in the early evening, when Gil and Spike were alone in the house, Gil received a text on his mobile:

J U L E S

## 16

Sunday 1 March

First, I must apologise.

J U L E S

Alright, I admit it's repetitive.

Well almost.

NB I deliberately changed all the letters to capitals just to add a soupçon of uncertainty.

I'm certain it couldn't have failed to grab your attention!

You wouldn't remember, but around the time I poisoned your pooch, I abandoned my observation of you for a short time. Needless to say, I was totally occupied. <u>It's not easy to befriend the friendless and unloved</u>.

Although, I can't tell a lie, it was less difficult than I'd anticipated. At first it was necessary to look like I wasn't really trying to gain his trust. Pariahs don't do trust and think suspicious thoughts about anyone wanting to make friends with them. So it demanded time, patience and skill.

Eventually, I had him eating out of my hand.

Not literally, I'm pleased to say!

I found him repellent, sad and sorry for himself.

I despise him.

Fortunately, my loathing and contempt is not reciprocated. Our friendship has brought him a new lease of life. He's even trying to drink less. Recently he confided in me that he's hooked on tranquilisers. He went on to solemnly swear to get help after we've gone into business.

Oh yes, we're going into business together!

At least, he believes it!

<u>Imagine</u>! He thinks we're going into business together to manufacture garden furniture. You see, I had to gain his trust. It started simply. I am so inventive. I complimented him on some garden furniture he'd made out of reclaimed timber. He's actually quite skilful at making things, can turn his hand to anything in fact, even mechanical things. Funnily enough, he'll shortly be doing a car repair for me. It seemed a waste to leave his garage empty. I'm certain he'll do a good job. Of course, there won't be anything wrong with the car, apart from the bits and pieces I've tinkered with.

His fingerprints will of course be all over it like a rash.

Anyway, I ran with the garden furniture idea. I praised his skills to the hilt. Took photographs of the stuff he'd made. All the time a plan was formulating. I asked him if he could think of other designs. He enthusiastically produced whatever I asked for like a performing seal. I told him I had a business acquaintance who owned a large share in a chain of garden centres in the north-east. I said I'd like to test them out on him, see what he thought.

From the look of gratitude on his pathetic puppy-dog face, you'd think I'd just saved the lives of his children (little bit of a sick joke there. Sorry!).

The next bit I teased out superbly.

"What did your friend say?" he kept asking with dog-like eagerness.

"Sorry, hasn't got back yet."

"Have you heard anything?"

"He likes them but he's not sure."

(Looks dejected)

"He'll need to show them to his Sales Manager before he can commit."

(Hope rises)

"Have you heard any more ... the Sales Manager?"

"Nothing. Sorry."

I kept him on tenterhooks for weeks.

I was a bit concerned he'd start blabbing. I needn't have worried. He's totally paranoid (the pills probably). He thinks everyone is out to steal his garden furniture designs.

The moron hasn't spoken to anyone about our business plan! What a sucker!

The night I dispatched the Blatts to the Great Children's Book Club in the Sky, I was thought by our friend to be in Newcastle, discussing garden furniture.

I'd arranged to call him at home at 9.45.

It was quite touching to hear the excitement in his voice when I told him we'd received an initial order for ten sets of furniture.

Then he suddenly went quiet. There was an awkward silence.

I thought perhaps I'd slipped up in some way.

I asked him what was wrong.

He confessed he didn't have any money to buy the materials and get started.

I told him, "What's the problem?"

So, I had to cough up for a load of timber he's having delivered on Wednesday. Expensive, but not too expensive, it's reclaimed timber because the project has an environmental angle. Anyway, like I said, "That's what friends do, Geoffrey."

"Maybe I can repay you by doing you a favour some time?" he said.

"Well, there is one thing ... <u>I wonder if you could take a look at an old Ford Galaxy I've got</u>?"

17

The police wasted no time investigating the text message. Unfortunately very little could be ascertained from it. The word JULES had been sent via a pay-as-you-go phone, and the sim card proved untraceable.

A day later, Gil received a second text: 'an eye for an eye – tooth for a tooth'.

However, Mullings and Jackson appeared to be less than certain about the authenticity of either of the messages.

"It must be him!" insisted Gil.

"It's possible," replied Jackson, "It was sent via another pay-as-you-go mobile."

But Mullings clearly remained unconvinced.

"It has to be the killer ... both the texts," stated Gil, now staring incredulously at Mullings, "Who else, then? He deliberately chose my wife's nickname, just like he scrawled it across her portrait ... to let me know he'd got into my computer!"

Mullings didn't share this certainty at all, "The damage to the portrait has recently been reported in the media. In the first text, your wife's name was written in block capitals. Passwords are generally case sensitive, and on your computer it was only capitalised in its first letter. Our killer adopted this form exactly when the portrait was defaced. We deliberately misinformed the press that your wife's name was scrawled over the painting in upper case, but the killer would certainly recognise this as incorrect."

Gil was exasperated by what seemed rather simplistic reasoning. "So you're saying these were hoax texts?" Gil could feel his hackles begin to rise.

"Mr Harper, I'm trying not to make assumptions ... but I think you are. As for hoax callers, sadly, a lot of investigations are hindered and many hours lost, dealing with them. It's hard to believe but there are people who think it's amusing to feed the police misleading information."

Since the murders, Gil had acquired a haunted expression and more grey in his hair. He feared many things at this time. But ironically, one recurring thought that troubled him a great deal, was that the killer had finished with him and he would have to spend the rest of his life in a state of limbo; never being certain, constantly checking over his shoulder, forever anxious for those he cared about.

Gil took in a deep breath and sighed, "It just felt like him, that's all."

"It may well be," replied Mullings. "Assuming it is, not some prankster having fun, we need to ask why? Why does he choose to communicate with you at this moment, and why in this particular way? What does he want us to think? Is he trying to manipulate us, get us to believe something?"

Jackson spoke next and voiced exactly what Gil was thinking, "Certainly, 'An eye for an eye' etc sounds like vengeance, retribution."

"It immediately made me think of the accident," said Gil.

"But that doesn't make sense," said Mullings. "Seeking vengeance for an accident nobody ever believed was your fault in the first place? And if vengeance really was the motive, why was Michael Chilvers killed?"

"To get me convicted for murder," retorted Gil.

"No. We've been over that," stated Mullings, showing a little exasperation himself now, his voice uncharacteristically raised. The case was taking its toll on everyone. He paused, his tone less strained when he spoke again, "Whoever killed Mr Chilvers planned meticulously. They knew you'd be at the Paddicks' party. They wanted to get you rattled, leave their calling card, but didn't want to land you in too much trouble. They made sure you had a cast-iron alibi."

Gil shook his head despondently, "Christ, what's he after?"

"It's like a vendetta," interjected Jackson.

Mullings immediately glanced across at his colleague. "Vendetta? A vendetta is personal. Is it really personal ... or does the killer want us to believe it is?"

"There surely has to be a reason, some motive?" said Gil, horrified by the idea of murder without cause.

"Oh, there's definitely a motive ... in the mind of the killer," said Mullings.

## 18

Three days later, a third text arrived. Unlike the first two, this one came via the landline.

Gil glanced at his watch when the phone rang. It was 9.47 pm, too early for Sally. He hesitated. Ever since the call from the bogus doctor, Gil had flinched whenever the phone rang, especially in the evenings with just him and Spike at home.

He picked up the handset. He'd got into the habit of not speaking first.

The messaging service informed there was a voice text. It reeled off a mobile phone number then gave the time Gil had already noted.

Another automated female voice then went on to deliver the actual message with robotic precision:

*'This is where it ends.*

*'You will never be able to understand why I did this.*

*'You took three lives precious to me. It doesn't matter who was to blame. I've suffered, served my sentence. I wanted you to understand how I've felt the past five years.*

*'Now we're quits. Your wife, Felix and Kate Blatt. Three for three. I'll let you keep the dog. Do you remember our dog was in the back of the truck with my children and had to be put down?*

*'I'm sorry about Chilvers. A red herring, to throw everyone off my scent.*

*'It's over.*

*'I hope you live a long and painful life.'*

Once the message ended, Gil was left reeling like a drunken man. He was finding it hard to breathe, the blood was screaming through his head, ears ringing, heart pounding. Spike, recognising something was not quite right with his master, made small circular manoeuvres about his feet and began to whimper.

Gil covered his mouth with his hand until the shock had subsided enough to replay the message. The main gist of it was straightforward, but the unusual stresses and inflections of the automated delivery had made parts of the message difficult to grasp first off.

But this time its meaning was crystal clear.

He muttered Geoff Owens' name under his breath, in a flat, passionless tone.

Despite any assertions made by the police to the contrary, Geoff Owens was the only person it logically could be. Gil could see this.

From that moment, Gil behaved like a man in a trance. He took his jacket from its peg in the hall and put it on.

"Stay here," he told Spike. The poor dog was unusually agitated by the sight of his master getting ready to leave the house.

The Skoda was parked on the drive. Gil hadn't liked using the garage much after it had been the focus of so much forensic scrutiny. In fact, whenever he stood inside its four walls he immediately felt anxious and trapped.

He started the engine, turned on the headlights and exited the drive; giving no thought for the plain-clothed policeman he knew must be out there somewhere.

## 19

The drive to the village of Speldhurst took less than twenty minutes. He took the A21, came off at Tonbridge, headed through Southborough, then turned off for Speldhurst.

He knew the way. For nearly two years after Julia's death he had been compelled to make this journey quite regularly. Sometimes he'd parked in the woodland a discreet distance from Owens' cottage where he'd sit for an hour or so. At other times he had merely driven past the cottage. He had never understood why, particularly since Owens was in prison at the time. But while the thing lasted he'd been utterly compelled to do it.

Gil had made reference to these nocturnal visits in his journal only once:

> ... I suspect they must have had something to do with the arbitrary nature of existence and the devastating impact one single moment, bad timing and sheer error of judgement can have upon so many lives ...

He had never spoken directly to Owens. They had each, of course, observed the other, at the inquest and at Owens' subsequent trial, but there had been an almost tacit agreement never to approach. Neither man could have said anything the other would ever want or hope to hear.

Gil made no attempt to hide his presence now. He left his car on a weed-infested patch of tarmac on the short neglected driveway which led to a badly dilapidated, pre-fabricated garage. The wretched building stood about ten yards to the side of Owens' cottage. The main building was itself in need of renovation, and had deteriorated considerably through neglect since the days of Gil's first visits. The ground about the cottage told of Owens' former livelihood as a landscape gardener, with rusting machinery, old railway sleepers, mounds of stone, brick, slate and other materials, partly hidden beneath bramble bushes and overgrown vegetation.

Owens had failed to be consistent at anything since the accident, and now his cottage, sited on one of the back lanes of the village and standing alone in a depression at the base of two small hills, was in chronic disarray.

As Gil stepped from the car an owl hooted, and somewhere in the darkness of the surrounding woods a small creature shrieked before all lapsed into silence again. The night was icy and still, eeriness seemed to ooze from the cottage. Every window was illuminated and light spilled from the hall through the open front door.

Gil didn't even hesitate. A few weeks ago, before Felix and Kate, before Chilvers or Spike's poisoning, he wouldn't have left the safety of his car. He no longer cared; he was here for closure, whatever the cost. As he reached the garage he saw one of its doors was slightly ajar. He noticed, without displaying any emotion, that it contained a car very like the one he'd seen on Sevenoaks High Street.

Despite finding it difficult to think straight and engage in any clear or rational thought, Gil appreciated he was meant to see this. That it was all for him, meticulously arranged, like a piece of performance art. He didn't linger at the garage. He was being drawn, as if by magnetism or some other force, towards the front door. Alongside the garage he passed a neatly-stacked pile of timber, out of place in the shambolic chaos surrounding the cottage.

If Gil heard the car stop behind him and the police officer call out his name, he gave no indication of it.

Nothing could make him stop now.

He reached the front door, a solitary, forlorn figure, accentuated by the light spilling from the hall and stairwell.

"Mr Harper, please, wait ... DCI Mullings is on his way!" called the policeman.

Gil paused. His head inclined briefly at the mention of Mullings' name.

Then he walked into the cottage.

## 20

"Fuck," mouthed the police officer under his breath. It would be at least ten minutes before back-up arrived; waiting didn't seem like an option. At that moment he was grateful that due to the brutality of the Blatts' murders he was carrying a gun. He withdrew it from its holster, checked the safety catch and followed the path Gil Harper had taken.

When he reached the front door he saw that Harper had almost ascended the flight of stairs ahead and was just turning right onto the landing. He decided against calling out again. He cautiously entered the hall. It was an advantage that everywhere was so well-lit. The two rooms right and left of the hall had their doors wide open. The policeman took no chances as he checked both these rooms before resuming his pursuit.

As he began to climb the staircase the officer became aware of water dripping onto the worn-out stair carpet from the landing above. The further up he went, the wetter it became. The water was not clear, appearing brown against the muddy green colour of the carpet. There was too the sweet metallic smell he always associated with blood. It caused the hairs at the back of his neck to rise.

The police officer reached the top step and turned right. Gil Harper was less than ten feet away, standing completely still, staring into a room through its open door. Judging from the sound of taps running and the amount of water swishing around his feet it was a bathroom.

The policeman approached tentatively.

Gil's face was devoid of readable emotion. But the officer noticed that tears were freely flowing down his cheeks.

When the policeman was almost level with him, still taking no chances, he suddenly sprang forward to check the room. "Christ!" he gasped. His free hand flew involuntarily to his mouth.

It was indeed a bathroom. Lying in its overflowing tub with both taps open was Geoff Owens; his eyes wearing the dull, filmy stare only the dead possess. One arm had floated above the water and was dangling palm-up over the edge of the bath; the lacerations to the wrist were deep and the flesh had drained parchment white around the wounds.

There was nothing that could be done, except turn off the taps, get Harper out, and help preserve as much evidence as possible.

## 21

From the dark interior of a police car, Gil watched with hypnotic fascination as evidence gatherers, like bees around a hive, secured the crime scene. Although he couldn't stop shaking, he was not quite as distraught as he had been when he'd come upon Owens' reclining corpse, bloodless and still, an alabaster statue in the overflowing tub. Mullings was amongst the first to arrive at the crime scene and they had spoken together briefly. Later, Gil retained only the haziest recollection of this meeting.

Shortly afterwards, Gil was taken to Maidstone Police Station, where he spent a good deal of the remaining night.

The experience was considerably different to his first visit to Maidstone Police Station, when he'd been suspected of running down Michael Chilvers. This time, he was regularly asked if he was okay and taken to the canteen for rests and cups of tea. PC Amy Shaw, who had sat with him throughout the night Kate and Felix were murdered, was assigned to him again. It was comforting to have a friendly face at his side.

A doctor was called out to examine him and presented him with a pill, which he dutifully took without any resistance. Whatever the medication was, it certainly worked, and after a short time he felt far less emotionally fraught. In due course, he was able to answer questions and went on to give a statement.

## 22

It was 6 am when Mullings and Jackson left the incident scene in Speldhurst.

It had been a demanding night and DCI Mullings did not look entirely at ease with himself. He sensed he was out of step with a prevailing view amongst his colleagues that the case, bar a few loose ends, was over. Indeed, Mullings, as the person with overall responsibility, could not recall working on such a case before, or one that had caused him quite so many sleepless nights. Yet, despite these frustrations, he retained powerful misgivings about the conclusions everyone now seemed so eager to embrace.

On the journey to Maidstone with DI Jackson, Mullings confided, "It's too damned neat, too perfect."

Jackson's eyes remained implacably fixed on the road ahead. He volunteered no opinion.

DCI Mullings took this to mean that his young colleague did not intend to be drawn in. They had finally been given a break; let sleeping dogs lie.

Mullings used the next minutes, spent in silence, to review the recent developments in the case. There had been a confession, at least something closely resembling one, comprehensive and detailed. If this was true, then Geoff Owens had recorded his nefarious activities on a laptop, a piece of equipment nobody had previously known about. The account was written intermittently in a diary format and it described in detail the surveillance of Gil Harper, the opportunistic break-in of Harper's home and the acquisition of the diary and security codes. It went on to record the poisoning of the dog and how Michael Chilvers had been run down using Harper's car. Then, perhaps more significantly if this vengeance driven account was to be upheld, it described in chillingly casual detail the murders of Kate and Felix Blatt.

It was a factually plausible account that covered exactly two months, from 5 January right up to 5 March. The last entry had been written approximately an hour before the final voice text was sent to Gil Harper, and included the following:

... Since the accident that robbed me of my two beautiful children and drove my wife to take her own life ... the only way I could carry on was by knowing that one day I'd set things right with Harper. I never accepted that judge's verdict. How could I be responsible for everything? How is it possible for two cars to collide but for only one driver to be to blame? They said I was drunk which is rubbish ...

After a while, DCI Mullings spoke again. Jackson presumed that the words were directed at him; his senior officer was in fact merely thinking aloud. "But it still couldn't have been Owens on the M25," he said. He was referring to the fact that Geoff Owens had an alibi over the Christmas period, when he'd spent ten days with his sister and her family in Hastings.

"Alibis have a habit of falling apart once the solid evidence stacks up," replied Jackson.

"That's always a possibility," replied Mullings, "But if he had done it, don't you think he'd have mentioned it? Owens was pretty candid on the laptop about everything else."

"Perhaps the answer is we'll never know. I mean, maybe that particular incident was down to Michael Chilvers after all?" said the younger man, with an air of impatience.

"None of the prints on the paint-can matched either man, Owens or Chilvers. But, I don't know … Chilvers had an impetuous nature, if the paint really was down to him, then I'd be surprised not to find something, wouldn't you?"

Jackson shrugged his shoulders and grunted.

Mullings, unperturbed by his colleague's offhanded response, went on, "But imagine the planning and co-ordination required … whether it was Chilvers or Owens on that road? They'd have needed to pursue Harper all the way from Somerset! Not an easy feat."

"Perhaps it was a joy-rider then, after all!" said Jackson.

"If so, it was an enormous coincidence, don't you think?"

Jackson said nothing.

Mullings closed his eyes while he turned over in his mind the statement he was about to make. His eyelids remained shut as he said, "There is of course always a possibility … that our killer wasn't Owens."

The silence afterwards seemed to be electrically charged.

Mullings predicted the younger man's reticence would prove to be an accurate gauge of opinion amongst his colleagues. After all the bad publicity the investigation had attracted, it wouldn't be hard to picture the top brass's eagerness to kiss it goodbye. Mullings, a lifelong church-goer, a man whose life was founded on faith and belief, suddenly found himself in the position of heretic.

Then, after what seemed an interminable silence, Jackson stated categorically, "We've got Owens' confession."

Mullings pursed his lips. As he sat shrouded in the dark of the passenger seat, he knew that if he persisted with this he would be out on a limb. Jackson's view would remain the unshakeable position of most of his colleagues, and it could be taken as read that at the senior management end a huge corporate sigh of relief would be heard. There would be no burning desire to challenge the authenticity of the laptop account; in fact, even Mullings found the arguments in its favour compelling. He wanted to believe, but then, he had a policeman's nose; something just smelt wrong.

As for Jackson's opposition, it wasn't personal. He was only doing what politicians the world over did instinctively. He was simply distancing himself from any perceived errors it must now be assumed were made, during an investigation that had allowed an obvious suspect a free rein to commit three murders.

Mullings considered the matter too important to let it drop, "Don't you think it's a little unusual to be handed so many answers in one go? The difficulty all along has been a lack of physical evidence. Up until a few hours ago we had nothing, absolutely nothing, on Geoff Owens. Suddenly, we have the car, the knife, boots, clothing … even Harper's driving licence ... as well as a laptop confession linking him with all three murders!"

Jackson came back at once, "Owens wanted to rub our noses in it, let us know how clever he'd been, show us what meticulous planning he'd done. It sounds to me like you just don't want to accept he wrong-footed us!" There was a detectable note of anger in his voice as he reiterated, "We have his confession!"

"No!" stated Mullings emphatically, "We've been given a plausible, and I daresay authentic account, but we're having to assume it was Geoff Owens who wrote it!"

"I think that's very unlikely ... I mean, what would be the point?" enquired an incredulous Jackson. There was a pause, then he added "And there's nothing, no evidence, to suggest Owens didn't take his own life!"

Mullings made no reply; he merely nodded in the darkness.

## 23

Friday the sixth of March was the London first night for Verdi's *Macbeth*.

As soon as she heard, Sally dropped everything, abandoning her links with the production at the very last minute. It didn't matter, as far as she was concerned her feelings for Gil far outstripped any ambition she possessed.

Sally's colleagues were supportive and understood completely. And Klaus was expressing the views of just about everyone in the company when he assured her, "Don't you worry about us, darling. That lovely man of yours needs you far more than we do. Anyway, you've done everything ... the cozzies look marvellous! No, darling, it's all over now, bar the fucking songs!"

Just as before, Gil could be difficult and short with Sally at times and often gave her the impression she was in his way. Megan continued to provide stalwart support to both of them, and without her, the relationship might not have survived the particularly dreadful days that followed Geoff Owens' shortly to be confirmed suicide.

There were days when Gil went off alone, not even taking Spike. He would sometimes return hours later, offering no explanation of where he'd been; the state of his footwear suggesting walks over muddy tracks. The former intimacy between Gil and Sally had all but ground to a halt. Apart from an undemonstrative kiss at bedtime and the fact they shared a bed, they might have been close friends. For Sally, shedding a tear on Megan's shoulder remained a daily occurrence.

When the bodies of Kate and Felix were released for burial, the solicitors acting as their executors approached Gil, as the will's main beneficiary, to assist with funeral planning. Of course, he immediately agreed to help. The organisational process required him to contact large numbers of people. And many of these, perhaps to relieve their own sense of horror, wanted to discuss with him in some detail what had happened.

This in turn forced Gil to open up, and the process became in some ways a kind of talking cure.

## 24

The post-mortem on Owens was concluded swiftly. The large quantities of alcohol and tranquilisers found in his bloodstream were consistent with the description, assumed to be in Owens' own words, of his final act of violence, this time against himself. In fact, suicide was referred to several times throughout the laptop account as 'taking the Roman option'. Thus far, nothing had come to light to question this.

After the Owens post-mortem, Mullings was summoned to the office of the Deputy Chief Constable.

"The papers will no doubt make out we behaved like Laurel and Hardy," commented the Deputy Chief Constable acerbically.

"Every single lead was methodically pursued," replied Mullings, unabashed. "The killer covered his tracks very carefully."

"I appreciate that, John," the DCC replied haughtily, "However, the press can be relied upon to highlight our failure to apprehend Owens earlier. They are extremely focused on this case ... Felix Blatt was a national celebrity."

"They should study the course of the investigation. Nothing suggested Owens could possibly be responsible. In fact, nobody has yet come forward to say they saw him in the vehicle he claims to have used ... or, for that matter, ever saw him in any vehicle at all after he was banned from driving!"

"He was extremely cautious, by his own account the car was hidden in woods near his home."

"But where exactly, and why haven't we found the tracks? And why didn't anyone notice it hidden there?"

"Are you actually disputing the evidence, Chief Inspector?"

"The only *evidence*," answered Mullings, "is what we've been told to believe, by a laptop, conveniently found at Owens' house."

"Come, come!" was the immediate response of the DCC. The man's naturally sanguine features suddenly grew in depth and shade to a colour resembling tawny port, "Unless you can back up these views with some compelling evidence, I'm afraid your reservations sound like bitterness and sour grapes."

Mullings opened his mouth to interject but thought better of it. Nothing would be gained.

The Deputy Chief Constable changed tack. He smiled understandingly, his high colour fading to a less dramatic hue, "This situation isn't easy, John ... not for anyone. Your record is first-class and it isn't being disputed. However, I've heard it said in some circles, and believe me, I'm not personally in agreement with this view, that two lives may have been saved had certain questions been asked."

Mullings really disliked it when the top brass became all reasonable and cuddly.

The Deputy Chief Constable paused to smile with shark-like sincerity, "Under the circumstances the authority would understand entirely, and indeed wish to back you up, should you choose to take early retirement."

Mullings wasn't entirely surprised. Even so, it still came as a shock. He felt his hands trembling with emotion as he replied, "I wish I'd been able to prevent the deaths of Mr and Mrs Blatt, sir. However, I remain satisfied with the investigation I led. I believe the right lines of inquiry were pursued, and I have no plans to take early retirement."

The DCC looked across the table at Mullings with a face like thunder, "Then I have to advise you, should any discrepancies or shortcomings in your current investigation be uncovered, the authority may have no option but to take disciplinary proceedings on grounds of incompetence against you. This may result in loss of rank, or possibly dismissal. I should remind you too, that such a situation may prove detrimental to any final salary pension, which would be a shame, after so many years of loyal service."

Mullings swallowed hard and nodded.

## 25

The date fixed for the funeral was Wednesday the eighteenth of March.

The evening before, Gil took Sally to dinner. It was the first time they had been out together since those happy few days in Manchester, which now seemed eons past.

"I wanted to say thanks for sticking me out," said Gil, "I know I've been difficult."

"If you weren't affected by what happened to you, then you probably wouldn't be someone I'd care about much," Sally replied.

"I've been selfish," he said.

"You were traumatised," replied Sally, dabbing at a tear that was forming in her eye with the corner of a napkin.

"It's not only me though, is it? You were caught up too … when Michael was killed."

Sally nodded, "I'll admit, it wasn't easy … but then I wasn't the one who found him! And let's face it, I didn't have too many warm memories of Michael," she said, before adding, "Even so, I still wouldn't have wished what happened …"

"'Course not."

"I break out in a cold sweat to think my friends could believe for one minute I might have done it!"

"They were only trying to protect you."

"I know," she replied, "but it makes you wonder, what do people imagine you're capable of?"

Gil shook his head, "Who knows what any of us is capable of under certain circumstances? When I drove to Geoff Owens' house that night …" he stalled momentarily before going on, "If he'd been alive … I really don't know what I'd have done."

For a moment, the haunted expression that had taken possession of him for so many days flickered back into his eyes.

"Poor love," said Sally, taking his hands in hers. Her eyes were filling up with tears again. "And you've got the hardest day of all tomorrow," she said, meaning the funeral.

"Not hardest," he replied, "I'm not looking forward to it … but I know from experience, it'll at least bring closure."

Sally understood this and nodded.

"I wanted to talk to you about after the funeral," he began. "I wanted to ask if you'd still consider coming away to Wales with me … like we'd planned once the opera opened."

Sally smiled, "Yes, yes of course, I'd love to," she said. She hadn't forgotten their plan, but the opera's opening night was now almost two weeks ago, and she assumed Gil had given up on the idea. Sally would have been in favour of anything that might help rekindle their relationship.

"I'd understand if you didn't want to!" put in Gil, "I've been such an almighty pain … I'd understand if you …"

"Gil?"

"Yes?"

"Just shut the fuck up! I'd love to come."

Gil smiled. He felt happier at that moment than he had done in weeks.

"Where is it again?"

Gil laughed, "West Wales, near a place called Llangrannog, on the Ceredigion coast."

"Sounds lovely."

"I wouldn't describe it as lovely. It's pretty basic - a tiny farm labourer's cottage - but I've always loved it. The coastline is stunning - rugged and very beautiful."

If Sally had any reservations at all she didn't show it. "I can't wait," she said.

## 26

Gil had given the funeral planning a great deal of thought. It was a practical way of expressing his love and respect for Felix and Kate. Opting for a joint funeral seemed an obvious choice for two people who had spent such a large portion of their lives together, and what's more, the thought of two separate funerals seemed like an unnecessarily grim prospect.

Those attending were met by an excerpt from Faure's Requiem, and they would exit the church to The Song of the Birds by Pablo Casals. Gil found the picking of the hymns enormously difficult and he enlisted Megan's help here.

It was touching to witness the large number of children accompanied by a grown-up who came. The church itself barely managed to seat those invited, let alone accommodate the three to four hundred fans who arrived. However, Gil had anticipated this and organised speakers to be set up in the churchyard.

The intimacy of the church magnified the presence of Kate and Felix's coffins, which lying side by side left barely enough room for participants to pass to the pulpit. The vicar led the service, and there were three eulogies delivered before the final hymn; Felix's nephew went first, then Patrick Small, and finally Gil.

Gil began by explaining his choice of venue, "In case you were wondering why I chose All Saints' Tudeley, and not something bigger … it's because it was Kate and Felix's favourite church …"

He went on to explain how Felix, who had always derived great pleasure introducing his young colleague to new experiences, had brought him to Tudeley church some fifteen years earlier, "I remember how excited he was at the prospect that I'd never been here before. As we walked from the car he told me, 'Harp, you're about to see a jewel.' And of course, Felix was rarely wrong about such matters ... I'd never have told him that though."

At this a gentle ripple of laughter passed through the congregation.

"And on that, my first of many visits here, we sat together in silent appreciation of these wonderful windows." Gil was referring to the stained glass of Marc Chagall that bestowed a sublime benevolence over the setting.

"I worked closely with Felix Blatt for nearly twenty years. He was an inspiration: colleague, friend, mentor … as the illustrator of his books, he provided me without fail with a rich vein of pure gold.

"I am forever in his debt.

"As friends, Kate and Felix proved themselves constant and unfailing. I met them at the same moment in time, and across the twenty years that followed, I doubt if more than three days ever passed without some communication between us. At the Blatts' home, I never received anything but the warmest welcome … they were the kindest of people.

"Five years ago, when my wife Jules died in a car accident along with our unborn child, I didn't know quite frankly how to continue living." Gil looked for a moment like he was struggling to speak, "It was only the perseverance of my friends, like Kate and Felix, who didn't give up on me, and refused to let me become reclusive, which got me through. Their love and support slowly guided me back to life.

"Nobody should ever die the way they did …"

At this point there was a tremor in Gil's voice.

Sally, already moved to tears herself, feared he would be unable to continue.

But he drew breath and found the strength to go on, "… and it seems particularly unjust that two people who abhorred violence, should die in such a terrible way.

"Kate and Felix adored children. And although they rarely mentioned it, not having children was an acute sadness … perhaps the only sadness in otherwise content and happy lives. However, they compensated for this only real disappointment in their lives by the work they did for children's charities. Their philosophy was a simple one ... happy children from happy childhoods become happy adults who in turn contribute to a better society. Felix's books were properly anarchic and irreverent, adored almost universally by children ... the number of children here today testifies to that.

"Our collaboration was about to naturally conclude ... our final work is with our publishers. But what I'm forced to say goodbye to here today is far more important than any book ..."

At this point Gil's lip trembled and a single involuntary tear ran down his cheek.

"They leave me with a hole ..." he stretched a hand out across his heart, "here ..." At this point Gil stopped. He had written a couple more sentences but knew that he could not deliver them. He looked up at the bowed heads of the congregation through blurry eyes and told them with a gentle smile, "They were my friends."

When the service was over and the coffins were borne out into the churchyard for burial, the skies suddenly burst open and a torrent of rain poured down onto the mourners. It was completely unexpected. When they'd walked into the church an hour earlier, blustery winds had been blowing fluffy white clouds across a blue sky.

"Felix will have organised this," Patrick Small whispered in Gil's ear as they followed the coffin bearers through the deluge, "Far too much reverence and respect!"

Gil smiled.

Fortunately, some people had come prepared, and a rather garish golfing umbrella was passed to them before Gil, Patrick and Sally got too soaked.

The funeral attendees were now hunched and huddled together under an assortment of jackets, kagouls, rain-coats and umbrellas.

It caused Gil to chuckle inwardly as he thought, 'The old bugger will be loving this!'

The coffins were committed to the earth in the same grave. The vicar's ministry, respectful but thankfully succinct, was succeeded by a faster than usual exit by those present from the churchyard to the car park; half walk, half sprint, it was the kind of human foible Felix loved to parody in his writing.

It was touching to see how many of Felix's fans remained after the downpour. Gil felt it was only fitting to stop and talk to as many as possible, and he shook a lot of hands. Many of the children were carrying posies of flowers to put on the grave. Everyone seemed to want to express how sad they felt.

"Felix Blatt was a fantastic writer."

"Will you continue to draw pictures?"

Many of the grown-ups voiced how glad they had been when the Blatts' killer was finally identified. Some began to re-iterate what the papers had said about police incompetence. Gil didn't want to get into a debate on the subject, which prompted him to head for the car.

As he stooped to get into the black funeral car, a hand suddenly gripped his elbow with unexpected determination.

"Could you sign this, Mr Harper?" asked a male voice.

Gil looked up in the direction of the person who was holding on to him. The first thing he noticed was branded white trainers and navy-blue track-suit bottoms, white-striped along their sides. The man was dressed in a soaking wet grey hoodie pulled down over a red peaked baseball cap set low on the forehead. It obscured most of the face apart from the mouth. The man was grinning, revealing teeth with quite large gaps between them. He held out a copy of *The Rotten Trotters*, Gil's first collaboration with Felix.

Gil was momentarily flummoxed, "I … er … I … d … d ..." he stammered.

Patrick, already seated in the car, came to Gil's rescue by poking his head out and stating unequivocally in his most commanding Old Etonian tone, "I'm sure you can appreciate that under the circumstances, Mr Harper is not signing autographs."

The man immediately released his hold on Gil, "Aw … right … s-s-s … s-s-s … s-sorry," he replied.

Gil got in alongside Sally and Patrick.

"The cheek of some people," said Sally.

"Pretty insensitive," commented Patrick.

As they moved off, Gil strained to look back through the rear window but the man had already evaporated into the crowd. "Was he taking the piss?" he asked.

"One born every minute!" exclaimed Megan from the seat in front.

## 27

Some refreshments were organised for those invited to the funeral at a hotel in Tonbridge. A number of people expressed how moving they'd found the service, especially Gil's heartfelt eulogy.

Later that evening, DCI Mullings visited Gil's house unannounced.

Some friends had come back after the funeral and half a dozen people, including George and Marjorie who had travelled up from Somerset, were staying overnight. Megan too was putting up funeral guests; in fact, she had courageously volunteered to put up Felix's nephew and his dreaded wife for the night.

Gil took Mullings into the study.

"I just wanted to offer my personal condolences, Mr Harper. I didn't get a chance to speak to you at the funeral."

"I'm sorry, I didn't realise you were present."

Mullings shrugged, "What you said was very moving ... powerful."

Gil acknowledged the compliment with a diffident nod.

There followed an awkward silence before Mullings continued with, "It was an extremely sad occasion ... an ordeal for everyone."

"The way they died didn't allow much room for positive spin," replied Gil.

"No, no indeed ... it's been a shocking, bewildering case."

Gil nodded again, then after a pause, he said, "I just want you to know, I didn't agree with the tabloids. I believe you did everything you could have done under the circumstances."

Mullings looked genuinely touched, "Thank you, I really appreciate you saying that."

"Can I offer you something to drink, Chief Inspector? Tea, coffee - something stronger?" he pointed to the scotch and ice in his own glass.

"No thanks, I won't take up any more of your time. I'll let you return to your guests." As Mullings approached the door he turned to say, "But, if anything should occur, anything to do with the case, however inconsequential it seems ... don't hesitate, contact me." Mullings seemed uncharacteristically edgy; he was looking at his feet, shuffling about as he spoke. "There are parts of this inquiry that still remain hard to get into perspective," he added. "Anyway, you know how to reach me."

"Yes, of course," said Gil.

"Any immediate plans?" asked Mullings.

"The day after tomorrow, Sally and I are going away for a couple of weeks."

"Abroad?" asked Mullings.

"No. I have a cottage in Wales, on the Ceredigion coast. I haven't been there for years, since before my wife's death. Megan has all the details."

"I'll take the telephone number," said Mullings, reaching inside his jacket for a notepad.

Gil shook his head, "Sorry. We never had a phone line installed. It was our bolt hole, away from civilisation. It's on a wild but quite stunning stretch of coastline."

"Plenty of fresh air then," responded Mullings, returning the notepad to its pocket, "Anyway you'll have your mobile with you."

"Yes, but unless things have changed in five years, it's generally out of range of the mobile networks. I usually phone Megan each day from a town."

Mullings raised his eyebrows and smiled, "Sounds enviably peaceful," he said.

1 3 5
2 4 R

# FIFTH

20 March - 1 April

## 1

A plan to set off early for the cottage went awry when, out of the blue, Sally declared a little shame-facedly, "I'm sorry Gil, but I must sort out a few things before I can leave."

"What sort of things?" he asked, nonplussed by the suddenness of the announcement.

"Well, I definitely need some toiletries and stuff."

"Can't you pick them up when we get there?" he asked, holding back an urge to add it was Wales they were headed for, not the Hindu Kush.

"They may not have exactly what I need."

Despite his own raw emotional state, Gil had observed how tense, distracted and almost secretive Sally had become over the preceding few days; not altogether surprising perhaps in light of recent events. Even so, a sudden change in her naturally cheery demeanour had left him feeling slightly confused. She'd given him the impression that she was trying hard to rein in and keep the lid down on her own emotions. Her behaviour seemed uncharacteristic. She had spent an age in the bathroom that morning, so long, in fact, that Gil had taken a shower in one of the other rooms. And when she'd finally emerged, didn't want any breakfast and looked quite unsettled.

Her appearance prompted Gil to ask, "Are you sure you still want to go to the cottage? I'd understand …"

"I do, I really do" she countered, "I want to be with you more than anything."

Gil felt reassured. This was before Sally mentioned the need to delay their departure for the sake of toiletries.

Gil offered to drive her up to the shops.

"No, I'll be better on my own. And I really ought to go across to my house … pick up any mail and stuff."

"I thought you'd already done that … never mind, we can easily call on the way."

Sally winced sheepishly, "I have to get a prescription … anti-histamine, my hay-fever, in case it starts playing up. Sorry Gil, I should've sorted it out before. The surgery receptionist is a bit of a Tartar and wouldn't let me have a repeat prescription without seeing my GP, but I managed to get an early appointment."

Gil reconciled himself to a late start and surreptitiously widened his eyes in the direction of Spike, who didn't get the transmitted signal and responded by angling his head at Gil with enquiring confusion.

## 2

It was shortly after 11 am when Sally returned. Gil, trying to be philosophical about it all, was strolling in the garden with Spike. He only realised she'd arrived back when he happened to glance up at Megan's window and saw the two women framed there. Megan had her arms around Sally and appeared to be offering the younger woman words of comfort. Despite his own emotional absence of late, Gil had noticed the bond that had grown between these two. Sally had sought out the companionship of the older woman many times during those miserably dark days, when he'd sometimes been too downhearted to speak. He suddenly felt ashamed of himself; it might be easy to justify his mood swings, but it could only have been dreadful to live with. He wondered if Sally was experiencing misgivings about their relationship, apprehension perhaps at being alone with him in an isolated setting if his depressive state returned. The thought of upsetting Sally, perhaps losing her, made him feel quite desolate.

He returned to the kitchen and began to make some coffee. When the two women appeared a few minutes later he didn't draw attention to either the time or the redness around Sally's eyes.

"Sorry I was so long."

"No problem," he reassured.

"But now we won't get there till after dark!" she exclaimed, aware Gil had meant to reach the cottage early enough to deal with any unforeseen problems.

"It'll be fine. The Pritchards keep an eye on the place. Anyway, if the roof's blown away or something we can always find a hotel for the night."

Megan took one each of their hands in hers, "Just enjoy. And relax. It's been an awful time. Things can only change for the better."

## 3

It was long after dark by the time they arrived at the cottage, some eight and a half hours later. Gil had driven all the way, despite Sally's offers to relieve him. They had taken frequent breaks, for lunch, afternoon tea and an evening meal, so neither felt too frazzled by the journey.

The cottage was roughly midway between New Quay to the north and Llangrannog to the south. They had opted, after long hours on the M4, to take their evening meal at a place east of Carmarthen. It was listed in the restaurant guide Gil kept in the glove compartment. Spike had no objections to being left in the car, as this afforded him an opportunity to guard his personal property. In fact, Spike behaved in an exemplary fashion throughout the journey and had even accepted relegation to the back seat with good grace; most probably this was because he liked standing on top of the mound of new bedding they were taking to the cottage.

They chatted intermittently. Sally took several naps, as did Spike whenever he judged it safe to abandon his vigil at the window. They talked for a time about the happiest things they recalled from their respective childhoods. It was a safe place to inhabit, and there was a positive sense of moving away from the pain of recent weeks. It felt as if they were creating a bubble in time, an opportunity to step away from the grieving, hurt and sense of loss that had become their life.

After Carmarthen they left the main carriageway and took an A road to the small town of Llandysul.

"I used to love it here," said Gil as they drove through its quiet streets, "This is where my grandparents lived. I came here every summer holidays. I felt free … an adventurer."

"Shame it's dark," said Sally. "My fault, taking so much time this morning."

"It would be dark anyway. It's a long drive."

"Perhaps we could come back in the daytime?"
"Not much to see, just a little house."
"But it was important to you once ... that makes it important to me," said Sally, reaching out her hand and stroking the side of Gil's face.
Gil smiled. Perhaps everything might be okay again. He hoped so.
Once they had left Llandysul they continued north for a while along a B road. After a lot of ups and downs, very bad for Spike's balance, they joined a major road again. However, they only pursued this road for a brief time, before veering off to proceed along some very narrow lanes for the last few miles. The road twisted constantly and was just wide enough to take a single vehicle, but they met no other traffic. After what was probably only two or three country miles but seemed more like ten, Gil pulled up before a metal gate.
"I wasn't sure I'd actually remember," he said. Sally heard the excitement in his voice.
Gil got out and opened the gate. With the car door open Sally could smell ozone, and perhaps after so much talk of earlier times, it rekindled in her the thrill of arriving at the seaside and its drawing power over children.
Gil returned, drove the car onto the track then pulled up again.
"Let me," said Sally.
"No, it's okay, the path can be a bit of a cowpat obstacle-course."
He closed the gate, got behind the wheel again, and proceeded to drive slowly, bumping along the rough track for the final quarter of a mile.
The meandering road, definitely not the handiwork of ancient Romans, ran beside a high stone wall.
"This is great," exclaimed Sally, opening her window to feel the sea breeze on her skin and riffling through her hair.
"It can get pretty fierce along this coast," laughed Gil, taking pleasure from her excitement. From the back seat he could hear Spike as he sniffed and whiffled, "Sounds like Spikey might recognise the local smells from his puppy days."
Along the driver's side there was hedging and a few gnarled trees, stunted and disfigured by the unceasing winds blowing across the Irish Sea.
Sally pointed over to the right, at the silhouette of a building that stood dark and solitary on the brow of a hill. "Is that it?" she asked uncertainly. The house looked too big, rather unwelcoming and didn't seem to fit the description Gil had given her.
"No," he replied, "that's a ruin. My place is further down the hill."

After a couple more minutes of slow progress they came to a stop. It was as far as it was possible to go. Ahead there stood a fence of wire stretched across posts and a wooden stile that met and adjoined the stone wall. The lane itself quadrupled in width at this point to allow for turning and parking. But Sally still hadn't seen any sign of the cottage yet.

"Where is it?" she asked.

"Just over here," Gil said, indicating right.

They left their bags in the car and Gil, who had come prepared with a torch, lit the way ahead, already being pioneered by Spike. An opening between a row of weather-beaten rowans led up six irregularly-spaced steps to a path that swiftly brought them to the front of a farm-labourer's cottage. The small early nineteenth-century building was silhouetted against the most stunning backdrop of stars Sally could ever recall witnessing. Despite the mildness of the night, the air was redolent with the might of the Atlantic, its sounds and saltiness filling Sally's head, energising her whole being.

Gil fumbled in a pocket for his key, opened the front door, and groped with a hand for the light-switch.

The cottage was warmer inside than anticipated, soon explained by the coal fire lit in the living-room fireplace.

"The Pritchards!" exclaimed Gil with an appreciative smile.

There was a note on the little dining table, which Gil read aloud, "*Dear Mr Harper* … They always call me 'Mr' … I've given up telling them to call me Gil … *Siriol has replaced the empty gas canister for you. I've had a fire going the last few days, since I knew for certain you were coming, to get the place nice and aired. I've also left you an old fan-heater from our attic up in the bedroom. You said you'd be bringing bedding but you didn't mention towels, so I've left two bath and a bar of soap. Hope the journey wasn't too tiring, Gwyneth P* ... Then a P.S. ... *Pint of milk, loaf of bread, quarter of tea and pack of butter in kitchen*."

"That's so thoughtful," said Sally, "Do you pay them to look after the place?"

"I've tried, but they won't take anything. I suppose they consider it fair because I let them use the cottage whenever they want to put up relatives or friends."

"So the cottage hasn't been totally empty all this time?"

"No, the Pritchards would have had the odd relation staying."

Sally insisted on a guided tour of the property. Because of its size this didn't take long; it was a very simple two-up, two-down. An entrance porch had been tacked on at the front, to lessen the impact of the sea which had previously blasted the living-room every time the front door opened. Directly opposite the entrance to this sole reception room there was a flight of stairs to the floor above. On this upper storey there was one bedroom and a bathroom. Back on the ground floor there was also a kitchen, small but perfectly versatile behind the living-room, and beyond this there was a small utility room that Gil and Jules had added when they'd done away with the outside toilet.

"This is utterly brilliant," said Sally some time later after a cup of tea. They had arrived upstairs again and she was perched on the edge of the unmade bed, "Perfect!"

"I love it here," said Gil, "Thanks again for agreeing to join me." An expression of some sadness suddenly crossed his face.

"It must hold a lot of memories," said Sally.

He shook his head from side to side, "I just wasn't able to come near the place … even after all this time. I thought about selling … been on the verge of doing so on several occasions." He sat beside Sally and took her hands in his, "You're the only person I've ever wanted to bring here since Jules."

"Did Jules love it too?"

Gil's eyes misted slightly, then much to Sally's surprise, he let out what was for him an unusually big laugh, "She always insisted that she did … I think she liked the idea of it more than the reality ... probably felt she had to, because she knew I absolutely loved it here."

"Why was that, then? Just not her thing?"

"All Jules' energy was geared up for the world of problem-solving. She thrived on difficult meetings, enjoyed nothing better than making awkward people come round to her point of view. I've never met anyone who just loved negotiating deals so much. A weekend at the cottage and Jules would claim to feel so happy she never wanted to leave ever again. After about five days though, her eyes had started to glaze!" Gil smiled in recalling his late wife's foibles, "Once it got to about ten days, it became really tricky … it was like being holed-up with a sad wild creature that had lost the will to live."

Sally laughed, "Poor Jules having to suffer rural bliss for the man she loved."

"I guess we were attracted like opposites are."

"I don't think I'll be fed up after ten days. I'm afraid you'll have to call in the bailiffs to evict me. When I see a nest I want to curl up and forget all the problematic stuff."

"Me too," said Gil. He stroked her hair then gently kissed her mouth. Her face had an almost luminous glow about it.

He felt powerfully drawn to ask her to marry him there and then, but he knew it wasn't right; not there, not after talking about Jules. Anyway, his instincts told him there was something bothering Sally, perhaps it was to do with their relationship. Whatever it was, it would have been wrong to pressurise her. "I'd better fetch the rest of the bags and stuff," he said.

"I'll help."

For the next half an hour they busied themselves with what needed to be done. They made up the bed with new bed-linen, and while Sally put their clothes away in the bedroom, Gil went outside to fetch some coal to bank up the fire for the night. The ordering of fuel was another thing the Pritchards had done, at Gil's request.

The coal bunker was just outside the back door, and as he bent to pick up the scuttle to return inside again, out of the corner of his eye Gil thought he glimpsed a light in one of the upstairs windows of the derelict building above on the horizon.

He froze. The hairs on the back of his neck immediately sprang to attention.

He stood transfixed, staring up at the deserted house.

Nothing … just darkness, exactly as it should be.

Then, away in the distance, he heard the vague hum of a car engine as it travelled the road beyond the old house and illuminated the horizon for a split second with the glow of its lights.

Gil sighed with relief.

He was still a bit jumpy. It was perfectly understandable after everything that had happened. There was nothing to worry about.

He felt an involuntary shiver run through him. The night was turning cold.

He picked up the scuttle and went back inside to the warm.

## 4

When he woke next morning, Gil was surprised to discover he was alone in bed. He suspected this meant it was quite late. The quality of the light streaming in through his bedroom window confirmed this. Without seeking out his watch, he guessed with astonishing accuracy, about ten-thirty. He lay quite still for a moment, listening for sounds from inside the cottage; turn of a tap, clink of a spoon on a cereal bowl, a match being struck. This required him to block out the cacophony beyond its walls; the breaking of waves, the caw, screech and squawk of gulls and the unceasing flight of the wind about the eaves and chimney-pots. All was silent.

The absence of domestic noise provided the impetus to rouse him from bed. He paused a moment to yawn, then got up, stretched, and shuffled over to the window. The curtains had been left open during the night and as he gazed out on the day he was struck by the brilliant vastness of sea and sky.

Sally was leaning against the stile at the far end of the lane, close to where the car was parked. She had wrapped a long cardigan around herself and was gazing thoughtfully out at the sea. Spike was sitting happily by her side taking in the day. Not conscious of being watched, she occasionally took a sip from the mug in her hand. Gil thought how beautiful she looked on that fine spring morning.

He quickly drew on a sweater and a pair of jeans, attached a long-forgotten pair of moccasin-style slippers to his feet, and padded off downstairs. As he left the cottage and entered the magnificent day, the need to pause, take in a deep breath and smile, was irresistible. As ever, there were the incessant calls of sea birds, soaring high in a cloudless sky above shimmering waves. It was one of those mornings when sea and sky blended seamlessly, and plotting the line of the horizon became guesswork.

Not visible to Gil from his current vantage point, down the steeply sloping grassy bank, about thirty feet below the cottage, was the Ceredigion coastal path. The route, popular with walkers, pursued the course of the dark grey cliffs that rose a hundred feet above the jagged rocks and boiling sea at their feet.

Gil took the steps down to the lane. Spike, tail wagging a little sheepishly, came across to greet him. Sally was still unaware he'd arrived and appeared to be deep in thought.

"Enjoying the view?" he called out.

Sally nearly leapt out of her skin.

"I ... I ... I was just looking at the sea," she explained, quite flustered, face reddening with embarrassment.

"That's okay. No charge for it!" he joked.

She laughed and said, "I wasn't expecting you ... you gave me a shock!"

"Sorry."

From her reaction, Gil suspected he'd interrupted a thought process that involved him in some way. He also recognised that whatever the problem was, she wasn't ready yet to voice it.

"I left you lying in bed, dead to the world you were! See, should've let me share the driving yesterday ... silly old thing!"

"Easy with the old," he scowled. "I'm just fine and dandy," he said coming up beside her to steal a kiss and then the mug from her hand.

Without examining its contents, Gil took a large slurp, only to immediately grimace and exclaim, "Urgh!" He didn't mind an occasional herb tea, if he knew what was coming, but he'd been expecting coffee.

Sally laughed.

"You might've warned me!" he said, making an exaggerated face.

"You shouldn't go round pinching other people's drinks!"

"But you drink coffee in the morning!" he protested.

"I bought some herb teas when I went shopping yesterday."

"What is it?" He asked the question like he meant to file it away for future reference.

"Ginger and ginseng."

"Mmm ... should carry a health warning."

Sally wrapped her arms about him and kissed his cheek. For a few moments they stared out across the cliffs, absorbed into the great seascape before them. As they shared the moment, they felt some of their tensions dissipate. It had been a good choice, to come here for renewal.

Gil sighed with satisfaction and leant his free arm on the wooden fence-post in front of him, only to find, much to his surprise, that it immediately gave way. However, the post, wired to a series of other posts, remained upright despite breaking at its base.

"Blimey! Completely rotten!" he exclaimed, pointing a foot at the place where the wood had decayed. This prompted him to check out the other posts, only to discover they were in a similar state of deterioration. "The Pritchards will know someone who can fix them. Not even the stile looks like it's got much life left in it."

Beyond the stile the path descended steeply before it joined the route below.

"Is it a public right of way?" asked Sally.

Gil nodded, "Joins the coastal path," he replied, pointing down at its seaward edge.

"Does it get busy?"

"Not really. There's a bit of extra footfall in summer. The Pritchards rent out a small field for camping."

"Ooh, hello sailor!" said Sally, responding in time-honoured theatrical tradition to the word 'camp'.

Gil playfully swiped a hand across her hair, "Just a few tents and half a dozen touring caravans."

"Is that a nuisance?" she asked.

"Never," replied Gil. "People who drop litter and let their children go insane aren't interested in remote spots and long coastal walks. Almost everyone who goes by is nice and polite ... usually serious walkers, some families, mostly husbands and wives out for a trek."

"Ah, yes!" exclaimed Sally, "The noble British walker and his mate ... chirpy and gregarious."

Gil smiled and took up the idea, "A plain, though not wholly uninteresting species," he went on, emulating the style of a guide book, "Homo brittanicus pedestrianus, can be spotted in many parts of the world ..."

"And easily identified by their sturdy and sensible socks," put in Sally.

They laughed. Gil smacked a kiss onto her forehead.

"Making up Latin before midday ... I need coffee!" said Gil.

## 5

"So how did the Pritchards come to sell the cottage to you and Jules?" Sally asked as they trudged uphill along the track.

Gil was taking her to meet them. It was a nice afternoon, so they went on foot.

"Liked our friendly young faces, I guess," he replied.

It was an exhilarating climb. They held hands as they walked. Spike was up ahead on an extendable lead operated by Gil. This was because Spike wasn't a hundred percent trustworthy when it came to farm animals like sheep that always ran away so agreeably.

Gil was glad he'd thought to use the lead, as they soon discovered the field where the derelict house stood was heaving with sheep. Spike stood at its gate barking.

"Strange," said Gil, as they caught up, "It's his 'stay back' bark."

"Telling off the sheep?" asked Sally.

"Don't think so ... quite likes sheep, even though he'd love to get in there and chase them about."

"He doesn't seem to be looking at the sheep," said Sally, "I'd say he's barking at the house."

Gil looked concerned for a moment. Then, much to his relief, about two dozen starlings suddenly ascended skywards out of a hole in the roof of the run-down building.

Spike followed the birds as they soared up into the air and he stopped his noise.

"Spike's never been keen on our feathered friends."

Gil and Sally moved off. However, Spike remained grumbling at the gate and Gil needed to give a few sharp tugs of encouragement before he joined them.

"Who does the house belong to?" asked Sally.

"The Pritchards."

"Do they plan to sell it?"

"I don't think they ever would."

"Why not?" she asked.

Gil anticipated the answer might dampen their mood and gave a short involuntary sigh. After this, he had to explain. He began, "Gwyneth and Siriol Pritchard used to live there. Siriol's parents had the main farmhouse ... where we're headed." He paused briefly then added, "Gwyneth told Jules about it once. Anyway, after Siriol's mother passed away, the farmhouse became too much for his father ... so Siriol and Gwyneth moved into the bigger house, while the old man moved in here."

"That would make sense."

"Apparently, the old man started to lose it a bit. They asked him to come and live with them, but he was fiercely independent and wouldn't hear of it. Anyway, one night he accidentally set fire to the kitchen. One of Siriol's sons saw the smoke ... they rushed down ... managed to put the fire out before the place went up completely ... but unfortunately, too late to save the old man."

"How terribly sad."

"According to Gwyneth, Siriol wouldn't dream of selling."

"I can understand that," said Sally.

The story inevitably brought them down and they walked on for a minute or two in silence. However, they seemed determined not to allow dark thoughts to blight their day. And by the time they reached the gate onto the main road they had recovered their good spirits.

The Pritchards lived just five minutes on from here. Apart from grazing a few sheep, they were really dairy farmers, and the closer Gil and Sally got to their farm, the more potent became the smells associated with their line of work. The farmhouse itself was unprepossessing, utilitarian, and without a doubt not the domain of hobby farmers. On entering a cobbled yard, enclosed on three sides by buildings with the house directly ahead, a trio of sheepdogs suddenly sprang out from an open doorway.

Three dogs, all barking at once, are always challenging. Gil and Sally took it from the dogs' stances that they were being instructed to walk to the house, without veering off course. The dogs didn't pay Spike any special attention, him being a dog and all. Poor Spike looked uncharacteristically chastened by their presence.

A short but powerful-looking man in his mid-twenties, dressed in a blue boiler-suit and black wellingtons appeared in the doorway where the dogs had rushed from, and said commandingly, "Dewch nôl!"

The dogs ceased barking at once and returned into the building. The young man, Gwyneth and Siriol's middle son Emrys, smiled and waved before disappearing again.

"Why don't you ever listen to me like that?" Gil asked the unusually humble Spike, who for once looked grateful to be on a lead.

Having been alerted by the dogs, Gwyneth Pritchard was on the doorstep by the time her visitors had crossed the last few yards to the house.

"Mr Harper … long time no see … welcome back," she greeted, taking Gil's hand.

"It's lovely to see you again, Gwyneth," he replied, before making an introduction perhaps a little more formally than usual, "I'd like you to meet Sally … Sally Curtis."

"Very pleased to meet you," said Gwyneth, solemnly shaking Sally's hand, "Miss Curtis."

"Sally."

"Oh!" said Gwyneth uncertainly.

"Please call me Sally. I wouldn't know who you meant if you called me Miss Curtis," she said warmly.

Gwyneth smiled, "Sally, then. Come inside both of you. Welcome. The kettle's just boiled."

Gil, leading Spike, followed them in with a bemused expression on his face. He couldn't quite work out how Sally had got Gwyneth to call her by her first name in under a minute, after he'd consistently failed to do the same thing in nearly a decade.

Gwyneth Pritchard was every inch of her a farmer's wife. When you met her you felt her genes and chromosomes had been filtered through layers of Cambrian rock over generations. She was tall, broad, large-breasted and carried a little extra weight around her middle. Her shoulders looked so strong you felt she might easily pop a sheep or two under each arm. Two of her three sons, not Emrys, who was slighter and took after his father, had inherited her build and played rugby at a fairly high amateur level. Despite Gwyneth's ample proportions she was every bit a lady too. Her voice was softly feminine with gentle Welsh cadences that Sally immediately adored listening to. In her early-sixties, Gwyneth had succumbed to the modern pressure to remain youthful by dyeing and perming her naturally brown, now greying straight hair, strawberry blonde, which didn't really suit her.

"Siriol said you'd drop by today, so we were expecting you!"

Gwyneth led the way into the large farm kitchen, where she'd been baking. Gil could not recall calling on the Pritchards at any time when Gwyneth had not been baking. The smell of bread and cakes was mouth-watering.

"Gil's told me lots about you," said Sally.

"Really," said Gwyneth, with a tiny twinkle in her eye, "I'm sure there's not much to say about us. Mr Harper told me on the phone you're in the theatre, Sally, that sounds exciting!"

"I'm not an actress or anything," said Sally, "I make costumes for shows."

"Mmm, sounds a lot more glamorous than anything Siriol or I have ever done."

They were directed to sit at the large oak table which might easily have accommodated a dozen more. Gwyneth, her senses highly tuned over half a century to the smells of baking, exclaimed, "Something's burning!" and excused herself while she went over to the cooking range and skilfully attended to a batch of Welsh-cakes that were browning on a round black griddle.

Despite this disruption, within five minutes of being seated they had cups of tea placed before them. Gil had never left the Pritchards' house without drinking at least one cup of tea and eating something. He had forewarned Sally about the need for stomach space when on a Pritchard visit.

After pouring the tea, Gwyneth explained her husband's absence by informing them, "Siriol is doing the dreaded paperwork!"

After this she left them briefly, went into the hallway and called upstairs. She spoke in Welsh, seamlessly gliding from one language into the other. The family only ever spoke their mother tongue between themselves.

A man's voice immediately replied back in Welsh. Shortly afterwards, in his stockinged feet, Siriol came down to greet the guests. He was accompanied by his best sheepdog, Sian, the only dog ever allowed inside their house with the exception of pets like Spike.

Siriol's first words to his guests were, "Welcome ... sorry for not being here to greet you, it's the afternoon for the dreaded paperwork."

Siriol Pritchard was a head shorter than his wife, built on a wiry frame with grizzled hair, his complexion ruddy and weather-beaten. He spoke in Welsh rapidly, but clearly found such unguarded fluency in English more difficult. Although he was always polite, he was less formal than his wife. He had a dry Welsh sense of humour, and you always had to look beyond an impassive face to catch the twinkle in the eye.

Sally took to him immediately. And he too, like his wife, called her by her first name from the start. Over her second cup of tea Sally told him, in praise of the large slice of homemade sponge she was eating, "I'm sorry to say I'm a dreadful cook me, absolutely hopeless. You're a lucky man to have a wife who's so expert in the kitchen."

Siriol responded by telling her, "Yes, Gwyn's very good, fair play … but of course here in West Wales we all take cooking very seriously. I'm a very good pastry chef myself. In fact, Gwyn and I tend to bake on alternate days."

He said all this with such a completely straight face that Sally replied earnestly, "That's very interesting."

"Don't listen," interrupted Gwyneth, "He's pulling your leg … couldn't boil an egg to save his life!"

Sally narrowed her eyes and gave Siriol, who was sat beside her, a nudge in mock annoyance.

"No," chuckled Siriol, "I burn water, me."

The Pritchards were clearly quite taken with Sally. This was strangely important to Gil, as they had been so very fond of his wife. When Jules had died, despite always being extremely busy on the farm, they had insisted on making the journey to Kent for the funeral. Up until today, that had been the last time he'd seen them.

Gil had talked about the Blatts and everything that had happened during a long telephone conversation with Gwyneth. And, of course, every detail had been covered and minutely analysed by the papers. So, that afternoon, much to Gil and Sally's relief, only oblique references needed to be made to recent troubles. The Pritchards were not the sort to pry.

Sally found them every bit as charming as Gil had described and particularly loved their old-fashioned formality. They stayed comfortably chatting around the kitchen table for nearly two hours. Only Spike felt uneasy, observed by Sian the sheepdog as she lay flat to the floor at her master's feet, her alert eyes carefully watching him the whole time.

# 6

The days ahead provided the much-needed opportunity to relax. Inevitably, Gil was sometimes drawn into the dark memories that lurked in his mind. Sally instinctively stepped back at these moments and gave him space to work it out. It would never be possible to completely forget, he knew this, but he hoped that with time the horrendous pictures in his head would fade, and he'd be able to live his life with less intrusion from them. Quite often, especially when he stood under the stars at night, he found himself wishing to thank whatever universal force was in charge of everything for providing him with Sally.

Each day they rose early and enjoyed brisk walks along the cliffs. It never failed to amuse Gil, how, once Sally had climbed over the stile, she invariably verbalised her descent down the bank with, "Ah … Ah … Ah!" in the hope she'd be able to apply the brakes and stop her legs before careering over the edge. Of course she always knew she would stop, and after the first time this display was only repeated for Gil's amusement. Actually, once safely on the path, holding onto Gil for added courage, she couldn't resist stealing cautious glances down at the rocks and sea. An almost vertical drop was only interrupted by a faultline, which had produced a narrow ledge that ran about ten foot below the top of the cliff.

"I suppose if my legs didn't stop in time, I'd have one last chance to save myself if I grabbed hold of that," Sally joked.

"If you're a bit scaredy-cat, you can always bring a parachute out on walks."

"You don't think I'd look silly?" asked Sally playing along with the idea.

"You could never look silly!"

They had an appetite for long, vigorous walks. They tended to get back in time to drive off to a pub for lunch. In the afternoons they generally visited a town, historic site or sometimes took another walk. They made any necessary phone calls in the afternoons too; there had been no improvement in reception over five years. Occasionally they went out for an evening meal, but more often preferred to eat simply at home.

Each day, the decision whether to take the coastal path north or south was usually made on the spot, after crossing the stile. They tended to go south mostly, when they would walk along the cliffs down to Llangrannog. It became their special walk. The sea and air at Llangrannog was always spectacularly potent. They loved to simply stand before the surf, and watch the broad field of charging white horses as they came thundering down onto the beach.

The very first time Gil had taken her there, the sea was uncommonly placid and he'd felt a little disappointed. It was the wildness of the West Wales coast he loved most and he'd wanted to share it with Sally.

Sally, however, was utterly enthralled even by this relatively gentle day, "It's wonderful. What's the word Hindus use … prana?"

Gil nodded and smiled.

"It makes me feel so alive!"

"Believe me, this is soft core for Llangrannog," he said. "I love this place. My grandparents used to bring me here with my bucket and spade … it meant escape!" He broke off for a moment before adding, "My grandparents were always a lot more fun to be with than my mum and dad."

"What makes people be like that?" she asked. "Do you think it's fear … makes them deny themselves the best life has to offer?"

"I guess it must be," said Gil, "a kind of fear at least. I think my parents were restrained by a deep-seated belief that they weren't quite good enough. They were dreadful suburban snobs … aspired to be part of a class they didn't feel worthy of."

"What a waste of life," said Sally, "to impose such limitations on yourself," she paused almost imperceptibly, before going on, "I can't talk. I stayed with Michael even though he treated me like a piece of rubbish. I know what it's like to be afraid … to feel not good enough … to feel that you're unlovable."

"How could you of all people believe that of yourself?" asked Gil.

"Easy I suppose, if you've had the right schooling."

Gil nodded, "Makes me feel grateful I'm nobody's father … can't be held responsible then for fucking up anyone else's head but my own!"

Sally had a look of deep sadness in her eyes as she turned and looked at Gil. The conversation had made them both feel a little maudlin.

They returned their attention to the sea as it undulated and bobbed beneath a clear blue sky. The waves that day dramatically materialised only about ten yards out. They appeared to grow in strength and power as they surged forward, before crashing with a profound energy onto the beach.

After a few minutes of watching, Gil said, "Let's get a coffee," pointing to the café just above the beach.

# 7

The first week at the cottage passed quickly. During this time they enjoyed phenomenal luck with the weather. For eight days in a row the sun beamed benevolently down on their daily walks.

It was 3 pm on Sunday afternoon. They had returned home after consuming a large Sunday lunch. Gil was keeping at bay any soporific yearnings by working on his laptop at a small plastic table in the cottage's tiny rear garden. Sally was fast asleep, gently snoring on a reclining chair at his side, while Spike, also asleep, lay with shameless abandon in the crook of her arm.

Gil had just written in his diary:

> In the intimate moments we share, like after love making, or during our walks together, it often feels like we are one person and not two; however, there are also times when I sense Sally is distracted and troubled by her thoughts; at these moments she seems overcome by a deep unhappiness. My selfish worry (paranoia?) is that she is being kind, just sticking it out with me. And one day, when she senses I'm strong enough, she'll suggest we see less of each other. I fear that she'll go on some long theatrical tour and our relationship will gradually fade away.

Perhaps it was these anxious thoughts that triggered the idea that the house above was watching him again. He knew it was only foolishness, but he knew too, that he would need to put to rest his disquiet. After all, it wasn't the first time the empty house had troubled him.

Sally and the dog looked like they would remain sleeping a while. So, without any more thought, he found himself trudging up the lane. He went through the gate, passing what remained of the outbuildings until he stood before the house. The herd of grazing sheep from a week ago had been removed.

The house's ground floor windows were boarded up with galvanised sheeting, as was the front door. All the upstairs windows were open to the elements, the glass they once contained long gone. It was the front of the house that looked down onto the cottage. And from where Gil now stood, he could make out Sally and Spike asleep in the garden. It was when searching around the back of the house that he noticed the galvanised sheet concealing the door was loose. It required very little effort to lever the sheeting back far enough to allow him to enter.

Gil hesitated before going inside.

The interior was quite dark, and it took a moment or two for his eyes to adjust before he could see much. The floor was covered in fallen plaster and debris. The whole building reeked of damp and decay. Gil found his way out of what must once have been the kitchen into the hall. Here it was possible to see a little easier, because part of the roof was missing. The staircase had been removed, offering no means of access to the floor above. Gil was able to form a picture of how the place must have looked in times past from the wall light fittings and faded red flock wallpaper that had once ascended the stairs.

It was at this point that Gil noticed the wooden ladder lying on the floor next to the longest wall. Before he considered the sheer foolishness of looking around the upper storey of a derelict house, Gil had raised the ladder, which seemed quite sound, and placed it against a ceiling joist.

He began to climb.

He made it until his foot came into contact with the ladder's third rung, when it immediately collapsed under his weight. Fortunately the rung supporting his hands held, as did the second rung beneath his feet. He escaped with a scratch to his cheek and a bruised ankle. The main casualty was his ego as he limped back to the cottage.

He told Sally that his very minor injuries were the result of a sense of adventure for exploring old houses. He didn't want her to know the truth, of course, that he'd been harbouring irrational fears about being watched. Their situation at the cottage was not really conducive to that idea, and it seemed daft to get her spooked for nothing.

"You might have broken your neck," Sally remonstrated, as she finished cleaning the scratch on his cheek, tossing him a tube of arnica cream to apply to his ankle, "Men can be so effin' stupid sometimes!" she scolded, concerned that he might have been seriously hurt.

## 8

Sunday 29 March

I'd have been very disappointed if you'd forced my hand today.

I would, of course, have had no option but to club you round the head with the concrete lintel I was holding. If you were still alive by the time your body hit the ground, I'd have been so angry with you for interfering with my plans, there would have been no stopping me.

I can picture it: me smashing the butt end of that lintel again and again into your face until it resembled a bag of pulped tomatoes.

No room for any subtlety after that!

Then, I expect I'd have gone down to your cottage in a wild rage and turned it into a slaughterhouse.

Not a nice picture, is it?

To be honest, I wasn't very surprised when you came up to the house today. I can appreciate, after everything that has happened, how unnerving it must be staying in such a remote spot. Even so, I'm still confident you believe Geoff Owens was the mastermind behind the entire nefarious goings on!

As for the ladder, in case anyone decided to take a look upstairs, I'd taken the precaution of weakening the third rung at each end. Of course, there was always a possibility my saw cut wasn't quite deep enough and the rung might have held.

Anyway, it broke, which fortunately for you meant you didn't have to die!

Strange, when I think about you and your whore, I'm filled with thoughts of my own omnipotence.

I suppose I do exercise a truly god-like power over you.

## Hallelujah! Praise the Lord!

In fact, the only real difference between me and God is that only one of us exists.

## Guess which one?

I had an unshakeable conviction that you'd stick with your plan and bring the bitch to the cottage.

On a positive note, it's the only thing that's kept her fit and healthy up until now. If I hadn't chosen it as the setting for my finale there's no possibility she would have lived this long.

Of course nothing was ever certain. For starters, I had to keep my fingers crossed that the relationship would survive, and what with funerals, post-mortems and everything, it's all run on a couple of weeks later than anticipated.

Such a lot has happened since you first mentioned coming here in your diary. January seems so distant now. Of course, I no longer enjoy the benefit of reading your diary. Although I do pride myself on knowing how you think. You're a bit like a steam locomotive, Gil old chum, chugging along the track set out before you.

Yes, I've done a great deal of careful planning. Imagine my anxiety, wondering if I could gain Geoff Owens' trust in time?

<u>Nothing to worry about there of course</u>!

In fact it really makes me smile to think of his trust. The uncomprehending confusion in his eyes, when in a semi-comatose (but still just conscious) state, I cut open his wrists.

<u>Imagine executing a pet spaniel and you get the picture</u>.

Such loyalty!

Talking of backside-sniffers, I haven't forgotten or forgiven your little pest. To be fair, I don't honestly know why I feel quite so vindictive towards him. I'm probably still angry he survived my attempt to dispatch him to the great Veterinarian on High. As you know, I detest failure!

By the way, I really liked your cottage. I spent two nights there during the days leading up to the Blatts' funerals. Believe it or not I actually slept in your bed. I forced the small window in the utility space behind the kitchen to get in. It wasn't very secure, and I patched it up again when I left.

I set this place up for myself during that time.

There's just one thing I haven't been entirely certain of up until now - the timing of the final scene in this little drama of ours!

I know, I know, I've been holding back. No good of course. Although, it's understandable, after all, I'm only human. But I confess I've let sentimentality get the better of me.

I know the longer I delay, the greater chance there is of something going wrong - like almost happened today!

<u>Sobering thought</u>: two more steps on that ladder and you were a dead man!

So, we're nearly at the end.

Ready?

I very much doubt it!

Did you know today is officially the first day of British summertime?

Tonight will be your tenth night at the cottage.

I notice the nice weather we've been having is forecast to change, with strong winds and rain due to blow in from the west.

It only seems fitting that it should be raining in Wales – after all, it's such a dreary place! It would also tie in rather neatly with all that rain on the motorway when we first met, and later when we had our nice little chat together at your friends' double funeral.

<u>See. I've gone all sentimental again</u>.

Tomorrow it is then! A rainy day (we hope!).

## 9

The weather forecast they listened to over breakfast said a cold front was heading inland and promised a storm later. However, the report also predicted that the day would remain bright and sunny until the afternoon, and, because of this, they saw no reason to deny themselves the pleasure of a morning walk.

They took their favourite route along the coastal path to Llangrannog. As usual, they maintained a good pace. In fact, they only broke off once round mid-journey point, to watch a group of seals frolicking in the surf off Ynys Lochtyn.

"Don't you sometimes wish we could be like that, Gil Harper? Demonstrate the sheer joy of living, put our magnificent brains on standby occasionally?"

Her words not only rang with conviction but had a certain wistfulness about them. This only confirmed to Gil that his observations were correct; whatever had been troubling Sally for the past week hadn't gone away and was still playing on her mind. Even so, he still couldn't quite bring himself to ask what the problem was, probably because he feared the answer.

The seals were trying to outdo each other by demonstrating all kinds of watery acrobatics. Sally glanced at Gil and laughed. They were sitting side by side on the cliff top grass. "It's infectious … impossible not to smile at their antics!"

They continued to watch for several more minutes. However, the next time Sally looked at Gil, she saw that his eyes were no longer trained on the seals but fixed on her.

"Hallo," she said.

"I love you," he said.

Tears immediately began to form in her eyes as she whispered, "I love you too."

Gil took Sally's hand. The moment for candour had arrived. He said, "Most of the time we've been here you've seemed happy … but from time to time, I've sensed sadness too …"

At first she looked ready to deny this, but checked herself and replied, "Am I really that transparent?"

"You haven't been difficult to be with, or anything," he reassured her, "But I've noticed you deep in thought at times. The day we left Sevenoaks, I was in the garden … I didn't realise you'd got back … you were talking to Megan in her office. When you came downstairs, I saw you'd been crying."

Sally nodded, "You're right, Gil … something has been on my mind."

"Is it to do with us?"

She sighed, turned her face away from him and looked out to sea.

Gil felt his guts tighten as he waited for the explanation.

The moment was suddenly interrupted by Spike, who rushed past them barking. Gil felt some uncommonly vindictive thoughts towards his four-legged friend. Needless to say, Spike missed the gull he was after by a mile. It didn't matter; forever the optimist, he immediately gave chase to another, then another. Once he'd finished policing the now gull-free cliff top, he sat panting with an air of contentment.

They couldn't help but laugh.

Sally gripped Gil's hand tightly and rested her head against his shoulder. Once again she turned her attention to the seals. She said, "Let's talk tonight over supper. Do you mind?"

"Not at all," he lied.

## 10

John Mullings was no longer partnered by DI Jackson or assigned to the Harper/Owens case. As far as the Policing Authority was concerned he was persona non grata. He just hadn't played the game. Not only had he refused to take the blame for failing to put the finger on Geoff Owens sooner, but he'd refused to accept the role of sacrificial victim. His cussedness had been met by a severely cold shoulder. The tribal elders were letting it be known how unwise it was to go against their will; he was outcast. In terms of work, he was being tossed scraps and titbits, the loose ends of workaday cases others had begun, far beneath either his ability or status as a Detective Chief Inspector.

He spent the morning of Monday, thirtieth of March, interviewing five middle-aged women in the personable company of PC Amy Shaw. These five had all suffered the misfortune of being accosted by a man in his mid-twenties who'd exposed himself to them. They had each described the perpetrator as badly dressed and not physically very imposing. Three of them had gone on to suggest that he may have had learning difficulties. The incidents had occurred over three weeks, in four different villages around the Maidstone area.

The interviews had overrun and lunch was skipped to keep an appointment previously arranged for them with a consultant psychologist. Amy Shaw found this meeting interminably dull. The psychologist woman just droned on, expounding theories and quoting various studies. All Shaw could think about was her rumbling stomach. She wondered how the DCI managed to look so interested. In fact, only once did Mullings show the tiniest chink in his armour. Shaw observed an almost imperceptible twitch in his left cheek as the psychologist pronounced, "It's typical of an inadequate male, who tends to believe any female can be made subservient if he waves his penis about at her."

On their way back to the station, Shaw said with a wry smile as she drove their car, "I'm going to tell my boyfriend it's no good trying to make me subservient by prancing round the flat in his boxers."

John Mullings allowed a smile to flicker across his mouth.

Shaw considered it a privilege to be working with Mullings. In her opinion he was being treated disgracefully.

"You know, Amy," began Mullings, "I don't think we'll be hearing any more from our flasher ... not for a while anyway ... not after Mrs Bovey."

Shaw looked over and caught the amused look in Mullings' eyes. After that, neither of them was able to restrain their laughter.

Dorothy Bovey, a forty-seven year old housewife, a dinner lady at the local primary school, had been taken aback when a slightly-built man raced out from an area of shrubbery next to her village green. She'd told them, "My glasses were at the opticians being repaired. For a second I couldn't quite make out what he was doin'. But once I saw what the dirty little sod was waggling at me, I saw red, didn't I? 'Don't you wave that pathetic thing at me', I said, 'That ain't nothing to boast about,' I told him, 'I've picked bigger slugs off my lettuces.'"

Matters then took a turn for the worse as far as the perpetrator was concerned when Mrs Bovey suddenly gave chase. "I'd have caught him too," she said, "Only I was weighed down with two bags of heavy shopping."

Still smiling about it, Mullings took his leave of Shaw in the staff canteen, after purchasing a sandwich and coffee.

On the way through to his office he exchanged a greeting with Sergeant Cutler, the office manager.

"Have a good morning, John?"

To this Mullings responded with a raised eyebrow.

"Like that, was it?" said Cutler.

Mullings sat at his desk and cast a jaundiced eye over his in-tray. At first glance nothing seemed to have altered. Then he noticed the forensic file tucked into the middle of the pile. He was ninety-nine percent certain it hadn't been there before. The first question he asked himself was why a file for the Harper/Owens case had been left on his desk? It was dated 23/03.

His first impulse was to call Frank Cutler and send it away again. But there was something odd about the way it had materialised. Mullings' curiosity got the better of him. As he opened the file and scanned the page before him, he distractedly tore the cellophane cover off his sandwich pack. The prawn mayo sandwich never reached his mouth.

As Cutler walked by his office door, Mullings called to him, "Frank, this file, where did it come from?"

The police sergeant stared at the object in question with complete detachment and replied with innocence worthy of a choir-boy, "Dunno, sir!"

In Mullings' experience, Frank Cutler knew the whereabouts of every paperclip and post-it note in his domain, what's more, using the word sir made his reply thoroughly unconvincing. These two had been friends for twenty years.

Mullings glanced at the office clock. It was 3.30 pm. "Is the Deputy Chief Constable still around?" he asked.

"In his office, I believe."

"Tell him I need to see him, pronto."

"What'll I say if he's busy?"

"Tell him, if he doesn't see me, he may be looking at early retirement."

Cutler's eyes widened, "I don't expect I'll tell him that ... but I daresay I'll find a way to convey a sense of urgency."

## 11

They drove north in search of lunch to the coastal town of Aberaeron. Spike, always ready to take a snooze after his morning walk, was left at the cottage. Gil had been to Aberaeron many times. He parked overlooking the sea and led the way through the town's narrow streets.

"I'm famished," said Sally as they walked along.

The bright clear sky was already beginning to cloud over.

"It's not far," said Gil, who had promised Sally some really good fish and chips for lunch.

The restaurant was near the quayside. Gil ordered cod and chips with bread and butter and tea for two.

Once they'd hungrily put away the massive portions that arrived, Sally, with a look of satisfaction, patted her slightly distended stomach and said, "You weren't wrong - those fish and chips were in a class of their own ... seriously good!"

After lunch, Gil rang Megan, as he'd done every day. There was nothing of any pressing importance happening at home.

On their way back to the car, they walked along the seafront and bought ice-creams sweetened with honey. And as they sauntered along licking their cones, they watched in awe as the heavens darkened and every trace of the morning's bright blue was superseded by the colours in a deep, dark bruise. By the time they reached the car park, the sky looked very threatening, but it hadn't yet started to rain. A roll of distant thunder was heard and a fork of lightning dashed through the clouds far out to sea.

They decided it would be wise to head for the cottage.

When they were approximately halfway there, Gil timed the gap between lightning strike and thunderclap, "Reckon about twelve miles … but closing."

"That sky is truly awesome," said Sally, "Worthy of Cecil B De Mille!"

Much to their surprise, they managed to drive the remaining seven or eight miles and were safely indoors before the downpour began.

"Now that's what I call torrential rain!" commented Gil.

"Nice for ducks!" added Sally.

The ground outside the cottage was immediately transformed into a quagmire. They felt lucky to be inside; warm, dry and above all safe.

## 12

Mullings got his audience.

The Deputy Chief Constable's secretary condescendingly informed him that her boss was very busy, and advised keeping the interview brief. Mullings shrugged; he was not in the mood for diplomacy.

When he went in the DCC was wearing an expression of magnanimous smugness. He clearly believed Mullings had reconsidered the offer of early retirement and had come, tail between his legs, in supplication.

This only served to make Mullings feel more aggrieved.

"What can I do for you, John?"

"You can take a look at this," he replied, almost throwing the file down onto the desk. The Deputy Chief Constable was noticeably taken aback by Mullings' audacity.

"This is an evidence file for Harper/Owens … you're no longer …"

"Yes, yes, I know," interrupted Mullings, "No longer on the case. Just take a look - first page."

The Deputy Chief Constable didn't much care for the Chief Inspector's tone. He flicked open the file testily. His body language said this had better be important.

The DCC surveyed the page in question. As soon as his face began to turn a deep, satisfying shade of purple, Mullings knew he'd hit the mark.

"Quite a cock-up, don't you think, sir?" It was hard not to sound condescending.

By this point, the Deputy Chief Constable was doing a fair impression of the incredible shrinking man in his oversized leather chair. "How the hell could this happen?" he asked angrily.

"Don't ask me. I'd been taken off the case before this evidence appeared in the file ... I suspect it either wasn't read properly or got filed incorrectly. Someone hadn't joined up all the dots."

"Christ Almighty!" exclaimed the DCC.

"There can't be any doubt, can there? A thumbprint from the paint can on Harper's car ... making an exact match with a thumbprint on Geoff Owens' bathroom door. An incredible stroke of luck we found it at all ... it wasn't on the door handle but on a panel."

"Contact Harper ... send an officer round immediately ... explain new evidence has come to light ... he may be in some danger."

"Some danger?" echoed Mullings not attempting to disguise his incredulity, "I already tried to contact Gil Harper ... he's not at home, he's in Wales taking a break with Miss Curtis ... somewhere remote and difficult to pronounce ... no landline ... and mobile phone reception is a complete washout."

"What do you suggest, John?" asked the Deputy Chief Constable, whose humbleness of voice didn't quite match the look of violent enmity in his eyes.

## 13

Neither Gil nor Sally much cared for the lightning when it started, and poor Spike was thoroughly terror-stricken. Being in an isolated cottage on a cliff-top in the far west of Wales during a storm that was picking up momentum had a precarious feel about it. Sally certainly felt a little bit spooked. As for Gil, the downpour started him thinking again about that awful drive home on Christmas Day.

To take his mind off such potentially dark thoughts, he put on his waterproofs and went outside to fetch some coal. After doing this, he set about building a fire for the evening. Once he'd got it blazing away, the fire had a calming effect. It made the room seem far cosier and, quite illogically, they immediately felt more sheltered and protected from the storm. They sat in armchairs opposite each other and read their books companionably for a while. But before long, the combined effect of lunch and the heat from the fire caused them both to doze off.

# 14

Gil woke first; they couldn't have slept for long, his watch read 5.20 pm. It shouldn't have been dark, but to all intents and purposes it was.

When he tried to turn on the lights, nothing happened.

"No light," he mumbled, stating the obvious.

This didn't come as much of a surprise; the cottage's power supply had always been unreliable during bad weather. Because of this, he and Jules had always kept a couple of storm lamps and candles handy. Except that was over five years ago, and for all he knew the Pritchards' relatives could have exhausted his stash and not re-stocked. After a few minutes fumbling about in the dark, he found his back-up lighting supply intact in a kitchen base unit. He spent the next minutes filling and lighting the lamps and attaching candles to any old saucers he could find.

Gil left one of the storm lamps in the kitchen but took the other one on a tray along with half a dozen candles through to the living room. He placed the lamp on the little dining table and set the candles up at various points around the room. The lightning and thunderclaps were very close together now, and a large flash and rumble caused Gil to flinch as he shut the front curtains. Poor Spike didn't appreciate either the howling wind or thunder and lightning; he remained cowering beneath Gil's vacated chair and from time to time gave a heartfelt whine.

Gil was shovelling a few more coals onto the fire when Sally awoke.

"Hallo …what's been happening?" she asked, surprised by the new lighting arrangements.

"Power's gone off," replied Gil, "Sometimes happens round here … but we've got plenty of candles."

They were so full of fish, chips and ice-cream that they weren't able to contemplate anything to eat or drink for a while. So, Gil did what he and Jules had done many times on rainy evenings at the cottage: fished out the Scrabble board.

"Want a game?" he asked, showing Sally the box.

"Yeah … okay …" said Sally sounding uncertain.

"Don't you like Scrabble?"

"Yes … but I've only played once or twice … ages ago … I won't be any good … I don't think I can remember the rules … you'll win easily."

"I'll explain as we go along," promised Gil.

At the start of the game, Gil was helpful and attentive. But as the game proceeded he became increasingly unconvinced by the claim she'd made about being a novice. Halfway into the game, Sally took the lead by using up all seven of her letters on a triple word score.

"That's fifty extra points too, isn't it?" she asked perkily, all of a sudden less uncertain about the rules.

Gil scowled suspiciously, "You're doing remarkably well for someone who's only played once or twice, long ago. Did you mean once or twice a week?"

"Mmm," she smiled, "Funny how things just come back to you, isn't it?"

Gil shook his head and laughed, "Right," he said feigning seriousness, "It's Scrabble war ... no more Mr Nice-Guy!"

Sally chuckled wickedly as Gil perused the set of mediocre letters before him in the vain hope of producing something impressive. He frustratingly rearranged them several times, even found a seven letter word, but couldn't find anywhere to put it.

"Come on!" she teased, "Haven't got all flippin' day!"

Gil grunted in her general direction.

It was then that a particularly loud clap of thunder and simultaneous lightning flash lit up the cottage's porch. The great bang that accompanied it caused them both to jump. They stared at each other like a couple of shell-shocked battle veterans for a moment.

"Bloody hell that was loud!" exclaimed Sally, clutching at her chest.

"Bolt must've landed close by ... hit a tree or something."

"Glad I'm in here, not out there," she gasped.

A moment after Sally had uttered these words, Spike made them both jump again, when he began to bark ferociously. He rushed out from his hiding place and literally hurled himself at the front door in an unprecedented manner.

"What on earth's up with him?" Gil exclaimed, wincing at the deafening sound his dog was making.

"Poor Spike," said Sally, "That last bang must've really frightened him."

Spike's barking increased in volume and intensity; the noise was unbearable.

"Be quiet!" shouted Gil, unusually sternly.

The command, if heard, was completely ignored.

With nerves still jangling after the lightning blast, and teeth set on edge by Spike's barking, when a shadow projected itself across the cottage's porch, their fight or flight mechanisms hit red alert. Sally couldn't help releasing an involuntary shriek.

Gil sprang to his feet and approached the front door. Spike's barking was making him feel extremely nervous.

"Spike! Quiet!" he tried again, still to no avail.

As the shadow metamorphosed into a living person, Spike hurled himself at the door even more aggressively.

The first words spoken by the man outside could not be heard above the cacophony of storm and dog.

"Shut up, Spike!" shouted Gil.

Their caller tried again. This time Gil caught, "PC," and at once connected this with the outline of a uniform. Gil instantly felt relieved and unlocked the door. It was only the sight of Spike baring his teeth, ready to attack, that caused him to stall.

"I'm sorry," Gil said through the door gap, "It's the storm … he isn't normally like this."

"Not to worry … quite the little guard dog, isn't he? I need to talk to you, Mr Harper. Is there somewhere the dog could go, another room perhaps?

"Just a minute!" Gil told the policeman.

He attempted to pick Spike up, but the little chap was in such a distressed state by then, that he did something he'd never done before, and snapped at his hand.

"Can you get his lead?" he told Sally, as he held Spike by his collar. The dog was still snarling at the policeman outside.

Gil shut the door momentarily while he attached the lead to Spike's collar. He then dragged the small protesting dog away from the door. All the while the poor creature continued to bark, growl and fight the lead. And once Spike realised he was going to be locked up in the utility room, he made a last ditch attempt to scramble free as Gil slipped the lead from his collar.

As Gil walked back to the living-room all he could hear were Spike's doleful whines.

By this time, Sally had let the policeman in.

"I don't normally have such a dramatic effect on dogs," the man said in a pronounced Welsh accent. His overcoat was dripping wet.

"What are you doing here?" asked Gil in an uncharacteristically blunt manner. He was noticeably shaken after witnessing Spike's behaviour.

"Ah yes, Mr Harper, Miss Curtis … forgive the intrusion. I'm PC Glyn Davies. We got a call earlier from our colleagues in Kent … a DCI Mullings, is it?"

"Yes," said Gil, reassured by the mention of Mullings' name.

"He's making his way here … he asked my Inspector to send someone out, to stay with you until he arrives."

"Why, what's happened?" asked Gil.

"Sorry sir, couldn't tell you … he spoke to my boss, not me … something to do with new evidence, I think."

Gil turned to Sally, whose face mirrored the bewilderment he felt.

"Hope I didn't give you too much of a fright, Miss Curtis?" the policeman told Sally. "Playing Scrabble, is it?"

"Trying to take our minds off the storm," she replied.

"Worst I've known in a while," replied the policeman, "Caught myself flinching once or twice driving down that hill."

"Can I take your wet coat, Constable Davies?" asked Sally.

"Might as well keep it on for a bit … neither my handset's working nor the car radio … must get through to control, say I've got here … storm, see … playing havoc with communications right across Wales ... I'll need to go back out to the car in a bit and try again."

"Your accent," said Gil, "It's not from these parts." He was by no means an expert on the accents of Wales, but his long association with Ceredigion made him question the Constable's way of speaking.

The man smiled, "Fair cop, guv … you tumbled me, Mr Harper. I've been here a good few years now, more than ten in fact … expect the accent's got a bit mixed-up … I'm from East Wales originally … Monmouth way … know it round there?"

"No."

"Shame … lads in my station take the Mickey quite a bit at the way I talk … I have in turn been known to refer to them as 'woolly-backs' … 'mongst other things!" He went on to laugh at the idea of this.

Gil and Sally weren't in the mood for joviality. The storm, Spike's extraordinary behaviour, and the policeman's sudden arrival had unnerved them.

"So you've no idea what's bringing DCI Mullings here?" asked Gil.

The man immediately fell silent, and with a look of gravitas that suggested training he said, "My chief mentioned new evidence … nothing more … sorry."

"Any idea when he's likely to arrive?" asked Sally.

"The roads through Wales are very precarious at the moment … flash flooding in parts. The emergency services are rushed off their feet. There's been an accident on the M4 near Swindon, and speed limit is down to forty due to poor visibility round Bristol. I doubt we'll be seeing Chief Inspector Mullings until well after midnight."

There was a sudden flash of lightning and another loud strike nearby.

Spike resumed barking.

"That sounded close," laughed their visitor, "Tree I expect, in one of the fields above."

"I'm with Spike," said Sally, "I've decided I hate storms."

"Can't say I'm keen either," agreed Gil.

"You get used to them living out here," said the policeman.

"Can I get you a hot drink, Constable Davies?" asked Sally, rolling her eyes to add, "Maybe I'll have a drop of brandy in mine."

"Not for me, Miss Curtis … I wanted to come by and introduce myself but I'd best get back out to the car and radio control. But I'd love a cup of something once I get back."

"Okay," said Sally, "I'll make us all hot drinks when you return."

"I shouldn't be long," he said as he opened the front door and went back out into that terrible storm. PC Davies' stoicism and sense of duty were impressive.

## 15

As soon as they were alone, Sally asked Gil, "Why do you think Mullings is coming here?"

"I really can't imagine. Something to do with Geoff Owens, perhaps?"

"Why send us a chaperone?"

Gil shook his head, "Dunno … some kind of police procedure perhaps … guess we'll just have to wait for Mullings to explain."

Without any specific information or facts, beyond conjecture there was little more to say. However, their imaginations were unable to let the matter drop. But for the sake of the other, they tried to look relaxed as they completed their game.

Sally maintained her lead, and although Gil played valiantly, in the final tally he was twenty points behind.

"Only played once or twice!" he scoffed.

"I can't help owning a superior brain."

"I demand a rematch!"

After about ten minutes they began to wonder where PC Davies had got to.

"Do you think he's okay out there?" asked Sally.

"I expect he's still having trouble getting through … the storm seems to be moving away a little bit." Gil had counted a gap of four seconds between the most recent bout of thunder and lightning. Unfortunately each fresh burst set poor Spike off howling in the utility room.

Gil fared better in the second round. It amused him to discover that Sally was a competitive Scrabble player, "You lied didn't you about hardly ever playing before?"

"I wouldn't say lied," replied Sally grinning, a gleam in her eye, "I'd prefer the phrase, 'economical with the truth'."

They were beginning to feel concerned for PC Davies. He'd now been gone half an hour. Gil's watch said 6.35.

It showed the state of their nerves, when, despite the policeman's return being long overdue, they both jumped at the sharp rap on the front door. They turned and saw through the door's frosted glass panels a policeman's overcoat silhouetted against a fork of lightning. Spike must have heard the knock too because he commenced barking again.

Gil got to his feet, walked over to the door and felt a moment's hesitation about opening up.

"Only me!" called Davies cheerily.

Gil heard himself sigh with relief as he let the policeman back in.

"Any luck?" asked Gil.

"'Fraid not … still no reception whatever."

"Come in and take off your coat," said Gil.

"No point, I'll have to go back out to try again … just thought I'd come in for a bit of a warm … but seeing as I'm here, think I'll take you up on that offer of a hot drink," said the policeman rubbing his hands together to get them warm.

Sally began to rise, "I'll put the kettle on."

"No you don't. Sit down and finish your game," replied Davies, "I can do it …"

"You're our guest," answered Sally.

"Now sit down," countered Davies with a smile, adopting a commanding tone of mock seriousness, "I'm the policeman … you two carry on with your game."

Sally acquiesced and sat down again smiling.

PC Davies, en route to the kitchen, paused to ask, "I'm safe from the dog in here, aren't I?"

"Completely safe … he's shut away in the utility room," replied Gil.

"That's good to know," said Davies holding up and flexing the fingers on his hands, "I've grown quite attached to these boys."

The policeman went off into the kitchen area. However, he was only gone a few seconds before re-emerging again to ask, "What about you two, can I get you something?"

"We'll make ourselves some coffee once we've finished our game," said Gil.

"We make it in a cafetière," explained Sally, as if this was somehow a conclusive reason for declining his offer.

"Might just as easily make up a pot for three," replied Davies.

"Oh … Oh, okay," said Gil, "Mine's black, no sugar … thanks."

"Miss Curtis?"

"Okay then … thanks," replied Sally a little more hesitantly, "Milk in mine, please."

PC Davies left them. They could hear him filling up the kettle and searching the kitchen cupboards for the things he needed. Some five or six minutes later he returned holding a tray bearing a cafetière, three mugs and a small jug of milk. Gil and Sally were packing away the Scrabble. This time Gil had only lost by three points. They were laughing about the close finish and exchanging general banter about the game. PC Davies put down the tray on the sideboard where he plunged the cafetière and poured three coffees.

He placed the mugs down before them, and deposited a milk jug next to Sally's. As he did this he said with a smile, "I put a drop of something extra into them."

"How do you mean?" asked Gil uncertainly.

"I saw a bottle of brandy on the side and poured a drop into each mug … like you said, Miss Curtis."

"I'm not sure I was entirely serious … but thanks," she replied.

"I can easily change them?" said Davies, eager to correct his mistake.

"A drop of brandy's always welcome," said Gil, "We'll need sustaining if we've got to sit out the evening waiting for Kent Police to arrive."

"I only put in a drop … not enough to do any harm," reassured the policeman.

Gil took a sip from his mug. "Just the ticket," he said.

PC Davies found a space for his own coffee mug and what remained in the cafetière at the table. He pulled out a chair, sat down, tasted his drink, and then smacked his lips together with satisfaction.

Sally felt the policeman's eyes watching her keenly; waiting to see if the coffee met with her approval.

She stirred in some milk before tasting. "Lovely," she said.

Gil couldn't recall seeing Sally with a coffee even once during the past week. He'd put it down to some female dietary thing; Jules too had gone in for odd changes from time to time.

"I do pride myself on my coffee making. Sadly, I'm on duty," said the policeman with a good-natured shrug, "So just plain, mine."

The storm had moved further away. As they sat round the table drinking their coffees, Gil and Sally started to unwind.

PC Glyn Davies was about the same age if not a little younger than Gil. He was a little taller than Gil too, though only by a very small margin. The skin on his face was taut, the way that of runners or habitual exercisers often looks. His hair was short, a dark ash colour, thinning at the temples and on top. He had a rather unkempt beard, quite a bit redder than the hair on his head. Somehow the beard completed the rural policeman look. The man's eyes were bright, almost a translucent blue, and by far his most striking feature. The rest of his face was fairly nondescript: a very ordinary nose, neither too big nor small to warrant observation; his mouth was narrow, the lips thin; the teeth, only visible when he laughed, were irregularly spaced with large gaps between them.

"It took me a while for the penny to drop," said Davies, "That you had to be the Gil Harper I've been reading about."

Gil nodded; he took another sip of coffee, "We've had quite a time."

"I know the way facts get reported aren't always accurate," said Davies, "But it sounded like quite an ordeal."

Sally quickly swallowed a mouthful of coffee and put in, "Poor Gil was the victim of a total maniac."

"Total maniac, is it?" echoed the policeman.

"Geoff Owens must've been insane," she continued, "He murdered three people in cold blood."

"From what I've read … insane or not … he planned meticulously … seems like he fooled a lot of people?"

"I suppose plans had been festering in his mind over a long time," said Gil.

"So the killer's dead now, right?"

"I found his body … he'd left a confession on a lap-top."

"Convenient," said Davies.

At that moment the room flickered with a half-hearted burst of lightning followed by the distant rumble of thunder, now eight or nine miles away. It was feeble compared to what they had encountered earlier, but still enough to set Spike barking again.

"Listen to your dog! He's off!" laughed Davies.

"He's always been terrified of thunder and lightning … but I've never known him like this."

"Something must've got to him," agreed Davies.

"He'll settle down once the storm has passed."

PC Davies nodded. He took a mouthful of coffee, was pensive a moment, then asked, "If you could bear it … I only know the bits I caught in the papers … but I'd be interested to hear, from the horse's mouth as it were, what happened."

Gil took a large slug of coffee.

"Top-up?" asked the policeman, holding up the cafetière.

Gil held out his almost empty mug for a refill.

"Miss?"

Sally looked momentarily confused by the question.

"Coffee?" Davies asked indicating the cafetière.

She shook her head before taking another sip from her mug.

Gil began to tell the story. He started with the white paint on his car. He said, "I wonder if that's why DCI Mullings is coming here? Perhaps they've figured something out about the paint?" he directed this at Sally, who was staring wide-eyed back at him.

"Wasn't … what's his name … Owens is it … wasn't he responsible for the paint?"

"Not according to DCI Mullings … he said …" Gil paused. He suddenly felt uncertain about the exact order of events. He tried again, "Not according to D …C … D …C … Mull … Mull …" Gil shook his head in an attempt to expel the fog from it.

Something was wrong.

He looked over at Sally for reassurance. The unresponsive expression on her face hadn't altered at all since the last time he'd glanced across at her.

He looked at PC Davies' grinning mouth. There was something familiar about that grin and the gaps between his teeth.

Nothing was quite as it should be.

Gil staggered to his feet. The room was swimming before his eyes. Sally didn't appear to have moved at all.

PC Davies was now laughing uproariously in his face.

Gil's knees buckled under him.

Before he lost consciousness, Gil thought, 'Policemen … not meant to laugh at you like that … Spike knew … should've listened … should've listened to Spike …'

## 16

Gil couldn't open his eyes at first. His head felt like it had been boiled and tumble dried. He was seated, leaning forward, chin resting on something firm, his left arm raised. He gulped in the cold damp air, thought he'd throw up but was relieved when the sensation subsided. His mind began to replay images: the storm, Sally staring uncomprehendingly, the grinning policeman. His eyes burst open and he jerked upright, left hand grappling against its restraint.

Everything was fuzzy but he was conscious again.

He was in the driver's seat of a car, a Skoda he recognised, though not his own. His left hand was handcuffed to the steering-wheel.

Outside, the night was pitch-black, the wind high. The car windscreen was almost impenetrable through the constant rain. The driver's window had been left partly open and Gil's sweatshirt was soaked from the rain pelting through it.

It was at this point that he glanced in the rear view mirror and let out a gasp as he caught sight of the figure behind him. Through sheer panic he made futile exertions to break free of the cuff. His heart leapt in his chest. Then reason returned, flight was not an option; pulse racing, brain pounding, he peered into the mirror again. The figure hadn't moved; the neck and head were stretched right back.

He was scared for Sally.

Gil twisted round to the farthest extent his cuffed wrist would allow and peered intensely at the human form which remained completely still. This person was physically large with broad muscular shoulders, slightly overweight and male; not Sally. The man's chin was clean shaven and he'd been stripped to his underwear. Gil wasn't sure if he was breathing.

"Hello?"

The man didn't respond.

"Hello?"

He was either unconscious, or ... Gil didn't like to think about the alternative.

Gil felt acutely frightened. 'Once I turn round, he'll leap on me,' he thought.

This paranoia, undoubtedly exacerbated by his predicament, was also an after-effect of the chloral hydrate he'd unwittingly taken. He wrestled with his fears, reluctant to turn his back on an unidentified person, but reasoned it was important to explore his surroundings, glean whatever he could from them.

The car offered various clues to its identity: several pieces of Dyfed-Powys Police insignia, a smashed car radio; the cuffs on his left hand were the same type he'd seen used on detainees during his brief incarceration by Kent Police.

Drowned out by the heavy drumming of the rain, Gil hadn't heard the approach of feet. He spun round immediately as the rear door on the passenger side opened. It was the bearded man, no longer in police uniform but wearing a set of waterproofs. At first he looked surprised to see Gil awake. Then he smiled calmly and got in alongside the silent figure in the back seat.

"Welcome back," he said, Welsh accent dropped. "Sorry I wasn't here when you came round ... things to do."

"What's going on?" asked Gil.

"What's going on?" echoed the man "Tut, tut, tut … such a disappointing first comment! So clichéd!"

"Who are you?"

"Who are you?" repeated the man mockingly, "Not getting better, is it? I suggest you give a little more thought before opening your mouth again." The man leaned forward until he was only inches away from Gil's left ear. He adopted a soft, friendly, confiding tone, "Gil, if I told you who I was, I'd need to do unfortunate things to you, like I did to your friends."

Gil felt a wave of panic submerge him; at once he was terrified. It was like waking from a nightmare only to realise it was still running. His chest began to heave as it took rapid breaths. He was on the verge of hyperventilating. "What have you done to Sally?" he gasped.

"Gil, I appreciate you're anxious, but I suggest you breathe more evenly, otherwise you'll pass out."

In a peculiar way, the advice helped. Gil directed his breathing down from chest to abdomen.

"Very good. Those yoga classes paid off."

At the mention of yoga, another wave of fear momentarily overpowered Gil; he had once belonged to an all-male yoga class.

"Where's Sally? What have you done to her?" he asked, voice tremulous with fear.

"We've got a lot of catching up to do before we get onto the bitch," replied his captor.

"No! What have you done to her?" Gil shouted. "Sally. What have you done to her? Tell me!"

"Alright … relax … I'd hate to see you develop an embolism. If it'll put you at ease, the bitch is inside the cottage. I drugged her too."

"Is she okay?" probed Gil.

His captor, who had remained calm up until this point, suddenly lost control and without any warning lashed out with a fist. An explosion of white pain burst through Gil's left ear.

The man's speech was staccato when he spoke, "For-Christ's-sake! She's-been-drugged! Of course she's not *okay*!" After this there followed a pause as he sought to calm himself again. His voice was more controlled when he resumed, "She's been drugged. It'll wear off and should leave her system without causing any permanent harm. Is that what's troubling you … making you behave like a girlie-boy?" he added with contempt.

Gil took a deep breath; it helped to absorb some of the pain in his face. Hearing that Sally was alive gave him a little hope. Of course, there was no way to be certain the killer was telling the truth.

"I've never seen you before tonight. Why are you doing this?"

"Actually, we have met. Autograph hunter, Blatts' funeral. Remember?"

He did remember; that was why PC Davies had seemed familiar. Gil stared ahead, as though mesmerised by the water streams cascading down the windscreen. He realised how easily they'd been duped and shook his head in disbelief. Thinking aloud he said, "That was you?"

Gil immediately received a slap to the head, "I just said that didn't I? ... Duh!"

"But ... I don't know you!" Gil spluttered, trying to present a smaller target by shrinking closer to the open window. "I mean, why ... what have I ever done to you?"

"What have you ever done to me? Answer: nothing."

"Then why? What's the point?"

"Ah, yes, the point, where should I begin?" The man thought a moment, as if he considered his reply to be of the utmost importance, "Ever felt alone?"

Gil hesitated, he wasn't certain if the question was rhetorical. He didn't want to be struck again.

"Hello ... Planet Earth to Gil!"

"Alone. I've felt alone. Definitely," responded Gil.

"Thank you. Because if you'd tried to tell me otherwise, I'd have known you were fibbing ... all those indulgent passages, full of self-pity, about how your first bitch got her neck broken due to your lousy reactions ..."

Gil loathed the derogatory terms his tormentor used when he talked about Jules and Sally.

"*... I relive those last vital split seconds again and again in my dreams and sometimes during my waking hours ...*"

It took Gil a few moments before he realised the man was actually quoting from his own diary.

"*... I can't help thinking if only I'd done something different, perhaps Jules and our unborn child might have lived. At moments like these, I feel utterly wretched, dejected and alone.*"

Gil felt an ice cold shiver run down his spine. He was certain his jailer had just quoted the diary verbatim. Gil would have been unable to accurately quote a single sentence. He discovered himself involuntarily struggling against the handcuff.

"Very sorry for yourself weren't you?"

Gil made no reply; half expecting to be struck again he flinched in advance, but no blow arrived this time.

"Like you, I've felt alone too, but I'm glad to say never so full of self-pity," sneered his captor, "Inevitable I suppose that I should've felt isolated … I've always been an individual thinker." The man broke off to consider his uniqueness a moment, "We have a lot in common … the home life I endured throughout my early years was dull like yours. Even so, it helped instil in me self-reliance and an unshakeable belief that the vast majority of the human race exert about as much mental energy as plankton …"

The killer seemed keen to talk. From Gil's point of view it was at least better than being hit.

"Everywhere pettiness, bigotry, small-mindedness …"

Although the situation didn't allow much scope, Gil knew he had to try and think straight.

"A world of intellectual pygmies, weak and futile …"

Gil decided to learn as much as he could about his predicament. It was the nearest thing he had to a plan.

"I've read in every generation there are only a handful of worthwhile people. The rest, the unwashed masses … cannon fodder …"

Gil thought, 'I must seize any chance … get help … find Sally. Think.'

"Unfortunately, in the west, we no longer fight wars on the scale of the past … there isn't the stomach," he scoffed. "The worthless thrive …"

The other man who Gil had been watching intermittently through the rear view mirror still hadn't moved and didn't appear to be breathing.

"For years I went on … went to work every day … grinned, suffered the boredom … presented a face of affability even when dealing with inferior types."

It was mostly impossible to see through the relentless downpour landing on the windscreen, but from time to time it eased for a second or two. During these gaps, Gil realised the car was parked at the end of the track, facing downhill in the direction of the sea. He identified the stile, over to his left, and calculated it was little more than a yard from the car. However, it came as a surprise to him to see that the fence alongside it had disappeared.

At this point, for no apparent reason Gil's tormentor began to laugh. It had a curious self-deprecatory note about it, "You won't believe this, but I considered setting myself up in a shopping mall with various weapons and plenty of ammunition. Of course, the only way out of that one is death … but I didn't see why I should die along with all the useless trash I would have removed from the gene-pool. I reconsidered."

He leaned forward to confide, "I didn't want people to think I was crazy."

Gil didn't feel it was the right moment to correct this delusion.

"Over time, an idea evolved. For a few years I'd taken cars when the mood took me … I was always careful, wore gloves, set fire to them afterwards. My details aren't on any criminal databases. Impressive considering the things I've done. The point is it wasn't enough. Then one day it just came to me … I had to choose someone … someone who'd understand how I felt. Eventually, when conditions were right, I came across you …"

"Christmas Day," interjected Gil; it was really an aside to himself.

"Absolutely perfect … the rain, the occasion, a deserted motorway. I knew it had to be then! If I couldn't do it, I was a waste of space like all the rest."

"Geoff Owens had nothing to do with it! He was just another victim." Gil had been so certain of Owens' culpability; the realisation came like a revelation.

"Owens barely possessed the willpower to get out of bed each morning!" the killer scoffed, "He eminently deserved to die."

"But why?" asked Gil, trying to grasp the deranged logic, "If you'd chosen me … why kill the others?"

"You're missing the point, Gil. I never meant to kill you … well, not unless you forced me to. In fact, I've grown rather fond of you …"

The approval failed to engender pride in Gil.

"Let's be honest, you're not exactly MENSA material, but you did have integrity and were certainly a better subject than I'd expected. Perfect really."

"Perfect, for what?"

"To bring down and ruin."

A cold shudder ran through Gil's frame. "Why?" he asked, turning to look directly at his tormentor, "I don't even know you!"

"Exactly. I came to the conclusion a symbolic amends was owed me … penance, for all I'd suffered. You've heard the term, scapegoat?"

If there had been any lingering doubts, Gil was now certain his captor was one hundred per cent madman.

"I couldn't remove everyone who deserved to die. So I set about finding one … preferably someone I considered above average ... whose life I would destroy."

To Gil's mind, the argument sounded not unlike the orthodox Christian view on sin. He'd never been able to fully grasp exactly why the most perfect fleshly incarnation had to die in order to expiate humanity's sins.

"It's never been personal ..."

From Gil's point of view it wasn't easy to agree.

"It's an act of revenge ... a declaration of hate against humanity!"

Gil couldn't help himself. "You're insane," he said.

For his honesty, Gil received a blow to the left side of his head, which made his ear throb.

"I'm disappointed," Gil's assaulter whispered through clenched teeth in the painful ear, "I'd hoped for more than insults."

Unless he was prepared to receive more injuries, Gil needed to back-track, "I'm sorry. You'll appreciate I'm feeling quite threatened at the moment."

There was a pause. "I can understand that," agreed his attacker reasonably.

Gil couldn't take the tension any longer and had to ask, "Who's the man beside you?"

"PC Glyn Davies reporting for duty," replied the imposter in a Welsh accent more exaggerated than before.

"And is he ...?" hesitated Gil.

"Dead?"

"Yes."

"What do you think?" the man replied before going on to ask menacingly, "Your opinion, pray?"

Once again Gil wasn't sure if he was expected to answer.

"Yes? I'm waiting!"

"I think he may be dead."

"You *think* he may be dead?" his tormentor mocked, "Of course he's *dead*! Do I do things by half measures?"

"I thought perhaps you'd drugged him!"

"And how would I do that? Please drink this cup of coffee with chloral hydrate in it! Shove a valium up his arse? I strangled him with a length of electrical wire I'd stripped out of the house up there on the hill. I've been watching you two lovebirds from there for the past ten days."

Gil suddenly felt his anxiety level shoot up again. He was shivering from the cold; numbness had crept into his arms and legs. Despite this, he managed to ask, "Why did PC Davies come here?"

His tormentor laughed, "To wait for the cavalry, and deliver a message ... more or less what I told you, about Mullings being on his way and new evidence."

"How did you get him to tell *you* that?" asked Gil.

"Volunteered it ... thought I was you! 'Mr Harper?' he asked in his stupid Welsh accent. 'Yes', I replied, quick as a flash, wide-eyed and innocent."

"How could he make that mistake?"

"A track that only leads to one house … a man heading there during a storm. To his stupid Welsh peasant mind … I had to be you, I suppose!"

Gil shook his head from side to side; incredulous that his own hand of cards should have played out so disastrously.

"I was on my way to call anyway. The fact the police nearly made the right connection for once just makes it even better," laughed the killer. "I watched you get back just before the storm started. I put on my waterproofs and set off. I'd shut the gate to the derelict house only seconds before PC Davies arrived in this car. I admit I felt concerned … that is, till he lowered his window and with a big stupid grin asked, 'Mr Harper?'"

"So you killed him."

"Not just like that! Credit me with some subtlety!" said the killer reproachfully. "PC Davies was very obliging. First, he radioed control. The reception was terrible. The woman officer he spoke to told him the storm was messing up communications … it was possible they'd soon lose contact with him. After this, he was keen to drive me to your cottage. Of course, I couldn't let him do that.

"But I needed him to get out of the car. It's not easy to overpower someone in a car, especially a fat oaf like he was. I told him I'd been looking round the derelict house … thought someone had been watching us from there. That interested him, though he was less keen when I suggested I show him. He only agreed after I assured him I'd been all through and there was nobody there.

"I took him inside, quite dark it was, but he had a flashlight. I showed him the stepladder … not the one rigged for uninvited guests like you, a nice aluminium one I'd kept upstairs. He was about to step on the first rung, when I slipped the cable over his head and across his throat. He put up a fight … frankly, considering his size, a bit disappointing," he said dispassionately.

"I changed into his clothes … too big, of course."

"The reason you didn't take your coat off."

"Very good, Sherlock Holmes!"

Gil ignored the patronising comment, "How did you get him back to the car?" he asked.

"I levitated him!"

"Huh?"

"I carried him, you dolt!" his tormentor said irately, slapping Gil about the head like a school master from the pre-enlightened past.

Gil lurched forward "I meant … why not leave him? What was the point of putting him in the car?"

"Actually, at first I didn't. I went back and got him while you thought I was radioing control."

"You drove back to the farmhouse?"

"Yes, you didn't hear me arrive, so I reckoned you wouldn't notice if I left for a bit. Up at the empty house, the ground was sodden, there was nowhere to safely turn. I had to back in through the gate, couldn't afford to get bogged down. He was bloody heavy … must've liked his pies!"

"But why didn't you leave him where he was?"

"I like things neat. And I liked the idea of you in a car with a deceased passenger."

Gil nodded. No need to elucidate.

"I thought about leaving him next to you … but like I said, he was heavy, the back door was nearer. Anyway, I hadn't quite decided yet whether you'd be waking up with your current bitch dead at your side."

Gil gasped in horror.

"Nicely balanced and extremely shocking … but in the end I went with my Rohypnol idea."

"Rohypnol?"

"You are such a disappointment, Gil. Rohypnol … the date rape drug?"

Gil was probably more frightened then than at any previous moment. "What … what have you done?" he groaned.

"I told you before. I drugged her."

"Please, please don't hurt her. Do anything you want to me … I couldn't bear it if you …" Gil broke off, aware that by pleading he was doing exactly what he was meant to do.

"I haven't done anything unsavoury like raped her or anything. I hope you weren't thinking badly of me?" Gil's tormentor asked aggressively. "I'm not some common sex offender. I chose Rohypnol for its sedative qualities, and also because I particularly liked the idea of her passivity …"

"What have you done?" cried Gil.

The man sniffed the air in a very deliberate way, "Can you smell smoke?"

Gil turned his head in the direction of the window and sniffed. There was an acrid smell in the air. He nodded nervously.

"Unpleasant," the tormentor said, adding a fake cough. "I'm afraid I may have been careless and left a full pan of vegetable oil on the cooker, with all its burners lit … and a trail of towels soaked in oil leading right up to the gas bottle. By now I expect the cottage is full of smoke. Imagine poor Sally lying upstairs in your bedroom, unable to save herself … and you here, completely incapacitated. I expect a fire will start soon."

"Please don't do this," begged Gil, "I have money. Take everything I have."

"That's so generous Gil, but I don't need money. As I've already explained, this is not some common crime. It's an act of revenge against all that is crass … one man's battle against mediocrity."

Gil fought against his handcuffed hand, "You're fucking crazy!" he screamed; no longer caring if he got hit.

"Now you're getting unpleasant … must be time to leave," his tormentor replied contemptuously.

Without any warning, Gil suddenly felt the man's right hand grip tightly round his forehead. In the bottom left of his peripheral vision Gil saw the glimmer of a knife and felt its blade press into the soft skin of his neck.

"I used a similar knife on Kate Blatt. She put up a spirited defence, unlike her husband who died like a pathetic dumb animal. I considered slitting Constable Davies's throat with this … but too messy, and I wouldn't have been able to use his nice uniform then." The killer paused for contemplation, "If I drew this blade across your throat it would all be over in seconds."

"Do it," whispered Gil.

"I think you're just showing false bravado when you say, 'Do it', like that. I already told you I don't mean to hurt you … not physically. You see, I want to remember you sitting here waiting, watching the flames rise beyond those bushes, hoping for a miracle. Just think, soon every breath you take will carry the scent of your girlfriend's burning flesh. I've read that roast human smells quite a bit like pork. Imagine!"

Gil began to sob quietly.

The man removed the knife and his grip on Gil's head. A moment later he produced about two foot of thick metal pipe, slipped it over the handbrake, and by exerting considerable force, wrenched the mechanism out of place.

Gil felt the car immediately begin to roll forward and automatically responded by jamming his foot on the brake pedal. His tormentor then opened the rear passenger window and threw the piece of piping out.

"That's right, Gil, you'll need to keep your foot on the brake pedal – unless you fancy a swim!" he chuckled. "By the way, don't waste time thinking about the clutch and putting the car into reverse gear to hold it. While you were asleep, I did a bit of tinkering under the hood with my trusty scaffold pipe and detached the selector cable from the gear box.

The gear stick's completely useless!" The fact he was enjoying himself was self-evident in his voice. "You've got to keep your foot on that brake pedal until help arrives … unless you want to learn to fly that is. Unfortunately, your girlfriend will be slow-cooking while you wait."

"Christ, no!" cried Gil making a futile attempt to prise off the steering wheel, which only succeeded in leaving him out of breath and seeing stars.

"You may have noticed that the storm, with a little help from me, has cleared your path to the sea-shore by taking down the fence in front of us. So, you have an option: if your mental torment becomes too great, you can always take yourself and the good policeman off for a sky-dive," Gil's tormentor sneered. "I reckon you'll still be sitting here with your foot on that pedal when DCI Mullings arrives. I just wish I could be here to see it myself!"

Gil was certain he'd go mad long before the police reached him; his hopelessness and despair were all-encompassing.

His tormentor opened the car door ready to exit, "By the way," he said, "I found this in your girlfriend's handbag," he leaned forward waving a piece of paper under Gil's nose.

Gil made no response.

"I don't suppose you can read it in the dark. I'll tell you ... it's confirmation, your girlfriend's pregnancy test proved positive."

"What?"

"Congratulations!"

"You're lying!" exclaimed Gil.

"Now why would I lie?" mocked his tormentor. "You didn't know, did you? I had a feeling perhaps you didn't. Tut, tut, tut … secrets so early in a relationship! Tell me, do you deliberately let your pregnant partners die?"

"Kill *me*, let her go!" pleaded Gil.

"Asking favours now is it? A few moments ago you thought you'd be clever and hurl abuse at me!"

"Please!" Gil begged.

Satisfied with his achievements, the killer made to leave.

Gil removed his foot from the brake pedal at the very moment the man tried to exit.

Distracted by his own laughter, Gil's adversary didn't notice the car was moving. Over-confidence had made him blind to any possible danger to himself.

From Gil's perspective, it wasn't a plan at all. In fact, if it had been, it would have failed. It was instigated in a split second after hearing about Sally, when he literally saw red.

Gil aimed the car's passenger side at the stile.

It was one of those rare moments when every necessary factor required to work did so, and produced a result way beyond anything Gil could have imagined.

The killer's foot touched the ground at the exact moment the stile made contact with the car door. However, by the time he'd realised what was happening and attempted to remedy the situation, it was too late. The door clamped shut around his lower leg, causing excruciating pain.

Gil couldn't believe his luck; adding a turn to the steering-wheel before jamming his foot on the brake again. The car's nose was on the edge of the bank before it sloped down to the coastal path. The trapped man lurched forward, contorted in agony as he attempted to pull his leg free.

Gil turned round to look at his assailant, "Give me the key!" he screamed rattling the handcuffs.

"Okay, okay," replied his assailant, in a voice marked by pain but clearly stalling for time as he struggled to get free.

Gil eased his foot off the brake momentarily and jerked the steering-wheel left for extra purchase.

There was a sharp cry from the back of the car, "You'll pay for that!"

"The key, give me the key!" shouted Gil. Over his shoulder he saw his attacker sprawled across the rear seat like a beached turtle, "Pass me the key!"

Gil watched the man's hand reach inside his waterproof jacket a moment before it lunged forward, preceded by the knife. As he saw the blade coming at him he drew back. The blow could easily have been fatal if his attacker's coordination hadn't been impeded by an awkward position. As it was the blade scored a three-inch line along the bottom of Gil's jaw just above the neck. The weapon continued along its trajectory after cutting; Gil grabbed the attacker's hand with his own free hand, opened his mouth, and bit, hard as he could, on the other man's wrist.

The scream that followed proved the assault was successful. A second later, his attacker's hand opened, the knife was released and dropped beside the gear stick.

Gil released his teeth from the man's hand, which was immediately drawn back with a painful sigh.

"You'll pay for that too," warned the killer.

"The key, give me the key!" screamed Gil, spitting his enemy's blood from his teeth as he spoke.

"I dropped it on the ground outside … after I locked the cuffs. If you want it you'll have to let me fetch it."

"The key!" shouted Gil, "Don't fuck me about. Give me the key!"

"I told you, I don't have it!" he shouted back.

Gil considered the possibility of this. "Then we'll wait for Mullings," he said resolutely.

There followed, what was for Gil, an interminably long silence.

During this time his adversary continually struggled to get free. Gil could feel the blood from the wound on his jaw running down his neck, soaking into his sweatshirt but he was not aware of any pain. He could smell smoke; this was the thing he was most conscious of.

"Okay you waste of space, have your key ... but once you get free, soon I'll be free too, then you'll wish you were still handcuffed to that wheel."

"Why don't you just shut up!" said Gil, "The trouble with you psychopaths is you're so *boring*!"

Gil's off the cuff remark seemed to score a point. There was silence for a moment. When his assailant replied his voice had an iciness about it, "Okay, here it is".

The man held out the key. It was attached to a small round fob.

As Gil reached for it he let go the steering wheel which was still locked into the stile and inadvertently released pressure on the foot brake. The car moved forward. This caused his assailant great discomfort as his leg and foot were repositioned.

Gil had half expected his assailant to be malicious and let the key fall uselessly to the ground out of sheer spite, but fortunately he didn't. Gil took the small key with its two distinct ends precariously between finger and thumb. He was suddenly grateful for the hours recently spent in a police station, and especially glad he'd watched with interest as an officer had removed a set of handcuffs from a prisoner. He recalled noting how the cuffs were double locked; had observed how the pin-like end must be inserted into a hole on the flat surface of the cuff first before the key itself could be used. It was not easy to attempt something for the first time one-handed in the dark. He found the hole to take the pin, felt something click; after a few moments feeling with his fingers he located the key-hole.

Gil inserted and turned the key. He was aware of the noise of exertion coming from the back seat. The cuff fell open and slid down the steering wheel. At the same moment there came a painful shout from the rear, followed by the clunk of a door. A second after this Gil felt a pair of hands about his neck pressing into his windpipe.

"Said you'd be sorry didn't I?"

As Gil's head was jerked backwards, his foot lost its place on the brake pedal. The car began to nose-dive down the bank. His attacker held on; Gil was choking. The car was picking up momentum as it rolled towards the coastal path. Gil swung his fists about his head in the anticipated direction of his attacker, but to no avail. The police car was moving unexpectedly fast, Gil's feet were now out of reach of the pedals. His left hand fumbled around the gear stick for the knife; he touched its handle then raised it and jabbed behind him with all his strength. There was a sharp cry followed by the release of hands on Gil's neck as the man slunk back to nurse his wounded shoulder. Gil slammed his foot on the brake just as the car ploughed into the coastal path. The next moments seemed to play out in slowed down time as the car slid irrevocably towards the cliff. It seemed very possible it might not stop, but fortunately it did, the car's front end teetering precariously on the very edge of the cliff.

Gil felt for the door handle. As the door swung open he aimed for an area of cliff-top, took his foot off the brake and dived. He landed face down in a puddle of mud. He sat up, winded from the fall, gagging for breath after being half strangled. To his surprise he found he was still clutching the knife as he wiped the dirt from his eyes on his sweatshirt.

The police car seemed to hover a long time before it finally rolled forward; then it appeared to hang a moment in mid air. Gil thought he heard a door burst open a second or two before it plummeted. He scrambled to his feet and gazed over the edge. There was nothing to see through the incessant rain, just mist and darkness. A few seconds later he involuntarily shuddered at the almighty crash as half a ton of steel met rock and water.

Steadily clutching the knife, he searched the cliff-top through the haze.

There was no sign of the killer.

Gil had no idea how badly injured the man had been after he'd stabbed him. Perhaps his attacker was already dying as the car fell.

There was no time for reflection. He had to reach Sally.

Gil slid and slipped up the bank, which had become a mudslide. He tore his jeans and cut his knee on a stone but with his body running on adrenaline he didn't even notice. He sped past his own car and up the steps to the cottage. The smoke stung the eyes and became denser and more acrid the closer he got. He could see the flickering of flames behind the curtains of the living room although they were not yet alight.

Gil went through the porch, entered the front door and was immediately engulfed in a cloud of smoke that under normal circumstances would have sent anyone reeling in the opposite direction. He raised the front of his sweatshirt to cover his nose and mouth.

The house was filled with an eerie silence; he seemed to be immediately swallowed up by the smoke and darkness. The stairs were straight ahead and he groped forward, trying not to breathe in the noxious smoke, as he felt for the stair rail.

Once he'd located it he ascended as quickly as he could. When the steps petered out, he knew he'd reached the landing. The smoke was denser here. He searched with a hand for the door. Fortunately it had been shut, reducing the amount of smoke that had entered the room.

He heard coughing and was at once filled with hope.

As soon as the door opened and before the bedroom filled with smoke, he caught sight of Sally. She was lying on the bed asleep. He also noticed that her hands were tied to the corner posts of the bed. He thanked his lucky stars he hadn't discarded the knife.

He took in a gulp of the relatively clean air of the bedroom before becoming once again engulfed by the acrid smoke. He groped forward, reached the bed, felt for Sally's arms and the bonds attached to her wrists. The knife made light work of the rope. Once both arms were free, Gil let the knife fall. He dragged Sally to the side of the bed then hoisted her onto his shoulder. He groped his way back to the door. On the landing again, he felt for the stair rail. Ahead he could feel increased heat and the flicker of flames. There was nothing to do but proceed.

When he reached the bottom of the stairs the way ahead was outlined by the door frame which now presented a fiery rectangle to aim for. He scrambled out through the porch and was overjoyed to find himself in the pouring rain once again. His legs crumpled under him and he let Sally slip gently to the ground.

Rain was never more glorious.

He spent the next two minutes on his hands and knees coughing, gasping to get his breath back. Once he'd recovered enough to stand, he saw Sally's eyes were wide open; for a second he thought the worst. He was relieved to see her cough.

"You're safe now, Sal," he assured.

The glass in the cottage's windows had begun to shatter from the heat. The downstairs curtains were now ablaze as the fire completely took hold.

For the first time Gil remembered Spike.

He knew there was nothing he could do; that he had been incredibly lucky to reach Sally. He would find a moment to grieve for his old pal later.

"Sal, you okay?" he gasped.

There was no reply, just the same fixed expression and staring eyes as before.

Gil remembered the gas bottles in the kitchen.

There was a lot of heat coming from the cottage now. He dragged Sally into a sitting position and after a struggle levered her up onto his shoulder again. They were still coughing and spluttering as Gil staggered down the steps. There was a loud blast from the direction of the cottage as they reached the car; presumably the gas bottles. Gil leaned Sally against the passenger door, supporting her with his free arm while he fumbled for the keys in his jeans pocket.

He was horrified to discover that his keys were missing.

"Shit!" he cried.

Without really thinking, he tried the car door, found it was open and peering into the illuminated cab saw the keys on the passenger seat. Gil grabbed them without caring to consider how they'd got there.

He manoeuvred Sally round into a good position to get her seated. Her trance-like state was disconcerting, and if she was able to speak, so far she hadn't attempted to.

Gil noticed something register in her eye: a flicker, apprehension perhaps.

He turned just in time to side-step the length of scaffold pipe coming at his skull. But for Sally's signal, it would have been all over. Gil swerved, saving his head, however, the pipe still had momentum behind it and smacked into his left arm. There was a sharp explosion of pain, and Gil fell to his knees.

His attacker, overbalanced by the unexpected change of direction, hurtled forward. Gil, without giving it any thought, used the bunch of keys protruding from his fist as a weapon. The punch landed on his assailant's cheek and was accompanied by a squeal of pain. The man let the pipe fall as his hands flew up to protect his wounded face.

Gil, clambering to his feet, hurled himself at his enemy. They fell together onto the track, locked in bitter struggle. Not much advantage was gained by either man as they rolled about in the freezing mud. However, when Gil's hand probed the shoulder wound where he'd stabbed his attacker in the car, he did a thing that under normal circumstances would have appalled him; he inserted a finger into the wound and thrust. His enemy screamed.

Gil may have thought he was gaining the upper hand at this stage; but he'd already learnt he daren't let up. He smashed his forehead into his assailant's nose and blood tainted black with muddy water streamed down onto the man's teeth. Both men were very much weakened but Gil's attacker seemed so far to have come off worse. Gil knew that under normal conditions he would never have stood a chance.

The two men were almost exhausted by the combination of physical exertion and icy rain. Any blows that landed had lost almost all their power and it cost nearly as much in expended energy to give a blow as to receive it. Gil took a stomach punch and found himself gasping for breath. His assailant stood, dragging Gil up to a seated position, getting ready to strike again.

Gil's hand trailing through the mud caught hold of something thick and metallic, the scaffold pipe, and swung it in an arc at the other man's legs. The force behind the blow was comparatively weak; however, its effect was amplified because it met the leg already injured in the door. The assailant yelped as he stumbled forward but incredibly retained his hold on Gil who unfortunately lost his grip on the pipe. The two men went tumbling over the last few yards of track, before careering across what remained of the fence and down the bank. They landed with some force on the path below.

Gil had been in the most disadvantaged position on impact and was severely winded. He struggled for breath and tried to stand. His arms and legs had lost all power. He floundered about, punch-drunk, slipping and sliding like a child before it can walk.

His assailant was reeling and swaying too but managed to get to his feet. He spat a tooth from his blood-covered mouth before saying, "See, I did warn you … could've saved yourself a heap of trouble. Now I'm going to kill you … then I'm going to perform an emergency abortion on your girlfriend."

Gil cried out in agony as the man's boot connected with his injured arm. Then there came another kick, this time aimed at his stomach but which fortunately only made contact with his hip. He was unable to prevent himself from rolling towards the cliff edge.

Again Gil tried to stagger to his feet, only to collapse again when his attacker clubbed him with a fist. Gil was finished and he knew it. He was almost at the edge; what was coming seemed inevitable. However much he wanted to save Sally and himself, it was no good; he had tried, but now he had nothing left.

Gil's assailant pulled him to his knees, victory was plainly written on the man's face. The edge was so near, it would take only a small push to send Gil plummeting to his death.

The attacker drew back an arm.

Gil was vaguely aware of a shape flying down the slope through the darkness towards them. This unidentified form suddenly materialised between his attacker's legs with a flash of white. A terrible scream rang out across the cliff top, which for a moment seemed to top the howling squall of the wind and rain.

Gil, encouraged by the small dog's tenacity, somehow found the strength to scramble to his feet and stagger away from the cliff edge. He had to watch helplessly as his assailant viciously brought his fist down on Spike, who let out a yelp before falling to the ground. The punch was followed by a kick; after this Spike didn't move again.

By now, Gil had rekindled enough strength and loathing to throw a punch at his enemy's face. It was a feeble effort, and under normal circumstances it would have done little damage. However his assailant was much weakened too and it sent him floundering back, a couple of feet from the cliff edge.

Both men reeled about for the next few seconds, eyes fixed on the other trying to find the strength to stay standing.

Then Gil's assailant suddenly dropped to his knees. He looked up and grinned at Gil through bloodied teeth, "Stalemate," he panted.

Using the terminology of chess made Gil's anger flare up into an incandescent rage.

"Not a game!" he screamed, lunging forward with a punch that contained every remaining ounce of strength in his body; for Felix and Kate, the much-wronged Geoff Owens, PC Davies, even Michael Chilvers, and particularly for Spike.

The killer's arms flailed as he attempted to check his balance and save himself from falling.

Gil identified the problem and stepping forward applied a well placed shove to his assailant's chest, "Check-fucking-mate!" he said.

There was an expression of incredulity on the killer's face as he fell, arms floundering, trying to grasp thin air. This time there was no ledge directly below to save him.

Gil heard a dull thud as the man's body hit a rocky outcrop on its way down; swiftly followed by a more muted and distant thud as it reached the rocks at the base of the cliff; hurled, pummelled, regurgitated and then swallowed whole by the ferocious sea.

## 17

The small army of Welsh sheepdogs announced the Skoda's arrival as it juddered to a stop. The journey had been made without any gear changes because Gil's left arm was far too painful to use. He remembered Siriol and Emrys coming from the house as he staggered out of the car thinking, 'Thank God.' Beyond this he had a vague recollection of his legs turning to rubber but no memory of striking his head on the car door as he fell.

By the time he came round he'd been carried inside and Gwyneth was holding a pad against the free-flowing wound on his forehead.

"Sally?" he asked anxiously.

"She's calm," Gwyneth replied pointing to the sofa where Sally lay asleep under a blanket. "An ambulance is on its way, and a vet's coming out to see to your little dog. Take it easy. Rest now, Gil."

As he closed his eyes, he thought, 'She called me Gil … I must be in a bad way.'

The ambulance took them north to the Bronglais General Hospital in Aberystwyth. Upon arrival, they were wheeled off to be treated separately, and Gil didn't see Sally again for almost two days.

Quite soon after they were admitted, the Dyfed-Powys police arrived, eager for information. Gil managed to give them the bare details of what had occurred that evening. A police constable was assigned to him.

The first whole account he made was to Mullings and PC Shaw. They had reached the hospital about 1 am.

Gil told exactly how he remembered the events unfolding. He concluded his account by saying, "I pushed him off the cliff. After all the things he'd done, I just wanted him dead."

DCI Mullings glanced across at PC Shaw.

The three of them were alone in the hospital room. The local constable had only moments earlier been called away to the telephone.

Mullings peered steadily at Gil and said, "You mean he somehow got pushed from the cliff during the fight … an end he clearly intended for you."

"No, I …" began Gil, concussed and slow on the uptake.

"Clearly it was *self-defence* …" interrupted PC Shaw, as she paused in her note-taking.

Gil looked at them uncertainly. The penny dropped. He nodded.

"… those cliffs must have been awfully slippery on a night like this."

"Quite treacherous," added Mullings.

Gil was kept in the hospital for observation for thirty-six hours. During which time he appeared to possess an inexhaustible appetite for sleep. DCI Mullings and PC Shaw called in to see how he was progressing from time to time and kept him up to date with the inquiry.

"The Ceredigion division recovered the real PC Davies' body this morning. He was in the car, exactly as you described," informed Mullings.

"Poor chap," said Gil.

"He was a family man," added Shaw.

"Tragic," said Gil.

They all nodded in agreement.

Gil was understandably concerned about Sally. Mullings and Shaw made every effort to find out what they could and relayed this back to him. Unfortunately, there was little to tell, other than that her condition was stable. The hospital was not allowing visitors in to see her yet.

"She can't still be unconscious?" Gil asked, his face expressing deep concern.

"We really don't know," shrugged PC Shaw, "They've been running lots of tests on her … monitoring the effect of the Rohypnol perhaps?"

Mullings changed the subject. "The weather is set to remain fine. They hope to bring the police car up in the morning … tricky operation I'd imagine."

"And *him*?" asked Gil.

Mullings shook his head. "Still nothing … looks like the storm took the body out to sea …"

It seemed a cruel quirk of fate to think there might possibly be no body; no absolute finality to this matter after all.

"I'm sure he'll turn up. Bodies generally do," Mullings paused for a moment. "An exercise book containing his notes was discovered in your car, by the way."

"In my car?"

"He planned using it to get away from the crime scene," explained Shaw.

"Of course," said Gil, "Why it was unlocked and the keys were sitting on the seat."

## 18

Next morning, an uncommonly excited Mullings visited Gil with fresh information. A corpse had been retrieved from the sea, seven miles off the Ceredigion coast. The body was minus its head. It was believed this had become separated from its torso as it struck a rock on the way down the cliff. The corpse was wearing waterproof clothing and bore injuries consistent with those inflicted by Gil Harper: a knife wound in the left shoulder, contusions on the left calf, and puncture marks made by teeth to the right wrist. Most importantly, the hands were intact and exactly matched the prints the police had on file.

# 19

When Gil entered her hospital room, Sally's eyes were closed. He crept over to the bed and observed her face in repose for a few moments. He felt a mixture of emotions, but mostly a very deep sense of gratitude. His silent approach had left him with something of a quandary, and he considered exiting in order to re-enter the room more volubly, or emitting a gentle cough perhaps. These measures proved unnecessary, he'd been expected; Sally's eyes opened and her face lit up, expressing delight at seeing him. However, this first response almost immediately wavered as she took in Gil's injuries; the bruising and stitches on his face, his left arm in a sling. She couldn't hold back her tears.

Gil stroked her hair and gently reassured, "It's finished. We're free of him."

"You got hurt," she sobbed, reaching up to touch his face.

"I'm fine," he said, "It looks worse than it is." This was an understatement of course. It was less than forty-eight hours since the events at the cottage, and although Gil had taken lots of rest, his body ached comprehensively. He felt like he'd doubled in age overnight.

"How's Spike? The police weren't sure."

"It was touch and go. He had a collapsed lung, but he's on the mend. PC Shaw drove me over to the vet's to see him this morning. He saved my life – *our lives*!"

"Inspector Mullings said."

"Of course, he'll be unbearable to live with after this!"

"I can't wait to give him a hug," laughed Sally.

"PC Shaw said he should be nominated for an animal of courage award."

"I didn't know there was such a thing?"

"Apparently so, I don't doubt he deserves one … it's just the effect it'll have on us lesser mortals … left to deal with the consequences of his celebrity ego."

"I was told you were very brave too," said Sally.

"Not really," shrugged Gil, "It isn't brave, is it … fighting, when you realise you're about to lose everything that really matters to you?"

Sally wiped away a tear, "Sorry. I promised myself I wouldn't leak," she said, tears streaming freely from her eyes. "I remember you carrying me downstairs and a lot of smoke. Sorry, I wasn't much use."

"That wasn't your fault. You were totally out of it, in a trance or something. Anyway, you gave me the signal that he was coming up behind me. I don't know how you did it, but you got the message across."

"We got through it. Thank God," replied Sally.

"Yes, all *four* of us," replied Gil.

Sally looked sheepish.

"I wanted to tell you," she said.

"Why didn't you?"

"Because I knew you didn't want children."

"What?"

"You told me you no longer wanted to be a father. When I realised I was pregnant, I thought I'd better be sure … make up my own mind before I told you … I didn't want to blackmail you or anything."

"Blackmail? I'd never have thought that," assured Gil. "Since you mention it, I remember saying something along those lines … about not wanting to be a father."

He wanted to explain how everything was different now; how perception alters entirely once something becomes possible.

"What did you decide?" he asked tentatively.

Sally took a deep breath, "To have my baby," she replied uncertainly.

Gil looked down at his trembling hand, "I'm very glad you decided that. I've had something on my mind too … ever since we arrived here. It's got nothing to do with the baby … well, what I mean is, that's not the reason. It's just, I really love you, and for days I've been trying to pluck up enough courage to ask if you'd consider marrying me?"

Sally's eyes had started to leak again. She reached out and took Gil's hand.

"Well?" he asked.

"What do you think?" she said.

THE END

If you enjoyed reading *Roadrage* and would like to find out what Martin is currently working on, you can join him at these sites:

www.facebook.com/mj.johnson.author

www.mj-johnson.com